The Shadow's Reach

Keith Bond

Blatherbox LLC

Contents

For Heather,
who cheered for me, challenged me, and loved me through every chapter—
from blank page to final word.
Your love makes all things possible.

"We are all braver than we believe, stronger than we seem, and more capable than we imagine."

— Woodland Wisdom

Prologue

Deep below Thornwall Keep, a single crystal fell from the wall.

It was barely larger than a grain of sand. It came loose without a sound and drifted down to the floor. Purple light moved through the silver veins in the stone where it had been.

The chamber had been held still for thirty years, and the holding had not stopped. Crystal pillars rose in concentric rings, amber light and darkness locked against each other in every column. They gave off a low, continuous hum, the sound of stone under long strain.

Three other crystals lay on the floor near the northern arc, fallen the same way across the same years. The seventh pillar above them carried a hairline fracture. The amber in its heart ran thinner than it had ten years ago, and thinner than that ten years before.

The fallen crystal lay dark. The light moved on through the veins, and the hum went on with it.

The lock had been built by careful minds. The seven anchor points in the surface world reinforced one another, so that pressure on any single point tightened the remaining six. The conduit lines between them ran clean through the deep stone. The architects had understood what they were building, and they had built it well. The prison was woven through and around the anchors until they had become one thing. Thirty years of attention had not found a seam in it.

The lock had been built without slack. Each anchor sat in its place, the weight shared evenly across all seven so none carried more than its share. That was its strength, and it was also its requirement, that every anchor had to hold. Lose one and the other six had nothing extra to give. When one anchor's resistance changed, the other six adjusted to compensate, and the watching recorded every shift.

The fifth anchor had been changing for months. Its resistance was still there, but it had shifted, and the suppression no longer ran true through that line. The change moved through the other six like a shudder through a held weight.

A well-built lock could be read, and the eastern arc of the chamber showed the clearest record. Three pillars there where the amber light had thinned by fractions. One fracture too recent to have settled into the wall's older pattern. Two conduit lines that had come, over thirty years, to run almost parallel before their paths diverged. The architects had considered them stable, and they were a little less so each year. The angle between the two lines had been opening for a long time.

In each pillar the amber and the darkness went on pressing against each other. The watching continued, pillar by pillar, marking where the lock bent and by how much, and thirty years of it had not slowed the bending.

The influence moved through the surface world along paths already cut. The realm above was full of them. Streams running between settlements, wells drilled to the water table, the root systems of old trees reaching deeper than anything above ground knew, animal runs worn into hillsides over generations. The ordinary channels of ordinary places were all there, all of them open to whatever entered from below.

The influence moved through a stream north of a small settlement and found a farm on its banks. The crops had been struggling, grey-headed where the grain should have been full. A cellar foundation had a crack along its eastern edge, the stone around it faintly discolored. The mole who lived above had not noticed. The influence slipped into the crack, ran along the conduit line northeast beneath the bedrock, and continued. Then the fifth anchor completed.

It arrived as a small thing, a door closing, far away and at a single point. The prison felt the change. The suppressive force at that anchor collapsed inward and inverted. The remaining anchors adjusted. The eastern arc's amber shifted by a small amount, then steadied. The sound in the chamber dropped a half-note and found its new level. Five anchors inverted, the sixth flickering, the seventh holding.

The numbers were simple. Seven anchors, seven shares of the load. Five inverted meant the remaining two carried what had been divided seven ways. The seventh held. The sixth was uncertain.

The influence continued through the stream and reached the settlement itself, small, a market square, a fountain with purple-stained water from some accident years past, festival preparations of canvas and rope, a community making ready for an ordinary festival. The whole settlement asleep in its ordinary night, except for one thing.

There was a brightness in it, small and unsteady, that had been waiting in a dark place for a long time and had begun, faintly, to stir. The awareness knew this light. The same light had driven a blade through Malachar's form thirty years ago, and its resonance had run through every anchor at once.

That light had been fully awake and had known what it was. This one was smaller and uncertain, still folded into rust and sleep. The awareness touched the edge of it, briefly, then moved on.

It continued to the next settlement, to other streams and other farms with cracks running through their foundations. The fifth anchor was complete. The sixth was flickering. The watching of the eastern arc went on.

The small brightness in its small settlement slept on, and the awareness released it and returned to the watching.

Nibbles woke at nothing. The house was quiet. The dark was the ordinary dark of his bedroom, the square of window showing the same sky it always showed. The dream was gone before he could catch it, a sense of somewhere that had mattered, and then nothing, just the room and the blanket.

His paws were shaking. He lay still and let them. Whatever had startled him was gone before he reached it, and all that was left was the shaking. He breathed. His whiskers slowed.

The smells of the house came back one at a time. Old wool in the blanket. Pine pitch from the torch brackets in the hall. The dry warmth of the walls after a sunny day, faint but present. His mother's bread from yesterday, still there in the grain-and-fire smell that meant the kitchen had been used and was waiting for morning. He lay still and sorted through them, and underneath the familiar smells of the house there was something else.

Copper. Dry and metallic, the smell of an old coin pulled from a drawer that hadn't been opened in years. He turned his whiskers toward it and held still. It was not coming from the kitchen or the hall. It was just there, in the air, without a source he could find. His paws had started shaking again.

He got up. The floorboards were cold through his pads, and the room had gone colder than it had been when he went to sleep, the deeper cold of after midnight, when the fire in the hall had burned down to coals. He went to the window and looked out at the market square. The fountain stood in the center of it, its water darkened to near-black in the night, the purple stain invisible until morning. Nothing moved. The windows opposite were unlit, the baker's dark, the Festival grounds at the far edge still, the canvas barely shifting in the night air.

A board in the wall behind him contracted with a quiet tick.

He stood at the window. His whiskers moved slowly, reading the air. The copper smell had thinned, or he had got used to it. He couldn't tell which. His tail had curled against his leg, and he uncurled it.

The Festival was tomorrow. He had things to do in the morning, and standing at a window trying to find a smell that might have been nothing would not help with any of them.

He went back to bed and pulled the blanket up. The old wool smell came back around him, then the pine pitch from the hall, then the faint warmth of yesterday's bread, and the copper smell faded with him into sleep.

Chapter One

The Cheese Festival Incident

THE CANNON FIRED. IT fired in the wrong direction, north-northeast instead of north, which put the smoke cloud directly over the baker's stall and the lavender booth beside it. Someone in the square cheered anyway. Thimblewick had stopped expecting the cannon to fire straight three years ago. The cheer was for the smoke.

Nibbles Tumblepatch was already dressed. He had been dressed before the cannon, before first light, because today was supposed to be different and he wanted every minute of it. The cape was tablecloth, red wool, small embroidered edge, cut and stitched over three evenings in late summer because he had no other cloth and arriving at the Guild tent without a cape was unthinkable. The left side hung slightly long where his stitching had wandered.

The practice sword at his back was a mess. The grip fit his paw, three weeks of drilling in the dark against the back of a water trough had at least done that, but the blade was nicked and dulled along its length from too many fence posts. He stepped off his doorstep and walked toward the square.

Warm bread arrived first. The baker started at midnight on Cheese Day, and by morning the smell had spread through the entire western quarter. Aged cheese came after, the tournament wheels on the merchants' carts, wrapped and sealed. Underneath both, something else.

His whiskers caught it first. They were large for his head, embarrassingly so, and they pulled scents in faster than the rest of him could keep up with. Copper at the back of his throat, metallic, faintly bitter, there for one breath and gone. He stopped in the middle of the lane.

Nothing. Just bread and cheese and the distant shout of someone who had gotten the cannon smoke in the face. He kept walking.

The square was already full. Bunting between the posts in yellow and green. The fountain ran purple. The cleaning compound incident had been two years ago and the village had voted to keep the stain rather than pay for the bleach. Visitors were told it was enchanted, which was true in the sense that something had definitely happened to the water and the village had decided to call the something a feature.

He passed the lavender booth. A grey-furred rabbit was handing out sachets without looking up from her bundling. She handed him one. He tucked it into his pocket behind his three copper coins and the scrap of parchment he carried to write things down.

Today was supposed to be different. He had said this to himself twice before leaving home. He had meant it both times. He walked toward the tent.

He had first wanted to join the Guild at this same festival fourteen years ago, six years old, his mother's paw on his shoulder, watching a procession come through with a captain twice as tall as anyone he'd ever seen and hawk feathers in her helm. He had said *I'm going to do that*, entirely certain.

His mother had drawn a breath, and he had heard it settle.

"Nibbles," she said. Then, quietly, in the voice she used for things she actually believed, "Not for you. Not yet."

He had looked up at her. She wasn't looking at him. She was watching the last of the procession disappear around the fountain, and she was sad. Not disappointed. She had watched this before.

He had been turned away twice since then. The first time at fourteen, when corruption had broken out in the south fields and he had gone to it alone, before the warden assigned to that ground arrived. He drew the rot clean. He did it well. *The lad does not yet know his place in the line.* The second at sixteen, in the trial of bearing, when an Elder had pressed him hard and he had answered back the way an equal would, plain and steady. *He has the hands. He has not learned the hands are not his own.*

Both had been fair. The first time, he had run ahead of those above him. The second, he had forgotten whose he was. He had spent the years since learning the answer to both.

Today was the third.

The screaming went wrong. It came from inside the crowd. People shoved into each other, heads turning the wrong way, and a child was wailing somewhere he couldn't see. His whiskers flattened before he had turned.

The cheese wheel had come off the merchant's cart between the baker's stall and the second bunting pole. It was a tournament wheel, aged three years, the size of a wagon wheel. It had been tied at the wrong height, and the rope was gone. It was rolling, and it was picking up speed.

Between the wheel and where it was going stood a rabbit kit, four years old, a festival banner clutched in both paws. She wasn't moving. People around her were turning their heads, looking for someone to do something, and no one was moving yet.

Nibbles moved before he had finished thinking. He wasn't a fast runner, but he was low and quick, and he knew how to use gaps in a crowd. Under an elbow. Past a badger's knee. He reached her in three steps. His right paw found her far shoulder, the one that would swing her clear, and he shoved hard. She needed to be clear, and there was no time to be careful about it.

She went one way and he went the other, and the wheel found him before his feet had caught up to the shove.

The iron rim caught his left side. The impact arrived at his hip first, then ran up through his ribs in one hard wave he felt in his back teeth. His left paw was out, reaching for the ground, and the cobblestones took the paw and then his wrist and then the rest of him. He came to rest face-down on cobblestones warm from the morning sun.

The wheel was still moving somewhere to his left, slower now with the crowd in its way, and then there was a crash. The rabbit kit was crying. He stayed face-down and listened to the crying, then rolled over.

Blue sky above. Festival smoke drifting across it. The undersides of many pairs of eyes looking down at him. He found the kit from the crying. She was still standing where he had pushed her, festival banner still in both paws, crying at the banner.

"You're all right," he said, to the banner situation in general.

He got his knees under him. His left hip made its complaint clear. He listened to it and stood anyway. The thigh hurt sharply and was going to hurt for several days. The ribs were sore but nothing was broken. He had been hit hard enough to know the difference. Someone in the crowd had found the kit's mother and was threading her through, so he did not need to stay.

He checked his paws. The left pad was scraped from catching him, nothing that needed tending. He brushed them together. He fixed his cape, which had migrated. The cheese rind had found him; he could smell it.

His left thigh had opinions about the next step. He took it anyway and started walking.

Inside the Guild tent was chaos of three separate kinds.

The first was at the entrance, where a weasel in full plate armor was negotiating a sword exchange with the recruiter at the table, a young hedgehog with a clipboard who had clearly not been briefed on what to do when there was no procedure. The weasel had strong opinions about that gap and was sharing them at volume.

The second was in the center of the tent, where a squirrel in an apprentice robe had dropped something enchanted, and the fireball that resulted was three feet across and cooling on the canvas floor. The squirrel had gone very still. A Guild recruit was emptying a water bucket onto the fireball with the calm of someone who had done this before.

The third was the cheese wheel, which had arrived before Nibbles did. It was resting against the back desk. The wax coating had left a streak on the tent floor.

Nibbles stood in the entrance and took this in. The Guildmaster was behind the desk. Bristlebaum, old for a hedgehog, grey through most of his fur, quills somewhat blunt at the tips. His spectacles had been pushed up on his nose by some earlier event and sat at a slight angle. His paws were flat on the desk. His quills were extended at three-quarters of their full reach.

He was looking at the cheese wheel. Then he looked at Nibbles. His eyes went past the cape and the cheese rind to Nibbles' left side, the hip, the slight favoring of the leg, and then past Nibbles at the tent flap behind him. By the time his eyes came back, he had what he needed.

"You pushed the kit," Bristlebaum said.

Nibbles had a speech ready. It covered the cheese rind, who he was, and why he was here. He kept it.

"The wheel came from the baker's quarter," Bristlebaum said. "Her mother is outside." He looked at Nibbles' hip again. "How bad?"

"I'm fine."

"No doubt." He looked at the cheese wheel against his desk and then back at Nibbles. "Your name."

"Nibbles Tumblepatch. I'm here for my third Guild trial."

Bristlebaum picked up a ledger, opened it, ran one claw down a column. He didn't have to go far. "Turned away twice. Tumblepatch, Thimblewick." He closed it. "You're early."

"The cannon went off."

"The cannon always goes off. It never goes off straight." He set the ledger down and looked at Nibbles for a long moment without saying anything. "You pushed a child clear of a loose cartwheel," Bristlebaum said, "and then walked here covered in cheese rind."

"The rind is recent," Nibbles said.

"I can see that." Bristlebaum's quills settled a fraction. "Equipment is in the back. Shortswords are on the left side; they're sized for smaller paws." He said it without saying *like yours,* which Nibbles noted. "I'll be with you when I've finished with—"

He looked at the weasel, the squirrel, the fireball's aftermath, the cheese wheel.

"—this," he said.

Nibbles looked at the tent interior. Leather polish, something scorched, aged cheese. He had smelled worse.

"Is the fireball going to come back?" he asked.

"No," Bristlebaum said. "Go."

Nibbles went. The back of the tent was quieter. The real equipment, not the display pieces. Swords and tools on pegs, shelves labeled in careful handwriting. A table with maps. A row of packs along the far wall, buckled closed.

The shortswords were on the left side. Four of them, neatly arranged, the right size, blades clean and sharpened. In the corner, on the floor, was a chest.

Nibbles walked toward the shortswords, then past them, and stopped in front of the chest.

The chest was old. The joints had settled, and the wood around the latch had a groove worn into it, worn by a thumb or claw returning to the same spot over and over, pressing, checking, but not opening. Rust filled the keyhole.

Nibbles crouched down and put his paw on the latch. The chest wasn't locked. The latch lifted, and the lid opened on equipment wrapped in cloth gone grey with age. A practice dagger with its blade wrapped. A buckle from a belt that hadn't outlasted its last repair. A set of flint tools, still useable. And at the bottom, half-covered by the dagger's wrapping, a blade.

Rusted deep, the kind of rust that had worked its way into the metal over years. It was longer than the shortswords on the shelf. The hilt was wrapped in something that had been leather and was now closer to bark. A mark was worked into the pommel, a circle with lines through it, simple, the kind of mark someone had cut to mean something.

The grip was built for larger paws, a badger's, by the size and shape of it. He reached in anyway. His paw closed on the hilt with the wrap sitting wrong across his palm and the balance pulling forward.

The rust moved. It flowed back from the blade's surface, drawing toward the edges and then off them entirely. The metal underneath was silver-bright and clear. The rust had been a sheath, and it was coming off.

The blade reshaped as he held it. The length stayed, but the balance changed in his paw, the grip drawing in, the pommel settling. The whole sword was settling to him, and it was warm. The warmth came from inside the metal itself, not from sun or fire.

Then the light came. Cyan-blue, the color of deep water in the last moment before the sun left it, not from the edge but from the full length of the blade, outward. It wasn't fire. It passed through the canvas tent wall.

Nibbles held the sword at arm's length. A table caught someone's weight behind him, and he turned.

Bristlebaum was at the back of the tent. The weasel gone, the squirrel gone, Bristlebaum here, four feet away, with one paw braced against the edge of the equipment table. His spectacles had slid. His quills were fully extended, every one of them. He was looking at the blade. Nibbles looked at the blade, then at Bristlebaum.

"I wasn't going to—" He stopped. Bristlebaum wasn't listening. Bristlebaum was looking at the light, and at the blade, and at what the blade had just done. He opened his mouth, started a sentence, and closed his mouth again before any of it came out.

Then he put himself back together. The quills stayed up, but his spectacles settled. His paw came off the table. His chin came up. He looked at Nibbles, at the cheese rind on the cape, at the lit sword warm in his paw.

"Put it down," Bristlebaum said. His voice was flat.

"It changed," Nibbles said. "In my paw. The rust — and then the light—"

"I saw it."

"What is—"

"Put it down."

Nibbles looked at the sword. The light had steadied, warm and even. His palm was warm where the hilt sat in it.

He didn't put it down. He hadn't decided not to. His paw simply wouldn't move toward the chest. He looked at Bristlebaum, who looked back at him.

"It fits," Nibbles said. The hilt had drawn in to fit. "It changed to fit."

"Yes," Bristlebaum said, and the *yes* came out reluctantly.

"What is it called?"

Bristlebaum looked at the canvas above him for a long moment, then back at Nibbles.

"Whiskerbrand," he said.

Nibbles had never heard of it, and he said so.

"No," Bristlebaum said. "You wouldn't have." He pushed his spectacles back to where they belonged. He looked at the sword. "The shortswords are on the left side. Put that back and take a shortsword."

The sword was warm in his paw. The light moved through the metal at a steady pace. The grip sat against his palm the way it wanted to, not the way he was holding it. Nibbles looked at the shortswords on their pegs.

"What if I don't?" he asked.

Bristlebaum looked at him for a long moment.

"Then I have to explain," Bristlebaum said, "in a probationary contract, why you are leaving this tent today carrying a First Age blade that has been dormant for thirty years and that I have to list under Guild equipment as inactive."

"I could put it back," Nibbles offered.

"Yes," Bristlebaum said.

They both looked at the sword. The light went on moving through it.

"I could," Nibbles said.

"The sword," Bristlebaum said, "has not lit in thirty years. The last time someone held it, it did nothing at all." He kept his voice flat. "In thirty years, no one before you has opened that chest."

Nibbles looked at the chest, at the groove worn into the wood from thirty years of a thumb checking and not opening, at the rust no longer in the keyhole.

"Oh," Nibbles said.

Bristlebaum gripped the desk edge once, then let go. "The probationary restrictions," he said, "are going to be heavy."

Nibbles held the sword tighter.

The practice yard behind the tent was packed dirt and high fence, the Guild's working space, hidden from the festival crowd by planks and a hand-lettered sign telling anyone who tried the latch that the yard was private Guild property and not a shortcut to the cheese merchants. The latch had been worked from the wrong side enough times to wear it smooth anyway.

Bristlebaum pointed Nibbles to the center of the yard and put his own paws behind his back.

"Basic forms. Starting position." He looked at the sword, not at Nibbles. "I'm watching how the blade sits, not how you sit. You can be terrible."

"That should be easy," Nibbles said.

The hedgehog's quills came up half an inch.

"Starting position," Nibbles said.

His body moved without asking his mind for directions. Weight balanced between his feet, sword at guard. He had done the forms enough times on his own, against fence posts and grain sacks and the back wall of the mill storage in the dark, that the opening position arrived without his having to think through it.

The sword adjusted. His wrist moved with a small pressure at the hilt, and his wrist followed. One degree. The blade settled into a new angle, and he looked at where it was now and understood, from the angle alone, that this was where it should always have been. He had been holding it wrong for two years, and nobody had said.

"Move to the second form," Bristlebaum said.

He moved. The corrections came before the movements they were correcting. Not a tap on the shoulder afterward but a small pressure arriving a breath ahead, so that the first time through each form he was doing it right. He had never learned anything that way before. Every other thing he knew, he had learned by getting it wrong and then working back from the wrongness.

His footwork was still his footwork. The sword had no opinion on his footwork.

The seventh form was the pivot step. He had cheated the pivot for two years, back foot angled out past where it should be, a way of keeping his balance that was really a way of not trusting his weight through the full turn. This time he didn't cheat the step. The blade was sitting right, so his weight came down right, so the back foot landed where it was supposed to land. The seventh form finished level for the first time in his life.

He stood in the final position and looked at the wall of the fence in front of him. His right paw had blisters. Three sore spots on his palm that he would be feeling tomorrow. The hilt had drawn in to fit him, but his paw had two years of muscle memory for a different grip, and the two hadn't fully settled with each other yet. He looked at his right paw.

"Don't," Bristlebaum said.

"Don't what?"

"Don't change the grip to make up for them. Your paw will get used to it."

"I wasn't going to. I was looking at the blisters."

"They'll be worse tomorrow." Bristlebaum's posture hadn't shifted since they started. "Again from the first."

Nibbles set his feet.

The grin started somewhere in the fifth form. By the time he noticed it, it had been there for two full transitions, because the correction at his wrist had come again, the slight warm pressure arriving ahead of him, and this time he had felt it a full breath before he needed it. The sword was a step further ahead of him than he had realized. The grin was about something that had seen the motion before it happened and trusted him to follow.

In six years of practice, nobody had ever moved a step ahead of him. He kept the grin, and Bristlebaum saw it. The hedgehog watched, paws behind his back, and let the mouse work.

When Nibbles came to the final position the second time and stood still, Bristlebaum was quiet for a moment before he spoke.

"The restrictions," he said.

"Right."

"No blade in populated areas except on assignment." He raised one claw. "No purification work without Guild supervision." A second claw. "Field work at probationary grade. Guild-issued supply kit on every sortie. Evening reports." He paused. He looked at the sword. Then he looked at Nibbles. "At any point during your probation," he said, "you may return the sword to the Guild armory without losing your place. A warden who decides they are not ready may come back when they are." He paused again. "This offer does not expire."

He put his paws back behind his back. That last clause wasn't standard. Bristlebaum had built it just now, while he was standing there.

Nibbles looked at the sword. The light had settled to an even warmth. His palm throbbed.

"All right," Nibbles said.

"All right to which part."

"All of it. Including that one."

Bristlebaum looked at him, then turned for the service entrance.

"Inside. Quest Board."

Nibbles followed him. His left thigh had not forgotten the wheel. The sword sat warm against his back through the new leather sheath, steady and quiet.

The Quest Board filled the wall opposite the equipment shelf, ten feet high in a driftwood frame that carried the smell of salt and storm even here, forty miles from any coast. Notices covered the board in layers, the oldest gone yellow at the corners, newer ones pinned across their faces.

Bristlebaum worked through the lower section, the active local assignments with color-coded corners. He pulled a notice from the board and handed it over.

Nibbles took it. Nettleflint farm, Thimblewick region. Odd smell from the crumbleroot cellar. Two seasons of failed crops. Possible bad water from the old drainage channels, or from whatever had shifted in the soil below the southeast foundation. Look into it and report back.

He read it twice, folded it, put it in his pocket, and looked up at the rest of the board.

Merchant disputes. A missing sow. A bridge inspection pinned over a notice asking for the bridge inspection. A report on unusual weather near the northern ridge, marked as natural variation, with a question mark added after in different ink.

In the upper left corner, behind the edge of a moth-eaten campaign banner that had been used to pad out the frame's loose right side, there was a scrap of parchment. Half-burned, the right edge blackened and curled where someone had pulled it from a fire before it was entirely gone. Someone had pinned it up. Three words were still legible on it.

it is watching

The rest of the scrap was ash. Nibbles looked at it, then at the people nearby. Two candidates comparing notices on the right side of the board. The young recruiter at the table. The banner's edge covered the scrap for anyone not standing at his angle and his height. He didn't say anything.

Three rows up from the scrap, in the row marked for routine environmental surveys, blue-cornered, the blue faded to nearly nothing, there was a notice.

Millbrook village, northern pass road, thirty-second day of autumn. Fountain water violet-tinged. No illness reported. Mineral seepage from limestone deposits likely, common at altitude. Survey requested.

Bristlebaum was making a note on his clipboard.

"This one," Nibbles said.

Bristlebaum looked up, followed his gaze. "Mineral contamination. We'll have someone in the area within a month."

"It says violet."

"Limestone deposits at altitude can colour groundwater. It's been written down before."

"Our fountain is violet," Nibbles said. "From a cleaning compound."

"Different cause."

"Yes. But violet is a particular color." He looked at the date on the notice. Day thirty-two of autumn, six weeks ago.

Bristlebaum looked at the notice, then at Nibbles.

"Your assignment is the Nettleflint cellar," he said. "Millbrook is north. It's not your assignment."

"Can I ask why it hasn't been surveyed yet? It's been six weeks."

"Staffing," Bristlebaum said, and the word was carrying a lot. "We have six active field agents and an eastern corridor that is currently taking four of them. The northern road is a low-priority survey. We will get to it."

Nibbles looked at the Millbrook notice, then at the date again.

"All right," he said.

He looked at the rest of the board for another moment. The missing sow. The bridge inspection. The weather report with its secondhand question mark.

"The tin badge," Bristlebaum said. He held it out.

It was small and somewhat bent, and the Guild stamp had been worn shallow by years of reissue. Nibbles pinned it to the tablecloth cape and adjusted it until it sat level.

"Dawn," Bristlebaum said.

"Dawn," Nibbles said.

He took one more look at the Quest Board and walked out of the tent.

Outside, the Cheese Festival was exactly where he had left it. He had been inside (the tent, the practice yard, the forms, Bristlebaum, the sword) for perhaps two hours. The festival had not adjusted itself for any of it. The baker's stall had the same line in front of it. Minnow at the lavender booth was still bundling sachets without looking up. Three young recruits in new Guild tabards were crossing the square carefully, uncertain where to put their faces. A cart horse at the corner of the bakers' row had found a dropped roll and was sorting the situation out.

He bought one of the small nut-and-honey rounds from the festival cart, the kind that appeared only on Cheese Day. He had been looking forward to them since he was eight. He stood at the edge of the square and ate it.

The sword was warm and steady against his back through the sheath. His right paw had blisters, and his left hip was bruised hard from the cobblestones. The cellar notice was in his pocket.

He turned the day over in his head while he ate. The half-burned scrap, three words on a blackened edge, pinned where only a small creature at the right angle could read it. The Millbrook notice, six weeks old, violet water in a village on the northern road. The copper note in the morning air that had arrived before the cannon and faded before he could place it. And Bristlebaum's face when the rust burned away.

The lavender sachet from the morning was still in his pocket. He turned it over once in his paw, the dry scratch of the cloth, the smell coming sharp and clear, and put it back.

His mother's voice came back to him. *Not for you, not yet.* He had carried the second half for years; the first half he was still working on.

He straightened the tin badge on the tablecloth cape until it sat level, and left it there.

The festival moved around him. Bunting in yellow and green. The fountain running its permanent purple. The village at its loudest and busiest of the year. The baker was calling out his last round of the day. Two children were chasing each other around the fountain in a loop with no apparent endpoint.

The sword was on his back and the notice was in his pocket. He started walking.

Chapter Two

Into the Cellar

THE ROAD TO NETTLEFLINT'S farm ran northeast from Thimblewick's mill bridge, past the grain market and up through a stand of oak where the birds had gone quiet.

Nibbles noticed the quiet before he saw anything wrong. He'd been watching his feet (the blisters on his right paw pads had split sometime in the night and the first half-mile had been careful walking) but the silence reached him anyway. He knew how an oak stand sounded in late summer. The wren in the leaf litter. The recurring argument of wood pigeons. The starlings that moved through the canopy in a shifting mass when something startled them. He'd walked this road every week of his life, back from his mother's house on the other side of town.

The stand had birds in it. A wren on a lower branch, watching him. A pair of wood pigeons at the canopy edge, motionless. He stopped under them and looked up, and they looked down at him, and no one made a sound. The wren rotated its head as he passed beneath it without calling. He picked up his pace.

His left thigh ached where the cheese wheel had caught him yesterday. Whiskerbrand's hilt was pressing into the back of his neck. The sheath rode four inches too high for his frame, and he'd spent the first mile trying to adjust it before giving up. He had a list of things he needed, and the sheath was on it.

The south field stopped him at the fence line. Half the wheat was fine, full heads, the color grain turned when harvest was weeks away. The other half had given up. The heads were still full, the stalks still standing, but the color had failed to a dull grey. He got his notebook out.

The grey patches didn't follow the slope or the rows. They ran in a curve from the eastern fence to the old stone wall at the field's north end, tracking something under the soil he couldn't see from where he stood. He drew it as carefully as he could and wrote *pattern. not slope. not row direction. follows something underground.*

The fence post at the gate came next. Fence posts wear where gates swing, where ropes drag, where animals brush past on the outside. The groove on this one ran along the inside face, the side facing the cellar mound at the far end of the yard, low near the base, smoothed by repeated contact in the same spot over weeks. Something had been pressing against the inside of this fence over and over.

He was still writing when the farmhouse door opened and Nettleflint came out.

The mole was stooped through the shoulders and broad through the chest, paws gnarled from decades in the soil. His spectacles were thick and caught the light at an angle that made his eyes look doubled, the real eyes behind the lenses and the magnified versions on top.

"Guild tent sent you," Nettleflint said. It was not a question. He was looking at the cape.

"Nibbles Tumblepatch, probationary field agent." Nibbles put the notebook away. "I have a—"

"Probationary."

"Yes."

The mole studied him.

"My grain's failing," Nettleflint said. "Well water tastes of metal since the new moon. Three fence posts worn on the wrong side, something pressing at them in the night that I can't see in daylight. Guild sends me someone on probation."

"The Guildmaster sent me specifically. I'm the one carrying Whisker-brand." He paused. "That doesn't mean I know what I'm doing. I haven't done this before. What I can tell you is exactly what I find, whatever it turns out to be."

Nettleflint studied him a beat longer, then stepped aside and held the gate open.

"Cellar's at the back. Mind the vines on the door frame, they've gone sharp at the ends."

Nibbles stepped through.

The vines around the cellar door had dried from green to brown and pressed flat against the stone frame. Nibbles worked one loose and it crumbled in his pad, brittle all the way through. He crouched to look at the door itself.

The scratches were above the latch. They weren't key scratches (key scratches clustered around the keyhole) and they weren't wood splitting along the grain. Parallel lines, running horizontal across the planks, repeated every few inches up the door's face. He checked the inside of the door frame. Same pattern. He checked the outside face of the frame, and the scratches were there too.

Something warm was pressing against his spine through the sheath leather, a low vibration that had been there since the oak stand. He straightened and lifted the latch. The door swung inward on hinges that didn't squeal. Old cellar hinges should squeal. These had been oiled recently, and he didn't think Nettleflint had oiled them. He stepped across the threshold.

Whiskerbrand came free of the scabbard with a soft ring like a note struck on a bowl, and he hadn't pulled it. His paw had found the hilt, but the blade had moved an inch and a half clear of the scabbard before he caught it, and the vibration along his spine sharpened a half-step.

His whiskers caught the air first. Copper, iron, and something beneath both that he didn't have a name for.

He eased the blade back to the scabbard's catch, kept his paw on the hilt, and went down the steps.

The walls glowed. A faint purple radiance held steady in the mortar joints between stones. The light came from crystals growing in the joints, purple and faceted, each one catching the light of its neighbors. The light didn't move the way firelight moved. The mortar had dissolved where they grew, and the stones had shifted, settling wrong against each other.

Nibbles stopped on the third step from the bottom and counted. The south wall was covered from floor to above head height, crystals bridging the gaps between stones where the mortar had gone. The east wall was covered to roughly two-thirds. The west wall was a quarter done, the crystals there newer-looking, still finding their spacing. He went down the last steps and stood on the cellar floor and looked at the whole space.

The floor sloped toward the center drain, built to let water run down and keep the vegetables dry. The drain had the thickest crystal formation, a dense cluster built up at the lowest point. From the drain the growth spread outward in every direction, up the walls and across the floor, heavier on the south side, lighter on the north and west.

He looked at the northwest corner, farthest from the drain. Clean stone, bare mortar, the original work as it had been laid. He looked back at the drain and the dense cluster around it, and then back at the clean corner.

He wrote *drain at center. growth spreads outward from drain. northwest corner, farthest point from drain, clean. water flows to the drain.* He underlined the last line.

The smell was copper and iron and something beneath both, sweet and wrong. He looked at the shelves along the east wall. Clay jars, preserved goods, nothing disturbed. Whatever had been coming in here wasn't coming for the food.

His right paw was still on Whiskerbrand's hilt. The vibration along his spine had shifted from the low hum of the approach to something a half-step sharper.

He turned around.

The first spider dropped from the ceiling crossbeam and landed in a crouch three feet to his left, already oriented, all eight eyes on him before the motion had finished. The eyes were wrong. They should have been dark reflection, eight small points of caught light, and instead they were purple, full and luminous, lit from inside.

Nibbles' paw went to Whiskerbrand's hilt. The blade tore free of the scabbard before he asked it to, a snap of cyan-blue light in the cellar's purple glow, blazing briefly and settling to a cold brightness. He nearly dropped it. The blisters on his right paw pads had split during the morning's walk, and the leather hilt hit exactly where the skin had opened.

He adjusted. Left paw up to help carry the grip. He had been practicing this for one day.

The second spider came from behind the drain cluster, moving left. The third came from the gap behind the eastern shelves, moving right.

He saw all three at once. Front pressure and two flanks, placed in a triangle with him at the center. Spiders don't hunt in triangles. They don't coordinate flanks. Then the front spider moved.

He swung Whiskerbrand in an arc he hadn't planned. His paw had moved the blade before he chose to move it, coming around low and fast. The front spider lunged into the arc and the blade caught it across its forward legs. It went sideways into the crystal cluster near the drain with a sound like crockery hitting stone and stopped moving.

The left-flank spider came. He turned right. Wrong call. The left-flank spider was faster than he'd judged and closed the distance before he corrected. He was inside his own swing radius, no room for the blade, and he pulled Whiskerbrand back left too wide and too slow. The grip rotated in his paws. He went with it rather than fight it and lose the sword. The blade came back inward and caught the spider on its carapace with the flat, a redirect rather than an edge hit, enough force to drive it hard into the west wall. It hit stone and stopped moving.

Nibbles moved to the center of the cellar, away from the walls and the shelves, into open ground. The fourth spider dropped from the crossbeam above him.

It landed on his left shoulder at the junction of shoulder and neck and bit through his coat before he could do anything. Two points of pressure, hot and fast, and then the spider was in his grip, heavy and hard-shelled, and he threw it against the stone floor. It hit hard and lay still.

The shoulder burned. He had been bitten by spiders before, and burning was what spider bites did. The cold spreading outward from the puncture points was not. It moved slowly into the muscle, with purpose. He kept his paw on the sword and kept his feet moving.

The first spider had righted itself in the crystal cluster and was coming again. He held his ground this time, sword up. Whiskerbrand followed the spider's approach, a slight pressure in his palms redirecting the angle, the blade settling a half-beat ahead of the spider's next move. He followed the grip. The spider broke left at the last moment into a blade that was already waiting for it. He ended with Whiskerbrand's tip through the spider's body, pinned to the stone floor beside the drain. He pulled the blade free.

The second spider had recovered from the wall. He engaged it directly, standing where he chose to stand. The angle was wrong on the first pass and wrong again on the second, but Whiskerbrand held the line on both even when his arms weren't doing what he intended, and on the third exchange the spider stopped moving. The third spider backed into the corner under the east shelves and crouched there.

Nibbles stood in the center of the cellar and breathed. His left shoulder burned above the collarbone, and the cold from the bite had reached some-where between his shoulder and his elbow and settled there. His left thigh had seized from overextending the wrong way twice during the second spider's rush. His right paw pads were bleeding. The blisters had opened fully against the grip. Four spiders. Three down, the fourth where it had fallen.

He looked at where the three had positioned themselves when they came at him. Front pressure, two flanks. Someone had taught them that.

The crack was at the base of the south wall, in the section where the crystal growth was densest. He'd missed it at first because the crystal formation had grown high on either side, purple facets framing the gap. But the crack itself was open, a line through the stone and the mortar and into the bedrock below, wider at the center and narrowing at each end. The stone around it had a color the rest of the cellar floor didn't have, a purple barely visible, seeping upward from somewhere below the crystals, down through the rock itself.

He crouched in front of it. The crystals spread outward from the crack in every direction he'd mapped. Toward the drain, up the south wall, east and west. The drain was where the growth concentrated because that was where water moved, but the crack was where it came from. Whiskerbrand hummed against his spine in a rhythm slower than the fight-sharpness, and deeper, a vibration he felt in his sternum.

Nobody had given him instructions for this. The Guildmaster had handed him a quest scroll, a sheath that didn't fit, and the information, delivered in a clipped tone at the end of the practice session, that the sword would know what to do when it needed to. Nibbles took Whiskerbrand in both paws. His left shoulder was still burning above the collarbone. His right paw was wet with blood from the fight. He put both paws on the hilt anyway, left covering most of the right, and crouched lower in front of the crack.

The sword pulled his paws forward, a pressure on the hilt, the weight of something leaning into him heavier than it looked. He let his arms extend. The tip of Whiskerbrand touched the stone at the crack's edge.

The hilt burned. A brightness moved from the hilt through his paws and up his forearms, through his shoulders and into his chest, and Whiskerbrand blazed cyan-blue, flooding the cellar so hard that the purple glow of the crystals disappeared under it. The walls went white. The light poured down through the crack the way water pours into a drain, following the gap, going down through the stone and into whatever was below.

The hollow opened in his chest. He had expected pain, and this wasn't pain. It was an absence, and the cold of it spread outward from his chest. His vision dimmed at the edges, the cellar walls softening and receding, but the crack in front of him stayed sharp and clear and still bright with the light going into it. He counted his heartbeats because he needed something to count.

Something pressed back through the connection. Through the crack, through the sword, through the light running downward into the stone, something became aware of him. He felt it. An attention, focused and cold, arriving from very far away at very high speed, from something that had been in the dark for a long time. It had been doing something when he interrupted it, and now it was looking at him. Its curiosity was specific. *What are you, what are you carrying, what are you doing here.*

He held on. Letting go felt like giving it what it wanted, so he didn't.

The light kept going down through the crack. The hollow in his chest stayed open. His vision had narrowed to the crack and the blade and the brightness. He could feel his heartbeat in his right paw, in the split skin against the leather.

The thing on the other side of the crack examined him, and he held on.

Whiskerbrand cut the light off. One moment blazing, then not. The hilt cooled and the hollow in his chest closed at the same time, the closing hitting him like a heavy door dropping into its latch. His knees buckled. He caught himself with his left paw on the stone floor before he went all the way down, and he stayed there, paws on cold stone, head down, breathing.

The crack was still there, but the crystals had pulled back from it, two inches on each side, the stone visible beneath, the purple glow dimmer than before. The dense cluster around the drain was thinner. The south wall still glowed, but less.

In the last moment before the light had died, the brightness had gone deepest into the crack and shown him what was below. A flash, barely a second, the light illuminating the bedrock beneath the cellar floor. Lines cut into the stone. Carved lines, not natural fracture, running in a pattern through the bedrock in narrow, precise channels. The kind of channels someone cuts on purpose, knowing in advance where they want something to flow.

He didn't know what they were. He wrote it down. *Lines in bedrock below crack. carved. patterned. not natural fracture.*

He put the notebook away and stood up. The hollow had not fully closed, a soreness at the center of his chest. His left shoulder still burned above the collarbone, and the cold from the bite had reached somewhere between his shoulder and elbow and settled there. He climbed the steps back toward the daylight.

The light hit him when he pushed the cellar door open, and he stood at the top of the steps and breathed air that was not copper and iron and that wrong-sweet smell underneath both. The farmyard was quiet. The late morning was warm. He could hear the sounds of the farm. Wind through the drying racks on the south fence. The low complaint of sheep from the far field. Nothing that shouldn't be there.

He pulled the cellar door closed and turned toward the farmhouse. Nettleflint's wife was at the kitchen window with her paw flat against the glass, watching him without moving. Behind her, through the wavy kitchen glass, he could see a bread board and flour dust hanging in the warm air.

He stopped. He looked down at himself. His right paw wrapped in Nettleflint's cloth, already spotted through with blood where the split blisters had opened against the leather grip during the fight. The tear in his coat at the left shoulder, two puncture points through the fabric above the collarbone. The careful way he'd been carrying his weight since the second spider's rush, his left thigh still seized across the muscle from overextending wrong twice during the fight.

He looked back up. She was still at the glass.

Nettleflint came around the south corner of the farmhouse. He looked at Nibbles once, then up at his wife in the window. She gave one nod and stepped back from the glass. Nettleflint turned back to Nibbles.

Nibbles gave the report standing in the yard. Three spiders, possibly a fourth. The coordinated flanking, triangle placement, positioned before he'd seen them. The crystals in the mortar and their spread from the drain outward. He described the cleansing as carefully as he could. The hilt burning. The light going down through the crack. The hollow in his chest that had not fully closed. He described the void-touched bite on his left shoulder and the cold still in the arm below it. He said the crystal formation should recede over the coming days, that the grain might improve once the source crack was sealed, that he couldn't promise a timeline.

Nettleflint listened without interrupting. He was looking at Nibbles' shoulder, and then at his paw through the cloth, and then at the cellar door.

"Come in and wash that out properly," the mole said.

"I can manage in town—"

"Now." He paused. "My wife has bread out of the oven. She'd take it as a slight if you left without any."

He went back toward the kitchen door without waiting.

Nibbles tucked Nettleflint's cloth carefully into his pocket and followed the mole through the kitchen door.

He found the trail when they came back out through the yard twenty minutes later, his shoulder cleaned and packed with a cloth soaked in something that stung, a wrapped heel of bread in his coat pocket that the wife had put there without comment.

He was watching his feet crossing the flagstones because his left thigh was still seized and the gaps between the stones were uneven, which was how he saw it.

Fine particles of cellar dust, the light grey dust that built up in the mortar channels over years and came loose when crystals dissolved, displaced in a narrow line from the east foundation wall outward across the flagstones. Half an inch wide. The particles on each side were undisturbed. Whatever had made the line had moved carefully enough to disturb only what was directly beneath it. The line ran straight to the east foundation wall and stopped.

He crouched. At the base of the wall, between the second and third courses of foundation stone from the ground, there was a gap, two inches wide, a little over an inch tall, the edges worn smooth. The trail went into it, and nothing had come back out.

He counted the spiders. The one pinned by the drain. The one driven into the west wall. The one he'd worked to a three-exchange finish. The one from the crossbeam that had gotten through his coat, that he'd thrown to the floor. Four in the cellar. But when the cleansing had needed both his paws and all of his attention, the third spider had been in the corner under the east shelves, and his back had been turned to the east corner the whole time.

He straightened, carefully, and turned to find the farmer.

"One of the spiders got out," he said. "Through the east foundation wall. Gap in the lower stones, second course from the ground." He pointed. "The trail is there, from the corner under the east shelves to the gap. It carried the same corruption as the others."

Nettleflint crossed to the east wall and looked where Nibbles was pointing. The thick spectacles caught the morning light wrong and turned white at the angle. The mole bent lower, tilting his head.

"I'll take your word for it," Nettleflint said.

"The gap needs filling today. Mortar if you have it, stone if you don't. And don't go into the cellar until I come back with someone who can tell me what the bite on my shoulder means." He paused. "I don't know where the spider is in the foundations."

Nettleflint looked at the gap.

"I'll fill it," he said.

Nibbles wrote the location in his notebook (*east foundation wall, 2nd-3rd course from ground, gap approx 2in wide, third spider exited here, void-crystal corruption, present location in foundations unknown, farmer advised. fill today*) and drew the gap's position on his exterior foundation sketch. He put the notebook away.

He made it back to the Guild tent three hours after leaving the farm, with the afternoon going gold through the canvas and the quest board throwing long shadows across the floor that nearly reached Bristlebaum's desk.

The Guildmaster was working through a stack of requests when Nibbles came through the tent flap. He looked up, turned the topmost page face down, and waited. His quills were at the slightly raised position they held when he was working something out. Nibbles came to the desk.

"Three spiders in the cellar, possibly a fourth. I'm counting the one that escaped separately. They coordinated. Front pressure and two flanks, triangle, already positioned when I entered. Someone taught them that." He set his notebook on the desk, open to the cellar sketch. "Crystals in every mortar joint on three walls. Spread outward from the foundation crack in the south wall, heaviest around the center drain. The northwest corner was clean, the farthest point from the drain."

Bristlebaum pulled the notebook closer and looked at the sketch. His claw moved along the drawing, pausing at the drain cluster, the crack location, the clean corner. He turned to the next page. The exterior foundation sketch with the gap marked.

"Third spider escaped through the east foundation wall before I finished in the cellar," Nibbles said. "Gap in the lower courses, I've marked it. I've asked the farmer to fill it today. The spider is somewhere in the foundations and I can't tell you where." He touched the notation on the sketch. "The farmer's well water has been running wrong since the new moon. Fence posts worn on the inside face."

"The bite," Bristlebaum said.

"Left shoulder above the collarbone. Two points, void-touched. Cold spreading from the punctures outward during the fight. It's settled between the shoulder and the elbow now and it's still there." He pulled the collar aside so Bristlebaum could see the packed cloth. "I'll need someone to look at it."

Bristlebaum looked. "Tonight," he said.

"The cleansing." Nibbles had arranged what he wanted to say on the walk back, putting it in the order he needed to deliver it. "I drove the blade into the crack. Both paws on the hilt. The hilt burned. It felt more like heat going in than out, no pain in it. The light went down through the crack into the stone below, following the gap. I could see it going through." He paused. "A hollow opened in my chest while the light was running. An absence, like the opposite of something being there. My vision went narrow at the edges. Whiskerbrand cut the light off when it finished. Crystals pulled back two inches on each side of the crack. The drain cluster is thinner than before."

The canvas of the tent moved faintly in the afternoon air.

He had words for what came next. He'd put them together on the walk back, working out a sentence that was honest about what he'd felt when something on the other side became aware of him through the connection. He didn't use it. Saying it would have meant Bristlebaum had to respond, and he didn't want the response to be Bristlebaum taking the sword back. He moved on.

"There are carved lines in the bedrock below the crack. I saw them in the last moment before the light cut off. Patterned, carved on purpose rather than natural fracture, running through the stone in narrow channels. I've written them down." He indicated the page. "I don't know what they are."

Bristlebaum had not moved since the cleansing description began. His claw rested on the desk edge, in the groove worn there over years of the same grip. He turned to the bedrock entry, looked at it, turned back to the cellar map. He took the regional map from the desk drawer and spread it flat.

It was large, the edges curling from being stored rolled. Crumbleroot Farm, Nettleflint's place, was marked in the eastern section. Bristlebaum's claw moved across it, then across the neighboring farms to the north, the wells that fed them. The farm road from the mill bridge. The stream that fed the wells and the smaller channels coming off it. His claw pressed briefly at each point and moved on. Nibbles watched the pattern, northeast to southwest, following the water routes. It wasn't random. It was a sequence, checking specific things.

The claw stopped on a point in the forest section northeast of Nettleflint's farm, and Bristlebaum pressed it flat against the map.

"'The seals have held for—'" Bristlebaum said, and stopped.

He pulled his paw back, rolled the map along its edges, squared the corners, and set it aside without finishing the sentence.

"Good work," he said. "Full follow-up requirements by morning."

He reached into his coat pocket and set the badge on the desk. Silver. Small. The Guild crest stamped clean into the face, a sword crossed with a quill.

Nibbles picked it up, and the metal was warm in his paw.

Chapter Three

Shadows in the Woods

THE SPARROW WAS ON the doorstep when Nibbles opened the door. He almost missed it. The morning light was still low, the shadow from the doorframe falling long across the worn stone, and the bird was tucked close to the left side of the threshold. Then he saw the eyes. Open. Faintly violet, the glow mostly gone but not entirely. The bird was dead. The violet wasn't.

The smell came to him a beat later. Faint, nothing like the concentrated wrongness of the Nettleflint cellar, but related. The same smell at a whisper. The residue of something that had passed through this bird on its way somewhere else. Nibbles stood in the doorway, holding still.

His left shoulder pulled when he shifted weight, the bandaging tight across the void-touched bite, still sore two days on. He had changed the dressing twice in the night and hadn't done a good job either time. The note rested against the sparrow's folded wing.

He crouched and picked it up without touching the bird. The paper was better quality than anything Thimblewick usually produced, pressed smooth, folded with the kind of care that took practice. A small dried fleck of lavender was caught in the fold of the seal. He opened it.

Mr. Tumblepatch,

The bird arrived outside my observation post three nights ago. Its eyes were clear then. I have been watching Wigglywood Forest and its environs for the past six weeks and can confirm that what you encountered in the Nettleflint cellar is consistent with a pattern I have been tracking since early spring. The infection has a source and a direction. I would ask that you meet me at the mill bridge before the seventh bell. I intend to introduce myself at that time. Bring the sword. This is not a training exercise.

A.A.

Nibbles read it twice. He thought about what had pressed back through the crack during the purification, that cold, curious pressure arriving in the last moment before Whiskerbrand's light closed the connection. He hadn't put it in his report to Bristlebaum. The right sentence hadn't come. The badge in his pocket was warm when he pressed his paw to it.

He stepped over the sparrow carefully, shut the door behind him, and went to find his vest.

The seventh bell was still settling into the morning air when he came around the bend in the road and saw the mill bridge empty. He slowed. The mill wheel turned at its usual pace, the stream running below in the low murmur of early morning, the bridge sitting solid and grey with lichen claiming the cracks. No one on it, no one in either direction.

"You are precisely on time," said a voice from the willows on his left.

Nibbles turned. The squirrel was standing at the near edge of the willow stand, and from the look of him he'd been there for some time. He looked comfortable. Green vest pressed sharp, every button aligned, every seam straight, the lapels lying exactly as they should. Whiskers groomed to perfect symmetry. Tail held still but not relaxed. A leather journal was tucked under his left arm. His amber eyes kept moving even when the rest of him was at rest.

"Agent Acornimus," the squirrel said. "S.I.S.S. A Guild intelligence body. Field operative, third class. You received my note."

"I did," Nibbles said. Then, because it seemed relevant, "A.A."

"Quite." Acornimus came toward him, each step placed. "I have been in Thimblewick for six weeks. You have been here rather longer. I thought it best to wait until the pattern reached the stage that warranted introduction. That stage arrived yesterday evening."

"What does your body do?"

"We track threats that arrive quietly. Before they reach the threshold for active Guild response." He came level with Nibbles on the road and stopped. His voice was even and clean. "In this case, I have been tracking signs that come before the obvious ones, livestock behavior, crop failure, water discoloration, birds. The Nettleflint situation confirmed routes I had mapped but not yet fully verified." He opened the journal. The visible pages were dense with small, neat handwriting and small, neat sketches, maps, timelines, columns of notation. "Two children are missing."

Nibbles's whiskers went flat.

"From Thimblewick?"

"Yes." Acornimus held the journal open. His right paw moved in a small, precise motion, reaching toward a clasp on the journal's cover, and stopped midway. He redirected the paw to a button on his vest, which he touched once and released. "Their names are Mira and Pip. Mira is seven years old. She wants to be a baker. She has been trying to persuade her mother to share the lemon-cake recipe since before midwinter. Her mother keeps telling her the butter temperature is too difficult for someone her age. Pip is five. He collects rocks. He has a collection he keeps in a box under his bed, each stone in an order he devised himself, and his older sister has been trying to rearrange it for months without success." A pause. "They went into the Wigglywood yesterday evening looking for spring herbs. They have not returned."

"We should cross," Nibbles said.

"Yes," Acornimus said. "I believe so."

They walked toward the bridge. The mill wheel kept turning behind them, the water lifting and falling under it.

"You said the infection follows channels," Nibbles said.

"I said it has a source and a direction. The direction I have confirmed. The source I have not." Acornimus's whiskers were forward and not moving. "Everything I have watched tracks the same underground routes, old channels beneath the valley floor, water paths, root networks. The sick zones lie on top of them. That is not coincidence." He paused. "Someone is pushing through existing architecture. Someone who knows where that architecture runs."

"Then it's directed," Nibbles said. "Not random."

"That is my conclusion, yes." Acornimus looked at him. "You reached it quickly."

"The animals in the cellar were following orders," Nibbles said. "Something was giving orders. I just didn't know what yet." They reached the bridge.

He stopped at the edge before stepping onto the stone. He'd started noticing the night before, on the walk home from the Nettleflint farm, when he passed the village fountain and caught for the first time that the permanent purple tint had a smell. Faint, nothing like the concentrated wrongness of the cellar crack, but related. He'd told himself he was tired and imagining. He'd woken this morning still thinking about it.

He crouched and put his bandaged paw to the stream. Cold. Moving. Stone and mud and the clean sharpness of water that had been running for a long time. He held his paw in for a slow count of three.

Clean. Different from fountain-clean, which was its own thing now that he was paying attention. The fountain had a mineral undertone he'd lived with so long it had become part of the background. This stream had no such undertone. This water was just water. He stood and dried his paw on his vest.

"You check water at crossings," Acornimus said. He had watched without comment.

"Started last night." Nibbles paused. "The fountain smells different from this. I noticed it walking home. I don't know what the difference means."

He wasn't entirely sure that was true. He had something forming, the wrongness strongest at the cellar, present but diluted at the fountain, absent at this stream. He couldn't prove it yet.

Acornimus's paw was already moving over a journal page. "The fountain draws from groundwater on the northern slope," he said. "That slope sits above the channel network I have been tracking. This stream draws from the eastern tributary, which does not." He kept writing. "Water moving through a healthy channel stays clean. Water moving through a corrupted one does not. The effect lessens with distance and dilution but does not vanish entirely."

Nibbles looked at the stream, then at the path beyond it. He was working out a way of telling what was underground by what came up through it. He didn't have a name for it yet, or any idea how far he could push it. He set the question aside and crossed the bridge.

The treeline was fifty yards past the bridge. Forty yards before they reached it, the birdsong changed.

Normal Wigglywood morning noise ran in every direction at once. Things calling, answering, alarming over small matters, singing for their own reasons. What Nibbles heard now came from one direction only, and the calls were warning of something rather than chattering about ordinary forest business. A steady alarm, patient, going on for a long time.

Whiskerbrand went warm at his back, the way it had in the cellar before the crack.

"The sword is reacting," Nibbles said.

"Noted." Acornimus wrote without slowing.

The undergrowth along the path was stiller than undergrowth should be. Plants angled toward the path rather than growing where they'd been seeded, the lean subtle enough that you only saw it once you were looking, a low pull toward the path that shouldn't have been there. The bark on the nearest trunks was pushing outward in places, bulging where something inside had been pressing for a long time. The leaves higher up carried a yellow-grey pallor. Five paces into the canopy, the air shifted. Same family as the cellar's wrongness, stronger with every step.

The bark-armored rabbit came out of the undergrowth on the left. Nibbles had grown up next to a field of rabbits. He knew their movement, the quick dart, the freeze-and-assess, the bolt away from anything new. This one came forward instead. Its shoulders had been replaced by a thick plating the color of dried bark, dark and hard, swallowing the filtered forest light instead of throwing it back. Its eyes were violet, the color solid and even and lit from behind like a torch. It moved at an angle that placed it deliberately in his path.

Two more emerged from the right.

"Left," Acornimus said, flat and clear, and moved right.

Nibbles drew Whiskerbrand. The blade came warm into his paw. His grip settled before he consciously adjusted it, the hilt finding the angle and holding him there.

The lead rabbit hit him at the knees.

The blow knocked him back half a step. His shoulder blazed, the void-touched bite going bright as he torqued to keep his balance, the bandaging holding the wound closed and doing nothing for the pain. He got the blade between them before the rabbit could press the advantage, and the warmth in the hilt shifted, a small direction arriving a half-beat early, and he let his wrist follow it. The redirect came out clean. The rabbit skittered wide.

Second rabbit, right side.

He tried to bring his left arm up and felt the elbow lock short. The bandage was doing its job and its job included preventing full extension. The block came up two inches shy of where he needed it. The rabbit's plated shoulder caught his forearm and knocked him sideways. He landed wrong on his right foot and his ankle complained sharply. He went to one knee.

Third rabbit, coming around behind.

The warmth in the hilt moved again, a tight pulse that was a direction, and he turned his wrist the way it indicated and brought the blade up in the arc it was guiding him toward. The flat of it caught the third rabbit across the side. The violet in its eyes guttered.

It stopped, and both of the others stopped with it.

Then all three together turned and walked back into the undergrowth at the same unhurried pace they'd used coming out.

Nibbles stayed on one knee for a slow breath, taking inventory. Shoulder hot, still working. Ankle, he could carry it if he was careful. Left elbow bruised on top of the bandage restriction, full extension still gone.

He could walk and he could fight. He would have to compensate for the elbow on the next one. He stood.

"The withdrawal was timed together," Acornimus said from ten feet away. He was writing already, pen moving, not looking at the page. A short dense stick lay at his feet. He had apparently persuaded his own three rabbits to leave without needing Nibbles to involve himself. "All three broke off at the same moment. None of them moving on their own."

"I noticed."

"The angles they came in on would have surrounded an isolated target." Acornimus tucked the stick away. "They are not simply infected. They are being directed."

"The children went northeast?" Nibbles asked.

"About a quarter-mile. There is a stream crossing before the old beech grove. The herbs they were collecting grow along that bank." Acornimus stepped over a root without slowing. "We should not delay."

The old beech grove came up quiet. Nibbles smelled the change before he saw what caused it. A gap in the corruption-smell more than a scent itself, a small radius around a dead oak where the wrong undertone was absent. Something living and clean had spent enough time near that tree to displace it. He adjusted his route without explaining why and came around the oak from the eastern side.

The hollow was at chest height, deep enough that the back of it was shadow. Mira was at the back of it. A young hedgehog girl. Her quills were flat, raised and lowered too many times since dusk and now simply down. She had been in there long enough that the first sharpness of fear had passed. Her small face found his the moment he came around the tree. She didn't move.

Nibbles stopped. He felt the pull to move toward her and put it aside. He crouched, putting himself at her level, settled back on his heels, and waited. She was watching him closely, weighing what he would do next. He waited a beat longer.

"I'm Nibbles," he said. He kept his voice at kitchen-table level, no urgency in it. "From the village. Your mother knows who I am. She's looking for you."

Mira's quills didn't move.

"Your mother told me about the lemon-cake project," he said.

Her quills came away from flat, settling into something between flat and watchful.

"She said you've been after the recipe since before midwinter, and she keeps telling you the butter temperature is too difficult for someone your age." He let that sit. "I think she's wrong. Most of the bakers I know started younger than seven."

"I'm seven and a half," Mira said. Her voice came out rough from crying and from however long she had been sitting in the hollow not using it.

"Right. So well past the point she should have handed it over." He shifted his weight, settling into the crouch rather than hovering over it, making himself comfortable and unhurried. "She'll be glad to see you. I expect she'll want to talk about the butter temperature again."

Mira's eyes moved to Acornimus, who was standing at the edge of Nibbles' peripheral vision with his paws clasped on his journal, making himself as small and unthreatening as a squirrel in a pressed vest could manage.

"Who is he?" she asked.

"He works with me. He helped find you. He's not going to cause you any problems."

She looked at Nibbles a beat longer.

"There was a rabbit," she said. "Its back was wrong. Plates, like bark grew over it. It went toward the stream. Where Pip is."

"I know. We saw those too. We got past them." He held her gaze. "Pip needs us to move right now. That means I need you out of this hollow and on your feet, because I'm going to need both paws free once we reach the stream, and I can't do that and carry you. Can you walk?"

She was quiet a beat, then came out of the hollow.

They heard Pip before they found him. It wasn't crying. Something smaller. A sound made in the back of a throat, soft and repeated, the noise of a child whose crying hadn't helped and so had stopped. Nibbles came through the last stand of ash trees with Mira behind him and saw Acornimus crouched at the water's edge with a small hedgehog boy against his chest.

Pip was five years old and small the way five-year-olds are small. His left arm lay across Acornimus's knee where the squirrel had set it carefully, and the arm was wrong.

The veins were violet. The color sat full and moving in them, pulsing along the blood vessels in slow rhythm. As Nibbles stood there, the leading edge advanced a half-inch up the inside of Pip's elbow.

He looked at Acornimus's paws.

Both of them were in contact with Pip's shoulders, and both had a tremor, small and constant, the shake of someone holding a position past what his muscles could sustain. Acornimus wasn't hiding it. He wasn't looking at his paws either. He was watching the advancing edge of the violet, counting inches.

"The advance," he said, when he heard Nibbles behind him. His voice came out even. "About one inch in the last eight minutes. Possibly less."

Nibbles moved forward, and the sword tore free of the scabbard. His right paw had been at his side. The hilt was in his grip and the blade was out and the light was present before his mind caught up to what was happening. It was full radiance this time, blazing and immediate, more light than the cellar's ten-second burst, and held without pause. The light fell across Pip's arm and Pip went rigid. He stopped the way a hand pressed flat against a wheel stops the wheel.

Nibbles tried to shift his grip and found that he couldn't. His paw was locked to the hilt. The hilt and his paw had become one thing. He heard himself make a sound that wasn't a word. His arm was shaking at a pace he could feel in his back teeth, and the hollow in his chest, the one that had not finished closing from the Nettleflint cellar, cracked wide open. Something cold was being drawn out of him faster than anything could fill back in.

He understood, in the same moment, that he wasn't doing this. The sword was. He was where the sword was doing it from. His paw was the contact point, his chest the source, and his job was narrow. Stay upright, keep the blade aimed at the arm, don't break the connection.

The violet retreated. He watched it happen. The leading edge pulling back, the color draining from violet to grey to the pale ordinary lines of a cold child's skin. Inch by inch, the advance reversing, Whiskerbrand's light pressing it back along the channels it had come up. The pulse in the veins slowed to a child's heartbeat instead of a corruption's.

The light stopped. The sword went from blazing to warm in the span of a breath, and Nibbles was on his knees in wet grass with no clear memory of going to them. His vision had pulled grey at the edges. His left shoulder was hot and sharp in a way he set aside for later. His chest had a cold in it that wasn't going to close quickly.

"Pip," he said. Half the volume he had intended.

"The child is clear." Acornimus's voice was close. "Do not try to stand yet."

Nibbles was in agreement with this. He became gradually aware that Pip was looking at him. Brown eyes, ordinary brown, the violet entirely gone. The boy had three small stones in his right paw, smooth river stones gripped tight. He had grabbed what was close and hadn't let go since. Mira was kneeling at the stream bank behind him, her quills flat with exhaustion, her gaze moving between Nibbles and her brother.

"Your rocks," Nibbles said.

Pip looked at them. "They're not from my collection. I found them here." A pause. "This one has a white line through it. I don't have one with a white line."

"That's a good one to keep," Nibbles said. His voice was coming back.

He sat in the wet grass another beat, taking stock. Left shoulder hot, still working. Left elbow bruised on top of the restriction, full extension still gone. Chest hollow, large, present, not a crisis if nothing required a fight in the next little while. He planned very firmly to require no fights in the next little while.

He got to his feet and said to Acornimus, "Pip's arm is clear."

Acornimus had opened his journal. "Confirmed."

What he didn't say (couldn't have said, exactly) was that his paw had locked to the hilt and he hadn't been able to release it, and that he hadn't done any of what had just happened. He had been the grip and the sword had done the rest, and he didn't have words for that yet.

They came out of the forest one foot and then the next, until the treeline was behind them and open road was ahead and the mill wheel's sound came through the morning air.

Mira walked beside Nibbles. Pip rode on Acornimus's back with the three stones still in his paw, which he had declined to pocket on the grounds that they were unfamiliar and required watching.

Acornimus began to speak. Not in the compressed mode from the forest. This was something else, measured and careful, six weeks of accumulated work finally being delivered to someone who could use it.

"The infection does not spread outward from a single point," Acornimus said. "It moves along existing channels, underground water routes, root networks, and paths through the earth that were laid down before any of the current settlements existed. The oldest channels in the valley. The ones the land used before anyone built anything on top of them." He let Pip shift his grip on his shoulder, then went on. "When those channels are healthy, they carry what they are meant to carry. When they are infected, the corruption moves through them the way any current moves, straight, fast, to wherever the channels run."

"Where do they run?" Nibbles asked.

"That is the question I have not yet answered fully." Acornimus's whiskers were forward and not moving. "What I can tell you is that the pattern of infection across this region (which farms fail, which wells, which sections of forest) matches the channel network beneath the ground. The Nettleflint farm sits above a junction where three of those channels converge. The crack in the cellar foundation was not incidental. It was the channel, finding the nearest surface."

Nibbles thought about the pressing-back through the crack. The cold, curious touch arriving in the last moment before Whiskerbrand's light sealed the gap. He hadn't put that in his report. He put it alongside this now.

"The channels have a name," Acornimus said. "Ley-line paths. Old practitioners used them to carry their workings through the earth itself. The ground as a medium." He shifted his grip on Pip without breaking his sentence. "To use these paths to move the infection requires knowing where they run. That knowing is not commonly held. The paths are old and the records that chart them are older still."

They came around the bend. The mill bridge appeared, and past it the first rooftops of Thimblewick.

"Someone who knows where the architecture runs," Nibbles said.

"Yes."

"And the Wigglywood Wardstone." He was working through it as he said it. "It sits on one of these paths."

Acornimus opened the journal to a page his paw found on its own. He held it where Nibbles could see, a map dense with notation and small marks. The village, the forest, the farm, and running through all of them in thin clean lines a network converging northeast of the treeline, toward a small X with three dates beside it.

"Yes," Acornimus said. "That is what I think."

They crossed the bridge. Nibbles crouched at the edge and pressed his paw to the stream's surface. Cold. Moving. Clean. He stood, dried his paw on his vest, and they walked into Thimblewick.

The baker was setting his board. The smell of bread came into the street warm and specific, flour and yeast and the sweetness of something made with honey that morning. Down the lane, two children were arguing about possession of a stick. The fountain ran in the square with its permanent purple tint, and underneath the fountain's ordinary sound Nibbles's whiskers caught the wrong undertone, faint and present.

Mira found her mother across the square, brief and fierce, before either of them had words yet. Arms around a child who was home. Pip was gathered up by an aunt who had been in the square since before dawn, her paws moving over his head and arms, checking that he was whole. He showed her the stone with the white line. She looked at it carefully and pronounced it sound.

Acornimus stood beside Nibbles and made a final mark in his journal. The square continued around them. The baker's customers. The morning argument resolved. A cart coming in from the east road with its wheels needing grease. Someone calling from a high window about a missing hat.

"The Guild tent," Nibbles said.

"Yes." Acornimus closed the journal. "I have six weeks of writing. Guild-master Bristlebaum will want to see it."

Chapter Four

The Guildmaster's Secret

THE FESTIVAL WAS OVER. The town had gone quiet. Bristlebaum sat at his desk in the command tent and worked through the day's stack.

Tonight's was ordinary. Reports on the clipboard, cross-referenced and signed. Supply tallies from the festival's final day. Acornimus's Wigglywood writing at the top of the active stack, ink barely dry. The teapot in the corner near the door had been closed for years. No one asked what had been in it.

He made three marks in the margin of the report, added a requisition to the bottom of the active stack, and pulled tomorrow's duty assignments toward him.

The courier arrived at a full run. He ducked under the tent flap without announcing himself, which was unusual for any courier and unheard of for priority dispatch, and stood in the lamplight breathing hard, his wings held slightly wrong. Bristlebaum set his pen down.

"Guildmaster Bristlebaum," the magpie said. He was young, barely past his first full-flight year by the look of him, and he had been told very clearly to deliver his message quickly and not very clearly to whom, and had been worrying about the difference the entire flight here.

"That's me," Bristlebaum said.

The magpie held out the letter and tried to do it steadily. When Bristlebaum reached for it, the courier's right wing flinched back half an inch before he caught himself and held still. The motion was involuntary.

Bristlebaum saw the flinch. He took the letter. "Where did you carry it from?"

"The Hollow relay, sir. The original courier, a crow, sir, they said he came in through the storm at half-speed. He's resting at the station. They handed it to me at first light yesterday and said run."

Bristlebaum nodded once. Someone had told this magpie the message was urgent without telling him what it contained.

"Dismissed."

The magpie left faster than he had arrived. The tent flap swung and settled. Bristlebaum turned the letter over.

It was sealed in pale green wax, a willow branch pressed into the surface, the impression clean and deep, made by a signet ring that had done this work for a long time. He hadn't seen that seal in thirty years, and he recognized it at once.

His quills shifted slightly, involuntarily, then settled. His claws didn't move for a beat.

The address on the front was in her handwriting, neat and unhurried, each word chosen before being committed to ink. His name. The tent designation. Below that, a single line underlined once. *Priority. Time-sensitive. The bearer has been told to make no delay.* She had pressed the underline hard enough that he could feel the groove through the back of the parchment.

Hazel Willowbark had not written to him in thirty years, and he had not written back. He had told himself this was mutual and agreed-upon, and he had held it as the passage of time in one direction. In the years after Shadowpeak, he had read every report she filed through official channels. He had never replied as himself.

Holding the sealed letter, he found he couldn't remember choosing not to write, which meant he had been choosing it the whole time.

He held it a beat, then broke the seal.

The wax cracked clean and the smell came with it, lavender first, the kind she kept in the parchment drawer to keep the paper from going brittle, and then beneath it, something sharper and green that he placed after a moment as feverfew. He had not smelled those together in thirty years. They arrived all at once. Her desk, her workroom, the smell of a place where things were carefully kept.

He smoothed the letter flat against his desk. His paw hovered over the first line, then settled, and he read.

Something fell out of the letter when he smoothed it flat. A small container, copper, thumb-sized, sealed with a cork and a ring of black wax, that had been folded into the letter's second crease and came loose when he pressed the page down. It landed on the desk between the lamp and the active stack. He looked at it.

Inside the container, something moved. He could see it through the fitted cap set into the container's mouth, dark crystal, transparent enough to show what was behind it. Through the crystal, faint as smoke behind glass, the contents shifted in slow turns. It wasn't the lamplight causing it. The lamp was steady and the tent was still, and the dust inside the container was moving on its own.

His paw had already moved back from the desk surface. He became aware of this after the fact, his paw resting two inches from where it had been. He had seen void dust before.

The last time had been thirty years ago, standing in a stone corridor three days after Shadowpeak while helping clear the summit site, when a sealed collection flask belonging to one of Aldric's mages had cracked against the passage floor. The dust that spilled had moved in still air exactly like this, slow, deliberate, turning with no wind to move it. Aldric had ordered everyone back at once. No discussion, no recovery of the flask. Three steps back and keep moving. Bristlebaum had asked why, already moving, and Aldric had said it in the flat tone he used when explaining only what needed to be said. *Void dust carries active essence. It does not stop because it is contained. It is patient.*

Bristlebaum looked at his paw, two inches from the desk surface. He didn't touch the container. He looked at it instead, steadily and from where he sat, until he understood what he was dealing with. The dust struck the crystal's inner surface, turned back, struck it again. In the thirty years since Shadowpeak, void dust in this state had been a rarity, something handled behind sealed archive glass, something that required a warded vessel and three signatures to move. Active void dust required closeness to a living void source, a corrupted anchor, something in recent direct contact with what fed Malachar's prison. Void dust didn't gather in open air. Someone had collected this near a Wardstone that had stopped being only a Wardstone.

Hazel hadn't sealed this into a letter as a curiosity. She'd sealed it in because she needed him to see it before he read the words.

He left the container where it was, between the lamp and the active stack, and read the letter.

The letter was one page. Hazel didn't waste pages.

Eight sentences. He counted them as he read. Each one said exactly what it was there to say and nothing else.

Brisk. The Ancient Willow at Whispering Hollow has void corruption in the root system. I have written it down through the whisper-net for eleven months. The three springs at the eastern edge of the Hollow show active void traces: void dust at the first, spreading strands at the second, and preserved creatures at the third that match what we found at Shadowpeak. One rune at my lintel went dark this past week. Five of the outer seals are in some stage of failure or at risk. The eastern seal is weakening on the schedule we expected. I would not write unless the matter required it. Bring Whiskerbrand.

He read it through once, then again.

Eleven months. She had been watching the corruption move through the whisper-net's root channels for eleven months before writing. Eleven months of observation, organized into evidence she trusted, then three weeks of certainty, then this. The dark rune at her lintel meant the perimeter wards on her cottage had begun to fail. The third spring meant the corruption pattern was no longer drift; it was the specific pattern they had seen at Shadowpeak, where Malachar's working had captured living things in void-stasis and held them. Hazel didn't write *match* unless what she had counted lined up to the exact mark.

Five of the outer seals in failure or at risk. Five of seven. He didn't need her to enumerate which ones. He had built the Guild over thirty years and read every report she had filed, every regional account that crossed his desk. He could fit the pattern to the geography without help. Wigglywood had been wrong for eight years, the southern confluence for four, the mountain pass for two, the eastern estuary inside two, the northern river confluence inside one. Five of the seven anchor points they had placed across the realm. He had read the reports as separate items, year by year, and never put them together. Hazel had put them together. That was the letter.

The sixth seal, the eastern one she had named, was weakening on the schedule they had once expected as the worst case. He knew the geography of that too. Ridgemarrow. The sixth stone sat on the low hill above that town. A practitioner there had been working alone for too long, in a region six months inside a failing zone. The seventh anchor she didn't need to name. The seventh anchor was beneath Thornwall.

The count worked in Bristlebaum a long time. Five inverted, the sixth failing, the seventh holding everything.

She had added a postscript at the bottom of the page in handwriting a little less controlled than the body of the letter. She had written for a long time and then gone back to add one last thing.

P.S. If the vendors at the Thimblewick market are still making their beetle crisps with the mountain pepper, bring some. I have been unable to match the seasoning, and after thirty years I have decided I will not solve the problem myself.

He almost smiled. It wasn't an apology for the silence. The silence had been right, the right discipline for the thirty years they had both kept without ever discussing it. The postscript said what the body of the letter didn't, that she remembered who they were, and the years hadn't changed it. She had always done that, and he had always understood.

He set the letter down.

Five anchors inverted. A sixth failing. A seventh that held everything. He had built the Guild carefully in the thirty years since Shadowpeak, built it into something real and good, something that saved lives and trained agents. He had been managing the gap when he should have been closing it. Five inverted anchors and a flickering sixth was the count of thirty years in the wrong direction.

The letter asked for the sword, and the sword meant Nibbles Tumblepatch. He had run out of reasons not to go back.

The summit chamber was a circle of dark stone, carved into the peak by old hands for old purposes. The ceiling was high and the air was thin and cold. The walls bowed slightly inward near the top, and in the final moments of the ritual the chamber seemed to breathe, long and slow, a pull inward and then a release.

Aldric had crossed the chamber toward Malachar with Whiskerbrand held level at his side. The blade blazed cyan-blue, even and total, light going outward without casting shadows. Brisk had stood fifteen feet behind and could see the entire chamber in that light, every crack in the stone, every face, every paw, every weapon held or lowered. The light left nowhere to hide. That was what he remembered first.

The fight lasted forty seconds. He had counted, after. Forty seconds of Aldric and Malachar, and when it was done, Malachar's form was broken at the chamber's center. The corruption fell in purple-black fragments to the flagstone where the blade had unmade it. The work of binding what remained was still to come, and would be done at Thornwall by the earth mages and the seven weaves they carried with them. The summit was where the blow had landed. Aldric was still standing when it was over. His sword arm hung wrong. Four clean lines opened in the forearm where Malachar's claws had closed on him, the split edges already gone the bruised-sky color of void contact. But he was standing. Brisk had thought *he's going to be all right.* He had thought *it's done.*

Aldric walked back across the chamber. Twelve steps. He held out Whiskerbrand and pressed the hilt into Brisk's paws.

The warmth arrived at once. The warmth was already in the metal, deep and ready, present before his paws had time to warm it. For one breath, Brisk held a blazing sword, and the blade was alive in his grip the way a banked coal is alive, warm and present and not refusing him.

Then it stopped. The warmth didn't fade. It stopped, like a lamp pinched out between two fingers, there one moment and gone the next. The blade went cold in his grip. The cyan light went out.

He looked at Aldric.

Aldric said, "The heart is what wakes the blade. Not the sword. The heart."

His voice had gone thin. There was no pain in the thinness. Something was leaving his body along with the light, and the voice was going with it. Then he dissolved.

It was slow, slower than Brisk expected, slower than he had time to understand before it was finished. The bone-white light that had been spreading through Aldric from the chest finally completed its passage, and his iron-gray fur dissolved into silver as the light reached it, the silver rising in the thin cold air of the chamber. Aldric's face was the last thing that remained, still there, still looking at Brisk, watching to see whether what he'd said had reached him. It had reached him. Brisk didn't yet know what it meant.

Aldric's face dissolved last, and Brisk reached into the motes as they dispersed, paw extended, the reflex of it, grasping for what had been there a moment before, and found nothing solid. The motes moved around his paw and continued rising.

By the time the last silver mote had passed through the chamber's walls and was gone, Whiskerbrand had rusted in Brisk's grip. The cyan was gone. The blade had pitted and dulled where his paws closed around the hilt, the weight of it sitting wrong, the metal already grown cold past the cold of the room.

Brisk stood with his paw full of nothing and a rusted sword in his other paw, and *worthy* settled into a question he would spend thirty years trying to answer.

Aldric had said *worthy*. Or he had said *right*. Brisk was no longer certain which. *Worthy* meant something you could measure, a permission you could delay until the standard was met. He had spent thirty years treating *worthy* as a permission he was never empowered to grant, and the blade had simply waited.

The tent after the memory was the same tent. The same lamp. The same stack. Bristlebaum's claws were resting in the grooves of the desk edge before he chose to stand, and he was standing before he had decided to. He paced the narrow lane between the desk and the equipment table, and the count went with him.

It had worked for thirty years. Agents trained under it had pulled children from flood water, contained early-stage corruption, settled a land dispute that would otherwise have collapsed into fighting. The Guild had saved lives. He could name most of them.

The other thing was also true. He had built the Guild's standards, in the first year after Shadowpeak, to make sure that no one bearing Whiskerbrand would ever be sent into a situation they weren't ready for. No one bearing Whiskerbrand. He had put Whiskerbrand in a chest. The standards had existed, the sword had been in the chest, and thirty years had gone by. He had called it prudence, and the wall had felt like a principle.

He stopped at the desk. The grooves were under his claws, and he pressed in until the wood gave back the resistance of years of pressing. He said it to the tent. To the lamplight and the closed teapot and the patched canvas. He said it quietly, because the saying was for himself.

"I gave up."

The words sat in the air. The lamp went on burning, the letter was still on his desk, the void dust still moving in its container, and none of that had changed. The giving-up had a name now, and that was the only difference.

He thought about Nibbles Tumblepatch. The mouse had come through the tent flap behind a cheese wheel that had no plans to stop. Bristlebaum had been sitting at this same desk when it happened. He'd watched the cheese wheel arrive, then Nibbles a half-beat behind it, then the mouse picking himself up from the ground in a way that suggested he'd been doing it long enough that the landing had become part of the walking. And then Nibbles had reached into the chest.

He had seen the sword's response from the first contact of paw against hilt. The warmth going outward. The rust burning off in a clean sweep. The blade reshaping at the edge. The light blazing up full and at once. It had arrived at brightness entirely, the way Aldric's blade had burned at the summit. He had recognized it. His first reaction had not been surprise, it had been relief, and his second had been to close the door again as fast as he could.

Every probationary restriction he had put on Nibbles since had been built for one purpose, to give the mouse enough institutional resistance to decide the sword had made a mistake and leave quietly. He had told himself otherwise. The boy needed more training. The situation required careful weighing. The materials had all been sound. The wall had still been a wall.

Nibbles had stayed. His writing was at the top of the active stack with three of Bristlebaum's own marks in the margin. Whiskerbrand was in whatever the mouse was using as a sheath, and the sword was awake. He had almost succeeded in pushing him out.

He pulled the regional map from the bottom drawer.

He found Ridgemarrow first. Northwest, three days' travel in clear conditions from Thimblewick, sitting at the base of the low hills where the sixth anchor's stone sat on an exposed prominence above the town. The map marked it as a settlement of about three hundred, which had been accurate two years ago. He didn't know what was accurate now, six months inside a failing Wardstone zone. Populations did what they did when things went wrong without resolution. They left. He marked it with a small x.

He found Whispering Hollow on the eastern edge of the map, in the river valley between the second and third hill ridges. Hazel had been working out of that valley for nearly thirty years, using the natural acoustics of the stone formation to extend her hearing along the ley channels. Her Ancient Willow was there. The sixth anchor's practitioner records were there. Hazel was there, waiting. A second x, the same size as the first.

He found Thornwall Keep last. It was in the northwestern corner of the map, barely within the cartographer's reach, marked with the notation reserved for discontinued Guild facilities, a small triangle in place of the settlement square, with the abandonment date printed beneath it in the small written-hand that meant the surveyors hadn't visited and were working from old record. The Keep had been a proving ground once, before Shadowpeak, before the Wardstones. Now it was where Hazel said the seventh anchor sat, three levels below the main hall, at the convergence point of all seven conduit lines. Now it was where the Herald was working.

He looked at the three marks. Whispering Hollow was closest, two days east, through familiar territory. Then Ridgemarrow, four days northwest from the Hollow. Then Thornwall, a full week beyond that through the border country, assuming the border country was still crossable.

He drew a line east to northwest, Hollow to Ridgemarrow, Ridgemarrow to Thornwall. The line passed through the region he knew from Acornimus's writing to be more corrupted as it moved northwest. Wigglywood was the fourth anchor's territory, and the fourth had been cold for eight years. The corruption in that region had been spreading for eight years. The route assumed it hadn't yet closed the roads. He couldn't be sure of that. He hadn't sent anyone into that region. There had been no reason to, until tonight.

This wasn't a single-agent job, and it wasn't a job that allowed the kind of preparation he would normally require. The timeline from Hazel's letter, weeks rather than months, left no room for full assembly. He had Acornimus here. He had Nibbles here, with the sword. The rest he would have to find on the road.

His claw traced the route once more. The point where the Wigglywood Forest track crossed into the border country, north of the mill bridge, where the corruption was thickest. The sixth anchor's location again, on the hill above Ridgemarrow. What Hazel had written about the practitioner there, alone, for too long. He hadn't sent anyone to Ridgemarrow in six months. The reports had come in, and he had filed them.

There was what he could still do, and he turned to it.

He wrote the warning in four lines. The raven's limit allowed no more. Trained messages couldn't exceed a standard dispatch card, and trained ravens didn't appreciate commentary. Four lines, used cleanly. An urgent warning, a single line naming the source as Wardstone corruption coming from the northwest, a recommendation to secure the sixth anchor site and pull the garrison back from exposure, and the instruction to hold position until the Guild team arrived.

He left out when the Guild team would arrive. He had no reliable answer. He also left out what the raven carried, as far as Nibbles was concerned. The mouse was presumably asleep, and this wasn't a conversation for tonight. He hadn't yet worked out what the mission was, hadn't settled in his own mind what Nibbles and Acornimus and the sword and Hazel's letter added up to. He would tell the mouse in the morning, when he had something coherent to tell him.

He folded the dispatch card to Guild specification and went to the raven post at the back of the tent.

The raven they kept for northern correspondence was a grey-shot bird named Finch. It wasn't his true name, only the one the Ridgemarrow warden had given him on his last posting, and it had stuck because no one had bothered to correct it. Finch was awake when Bristlebaum arrived, watching him from the perch. He had been roused from near-sleep and hadn't yet decided whether to be irritable about it.

"North," Bristlebaum said. "Ridgemarrow. Priority."

He attached the message to the leg strap, checked the clasp, and carried the raven to the tent's back flap. The night outside was still and dark, the festival grounds quiet at last, the cheese wheel memorial in the village square presiding over empty stalls and extinguished lanterns.

He opened the flap and held out his arm, and Finch departed. Three wingbeats to gain height, then the level purposeful flight of a trained dispatch bird that knew its destination and had no interest in delay. Bristlebaum watched until the raven cleared the roofline and was gone.

The warning would reach the Ridgemarrow warden by morning. Whether it would reach him in time was not something he could answer from here. He had sent what he could send tonight, and he let the flap fall.

He sat down at his desk. The void dust was still moving. He could see it through the crystal cap of Hazel's sealed container, the slow turns in still air, present and turning. Tomorrow he'd have Acornimus write it down properly and deal with containment. Tonight it could sit where it was and turn in the lamplight. The letter was under his paw.

He pulled a fresh sheet of parchment and wrote Acornimus's name at the top. Below it he wrote *Morning briefing. Early. Bring yesterday's report and do not eat first.* He set it in the message basket.

He pulled a second sheet and wrote Nibbles Tumblepatch at the top. He stopped. There wasn't anything he could say to the mouse that would fit on a message card. He would say it in the morning, in person.

He pulled the map back toward him and began to count. Agents available, equipment required, time from Thimblewick to the Hollow, from the Hollow to Ridgemarrow, from Ridgemarrow to Thornwall assuming the northern routes held. The void dust turned in its container, and somewhere over the village roofline the raven was already moving northwest.

Chapter Five

Into the Wigglywood

"Three-part entry," Bristlebaum said. "You hold right. Acornimus holds left. I take point. We match my pace."

The travel circle hummed beneath Nibbles's pads, a low vibration coming up through the stone, the outer rune-channels already warming. He had stood in the circle twice before during orientation, both times with the portal dark.

"Destination is Ridgemarrow," Bristlebaum said. "We assess the situation, establish contact with the local warden, and return before any further action. Clear?"

"Clear," Nibbles said.

"Abundantly," Acornimus said, opening his journal to a fresh page. "Though one notes the return timeline remains unspecified."

"Acornimus."

"Purely for the record."

"The record may show, we leave when we have what we came for."

Acornimus wrote something. It was probably that, but longer.

Nibbles checked the Whiskerbrand strap and the shoulder clasp. The sword was warm against his spine, had been since before they'd crossed the courtyard, an even attentive warmth oriented forward. His pads were still tender from the road. His shoulder had tightened overnight.

Bristlebaum was wearing a coat Nibbles hadn't seen before, heavier and different in cut. He had looked through a set of folded notes before the portal activated and put them inside that coat, and he hadn't mentioned what the notes said.

The air above the center of the ring thickened. The rune-channels brightened from amber to a warmer gold, the light spreading inward toward the center. The portal resolved into a vertical sheet of pale light.

At the outermost edge of the ring, where the carved channels ended and the plain courtyard stone began, a handful of sparks lifted from the rune-work and dissolved. Most of them were white. One at the far edge, barely visible in the brightening portal light, was not quite white. It went out before anyone was looking at it.

"Move," Bristlebaum said.

Acornimus went, and Nibbles went after him.

The transit was usually instantaneous. Nibbles had been told this more than once, described as a single step, as a blink, as something you forgot was happening before it had started. Step through, arrive. No gap between the two.

What he experienced had a gap. It was brief, barely long enough to form a thought inside, but the transit corridor didn't hold. The amber of the portal went wrong at the edges. A cold violet spread from the far margins of the passage, that same not-quite-white from the sparks, and his whiskers flattened hard against his face before he understood what he was seeing. He reached for Bristlebaum's arm. His paw found empty air.

The corridor went dark. It went in three directions at once, and then the ground arrived.

He hit on all fours, the impact driving through his heels into his knees and continuing until it reached his bad shoulder. It was sharp, the healing muscle locking hard in protest. He was upright before the pain had finished arriving, one paw at Whiskerbrand's hilt on pure reflex, cape swinging out to his right and catching around his forearm. He shook it free.

Trees. Dark-barked, widely spaced, with a canopy so dense that most of the sky was gone. The light that reached the ground came in narrow broken strips, pale and thin, crossing the undergrowth at shallow angles and showing nothing clearly. Dead leaves under his pads, soft earth beneath them, slightly too yielding. The air was cold and tasted of wet bark and something underneath it, iron, and a sweetness that had no place in any forest smell he recognized.

"Guildmaster," he said.

His voice went into the trees. He heard it go. He heard nothing come back.

He waited, counting to thirty. The forest gave him nothing back. No footsteps in the undergrowth, no answering call, no crack of a branch moving toward him. He could hear his own breathing. He could hear his pads shifting on the dead leaves underfoot. No birds, no insects, no creaking from the trunks. The trees were too still. There was no wind to explain it.

His whiskers worked fast, pulling at the air for anything he knew. The armor oil Bristlebaum applied in the same order every morning. The cedar-and-ink smell of Acornimus's satchel. He got wet bark and the metallic sweetness and nothing useful. His tail had curled tight around his left leg.

He turned a slow circle. The forest was the same in every direction. Same dark trunks. Same dense undergrowth. Same thin broken light that told him nothing about north or south. The space where the portal had been was empty. No shimmer, no leftover rune-light, nothing to mark that a portal had ever opened there. He had arrived elsewhere.

The portal fracture had put him somewhere wrong. Whether that meant somewhere next to the intended destination, inside the Wigglywood zone, or somewhere the corruption had already spread to, he couldn't say from a single position with no visible landmarks. The metallic-sweet smell was the same as what he'd run into near Nettleflint's farm. Beyond that it told him nothing.

He took stock plainly. He was intact, shoulder aching from the landing, pads stinging from hitting the ground before his feet had gotten fully under him, nothing new broken. Whiskerbrand warm on his back, present, oriented, not alarmed. Cape still attached. Badge still pinned at his chest. He had everything he'd stepped through the portal with. What he didn't have was Bristlebaum, or Acornimus, or any idea which direction led to Ridgemarrow.

He was afraid. He said the word to himself, because naming it was faster than working around it.

"Acornimus," he called, turning right and raising his voice. Then louder, "Guildmaster." He cupped his paws around his muzzle and pushed the sound as far into the trees as it would carry, turning north and then east.

He called once more. The trees gave him nothing back.

Staying still was waiting for the forest to find him. He adjusted Whiskerbrand's shoulder strap, shifted the weight forward of the injury, and moved north.

He moved slowly. One paw tested each step before his weight shifted, watching for soft ground hidden under dead leaves and listening for sound. He watched for a worn trail, a cleared path, any sign that something moved through this forest regularly and in a direction. The forest gave him none of it.

The wrongness built as he moved. The trees were too still. Beyond the absence of wind, there was no creak from the trunks, none of the slow complaints that old wood made under its own weight. Their bark was smooth where it should have been textured, and bulging in patches where something inside was working outward against the surface. Several trees near a stream he'd crossed had begun to lean toward the water, all at the same shallow angle, all oriented the same direction. The leaves drooped, jaundiced, their veining darkened toward the stems. The air smelled of iron, and underneath the iron something sweetish that didn't belong.

He was watching a cluster of ferns on his right when the bracken to his left turned. Three fronds, waist-high, at the edge of a thick stand. They moved slowly, the way something adjusts its attention. Rotating on their stems toward him. He stopped.

The bracken kept tracking. The motion was deliberate and paced, the movement of something following direction rather than wind.

The sword woke. The warmth against his spine that had been steady since the portal flared all at once, a sharp blaze that came through the sheath leather and the back of his tunic and arrived in his ribs like a door opening hard. The warmth pulled at him with urgency. He could feel the blade through the sheath, oriented ahead and right, the leather straining outward.

He didn't draw. He moved the direction the blade was pulling, faster, and the bracken tracked him until the trees closed between them.

He heard them before he saw them. They were quieter than footsteps. Two disturbances in the undergrowth, one to his left and one to his right, moving at the same careful pace, at the same distance apart. He stopped.

The rabbit on his left stepped into the gap between two trees. It had been a rabbit, or had started as one. Long ears, compact haunched body, the build of something made for speed and hiding. But its back and shoulders were plated in grey-brown growth that wasn't fur, overlapping panels, smooth and fitted close to the body, the same texture as bark. Its eyes were purple. Flat, unblinking. It moved toward him at a deliberate walk, unhurried, and nothing about that walk belonged to something built for fleeing. The rabbit on his right was the same.

Between them, fifteen feet ahead, the raccoon waited. Larger than a raccoon should be. Its right shoulder sat wrong. When it shifted its weight, a third limb shifted with it, shorter than the other two, attached at the joint in a way the original body hadn't planned for, moving in two joints that hadn't been there at birth. Its eyes were the same flat purple. It watched him without moving. They had placed themselves. Two flanking, one at center.

Whiskerbrand tore free. He hadn't made the decision. Or he had, but the sword made it first, the sheath leather releasing with a hard scrape, the hilt landing in his paw with enough force that his blistered pads felt it as a new pain on top of everything else. The blade blazed cyan-blue the moment it cleared the sheath. Tree shadows lurched sideways. Both rabbits flinched. The raccoon didn't move.

The left rabbit charged. Nibbles stepped to meet it and swung the sword across his body, and his left shoulder locked at the peak of the arc, the bad side refusing the cross-pull, the stroke pulling up short. The blade went wide. The rabbit ducked under it. It had known the angle. It came up inside his guard. Its teeth found his sleeve.

He got his left forearm between them and shoved. The rabbit lost its grip on the cloth but not its balance. It stumbled back, not far, and he followed the stagger with a downswing that overcorrected badly and hit nothing but air.

The right rabbit was still coming. He pivoted to track both.

The grip pulsed. A warmth rose into the base of the hilt, up through the metal and into his paw, adjusting his wrist angle before he'd chosen one. He was already in motion. He stayed in motion, and the stroke that landed was not the stroke he'd attempted. The blade hit the left rabbit at the gap between the bark-plating at its shoulder, where the growth hadn't grown flush with the body beneath.

Cyan-blue light discharged on contact. The rabbit unraveled from that point outward, bark plating crumbling first, then the corruption beneath dissolving, the shape of the animal coming apart in a cascade of silver dust that settled before it reached the ground. Empty space where it had been.

Recoil came back through the blade into his arms, a chest-deep draw, his vision dimming briefly at the edges.

The second rabbit was at two o'clock, unmoving. The raccoon remained at center, watching.

He was still looking at the empty space when he worked out what he'd been doing wrong. The grip correction in that last exchange. The sword had fixed a mistake he'd already made. He'd gone wide, pulled the stroke, and the blade had caught him after the fact. He'd been reacting to his own failures a half-beat late and the sword had been catching him. That kept him alive, but it wasn't the same as fighting.

The second rabbit hadn't moved. The raccoon was still at center, waiting. He didn't have time to think through this carefully. He had time for one decision. Stop being the thing the sword compensated for, and start doing this with it.

"Right," he said. Out loud, in a corrupted forest, to a sword. "We're both here. Partners."

The word came out slightly awkward. He said it anyway.

The warmth in the hilt changed. It wasn't the correction-pulse from the last exchange. This warmth settled in deeper and even, coming into the base of the grip and staying. He felt it in his paw and in his forearm. The blade's weight didn't change. What changed was the warmth. It stopped feeling like something he was managing and started feeling like a partner working with him.

The second rabbit committed. It came low and fast, angling to get under the blade before he could set an angle, the same approach the first one had used when his stroke had gone too high and left a gap. This one was anticipating the same gap. He stepped into it instead of back.

The warmth in the grip guided his wrist as the rabbit closed, a pull arriving while he was already moving, before the mistake could form instead of after. He came in from the rabbit's right side, where it couldn't easily redirect, and drove the blade in at the neck. The purification discharged lighter than the first kill, the hollow quick through his chest and clearing, his vision dipping for a moment and steadying. The second rabbit came apart in silver dust.

He straightened. His arms were shaking less. In that exchange he'd made choices rather than reacting to his own errors, and the sword had been meeting those choices rather than catching their consequences.

The raccoon-thing rose. It came upright from its waiting crouch to its full height, and its jaw unhinged past the angle a jaw was built to open, past the structural limits of the face, continuing until the gape was wider than the skull should allow. The third limb at its right shoulder extended fully outward, unfolding in two joints, reaching toward him.

There was no time to think. The raccoon came down all at once, a drop more than a charge, its full weight falling forward from the crouch, the extra limb sweeping sideways where he'd been standing a half-second before. He wasn't there anymore.

The warmth in the grip had pulled him left before he'd chosen left, and he'd gone with it, and the sweeping limb passed through empty air. He came up from the left and drove the blade at the raccoon's flank, the stroke shallow because his bad shoulder refused full extension at the top of the swing, the blade connecting at a lesser angle than he'd aimed for. It wasn't enough to discharge. The raccoon twisted away, that jaw still open at its impossible angle, and came around fast. He kept moving.

The raccoon's next strike came from the extra limb, low and fast, the two joints snapping outward in sequence. The warmth in the grip rose sharply. *Get the blade horizontal, block it.* He got it horizontal. The limb hit the flat of the blade and skidded off, the impact running back through the metal and into his paws, the blistered pads taking the shock sharp and close, separate from the ache his shoulder was already carrying. He stepped back one stride to absorb it, his left foot catching briefly on a root under leaves, then caught.

The raccoon kept pressing. He gave ground carefully, not in retreat but in controlled backward movement that kept the blade between them, watching for the moment the extra limb would overextend and expose the joint. It came when the raccoon turned its body to reangle the sweeping strike.

The extra limb's reach demanded that it swing wide on the outside of the turn, and for one beat it was committed to that arc and couldn't redirect. He stepped inside the sweep, got the blade's tip to the point where the third limb attached to the shoulder, the joint a wrong graft never meant to be there, and drove the stroke home.

The discharge came back through his arms harder than the two rabbits combined. The hollow draw hit deep and stayed, longer than the first two times, the cold settling in the chest and lingering as the raccoon came apart in silver, three seconds before his vision cleared and the edges of his sight stopped swimming. His arms were shaking. He was breathing fast and shallow through a clenched jaw. His bad shoulder had locked on the final stroke and wouldn't fully extend for a slow count of five while he stood in the silver dust and waited for the feeling to come back into the joint.

The hollow sensation faded to a low background presence, a new addition to the ache in his shoulder and the sting in his pads. Three uses. He could feel each one, stacked now and carried together. He didn't know how many more times he could draw that deep before the hollow stopped clearing. He set the question aside with the others and moved on.

He walked for a long time after that. The forest continued wrong. The leaning trees. The tracking bracken. The too-still trunks with their bark working outward in slow irregular patches. He moved carefully and watched his flanks and nothing else came at him.

Whiskerbrand stayed warm on his back, attentive rather than alarmed, oriented forward and slightly north. He had come to trust that orientation. When the blade pulled him toward something, that something was worth moving toward. When it had no opinion about direction, he picked his own and kept the blade's warmth as a running check.

He talked to it after a while. This was, on reflection, not the most dignified approach to navigating a corrupted forest. He talked to it anyway, because the alternative was the silence, and the silence in this place pressed in on him whenever he let it.

"I want to say that went well," he said. "I don't think it went well. I think it went acceptably, which I will take."

The sword stayed warm against his back.

"Bristlebaum would have handled those three in about forty seconds and then given me a very considered look," he said. "And Acornimus would have written up the encounter and added a footnote asking whether my footwork showed adequate technique."

The blade pulsed once, brief, something that might have been agreement. He had learned not to be too precise about reading the pulsations.

"Well." He was grinning even as he said it. "At least someone believes in me. Even if that someone is technically an enchanted blade with genuinely questionable taste in bearers."

He let the grin fade. He was afraid. He wanted to find Bristlebaum and Acornimus, or any trace of them, or any landmark that would tell him which direction held Ridgemarrow and which held more of this. He had three purifications behind him and a stacked cost in his chest and his shoulder and his pads, and he had no idea how far he had to walk before the forest ended.

He kept moving north, guided by the blade's warmth, watching the undergrowth.

A branch shifted above him. He had his paw at Whiskerbrand's hilt before he'd found the sound, holding contact, not drawing. The sword stayed warm. It wasn't alarmed. He looked up.

The crow sat on a low branch eight feet above him, glossy black feathers catching the thin strips of light that made it through the canopy. Sharp amber eyes aimed directly down at him. She had arrived in silence; he hadn't heard her come. She tilted her head, the angle steepening as she looked him over. He held still.

"Mouse," she said. "Sword. Guild badge." A pause. "Cape."

"It's useful," he said.

She tilted her head the other direction. He had the clear impression she was deciding whether that statement was worth a response.

"I've been watching you for an hour," she said.

He looked at the trees around him and went back over the last hour. She had been above him the whole time, no wingbeat, no movement in the canopy, nothing above the line of his own head while he'd been tracking the wrongness at ground level.

"You weren't at the portal," he said.

"No. I came in from the north two days ago. Scouting."

"Scouting for who?"

She looked at him for a moment. "Currently? You. The three you cleared in the lower hollow," she said. "I watched that."

He decided not to ask how she rated it.

"I can tell you there are more. Between here and the northern tree line, at least six clusters I've mapped, groups of four to six. They're stationed, not wandering. They hold position."

The coordination. He'd thought the same thing when the two rabbits and the raccoon had flanked him with deliberate geometry.

"Something is directing them," he said.

"That's what stationary clusters suggest to me, yes." She preened one wing feather without looking away. "I've also flown over a column on the ridge road north of here. Armed, moving northeast. Forty, maybe more. Moving with purpose. Not a patrol route, not a sweep. Moving toward somewhere."

Northeast. Ridgemarrow sat northeast of the Wigglywood zone. He kept that off his face.

"When did you see them?"

"This morning, before dawn. They had torches. They'll reach the ridge junction before nightfall."

Before nightfall. Ridgemarrow had a warden. Bristlebaum had sent a raven north three days ago. None of that felt like enough.

"Can you scout the route ahead, tell me what sits between here and the northern tree line?"

She was already looking north. "I can tell you what's in the air."

"That's what I need."

She tilted her head once more, studying him. He waited.

"I lost a mate and an egg to this corruption," she said. "Two seasons ago."

One sentence. Plain, no request attached. Then she was gone, no sound on the takeoff, only the branch above him dipping once from the push-off and springing back, and the canopy moving where she had been, leaves adjusting in her wake, the gap in the branches closing behind her as she climbed. He watched the canopy moving with her wings.

Chapter Six
The Slow Machine

Lark came back inside the hour.

She dropped from the canopy onto a low branch ahead of him, the same silent arrival she'd made the first time, and held there until he stopped walking.

"Two clusters between here and the tree line," she said. "I routed you around both. Your hedgehog and your squirrel are a quarter-mile northeast. Walking. The hedgehog is favoring his right side. The squirrel is writing."

The relief came before he could decide what to do with it, a loosening in the back of his neck and the place between his shoulders that had been holding since the portal fractured.

"You told them where I was," he said.

"I told them you were upright and moving. I assumed they could work out the rest." She was already adjusting her wings for the next lift. "Northeast. Stay below the leaning pines. I'll be ahead of you."

Then she lifted, and the canopy took her.

He found them at a stream crossing where the trees thinned just enough to let the light through in patches that did not quite belong to the Wigglywood. Bristlebaum saw him first. The Guildmaster had been crouched at the bank checking something at the water's edge; he stood when Nibbles came out of the trees, and his quills settled all at once, brief and complete. Nibbles had not seen them do that before.

"Agent Tumblepatch," Bristlebaum said.

"Guildmaster."

That was the whole of it from Bristlebaum's side. He looked Nibbles over once, the cape, the sword across his back, the way he was holding his shoulder, and brought his gaze back to Nibbles's face without remark.

"You drew the blade," he said.

"Three times."

A small pause. "We'll discuss it on the road."

Acornimus had risen from a fallen log where he'd been writing. His vest had a streak of mud down the right side that he had not yet noticed. He came across the clearing fast and not entirely with dignity, half-walking, half-running, committed to neither.

"You are intact," he said, arriving.

"Mostly."

"Mostly is acceptable. The portal fracture deposited the three of us across an arc of approximately two miles. The Guildmaster and I converged within forty minutes. You took somewhat longer." He had his pen out and was already writing. "I will need to record the encounters. For the report."

"Of course."

"Now would be best. While the details are recent."

"Acornimus."

"Purely for accuracy."

Bristlebaum was already moving. "On the road."

They crossed the stream and worked north along the route Lark had cleared. The Wigglywood thinned slowly. The leaning trees gave way to merely tilted ones, the bracken thinned back to ordinary undergrowth, the metallic-sweet smell fading by degrees until the air tasted only of wet bark and ordinary cold. By the time the trees opened onto the ridge road,

Nibbles had given Acornimus enough of the encounters that the squirrel's pen had stopped moving in protest and settled into a steady scratch.

Bristlebaum had said almost nothing the whole way. Once, when they passed a stand of trees that still leaned wrong, the Guildmaster had glanced at Whiskerbrand across Nibbles's back and said only, "Good."

They picked up the road at the ridge junction and walked five days. Lark stayed with them for two of those and then went ahead, scouting north with a brief tilt of her head that Nibbles had learned to read as goodbye-for-now. The road ran through country the corruption had not yet reached, ordinary forests, ordinary villages, ordinary innkeepers who did not ask why a Guildmaster was traveling with a mouse and a squirrel and a sword that did not match either of them. They slept in barns twice and a roadside common-room once. By the third night his shoulder had loosened.

On the morning of the fifth day they came up out of the lowland forest and onto the approach road, and Bristlebaum said, "Ironhold from the next ridge."

The approach road had been widening for a quarter-mile, and Nibbles hadn't worked out why until he crested the last ridge and the reason spread across the plain below.

Ironhold was built against a hillside the way a dam is built against a river, placed there to stop something. The outer walls were pale granite, thick and old. Arrow slits cut the face in patterns Nibbles followed without thinking, staggered, three levels of them, each cluster covering the gaps in the one below.

Silverpeak had felt large until now. The forecourt alone was the size of Thimblewick's market square. The main gate tower rose above it at the working height of something built to see a long way. A pair of guards watched them come down the road. Bristlebaum walked ahead without slowing. He got a quick nod at the gate, returned it, and led them through.

The gate passage ran thirty feet through the wall, dim and close, the daylight at the far end small. It opened into the courtyard, where the full size of the place arrived at once. From the western end of the complex, horses. Many horses, the smell of a stable built for a garrison rather than a household. Somewhere left of the main building, steel rang against steel in the disciplined rhythm of a training yard at work. Boots on stone from many directions, many sets, a steady drumming that rose and fell with the traffic.

Nibbles found his paw on Whiskerbrand's hilt without deciding to. The blade was warm against his back, quiet, only present.

"You've been dragging your jaw since the ridge," Acornimus said from his left, the vest impeccable after five days on the road. "It's not becoming."

Nibbles closed his mouth and kept moving.

The great hall inside the main building was worse. Vaulted ceiling, two stories up. Columns carved in the shapes of soldiers, load-bearing columns thick through the base, the carving a practical skin over stone meant to hold weight. Desks stood between the columns. Dozens, arranged in overlapping clusters, furniture that had collected there over years. Guild clerks moved the worn routes between them. At the far end, a quest board tall enough to need a rolling ladder was covered in papers, but the whispers that curled from its carved frame were thin. Fewer active assignments than the board had been built to carry.

Nibbles stood just inside the doors and worked out what was wrong with the room.

The ceiling height made sense for formations. The column spacing made sense for troops in full kit who needed to dress ranks without crowding the supports. The floor plan made sense if you imagined it empty, filling from the entrance in ordered lines. It had been a readying hall for armies, and it had been furnished since with the smaller work that came instead.

Bristlebaum had not slowed for any of it. He walked the hall along a direct line, the way a creature walks a room he knows. His quills were at the settled level that meant nothing was acutely wrong, and at the end of the hall they turned left.

The door to the Quartermaster's wing bore a small brass plate. REQUISITIONS, SUPPLY, AND RECORDS. The top of the lettering had worn down where passing shoulders had caught it.

Inside was different from the rest of Ironhold. The rest of the building had the working disorder of a large institution, maintained, workable, layered with the wear of long use. The Quartermaster's wing was different. Someone had cared for this room a long time.

Every shelf was labeled in handwriting that had not changed in what had to be decades. Every crate sat flush with its neighbor, with notches cut into the floor to show exactly where each piece should stand. Supplies were arranged by type, then date of receipt, then volume, and at the end of each row, a small notation board recorded outgoing inventory, what had left, when, by which unit, under whose signature. The smell was ink and clean rope and the dry cold of stone kept always free of damp. Nibbles had worked in clockmaker's workshops that were less well-ordered than this.

The desk edge had no grooves in it. Bristlebaum's desk in Thimblewick had grooves worn into the front edge from thirty years of the same grip. This desk was old, the chair-leg marks in the floor, the paper-smoothed surface, all of it spoke to decades of use, but the front edge was clean.

The badger at the desk was middle-aged, stocky through the chest and shoulders from decades of actual physical work. He carried the heavy frame of one who had moved supplies with his own paws long enough that it showed in how he sat. Classic badger coloring, white-grey fur on the face and head, darker grey-brown on the body. Pale blue eyes that took in the four of them at the door before anyone had spoken. A diagonal scar crossed the left side of his face from above the temple down to the jaw, old, clean-edged, a single cut. More scarring on his forearms where his sleeves were turned back, and on what Nibbles could see of his left shoulder. Practical earth-toned attire, with the Guild insignia at his left shoulder. He was setting down his pen as they came through the door.

"Guildmaster Bristlebaum." He rose, and the warmth in it was genuine, the warmth of an old association that had not corroded. "I expected you somewhat sooner, given the letter. Please sit." His eyes moved across the group. "All of you."

Four chairs waited at the angles that made sense for a group this size. Nibbles sat. Acornimus sat beside him, journal already open and pen uncapped, the reflex entirely involuntary.

"Merrick," Bristlebaum said.

Just the name. Merrick met the look and waited him out.

"You look tired," the badger said.

"Five days' march."

"Then let's not waste your time." He moved to the side table, where a stack of documents waited, prepared ahead of time. "Council authorization you don't have yet, I know. What you have is a Guildmaster's field requisition, which covers most of what you need right now."

He worked through the stack without ceremony. Traveling rations for eight. Nibbles counted under his breath and blinked. The right number for the party, which he had not told anyone. Field medical supplies organized by probable use. Four additional crossbow frames with a case of bolts, a careful notation on top reading *assigned north-route field agents.* A garrison supply manifest for Ridgemarrow, based on what the stationed unit had last reported needing.

"The garrison reports," Bristlebaum said.

"Six weeks out, not three months. I had a rider through the area on separate business last month. He noted no change at the garrison as of his passage." Merrick set the manifest with the other documents, small and exact. "The Council session is tomorrow afternoon. I've already sent your request for full intervention authorization."

"Without being asked."

"The submission window closed at midday. You were going to ask." Plain, not pointed. "They'll want the survey period. That's not mine to change from here."

"What if a survey team were already in the field."

Merrick looked at him. "If a survey team had been commissioned before the Council session and were already traveling north when the deliberation opened, yes, that would shorten the window considerably." A pause. "I can have the commissioning paperwork drafted tonight. You'd need to sign off this evening."

"I'll sign off tonight."

"Good." He lifted a rolled map from the side table and set it between them. "Corruption survey. Best current full coverage of the route north and the territories around Ridgemarrow."

Nibbles leaned forward before he'd decided to. The map was good, carefully done, the kind that required multiple passes to get the measurements right. Corruption advances were marked in degrees, pale purple for early-stage ground discoloration, darker for crystal growth, near-black for the full-capture zones he recognized from Wigglywood. The route north was annotated in the same hand that ran through all the records in this wing. The sixth Wardstone site was marked on its low hill at the settlement's edge, the corruption notation around it building across months in layers that told the story of progressive worsening. In the lower right corner, a date notation. Two weeks past.

Bristlebaum took the map without comment, rolled it, and added it to the stack.

Nibbles watched the exchange close out. Everything that had been asked for was in the stack on the desk. What was missing was the Council's signature, and neither of them was going to pretend the stack was enough without it.

"The party will be traveling with several field agents," Merrick said, settling back at his desk and returning to his daily log. "Requisitions for Riverclaw and Redstone are prepared. I've also set aside a fourth slot, unassigned." The pale blue eyes lifted briefly. "I expect you'll be picking someone up in the lower districts."

"Amend the paperwork when I have a name."

"Of course."

Acornimus had filled several pages in his journal over the course of the exchange. He looked up when it became clear the conversation had ended. "One appreciates," he said, with a quality of genuine feeling beneath the phrasing that surprised Nibbles, "the readiness in advance. The chairs in particular were a fine touch."

Merrick considered him with the pale blue eyes. "You're the S.I.S.S. operative."

"Third class," Acornimus confirmed, with the faint reservation he always brought to the *third class* portion.

"I know." Merrick returned to his log. "Safe passage, Guildmaster. To all of you."

The Council chamber was on the upper floor of the east wing, behind a door that required a guard's word and a second guard's key. Seven seats in formal arrangement, the founding Guild seals on the banners behind each member's position, the polished stone floor underfoot.

Bristlebaum had stood at this table on five separate occasions in thirty years, for different reasons. He laid the documents out in sequence.

The Willowbark letter first, thirty years of silence, ended now because the situation had outrun the silence. Then the corruption field reports from three stations, the pattern of advance, the specific sites of crystalline growth over the past eight months. Then the maps, Gareth Redstone's scout copies showing the corruption's generation points against the Wardstone anchor grid. Then the timeline, each stone's status, what the current rate of progress meant for the margin remaining.

He had prepared the presentation the way he prepared everything that came before this room. Strip it to sequence, remove what can be argued, leave only what can be demonstrated.

Nibbles was against the wall behind him, where Bristlebaum had placed him. The Council had requested the Whiskerbrand bearer attend, on the grounds that a legendary sword's waking after thirty years was a significant enough development to warrant documentation. Bristlebaum had agreed, and had told him clearly, on the walk from the Quartermaster's wing, what attending meant. Nibbles had agreed readily and looked nervous. His whiskers had been twitching since they'd entered the building. They were currently still.

Councillor Harwick opened the session. Grey-muzzled, deliberate. He was not adversarial.

"Guildmaster Bristlebaum. Tell us what you came to tell us."

Bristlebaum moved through the sequence. The Willowbark detection, void dust in stable-dormant form, the particle behavior that showed active void-essence rather than trace residue from decades-old corruption. The anchor pattern, generated at anchor points rather than spreading from a single source, which meant an active, directed corruption rather than a passive event. The Wardstone count, three fully inverted, two partially, the sixth under active attack. What the prison required to hold. What the current inversion rate meant for how much time remained. Each point once, then on to the next.

He watched the room as he spoke. Harwick's attention was full and level. He was following the argument carefully, listening rather than waiting for a break. Two of the other Council members were making notes. The fourth from the left had his paws folded and was looking at the Redstone maps. He looked genuinely concerned rather than procedurally skeptical. These were creatures who understood the information.

Harwick said, "Before we address the full intervention question — the survey team will need to verify the Ridgemarrow reports. I'd propose a two-week deliberation period while—"

"What happens to the sixth Wardstone if the corruption keeps progressing for two weeks?"

The mouse against the wall. Nibbles.

The room's attention shifted to the mouse with the tin badge and the ancient sword. He had asked a genuine question and was only now realizing he had asked it into the wrong room.

Bristlebaum's quills wanted to rise. He held them level through the slow, deliberate release at the base of each, practiced enough by now that nothing of it showed from the front.

The question was correct. Every creature in the room knew it was correct. Harwick's eyes had moved to the mouse against the wall, and the calculation behind them was not running in Bristlebaum's favor.

"Agent Tumblepatch," Harwick said. A pause.

"Nibbles," said Nibbles.

Bristlebaum moved before Harwick could build further on it.

"Agent Tumblepatch is present as a witness to the sword's waking," he said. "The Council has been generous in accommodating him."

Harwick took the opening offered him and let the matter drop.

"As I was saying," Harwick said, returning his attention to Bristlebaum, "a two-week survey period. The resources a Wardstone intervention requires are substantial. The precedent for committing them—"

"Requires survey confirmation," Bristlebaum said. "I know."

He did know it. The procedure had grown out of cases where the Guild had moved on bad intelligence and spent years paying for it. Harwick was not wrong to want confirmation. The procedure was a great deal of what had kept the Guild standing for two centuries. The corruption did not know about the procedure.

"I've commissioned a survey team," Bristlebaum said. "They move north ahead of my party and will report before the two weeks expire. That's authorized under field requisition." He paused. "I'd ask the Council to reduce the deliberation window to six days, contingent on the survey team's report."

Harwick looked at his colleagues. A brief exchange of looks, and that was that.

"We'll approve six days, contingent on the report confirming the preliminary information," he said. "If the report comes back uncertain, the full period stands."

"Understood."

Bristlebaum gathered the documents. The Willowbark letter went back into his coat. He rolled the maps.

Outside in the corridor, he stood a moment. Six days if the survey confirmed. Fourteen if it did not. Either was longer than he wanted. He tucked the letter inside his coat and went to find his party.

The corridor was quiet after the last of the Council attendants had gone through. Nibbles stood against the wall on the opposite side of the hall, where he'd ended up when the chamber emptied, the last one out, and tried to work out what he had done.

He knew the question had been correct. He'd seen it land on Harwick's face, the slight tightening around the eyes that meant the right thing had been asked at the wrong moment. He'd seen Bristlebaum hold very still, the way the Guildmaster held still when something had gone wrong and he did not want it to show. He had asked the right question, and he'd also made things harder.

His whiskers were flat against his cheeks. He pressed his back against the wall and was working through what had happened and what it had cost, when someone stepped into his path.

"You're Tumblepatch."

She was standing three steps away, between him and the stairwell. He hadn't heard her arrive. An otter, mid-build and strong through the shoulders, with warm brown fur and the short crossbow across her back, carried long enough that she did not adjust it when she moved. Hand-axes at her belt. Her eyes had already taken the corridor, exits, stairwell, the guard at the far end, before they settled on him.

"Yes," Nibbles said.

"Nori Riverclaw." She did not extend her paw. She looked at him and read him fast. "Your question."

He waited.

"It was the right question," she said. "And Harwick is going to bring it up for the next six months every time he needs to remind the Guildmaster that his operative can't read a Council room. That's what it cost. I'm not saying it wasn't worth asking. I'm saying that's the price."

He started to speak. She kept going.

"Smoothing friction isn't the same as resolving it." Her voice was even, not unkind. "The Guildmaster had a response prepared for Harwick's survey proposal. He was steering toward the timeline. Your question cut across that before he could land it. He got where he needed to get in the end, but he had to take a longer way around because of you. In that room, the long way around costs more than it costs out here." She paused. "That room runs on its own rules. Anything that doesn't fit the rules gets held against whoever brought it in."

Nibbles took this in.

"So I should have stayed quiet."

"In that room, yes. There's another place for the question, in the field, or with someone who has both the authority and the will to act on it." She glanced toward the stairwell, then back. "Arguing in there costs the Guildmaster his options. The room isn't wrong. It just isn't where that question goes."

She gave him the rest in plain language.

"You've been assigned to the mission," he said.

"Before the session." She looked at him without elaborating for a moment, then continued. "I had the northern routes mapped before anyone formally requested me. I put the work on the war-room wall because the corridor maps are six months out of date and I'd already done the update.

The Guildmaster walked through the war room yesterday morning and requested me by name."

"You mapped the routes before you were assigned."

"I knew the mission was coming. The corruption pattern in the field station reports has been building toward Ridgemarrow for weeks. Anyone reading them knew." A plain statement, nothing performed in it. "The three most likely failure points on the northern approach. The Brackley ford during high-spring runoff (we're four weeks into spring and the snowmelt is running heavy this year). The Ashwood garrison's patrol schedule leaves a gap on fourth-day mornings in the eastern coverage. The supply road into Ridgemarrow narrows to single file past the old mill, a bottleneck if we're moving as a group and someone's watching the approach. Those are the problems. I have answers for each."

Nibbles looked at her. "When did you work all that out?"

"Three weeks ago. When the fourth field station report came back with the same anomaly pattern as the third. That's when I started the maps."

He didn't have an answer to that.

"Why tell me all this," he said.

She turned to go. "Because you're going to be in the field with me, and I'd rather spend that time working than fixing the same mistake twice." She was already at the stairwell before she added, without turning back, "The question was right. The room was wrong for it. That's a difference worth knowing."

She walked away before he could respond. Her footsteps barely registered, the quiet of a creature used to moving where she was not meant to be heard. He stood in the empty corridor and let it settle.

The side room off the Quartermaster's wing smelled of old parchment and candle wax burned down to the nub. A table had been pushed against the far wall and covered in maps. They were hand-drawn work rather than the Guild's official surveys, each sheet cross-referenced in different layers, marks updated, marks overwritten, small notations in the margins.

Acornimus sat in the one chair the room offered, bent over the topmost map. He was not writing. He'd been reading the same map since they entered.

A fox sat on the edge of the table with his legs crossed beneath him, watching Acornimus. Red-brown fur, lean through the shoulders, the wear of someone who'd been on the move too long. A sheaf of field notes in his paw, already half-extended. The other paw rested on his thigh, tapping a rhythm, even, four beats and a pause.

He looked up when Bristlebaum came through the door and the rhythm stopped.

"Guildmaster Bristlebaum." He came off the table in one motion, not quite standing to attention but close enough. "Gareth Redstone. Scout and field analyst, two years unattached pending reassignment. I've been trying to get these in front of someone for eight months."

"Acornimus found you."

"I found him. He was asking the war-room clerks which field agents had been working corruption-adjacent assignments in the northern territories." Gareth gestured at the journal open in Acornimus' lap. "He's been reading for twenty minutes and he hasn't asked me to explain anything yet. That's new."

Acornimus looked up. "You're using the Wardstone anchor sites as a fixed grid."

"Yes."

"The corruption reports treat them as background infrastructure. They're not in the active survey work."

"They haven't been since Shadowpeak." Gareth moved to the table and turned the top map to face them. "Which is why every model the Guild has used for the past two years has shown the corruption spreading outward from a source in the northern territories toward population centers." He set a finger on the northern edge of the map. "There's no source. There's no outward spread. The corruption is being generated at the anchor sites themselves."

Bristlebaum was already at the table.

"Show me," he said.

Gareth laid three sheets side by side in the order they'd been accumulated, the first showing corruption advance as of eight months ago, the second four months ago, the third as of last week. At a glance, the picture supported the standard reading, growing zones, advancing edges, spreading from some center point. Then Gareth overlaid a fourth sheet, a tracing only, thin as the paper could be made, bearing seven marked points across the realm. The Wardstone anchor sites.

Nibbles stared at the overlay. The growing zones were expanding outward from the anchor sites themselves, each site the start of its own corruption radius, the radii spreading toward each other between the stones while the anchor cores darkened at the center. He'd been looking at it backward the whole time.

"The corruption is using the anchors," he said.

"The anchor network moves it through the realm," Gareth said. "It was built to carry the prison's suppressive field. Something is using those same channels to run the corruption through instead." He pulled the overlay off, then set it back precisely. "The inverting of the Wardstones isn't incidental. It's how it works. Invert the stone, and the channel it governs stops carrying suppression. It starts carrying corruption in the other direction."

"If that's true," Nibbles said, working through it, "then every stone that gets fully inverted makes the pattern worse for all of them. Each one that turns against the network is a new source."

"Yes." Gareth's voice was level. He had no satisfaction in it. "That's what I've been trying to submit for eight months."

Bristlebaum had not spoken. He was standing with his paws flat on the table, looking at the overlay, his quills risen exactly one degree.

"You submitted this formally," Bristlebaum said.

"I submitted formally in the autumn. I received a response that the submission had been received and would be reviewed." Gareth picked up the overlay sheet and held it without looking at it. "I submitted twice more. The fourth submission this month went to the Council clerk's office. I was told the Council had more pressing matters." He set the sheet down. "I understand the response time was institutional rather than deliberate."

The maps had been here for two years, the answer in them, and no one had looked.

"You're coming north with us," Bristlebaum said.

Gareth's paw went back to his thigh. The rhythm started, different now, faster and shorter, and stopped.

"I've been packed for two weeks," he said. "Nori told me the mission was coming."

"She was already rostered by name. You were the fourth slot."

"I know. She told me that too." A pause. "She said Merrick had already laid requisitions for a fourth unassigned position and expected you'd be picking someone up in the lower districts. Which meant she thought you'd need someone additional for the analysis work." He glanced at Acornimus. "Or you've covered it."

"S.I.S.S. operative," Acornimus said, without looking up from the map he was still reading. "Third class. Our ways of working complement each other rather than overlap." He turned a page slowly. He had stopped writing and started actually considering. "You read the field-station reports from the third-most-recent forward."

Gareth looked at him. "Yes."

"Most creatures read them chronologically."

"The pattern is readable earlier if you start from the third-most-recent and work backward."

"I know." Acornimus closed the journal. He looked at Gareth with the full quality of his attention. "The fourth-most-recent Ridgemarrow station report contains an anomaly that doesn't appear in the other stations. I want to know if you've found it."

Gareth's hand went back to his thigh. The rhythm ran four beats and stopped.

"Soil compaction along the sixth anchor's northern conduit line," he said. "Made by something passing regularly over the same ground for weeks running rather than by corruption."

"Yes." Acornimus opened the journal again and wrote two lines. "I wanted to be sure you'd found it."

"You didn't ask. You confirmed."

"I confirmed what I already knew. I wanted to know if you had it." Acornimus looked up. "You did."

Nori appeared in the doorway. She looked at the two of them for a moment, then turned to Bristlebaum. "The requisition paperwork is ready for your signature tonight. Merrick will need Gareth's name before then."

Gareth looked at her. "Did you just sign me onto the mission."

"You've been packed for two weeks."

"You didn't ask."

"You were going to." She glanced at Nibbles, a brief and exact look, then back to the door. "He has good maps and he thinks the maps make him a field agent. He's useful."

Gareth looked at Nibbles. "She's been saying that since the third month."

"The verdict," Nori said from the doorway, "is ongoing." She walked away before either of them could respond, the same quiet to her footsteps as before.

The lower districts of Ironhold had their own rhythm, separate from the fortress's upper half. Down here, the logic was older, too many creatures in too little space, getting on with it the way creatures always did.

Dash had been in Ironhold for three days. He'd spent the first afternoon mapping the covered market's layout and the second confirming what the first afternoon suggested about the bead merchant's back room, a window onto an alley with a courtyard at the far end that had no external connection to the upper districts. The merchant had stock worth taking, no obvious protection on it, and a front stall that kept him out of the back room for hours at a stretch. He had waited the third day to see if a better option turned up. It had not.

He went in through the window at midday, when the merchant was running his front stall and the noise from the covered market covered everything else. The room was more organized than he'd counted on. He'd planned for the standard back-room approach, loose stock, unsorted piles, things left where they sat because they did not look worth a glance. A well-organized room meant the valuable things were filed where their absence would show fast. He slowed, found a new angle, found the section with the small labeled boxes and worked through them in order.

The third box held what it looked like it held. Small enough to pocket. Easy to sell south of here. He took it and turned for the window. The door to the main stall swung open.

He was through the window before the merchant cleared the frame, moving low along the alley because north was the direction pursuers least expected. Left at the stack of crates, the narrow gap putting the crates half an inch from each ear, through the first junction and right at the second, which brought him parallel to the covered market's outer face.

The crowd was thick. He let the current carry him twenty steps before he turned to check. The merchant had stayed. The two who were following were faster than the merchant and not wearing a merchant's attire, and they'd split at the junction. One each direction. They had done this before. The back room had better protection than he had given it credit for.

Gap between two stalls and the outer wall. He took it, came out into the service alley behind the eastern market face. North again.

His left elbow caught the crate stack at the alley's corner. It was a brush, the outside of his elbow touching the top crate's edge in the turn, a contact so slight he was four steps past it before the first crate shifted. The second caught the first at the wrong angle. The whole stack came down across the alley's width in a loud uneven cascade. He stopped at the far end and listened.

The pursuers heard it. He tracked them by the way they answered, one coming around the market's southern face, one reading the noise as a clue. Eight seconds before the alley was closed from both ends.

He moved into the nearest doorway, which was unlocked, pushed through into a loading vestibule with two exits. The building would dead-end him. He stayed at the door and counted.

They went past in under ten seconds, the faster one first. He counted five more. Then he stepped out and turned south.

He was eleven steps from the covered market's outer face when someone stepped into the road ahead of him and stopped.

Squirrel. Green vest pressed too well for the lower districts at midday. A leather journal under one arm. He had placed himself ahead of where the pursuit would push Dash next, and he was not threatening anything.

Dash stopped. His right paw had gone to his dagger hilt without his deciding it. He counted. The squirrel in the path, nobody on either side, the pursuers still well behind. The lightning-bolt patch was showing at the gap of his coat. Nothing for it now.

"I haven't had a good look at what you took," the squirrel said. "I expect it's not worth what the next few minutes will cost you."

"Who are you."

"Agent Acornimus. S.I.S.S., third class." He opened the journal and wrote something before looking up again. "I'm engaged on a mission that requires someone who can do what you can do. I've known where you were since yesterday morning."

Dash looked at him. His whiskers were forward, working, no shift in the squirrel's weight, no hand near a weapon, nothing in him preparing to move. This was not an ambush, it was a meeting.

"You followed me."

"I had a look at your situation yesterday and waited to see if you'd find a better option." A pause. "You didn't."

"And so you're here."

"Here we are." The squirrel's whiskers were forward and not moving. "The mission runs north from Ironhold. Legitimate work, fully commissioned, authorized under field requisition. Guild rate for the duration." He tilted his head slightly. "We need someone who can move where the rest of us cannot. The specifics are for the briefing. What I'll say now is that the work is dangerous and it is necessary, and it needs what you can do."

Dash looked at him for a long moment. Then he took the small box from his pocket and set it on the crate to his right.

"Who else," he said.

"A Guildmaster. Two field agents. An S.I.S.S. operative." Acornimus wrote something else. "And a mouse with a legendary sword."

Dash ran each face he'd seen in the upper districts in the past day. The Guildmaster he had spotted from a distance, settled, slow to read, the kind he would have to spend time on. The otter with the crossbow, her eyes checked exits before faces, which meant she was not specifically looking at him. The fox with the maps was a map creature, and a map creature did not have time for a ferret in the lower districts. The squirrel in front of him was the easiest read of the four, precise, contained, interested in what he could see and write down. The mouse with the sword had been too occupied with the larger picture to fix on Dash as a problem.

He went through them again. He did not find, in any of them, the kind of opening he usually looked for, a habit to use, a weakness to press later. He found nothing he could name. That was unusual. He had not had a read this clean in three towns.

He heard the pursuit doubling back at the north end of the market. He moved his paw deliberately away from the dagger and let it fall to his side.

"When do we leave," he said.

"Tomorrow morning." Acornimus closed the journal. "Tonight you'll need to report to the Quartermaster's wing for the commission paperwork. We'll need your name on the roster before the signatures close."

Dash looked at the small box on the crate. Then he looked back at the squirrel.

"I wasn't planning on staying in Ironhold anyway."

He left the box where it was and followed Acornimus toward the upper districts.

They came out of the eastern building's lower exit in mid-afternoon, the light long and slant across the outer courtyard stone. Dash was four steps behind the group, his whiskers moving in small constant adjustments, the work of a new situation he had not finished reading. His paw had not gone near his dagger since the lower districts.

The courtyard held the party in rough assembly. Bristlebaum at the front, the requisition stack folded under his arm, his quills settled at the level that meant something had been resolved and he was not pleased with how. Nori was at his right, already looking north toward the main gate, hand-axes at her belt and the crossbow across her back the way she always carried it. Gareth had his map roll under one arm and was writing on the margin of a smaller notebook with the other, moving through the courtyard without watching his feet and managing not to walk into anything. Acornimus matched pace beside him, the journal already back under his arm.

They passed through the inner gate and into the long passage through the outer wall. Whiskerbrand was warm against his back, quiet. Nibbles had been in a crowd of strangers for hours and the blade had stayed level the whole time.

The outer gate opened into the forecourt and beyond it the approach road, pale in the afternoon light, running south toward Thimblewick and north toward Ridgemarrow.

Overhead, something shifted against the cloud cover. The small adjustment of wings correcting course, then Lark was banking left at the gate's height, coming around to pace them from above. She did not descend. She turned, caught a thermal off the gate tower, and angled northeast, counting them as she went.

Merrick stood at the Quartermaster's gate. The gate was a secondary entrance off the eastern face, the supply entrance, wide enough for a laden cart. He was standing at its edge in the same practical attire as before, the Guild insignia catching the afternoon light at his left shoulder. The daily log was closed. He watched them move through the courtyard, marking each of them once and not needing to write any of it down.

When Bristlebaum drew level, Merrick gave a half-nod, slight and precise. Bristlebaum returned it in kind. No words.

Nibbles glanced back once as they crossed the forecourt threshold. Merrick was already at his desk, the log open, the pen moving again.

The gates came together behind them, heavy and even, the sound the gates of Ironhold had made a great many times. They had a corruption-survey map two weeks out of date, a six-day deliberation window, and a party that had not existed this morning, and they turned north.

Chapter Seven
The Friction

THE ROAD NORTH FROM Ironhold ran straight for two leagues before bending west around a low ridge. Nibbles had walked it alone once. Walking it now in company was not the same road.

Bristlebaum walked at the front. Nori center-left, eyes moving in the slow rotation she ran on march, the short crossbow at her back, carried for six years and never reached for. Gareth behind her with a map folded under his paw, the tapping on his thigh meaning he was mid-pattern. Acornimus held the rear, journal open, pen moving in steady deliberate strokes. Lark somewhere above the eastern ridge, a black shape riding the air, banking, never quite still.

That left Dash. Nibbles had spent the first hour trying to work out where Dash was in the line of march and had given up trying to fix him to one position. Dash moved through the party on a path of his own. It wasn't random.

The first time Dash dropped back from point, Nibbles almost said something. He stopped himself. Nori had not reacted. Whatever that meant, he hadn't worked it out yet.

Dash had been thirty yards ahead of Bristlebaum's position, reading the road where it curved around a stand of old oaks. A reasonable place to send your fastest creature when you could not see ahead. What wasn't obvious was why he then dropped back through the formation entirely (past Bristlebaum, past Nori, past Gareth still writing) and settled thirty yards behind the rear, where the road bent back into sight from behind them.

Nibbles looked at Nori. She was watching the western treeline.

Forty minutes later, Dash was at point again. Nibbles had not seen him come up the column. His whiskers were reading the eastern hedge, both ears working independently, the left tracking the treeline and the right tracking the road ahead. When the hedge gave way to open country, he moved. The formation held its shape. Bristlebaum kept his eyes on the road ahead.

He walked another quarter-league before he had it. Dash wasn't keeping pace with the formation. He was reading the road, and his position was a side effect of that. When the front needed eyes, he was at the front. When the rear did, he was at the rear. Otherwise he was wherever the formation was thinnest.

On the next stretch, where the road dipped into a forested hollow and the trees pressed close on both sides, Dash moved to the left verge and held a position there at a pace just outside speaking range. Nibbles spent thirty minutes with his paw near Whiskerbrand's hilt, nothing coming through the trees, only the gap on the right side where his instinct kept expecting a body.

"Does he always do that?" Nibbles asked Nori, voice low.

"Yes."

"Does he know it creates—" Nibbles gestured at the gap that was no longer there.

"Yes." She was watching the treeline again.

The formation's problem wasn't Dash. The formation hadn't learned to be a formation yet. Given a few more days, the rest of them would work out where Dash tended to put himself and start covering the gaps without thinking about it.

Lark came down in the late morning. She dropped from the ridge's thermal without warning and caught a fencepost at the road's edge, wings folding with a single smooth snap. She held a moment before she spoke, the way she always did.

"The country changes ahead," she said. "Past the ridge bend. The fields are off."

Bristlebaum stopped walking. The rear of the column compressed as people caught up.

"Off how?" Bristlebaum asked.

Lark tilted her head, amber eyes tracking the ridgeline east before coming back. "The birds are present but they're holding to the high edges of the fields rather than working the low ground. The tree cover on the northern slope is the right color in patches and wrong in others. The wrong sections follow the lowest ground."

"Following water," Gareth said. He hadn't looked up from his map.

"Following the low ground," Lark said. "Whether that's water is your call."

She was not claiming water; she was reporting what she had seen. Nibbles watched her glance once at Gareth's map and then look away.

"How far?" Bristlebaum asked.

"Two leagues. Perhaps a little more, past where the ridge drops back on the western side."

Bristlebaum nodded once. Lark unfolded her wings and was back up before anyone else spoke.

Nibbles looked at the empty fencepost. The claw-marks in the weathered wood were fresh and pale against the grey.

She had described something he did not have a word for, but he had felt it before. Birds avoiding the low ground. Tree color wrong where the drainage ran.

The fields near Thimblewick had been the same in the weeks before the Cheese Festival. He remembered it now from the hauling runs to Nettleflint's farm. The animals quiet. The crops gone wrong at the low end of the field before they were wrong anywhere else. He had noticed it then without knowing what he was noticing. The only word he had ever put to it was *off*. Lark had just used the same one.

He wanted to say something about this to Bristlebaum. He turned toward the front of the column and found the Guildmaster already walking.

They stopped for the evening in a hollow at the road's edge where the ground was level and dry and three trees made a natural windbreak. The light was going out of the sky in long grey bars and the first chill was coming in from the north. Bristlebaum had held the pace since Ironhold without slowing, and everyone sat down with care, the way creatures sit down when they have spent the day finding out what their legs are capable of.

Nibbles set his pack down and stretched his back. The sheath straps for Whiskerbrand had worn a new line across his shoulder during the march. The blade sat warm against the leather, quiet.

Gareth closed his maps and worked the stiffness from his writing paw, knuckles flexing in sequence. Acornimus was still writing in his journal. He had not stopped writing, as far as Nibbles could tell, since the morning break. Nori ran through her crossbow harness in the same order she used at every halt, thumb finding each buckle and moving to the next without looking. Dash was sitting near the treeline rather than near the fire, eating from his pack, watching the road they'd come from.

Bristlebaum stood at the fire's edge studying Merrick's map. The evening light caught the parchment and Nibbles could see the map's edge from where he sat. Clean road lines. Settlement marks. Country that had been mapped at a desk.

He looked at Gareth's closed map case. The routes in Gareth's version were different. More corrections. More margin notes. He'd noticed this two days ago and hadn't thought about it further.

The party was tired. Road-tired, the kind that built up across a day of walking past the point where the body wanted to stop. Nibbles felt it in his feet and in the muscles at the backs of his legs. He looked around the fire and saw the same tiredness in every face.

An overnight march was coming. He had worked it out from the pace, from twice-noted observations during the afternoon that they were making better time than expected. Better time was only useful if they reached Ridgemarrow earlier than the sixth Wardstone failed. Telia Earthwhisper was at the stone alone, and the hours were not optional. Nibbles knew all of this. He spoke anyway.

"The pace today was harder than I expected," he said. He meant it as an observation, and it landed as something else.

Bristlebaum looked up from the map. His quills shifted, not to full extension, but enough to notice. Acornimus's pen paused.

"I mean," Nibbles said, "we've been on the road since before dawn, and if people had a chance to rest before we—"

"The overnight push is necessary," Bristlebaum said. His voice had the same tempo as his map consultations. He was not dismissing the observation. He had heard it, weighed it, set it aside.

"I know it's necessary," Nibbles said. "I just thought—"

Nori's paw closed around his arm, light but firm. She held there a moment, then moved to the left side of the fire and waited. He followed her.

"You're right that they're tired," she said, when there was distance between them and the group.

"I know," Nibbles said.

"So who does it help to say it?"

The honest answer was no one. Bristlebaum already knew. Everyone at the fire already knew. Naming it had not changed any of that. It had only made it harder for the Guildmaster to keep the schedule without looking as if he were ignoring his people.

"I wasn't trying to make things harder for him," Nibbles said.

"I know you weren't," Nori said. "But that's what you did. Smoothing friction isn't the same as resolving it. Smooth it and the group feels easier for a while. The friction is still there. The next time something presses on it, it presses harder."

Nibbles looked at the fire. Bristlebaum was back at the map. Acornimus was writing again.

"So I should have let it build," he said.

"You should have let it be. This group hasn't had its first real argument yet. When it does, it'll find out something about itself it doesn't know. Every time someone smooths things over before they can land, that argument gets pushed further down the road."

A lot in this camp had been smoothed already, Nibbles thought, and let it sit.

"You walked away before I could respond," he said.

"Yes," Nori said. She walked away.

Nibbles went back to the fire. The party settled into the small separate occupations that filled the space before decisions arrived. Nori at the east edge of camp with her eyes on the road's bend. Dash still at the treeline, pack moved to a new position. Bristlebaum at the map, working a count to himself.

At the far side of the firelight, Gareth and Acornimus had drifted toward each other without either of them announcing it. Gareth had a map open on a flat section of log; Acornimus's journal was open beside it. Nibbles sat within hearing range and kept still.

Gareth's map was one of the smaller hand-drawn ones, the margins packed with his compressed notations. He pointed to three marks in sequence. They fell in a loose arc across the northern farmland country, each with a date beside it.

"The growth pattern at these three sites follows the low drainage," Gareth said. He tapped each date in order. "The timing matches a single source point pushing outward at a steady rate. If I extend the radius backward from the outermost confirmed date, the source activation falls roughly here." He drew a fingertip in a slow circle in the empty country at the arc's center.

Acornimus studied the map. His expression did not change, but his paw moved to a page near the middle of his journal, turning to it without having to search. The S.I.S.S. notation system was different from Gareth's, finer marks, narrower columns, a key Nibbles could not read. But the shape of the marked locations was readable even from where Nibbles sat. They occupied the same ground. Several sat at nearly identical positions to Gareth's marks.

"Three of our candidate sites overlap with yours," Acornimus said. "One of our three source possibilities matches your origin point." He turned the journal so the column beside the marks was readable from Gareth's angle. "Independently verified, from field observation rather than projection."

Gareth read the column. The tapping on his knee started up, ran for several beats, changed, stopped.

"Your earliest confirmed date is two weeks before mine," Gareth said.

"Yes."

"That means the source was active before the first visible surface corruption by—" He ran the count. "Close to a month."

"Twenty-six days, based on our earliest observation."

Gareth looked at his map. He had been treating the first visible surface corruption as the starting point of the spread. Every radius, every projection, every rate guess had been built off that first visible date. If the source had been active a month before that, his rate was wrong, his radii were wrong, and the source point he'd located was probably off by enough to matter. He would need to redo all of it before morning.

"I'll need your field dates for the three confirmed sites," Gareth said. He was already reaching for his pen.

"I have them here," Acornimus said. He was already turning the page.

Nibbles watched them for a moment. Two pens reached two pages at the same time, different methods, the same problem.

Neither of them had expected the other to be useful. Gareth had treated pattern projection as more reliable than the Guild's institutional record; Acornimus had treated institutional record as more reliable than pattern projection from incomplete data. The overlap did not settle the argument between them. It only meant both of them now had more to work with than either of them had brought to the fire.

Nibbles looked up at the sky where Lark was somewhere in the dark, and thought, for the first time since the Ironhold gates closed, that this group might one day be a party.

Bristlebaum studied the map long after the fireside exchange had gone quiet. The fire dropped from flame to coals to dim embers, and the cold pressed in at the edges of the hollow, and Bristlebaum's paw moved along the road lines slowly, the way someone moves when speed is not the point. Nobody interrupted. By the end of a single day's march, the party had worked out that Bristlebaum at the map was not to be added to.

Nibbles sat with his back against his pack and worked through what Nori had said.

She was right. A correct observation at the wrong moment was not the same as a useful one. Bristlebaum had already accounted for the party's fatigue. He had to have, because arriving at Ridgemarrow with a party that could not work was not an option. Nibbles had not given him new information. He had given the rest of the party a reason to wonder whether the Guildmaster was hearing them, at the moment Bristlebaum could least afford the question.

Across the dying fire, Gareth had gone back to his revisions. His pen moved differently than before, shorter strokes, closer together, the tapping on his knee running and stopping as the new dates reset the count. When the tapping stopped and did not resume, Gareth wrote three lines fast and put the pen down. Acornimus sat with his closed journal balanced on one knee.

Nori was at the camp's eastern edge, her back to the fire, watching the road's bend south. Dash had shifted from the treeline to a position inside the camp's edge, not far, just past where the firelight became uncertain. His ears were working independently, the left toward the northwest approach, the right toward the road south. Lark was above, somewhere in the dark.

The coals settled lower, and Bristlebaum folded the map. One fold, then across, then into the worn leather case. He stood at the fire's edge and the embers lit him from below, the grey-streaked fur and the quills settled mid-register, the mace at his belt.

"We march through the night," he said. "Ridgemarrow by dawn."

He said it as a decision already made, the working set aside. He did not mention the fatigue. The sixth Wardstone was flickering, Telia was at the stone alone, and there were no hours to spare. What he had not said was that he knew what he was asking, and the body that carried the pack felt the difference between paying a cost and being asked to pay one.

Nori crossed from the camp's edge. Her thumb went to the left shoulder fastening of her crossbow harness, already set at the halt, checked again now, and moved through the sequence. Buckle, buckle, the tension strap at the back. The hand-axes at her belt shifted and settled to march weight.

Gareth closed the current map without finishing the line he was revising. He folded it, stored it, and stood, already on to the next thing.

Acornimus lifted his pack. A single measured breath as he set down the work and picked up the road. The pack went across his shoulders and his paws found the straps.

Dash was standing. He had been at the camp's edge and now was toward the column's front, the white lightning-bolt patch catching the last of the ember-light before the dark took it.

Lark was in the air before Nibbles finished resettling Whiskerbrand across his shoulder. The blade sat warm against the leather, quiet.

He looked at the cold coals, at the flattened ground where each of them had sat for an hour. Everyone here had known an overnight march was coming, and the march resumed.

The road at night was not the same road they had walked by day. The moon had risen by the time they left the hollow, not full, but enough to lift the pale stone of the road surface out of the dark. The hedgerows became dark shapes. The low country between them was darker still. Nibbles worked his whiskers without thinking about it, reading the air at the road's edges in sweeps, and got almost nothing back, cold air moving slowly from the north, old stone, dried grass. The night was still, and the party was a set of breathing shapes and footsteps and the occasional creak of Acornimus's pack harness moving north along a pale ribbon of road.

The first hour was easy. Tired legs carried themselves on the day's momentum. Then the road descended into a long shallow valley where the paving was older, subsided at the edges into mud where water had worked under it. His right ankle caught a sunken edge wrong, the foot turning before he corrected. The backs of his knees settled into the deeper ache of legs asked to keep working past what they had been ready for.

Somewhere ahead of him, Gareth was walking and writing. The sound of it reached Nibbles in the quieter stretches, the faint scratch of pen on paper between footfalls.

"Root," Nori said.

The sound of a foot redirecting at the last moment, the catch and push of a stride interrupted nearly in time. The pen kept moving.

"Thank you," Gareth said.

They walked. The pen scratched.

"Root," Nori said again.

"I see it," Gareth said.

He caught it anyway. The revision Gareth was doing was important. Nori was watching him. The matter was already in better hands than his.

Dash came through the column on the left side without warning, moving fast and quiet, and the white patch on his chest was bright in the moonlight for a moment before he angled into the shadow of the hedgerow. He stayed in the verge for a quarter-league, invisible except for the occasional shift of the upper branches against the wind. When he came back into view he was ahead of the column's front, not behind it. During the afternoon, a farm track on the left had connected through to a parallel road running north. Dash was checking whether it was still there and whether the parallel road was in use. Nibbles had not thought to check it. He noted the gap in his own attention and turned his eyes forward.

Then the shoulder. Low and specific. The deeper pull of something that had closed at the surface and not finished closing underneath, not the sharp edge of a fresh wound. He had felt this at Nettleflint's farm, going down toward the cellar crack. Briefly at Ironhold's lower courtyard, near training equipment that had touched a corruption-marked wall. The void-touch in the shoulder wound had been quiet since Ironhold. It was not quiet now.

Lark was above and she hadn't sounded.

The pull was low. He had been learning the difference between a signal and an alarm since Thimblewick, and this was a signal. The hedgerows had changed quality, still present, still dark, but no longer carrying sound up out of the gaps in them. He still did not have a word for it, but the shape of it was the same one Lark had pointed at by daylight, the same one he had felt at the cellar crack.

His shoulder was reading the country ahead of his eyes. The road climbed out of the valley on the far side and the surface improved. They passed the fifth league mark and kept going. Gareth was still writing. Acornimus was upright, pack settled, eyes ahead. Nori was where she was supposed to be. Dash was nowhere in sight, which meant he was working. Bristlebaum had not slowed all night.

The land changed before the sky did. The sky was still the dark that precedes dawn, the first thinning of the middle hours' deep black. The road ran north and the fields came in on either side. Nibbles read the wrong of them in his whiskers before his eyes had enough light to confirm it. The high ground on either side of the valley held animals, dark shapes on the ridgelines, and the low ground held nothing. No movement in the drainage channels. No night-birds in the low grass. The kind of silence that came over country with nothing in the low places.

Nobody said anything. They were past the part of the night where anyone had words for it.

A farmstead sat back from the boundary wall on the left, a lamp burning in one upper window, yellow and even, someone awake before dawn. He looked at the lamp and looked away. People had been living inside this country while it changed under them, and Telia Earthwhisper had been at the sixth stone holding the worst of it back. The lamp was what she was working for. His shoulder's pull was steady.

The road climbed a gentle rise, and at the crest the party stopped without anyone calling a halt. Each of them slowed as the view opened, one breath, then another, the cold air visible around them in the first grey.

Ridgemarrow lay below. A settlement's spread of rooftops in the valley floor, the dark shape of a mill at the water, the town quiet at this hour. On the hill to the north stood a standing stone, large, shoulder-high at least at this distance, leaning slightly forward where centuries had shifted it. The stone's surface held the first grey of the sky lighter than the hill behind it.

That was the sixth Wardstone site. The hill and the stone and the quiet valley and the fields on either side with nothing moving in the low ground. All of it the country Telia Earthwhisper had been working alone, her paws pressed to the stone for hours at a stretch.

In an hour, the morning would have come, and they would begin.

Chapter Eight
Ridgemarrow

THE PARTY CAME INTO Ridgemarrow before dawn, and the first thing Nibbles noticed was the silence.

He had been in enough villages since Thimblewick to know what they sounded like at this hour. Every town had its own noise before dawn, roosters, dogs, someone's cart wheel on stone. Ridgemarrow had none of it. The buildings were dark, the market square ahead held no movement, and the only thing he could see moving was an awning at the far end of the row, swinging in a light wind that nobody had come out to fasten against.

Nibbles was in the middle of the party line, where Nori had moved him three nights ago without comment, and he was tired enough that his paws were a step ahead of his mind, carrying him forward on habit. The shoulder was there. Always there. A dull pull he had stopped trying to ignore because ignoring it cost effort he needed for other things.

They came through the eastern gate and into the market square, and Whiskerbrand's warmth came through the sheath leather before he had looked at the fountain. Low and steady. He stopped.

The fountain was a stone basin at the square's center, fed by a pipe at the north edge. In the grey before-dawn light, the stone below the waterline glowed faint violet. The stone itself was stained all the way through, not the water above it. He crouched and looked at where the pipe met the basin's edge. The color went into the mortar.

Nori stopped beside him without being asked.

"Water's been tainted," she said.

"How long does stone stain like that?"

She looked at the pipe, the basin, the trickle coming in. "Months. Maybe longer."

The blade settled back to even warmth. Nibbles straightened and looked at the square properly.

Every third building on the south side was shut. Latched from outside. The people who lived in them had left and had not come back. The cart at the far corner had its load covered with canvas weighted at the corners, the kind of careful job done by someone who had expected to finish it later. The awning swung in the wind.

The livestock pens at the western edge held about a dozen animals. They were pressed against the far side of their pens, ears flat, none of them near the fence line, all of them watching the party, waiting to find out which way to run. No birdsong from any of the eaves.

Bristlebaum had stopped at the fountain. His quills were elevated, the same way they'd been since the party crossed into the sixth Wardstone's radius two hours back. He was looking at the north edge of the square, at a house with a Guild marker on the door. Dark and shuttered.

"The warden was supposed to meet us here," he said.

"Could be delayed," Nibbles said.

Bristlebaum kept his eyes on the ridge. Lark's call came from above, three short clicks for east perimeter clear. Bristlebaum acknowledged with a raised paw. The formation adjusted fractionally around Nibbles; he felt it without seeing it, the small accommodations of people who had been walking together long enough to know each other's positions.

He looked east. The hill at the edge of town was a low rise in the grey dawn, and at its crest he could make out the boulder-sized Wardstone, and at the Wardstone's base a figure crouched with both paws pressed flat to the stone's surface. Telia.

The badge was in his pocket. The town was empty in every direction the eye could see, and the only creature working at any of it was the groundhog alone on the hill.

"Nibbles," Bristlebaum said.

"I see someone at the stone," Nibbles said.

"Go."

He went.

Telia Earthwhisper felt the party arriving before she heard them. The stone told her first. A change in the conduit's pulse, three heartbeats of steadying she hadn't provided herself, the earth registering weight on the track up from town. A dozen bodies, maybe more. She felt it through her paws and through thirty years of practice. She opened her eyes.

A mouse was coming up the hill ahead of the rest, small even by mouse standards, wide-eyed, moving with care. He had a sword across his back in a simple leather sheath. The sword was warm. She felt that too, the same way she felt the conduit, an attention answering her own. She kept her paws on the stone.

The sixth Wardstone was boulder-sized grey granite at the crest of this hill, and its veins ran amber from the top down to about two-thirds of the way. Below that, they flickered, amber to violet and back, every few minutes, in the slow irregular rhythm she'd been tracking for eight weeks. The amber was the stone's own anchor, real and still working. The violet was what happened when the conduit lines running northeast lost too much energy to the inverted Wardstone that had claimed this region, and what the stone had left couldn't make up for the loss.

When the veins went violet she pushed and they went amber again, and after a few minutes they went violet, and she pushed again.

She had been doing it for two months. About four weeks in she had stopped thinking of it as holding, around the time she switched to sleeping in two-hour shifts because that was as long as the stone could be left.

The mouse stopped a few feet from the stone. He had the sense not to touch it.

"You're from the Guild," she said. Her voice came out rougher than she'd intended.

"Guildmaster Bristlebaum's party," the mouse said. "I'm Nibbles." He paused, then added, "The sword's called Whiskerbrand," as if that might be relevant information.

"I know," she said. "I felt it from the track."

A surge came through the conduit, longer than usual, violet climbing halfway up the lower veins before she caught it. She pushed, even, and the amber followed her channeling back down through the stone. The pulse subsided.

"That happen often?" he asked.

"More often than it did two months ago. When I first came, I could go two hours between surges. Now it's forty minutes. Sometimes less."

The rest of the party crested the hill. Bristlebaum was at the front. Hedgehog, older, grey-streaked, spectacles pushed crooked from the climb. He looked at the stone, at the amber-violet flicker in the lower veins, at her paws on the surface and the slight depression worn into the granite under them. His quills went to full extension.

"Telia Earthwhisper," he said.

"Guildmaster." Her paws stayed on the stone.

"Report."

"The stone is holding," she said. "I am helping it hold. The amber in the upper veins is the stone's own anchor. That's real, that's still working. What you're seeing at the base is the fight. The conduit lines northeast are bleeding energy toward the inverted anchor, and the stone can't make up the full loss on its own." The pulse came again, brief, and she caught it. "I've been filling the gap. Six weeks ago, the stone could cover half the loss by itself. Now it covers maybe a quarter. In another two months, less probably, it won't cover any of it."

"What does that mean for Ridgemarrow?" Bristlebaum asked.

"It means more corruption, faster. The town's already lost a third of its people, some dead, most left when the water went bad. It'll lose more." She met his eyes directly. "The answer isn't here. The answer is at whatever is inverting the anchors."

"Thornwall Keep," Bristlebaum said.

"Then go to Thornwall Keep."

He looked at her paws. At the depression worn into the granite. At the grey in her fur that had spread to her temples over the last eight weeks.

"You've been here alone," he said.

"Yes."

"Two months."

"Yes."

The otter came through the group without being waved forward. She simply came, moving around the other party members to crouch beside the Wardstone. She didn't touch the stone. She looked at the amber-violet alternation in the lower veins, then looked at Telia's paws on the stone's surface.

"How long between surges?" she asked.

"Usually four minutes. Sometimes three."

"And when it pulses violet, you push it back."

"Yes."

"What does it cost you?"

A direct question, practical rather than curious. Telia answered it the same way.

"More than it did two months ago."

Nori looked at her directly, at Telia rather than the stone. She gave a small nod, neither agreement nor disagreement, only acknowledgment.

"Where do you sleep?" she asked.

"Tent at the base of the hill. Two hours at night. The stone holds for two hours." A pause. "Most nights."

Nori nodded once and stood. She turned to Bristlebaum and began asking about garrison supplies and position assignments.

The pulse came again. Telia caught it and pushed it back.

She had been doing this alone for two months. The hard part, she was finding, was letting someone stand close enough to do it with her.

By the time Nibbles came back down from the hill, Bristlebaum had begun assigning positions and was moving toward the garrison building with Gareth behind him, unrolling maps as they walked. The south perimeter was visible from the hill's base (fence line, gate, the creek crossing beyond it) and at the edge of that line stood a figure in full armor, lance in hand, watching the party's arrival. A frog, from the build of him, and the way the armor sat on his frame. He was in no hurry to leave the post.

Nibbles went to find the garrison cistern, because Telia's cup had been empty.

Sir Leonardo Pondsworth III had been keeping the count since his first morning alone in Ridgemarrow's deserted garrison.

Four months. Three days.

He had started with months only. Months had felt imprecise. He had added the days when he caught himself checking the tally too often.

He was on the south perimeter when he heard the party arrive, making his morning check of the three positions he had reinforced last week. The attacks had changed shape; the reinforcements had been necessary; they had held. He had been making the morning check at each position to confirm they would hold again tonight. When movement came from the direction of the town square, he gathered his lance and walked to meet them.

More than he had expected. Bristlebaum's message had said a party; he had imagined four, perhaps five. There were more. Road-worn, tired from one overnight rather than from anything sustained, the kind of tired that sleep would address.

He stopped at a reasonable distance. He gave a formal bow, deeper than the situation warranted, and the plume on his helmet tilted forward into his field of vision. He caught it with his free hand before it fell.

"Pondsworth Credo," he said, not quite to anyone. "Dignity in the face of doom."

Bristlebaum's greeting was four words. Rank acknowledged, status requested.

"South and west are holding," Leonardo said, straightening. "East line had a breach three nights ago. I filled the gap with reinforced stakes, no recurrence since. North perimeter has held." He paused. "The attacks changed shape seventeen days ago. Before that they hit one position at a time, in sequence. Now they hit multiple positions at once."

"You have that written down," Bristlebaum said.

"Attack maps with approach lines. Last four nights charted separately." He had been doing this since the first week. Not for anyone else's reading. Writing it down was how he made the pattern hold still long enough to plan against.

"Briefing this afternoon," Bristlebaum said.

"Ready."

The party moved past him toward the Wardstone hill. Leonardo fell in at the rear.

He was glad they were here. He felt it in his chest, relief physical and real, and was immediately ashamed of the relief, because relief meant he could not have carried this much longer. He stopped that line of thought. He had held the perimeter for four months and three days. He was allowed to be glad there were more of them now.

The mouse had fallen into step beside him.

"Four months is a long time," the mouse said.

"It is," Leonardo said.

"You held it, though."

"Yes." A beat. "I'd rather not have needed to."

The mouse let that be the answer. Leonardo walked beside him for a few more steps, four months and three days of held perimeter still pressed in him somewhere he had not yet learned how to set down.

The party assembled below the Wardstone hill. Nibbles took his place, the badge in his pocket. The groundhog on the hill had been holding a failing stone alone for two months. The frog at the perimeter had been keeping his own count. Neither of them was holding their post alone anymore.

The day had a shape, and the shape helped.

Gareth set up at a table outside the garrison with his maps spread and his notes from Telia's reading alongside. He updated them throughout the morning, the conduit lines' current state, the amber-violet ratios, how fast the northeast quarter was losing energy by position. He did not tap his thigh while he worked. Once he reached for the map, adjusted a boundary line at the northeast corner of the Wardstone's radius, and went still for several seconds before going back to the map.

Leonardo's briefing was thorough. He'd spent four months writing the attacks down carefully. Approach lines were drawn in different colors. The last two weeks were drawn separately. The shift from sequential to simultaneous was marked with a note in different ink.

"They learn," he said, standing at the map table, lance planted beside him. "A position that held by a narrow margin on one night will see a different approach the next. They test, see what held and what didn't, and adjust."

"How quickly?" Nori asked.

"One night to change a direction. Two nights to abandon an approach entirely and find another." He paused. "Whatever is directing them is watching what happens and learning from it."

Acornimus had his journal open and his pen moving before Leonardo finished the sentence.

Dash wasn't at the briefing. Nibbles caught the absence the way he had gotten used to catching Dash's distance from the nearest exit, with Dash a known quantity in the corner of his attention, and missing from it now. He returned around midday and took his place in the loose formation near the south perimeter without saying where he had been. Nori glanced briefly at the south perimeter line when Dash came back. Then she returned to her work with Telia on the hill.

In the middle of the afternoon, Nibbles went to check the south line himself. Three of the positions Leonardo had pointed to on the attack map were different from that morning. The stakes at the east-facing angle had moved five feet north. The gap between the second and third fence sections had been reduced by a wedged post. A pile of stones near the creek crossing had been cleared, opening a clean view where one hadn't existed at dawn.

He stood and looked at the changes a moment. Then he went back to the hill without mentioning it. He did not yet have the words for what he thought he was seeing, and he had been learning that Nori only spoke when she did.

At the stone, Telia was still channeling. She had been at it all day. Nibbles brought water from the garrison cistern and held the cup at the angle that let her drink without taking her paws from the stone. She drank without comment. He went to refill it and came back without being asked.

The sun went down fast, and the livestock in the pens went completely still with it.

Nibbles found his position in the formation. The shoulder pulled hard for a moment. He shifted his weight until it eased.

Lark came in from the east, three clicks, east perimeter clear, and banked back up into the dark.

The Wardstone's amber-violet flicker was visible from the fence line. Telia's paws were still on the stone.

They came out of the dark in three directions at once. East first. Nibbles heard them before he saw them, animals moving in arcs instead of straight lines, cutting around toward the hill rather than running for it. Then north, out of the shadows past the last building in the row. Then south, beyond the livestock pens where the animals had been frozen for two hours.

Lark's call cut from above, two short, one long. Multiple approach, closing.

The formation came together. Bristlebaum moved to the south, which was the primary line. Leonardo moved to the east, between the approach and the hill, between the approach and Telia, still channeling at the stone. Nori took the right flank, between the east approach and the garrison wall. Nibbles held the seam between Nori's position and the south line, the gap that needed someone in it, and that was him.

The south wave hit first. Five animals came out of the dark, bark-plated across the shoulders and flanks, purple eyes, moving in the coordinated arcs Leonardo had been charting for four months. Bristlebaum's mace came up, tired and doing the work anyway. Two animals went down in the first exchange. A third pulled back.

The formation held for the first minute. Then Dash moved. He went left and fast, to the creek crossing, where three animals were trying to come around the outside of the perimeter fence in a wide arc. The move made sense. From the creek position he had angle on all three, and his daggers were out before he was fully set. But the flank he'd been covering was open.

Nibbles saw the gap. He was already moving toward it. The right flank was fifteen feet from his position. He covered it at a run, and the problem was clear the moment he arrived. The angle was wrong for his height against the fence line, and his left shoulder did not come up fully when he raised his guard on that side. He had known about the shoulder for weeks. He had been working around it in training; working around it in training and working around it under a charge were different problems.

The animal came through low and fast. Bark-plated across shoulders and flanks. Purple eyes fixed past Nibbles to the hill behind him. He was in its way. He got his left arm up. The shoulder did not finish the motion.

The animal hit him from the left, under his guard, and its teeth found the gap between his vest and his belt. The grip was meant to drag rather than wound. He dropped his weight and twisted right, wrong for the shoulder but right for breaking the grip, and the teeth tore through his left side as he went down rather than going where the animal wanted him. The pain was sharp and immediate. Left ribs, through skin.

He hit the ground and kept moving. Nori was already there. She had been moving before he hit, crossbow discharged at close range into the next animal pressing through the gap, bolt finding the neck above the plating, and her left hand-axe was already in her other paw for the follow-through. Her eyes were on the gap, and she filled it.

Nibbles got to his feet. His left side was wet. The shoulder was pulling hard. His paws were still working, and Whiskerbrand was still in its sheath. This was a hold-the-line fight, not a purification fight, and the line needed holding. He got back to the fence and held his position.

The south fight ran for another three minutes. Bristlebaum was methodical, mace finding the gaps in the bark plating, the neck, the belly edge, the seam between shoulder plates. Tired and working through it. Gareth was behind the garrison wall, not fighting, watching how the animals were moving together. Acornimus was writing in his journal one-handed, a short blade in the other paw.

Three south animals went down. Two retreated. One circled and then retreated. The formation pushed the line forward and held the new position.

At the northeast corner of the perimeter, past the fence line, at the edge of the torchlight's reach, something was standing.

It stood upright. It wore a cloak or armor that absorbed the torchlight rather than reflecting it, so that from this distance it read as an absence in the dark rather than a shape. No visible species. The figure stood still where the corrupted animals coordinated. Watching. Its attention was on the hill, on Telia at the stone, on the amber-violet flicker in the lower veins visible even from the perimeter's edge.

Lark's alarm came from overhead, a sharp three-note call, a pattern Nibbles had not heard from her before.

The figure was already moving. Unhurried, deliberate, stepping back from the fence line at the pace of something that had seen what it came to see. Three steps back into the dark beyond the perimeter, and then there was nothing there.

When it went, the coordinated part of the attack went with it. The animals broke off gradually, the arcing approaches falling apart over the next minute, each animal going back to scattered movement. Scattered, the party could handle. The formation pushed forward in the south, east, and west at once, and four minutes later the field was clear.

Lark banked a circuit over the northeast corner. Three clicks. Clear. The bell in Ridgemarrow's square began to ring, three long strokes, the all-clear pattern.

Nibbles sat down in the grass because his legs were not interested in any other option. His left side was wet and the shoulder was finished for the night, and across the formation he could hear people calling positions and checking each other. He pressed his paw against his left ribs and felt the torn skin beneath the vest. Bandaging next.

The field cleared in the ten minutes after the bell. Bristlebaum made his way around the perimeter positions, starting at the south and moving east, checking each in sequence. He kept a steady working pace. He worked the circuit the way Nibbles had watched him work a problem before, methodically and thoroughly, his quills at the elevated angle that meant he was still thinking.

Leonardo met the circuit at the east position with bandaging supplies from the garrison. He'd already bound his own left forearm, a claw-cut through the armor's gap at the wrist, shallow, cleaned and wrapped in the field. He moved to Nori first, who declined with a gesture toward Nibbles. Nibbles accepted the bandages.

"The left ribs," Nibbles said.

"I can see that," Leonardo said.

He worked without wasted motion. He found the tear, cleaned it, bound it firmly. His hands were steady.

"Thank you," Nibbles said.

"Pondsworth Credo," Leonardo said. "Leave the field better than you found it."

Nibbles was not sure the credo technically applied to bandaging, but the bandage was tight, which mattered more.

Bristlebaum came to the east position. He stood at the fence line and looked at the northeast corner, the dark where the watching figure had been, and his quills stayed high. He looked at the party assembled around him. Nori still running her check. Gareth already making notes. Acornimus with the journal closed but his pen uncapped. Dash returned from the creek crossing, his face giving nothing.

"Report," Bristlebaum said. He was still looking at the northeast corner.

Leonardo gave it. The same format as his afternoon briefing. Positions held, positions lost, positions recovered. Casualties none. His own claw-cut. Nibbles's left-side bite.

Then he said, "The gap that opened on the right flank was wider than it should have been."

Bristlebaum looked at him.

"The formation was slower into position than it would have been rested," Leonardo said. He was not looking at Nibbles or at any single member of the party. He spoke past the creek crossing, past the east fence line, into the dark beyond it. "The overnight march put everyone in place with less left in them than they should have had. Half a second slower on the right flank response is the difference between the gap staying manageable and what actually happened." He paused. "The overnight march was the decision that made tonight's gap inevitable."

Leonardo had never raised a tactical objection in front of the party. The east fence line was not the place to start. He had started anyway.

Bristlebaum's quills went to full extension.

His answer waited while his eyes moved (the northeast corner, Gareth's notes, the formation positions, Nibbles briefly, the bandaged left side and the shoulder held carefully) and came back to the east fence line.

"Your perimeter gaps were reinforced before nightfall," he said.

"Yes," Leonardo said.

"Written down for the full four months."

"Yes."

"The party held every position."

"The party held every position," Leonardo agreed. "With casualties that were avoidable." His voice stayed at the same level it had been.

Bristlebaum turned away. The turn was complete and deliberate, his back to the northeast corner, his face to the garrison and the dark buildings beyond it. His quills did not settle. He walked toward the garrison and nobody filled the silence behind him.

The party began to move. Gareth rolled his notes. Acornimus closed his journal. Leonardo stood at the fence line a moment longer, looking at the place where Bristlebaum had been standing, and then walked after him in silence.

Nori found Nibbles at the garrison wall. He was sitting with his back against the stone and his paws loose in his lap. The shoulder had given up cooperating for the night and he had stopped trying to make it. The bandage on his left ribs was holding. His vest was going to need significant attention.

"Let me look at the shoulder," Nori said.

She crouched and began unwrapping the shoulder binding without waiting for his answer. She worked carefully and quickly, the way she always worked when she had already decided what to do.

She pressed two fingers lightly to the void-touch under the surface of the healed skin, the cold underneath rather than the wound itself, the dull ache that had been there since it started.

"Still there," she said.

"Still there," he agreed.

"The bite tonight didn't reach this." She repacked the binding, replaced it with fresh, tied it off. "It's not worse."

"Good."

She sat down against the wall beside him, actually sat, not the compact ready posture she usually held, forearms on her knees, looking at the dark field beyond the garrison gate. She was tired. He could see it now, the stillness where she was usually moving, and she was letting him see it.

"You filled the gap wrong," she said.

He had been expecting something, just not that quickly.

"I know," he said.

"The gap was real. Dash moved without calling it and you moved to fill it, the right instinct. The problem was the angle." She turned her head to look at him directly. "You went straight for the middle of the gap. With your shoulder hurt and your height against the fence line, you needed to be five feet south and moving forward through the gap. The way you took it, you had no defensive reach on the left side and the animal was already coming through low."

He thought through where he had been standing. The animal coming through low.

"I didn't have time to read the angle," he said.

"No," she agreed. "You won't, in the moment. That's not the point." She turned back to the field. "The angle has to already be in your legs before the moment comes, so you don't have to think about it. Right now it isn't. Tonight it cost you."

He looked at his paws. "You said you'd teach me how to move rather than defend."

"I did." She was quiet a moment. "When your guard can't close on one side, the instinct is to raise it anyway. You did that tonight, you raised the left, and the shoulder didn't finish the motion, and you left exactly the opening the animal was looking for. The answer isn't raising it. The answer is moving so the opening you can't close faces something the animal can't come through. The fence post. Another party member. Terrain you've already put between yourself and the threat. The move has to be faster than raising your guard, which means it has to be a habit, not a decision."

He worked back through the memory of tonight and put the correction over it. The animal coming low, the fence post two feet to his right, the gap between the fence sections behind the approach. He could see the move now, clearly, where in the moment he had not been able to.

"You were already there," he said. "When I went down."

"I was already moving," Nori said. "I shouldn't have needed to be. Not for that attack."

He took this in. Both things were true. The gap had been real, and he had filled it wrong, and he sat with both of them.

"How do I practice the move?" he asked.

"Slowly, at first. The same way you've been learning to work around the shoulder, slow until your legs know it, then faster once they do. We'll start tomorrow morning at the garrison wall. Me giving directions, no pressure, no speed."

"And if we move camp tomorrow?"

"Then we start the morning after." She looked at him. "The teaching doesn't stop because we're on the road. It just happens somewhere else."

"Tonight I sleep," he said.

"Tonight you sleep." She stood, brushing the grass from her cloak. She held her paw down for him. He took it and she pulled him to his feet. "The shoulder needs rest and so does the rest of you."

He stood. His left side pulled, and he kept walking.

"The void-agent," he said. "The one that withdrew."

"I saw it."

"It was watching Telia. The stone."

"Yes." She looked at the hill, where the Wardstone still flickered amber and violet in the dark and Telia's channeling light held even at its base. "Gareth saw it too." She turned toward the garrison door. "Come on."

He followed her in.

Dawn came grey and slow, with a low wind from the northeast that smelled of turned earth and stone.

Nibbles woke when Lark's first circuit call came (three clicks, perimeter clear) and lay still a minute taking stock of what the night had done to his body. Left ribs sore, bandaged, holding. Shoulder stiff from being used past what it had left, sullen about it now. He dressed carefully, found his vest right-way-round on the first try, and put the badge in his pocket.

When he came outside, Telia was coming down the hill.

She moved slowly. The grey at her temples had spread while he had slept, barely visible, the line of it now above her eyes. She had her staff. She reached the level ground and stopped a moment with her paw flat against the nearest fence post, reading the earth through it. She saw Nibbles.

"The stone held through the night," she said. "Two surges. Both caught." She lifted her paw from the post. "The amber in the upper veins is steady."

"Good," Nibbles said. "Are you all right?"

She looked at him. "I can travel," she said.

"That's not what I asked."

A pause. "No," she said. "I'm not all right. The stone is better than when I arrived and worse than it needs to be when we return, and I have been awake for most of two months, and I am going to need to sleep through a complete day before we reach Thornwall." She looked at him directly. "But I can travel. And the answer isn't here."

"Bristlebaum told you we're going to Thornwall."

"I told Bristlebaum to go to Thornwall," she said. "I merely agreed to come along."

Nibbles thought about this and decided the distinction was probably accurate.

The party assembled in stages. Gareth came out with his saddlebags, then Acornimus with the journal already open, and Bristlebaum came from the garrison with his mace at his belt and his spectacles straightened for once. He walked to the base of the Wardstone hill and stood looking up at the amber veins holding in the upper third, the amber-violet flickering in the lower, for a long moment. Then he turned and began the loading check. His quills had come down a fraction from the previous night's full extension, though they were not going flat today.

Leonardo came from the perimeter on his fourth morning check of the reinforced positions, and stopped at the south fence to look at the assembly. He still had the parade-ground posture, the lance at his side, the plume sitting correctly in the dawn calm. He walked to Bristlebaum.

"The three reinforced positions will hold through tonight," he said. "Possibly the following night. After that, without reinforcement, the east gap will open again."

"Understood," Bristlebaum said.

"I will accompany your party." Leonardo kept his eyes on the middle distance between the garrison and the Wardstone hill, his voice the one he used for garrison reports. "The perimeter doesn't require a knight. It requires someone to hold it, and there are two families left in the south houses who understand the positions. A working company needs a working knight more than Ridgemarrow needs a garrison of one."

Bristlebaum acknowledged it with a nod and returned to the loading check.

The sun came up across the eastern hills. Gareth updated the corner of his map where the northeast boundary ran. Acornimus put his pen away and closed the journal. Dash was already at the gate.

Nibbles stood in the assembled formation and felt the badge in his pocket, smooth and cool.

The party had grown since the day before. The bite was under the bandage. The argument at the east fence line had not been settled and nobody pretended otherwise. Ahead of them the road ran north and west, through country the sixth Wardstone could no longer hold, and they went.

Chapter Nine

The Things That Can't Be Fixed

THE WOUND HAD BEEN manageable in the dark, and in the morning he could see what the dark had let him ignore. The bite along his left side had closed. The edges were doing something else.

Nori crouched beside him in the doorway of the building where the party had sheltered, her paw working carefully along the wound's border, tracing rather than pressing. Outside, Ridgemarrow was already moving. Voices down the street. A cart on stone. People putting the morning back together after a bad night.

Whiskerbrand warmed against his back. Lower and steadier than the sharp alert it gave near active corruption, the sword paying attention without urgency.

"Look here," Nori said.

The wound's center was doing what wounds should do, closed and red and angry-looking. At the border, the color changed. A faint threading of purple at the margins, deliberate and even, like dye worked into cloth from the outside. His whiskers went still.

"Void-touch," Nori said. "Stage 3 animals carry corruption in the bite. Most of it doesn't take hold in a clean body. At the wound's edge, some does."

"Is it going to spread?"

"Not if you don't aggravate it. Two or three days and it fades." She sat back, watching the wound rather than his face. "Watch for it moving inward. If the purple starts toward the center, tell me immediately. What you have now is the edge-touch. It slows healing. It doesn't stop it."

"What aggravates it?"

"Full extension on your left side. Anything that pulls the muscle through the shoulder, heavy lifting, swinging your left arm wide, reaching overhead to the left. That drives it deeper." She met his eyes. "You can walk normally. You can carry with your right arm if you keep your left side stable. Most things are open to you if you're careful about how you do them."

He flexed the fingers of his left paw. They moved, but a half-beat behind his right.

"There's a family north of here," Nori said. She was already standing. "Reedholm property. They came back this morning for what they can salvage from the farmhouse. They need another pair of paws." She looked at him. "Half a mile. You walk there, you carry things carefully, you walk back. It keeps you moving."

He took the assignment as given. "I'll find you when I'm back," he said.

He got to his feet slowly, keeping his left side from rotating, and adjusted Whiskerbrand's strap so the weight sat across his right shoulder rather than centering across his back. The sky outside was flat grey, the town smelling of damp stone. The Reedholm lane was half a mile north.

The Reedholm lane still latched at the bottom.

The gate was iron-hinged and old, sitting level in its frame, the latch catching without resistance. The hedgerows on either side had been kept to the same height for years. The lane's surface was packed earth, well-traveled, not cracked. From the road it looked like a working farm.

Up close, the soil gave it away.

Along the lane's edges, the ground had gone grey, the grey of soil that had been turned. Water would bead here rather than soak in. The grass along the verge still stood at the right height, green at the tips, but the stalks went wrong where they entered the ground. The farm was not dying. Dying would have meant the life failing. This was the life being turned the wrong way, everything still growing, all of it growing wrong.

In the yard, a mole and his wife were carrying things to a cart. They worked without speaking to each other.

The farmer was older, his spectacles thick, his paws gnarled from decades of work. He was at the barn door when Nibbles arrived, not moving, looking at the door itself. It was open. It swung gently in still air.

"You're from the Guild party," he said, without turning.

"Yes, sir. Nori Riverclaw sent me."

The farmer turned. He looked at Nibbles, at Whiskerbrand, at the way Nibbles was holding his left arm, and took it in without remarking.

"The grain's loaded already," he said. "What's left is household things. Good dishes, the winter blankets, the ledgers from the back room. Things that can be used somewhere else."

"I'll start."

The farmer stepped aside and Nibbles went through the kitchen door.

The farmhouse stopped him in the doorway a moment. He had been expecting something more obviously wrong, crystal in the walls, the smell of corruption, some visible sign. There was none of it. The walls were sound. The hearth was cold but intact. Two cups sat on the kitchen table where they'd been left the morning the family had gone.

On the wall beside the kitchen door, a hoe hung on its hook. The blade was clean. The handle had been worn smooth from use, then rubbed with oil and hung with care. It had been put away properly the last time it was used.

His tail curled around his ankle.

The farmer's wife came through the doorway with a box of folded cloth, working without looking up.

"Winter blankets are in the back room," she said. "Stack by size, please. One cart."

He went to the back room and began stacking. He worked for an hour. Blankets, folded and stacked by size. Two boxes of ledgers, carried carefully because they were heavy and he couldn't use his left arm to steady them properly. A tin chest of good dishes, wrapped in cloth. Each load out to the cart, set down, back inside. His left side tightened on the third trip. He adjusted and kept moving.

On the fourth trip back through the kitchen, he stopped and looked at the hoe again.

He had walked through farming land for most of this journey. He'd seen what the corruption did to crops. The greyness moving from the soil into the roots. The stalks growing in the wrong direction. The grain that looked whole from a distance and fell apart when you touched it. The Reedholm fields were no different. The irrigation channels running between this farm and Ridgemarrow's water carried soil that was past holding. The seeds in the ground were growing the wrong way.

None of it had touched the hoe. The hoe was still on its hook, ready for a field that no longer existed.

The farmer came in from outside. He saw Nibbles looking at the hoe and stopped.

"My father's," he said. "His father's before that."

Nibbles waited.

"I keep thinking I'll take it." The farmer looked at the hoe, then away. "My brother has good land in Millhaven, or he did a month ago. But he's already running two families off one farm. No room for another field." He was quiet a moment. "So where would I take it?"

He walked past Nibbles into the back room and picked up the last box himself.

Nibbles lifted the tin chest and carried it out to the cart.

He worked until the cart was full. When the farmer and his wife drove the cart down the lane toward the road, the gate swung shut behind them and caught on its latch without anyone having to close it. Nibbles stood in the yard and watched them go.

The farmhouse was still standing. The hoe was still on its hook. The gate still latched. None of it would be of any use to anyone again.

He had carried every box that could be carried. The cart had gone down the road. The farm was still here and still unworkable, and would be tomorrow, and the day after.

The hoe still hung on its hook through the open kitchen door. Nibbles turned south on the lane and walked back toward Ridgemarrow.

Nibbles found them at the Wardstone hill. The stone sat at the northern edge of Ridgemarrow on a low rise. Boulder-sized, grey granite, visible from half the town. The veins running through it should have been amber. Instead they ran amber and violet by turns, neither color holding even.

Telia was pressed against it, both paws flat on the stone's surface, her eyes closed. Her focus stayed on the stone as Nibbles arrived. Bristlebaum stood a few feet away, arms at his sides, watching her.

Nibbles stopped beside him and waited.

There was a depression in the stone's face where Telia's paws rested. A smoothing rather than a dramatic hollow, a wearing-away, the granite holding the shape of where her paws had been for hours and hours.

After a few minutes, Telia opened her eyes and stepped back from the stone.

"The field gaps," she said to Bristlebaum. "Three months ago, each break in the anchor field lasted for a count of ten before the field reasserted. Now they last for a count of thirty."

"What causes the breaks?"

"The conduit network carries suppressive force from each stone toward the prison. The five inverted stones are feeding void energy back into the network instead, drawing on the same lines but in reverse. The sixth stone makes up the difference. It generates enough force to cover its own share of the load and absorb some of what the inverted stones are pushing back through the lines." She looked at the stone, not at Bristlebaum. The veins flickered amber, then violet, held at violet for four slow seconds, then shifted back. "The gaps are the moments when the sixth anchor's flow drops below what the load requires. The field stutters. Then it reasserts."

"And the seventh stone," Bristlebaum said. "Under Thornwall."

"The other six hold the prison's suppressive field in place. The seventh is where the field is generated. The conduit lines from all six anchors converge there and feed into the prison's central architecture." Telia turned to look at him directly. "If the seventh falls, the prison fails. The remaining anchors become irrelevant. He knows this. He has always been working toward the seventh."

Bristlebaum took a moment with that.

"The sixth is buying time," he said.

"Yes. Without help from outside, the gaps lengthen faster. Each day I'm not here, the load grows without adjustment. The sixth stone won't fail immediately. It's been holding against this load for years. But the timeline shortens." She said it plainly. "Reaching Thornwall gives you the chance to stop the seventh before it falls. Staying here gives you more days before the sixth fails, but it doesn't stop the seventh."

Bristlebaum turned and looked at the stone. He stood there a long moment, looking at the flickering veins, amber and violet, amber and violet. He nodded once. He turned and walked back toward town. His quills were still at the angle they had been since the previous night.

Nibbles stood at the stone a moment longer. The depression in the granite caught the flat grey light the same way the rest of the surface did. You had to be standing where he was standing to see it. Then he followed Bristlebaum back.

Gareth had three maps spread across the table in the room they'd been given as a working space, weighted at the corners with field equipment, a compass, a folded knife, and a small wooden block that had clearly started as something else.

He was tapping when Nibbles came in. A quiet rhythm on his thigh, tap-tap-pause, tap-tap-pause. His eyes stayed on the maps. Nibbles pulled a chair over and sat.

"Third from the left is the current corruption boundary at each anchor site," Gareth said. "Updated four days ago. Second map is the same numbers from six months back. First is eighteen months back."

The maps were marked in red at each of the five inverted anchor sites, a rough radius around each stone showing how far the void growth had spread. On the oldest map, each radius was modest. On the six-month map, noticeably larger. On the current map, larger again by a proportion that was not the same as the first change.

"How fast it's spreading has been picking up," Nibbles said.

"Yes." Gareth pulled out a sheet of notes, columns of numbers, dates, measurements written in a small precise hand. "Each site spreads roughly as you'd expect for a stone that's been inverted as long as that one has. Longer inversion, more spread. The rate for each site holds with its own timeline." He tapped a column with one claw. "Except here." He moved to the second map, then the third. "Six months ago, the spread at all five sites picked up at the same time. Each one, by roughly the same proportion."

Nibbles looked at the maps again. "That doesn't happen on its own."

"No." Gareth reached for his pen and wrote *Six months. All five sites pick up, at the same time. Source?* He underlined *at the same time* twice, pressing harder on the second pass. Then he circled the time notation. Twice. He set the pen down and looked at what he'd written. The rhythm on his thigh had changed. Slower now. Tap. Pause. Tap.

"What does it mean?" Nibbles asked.

"If it picks up at all five anchor sites at the same moment, it didn't come from the individual stones. They're in five different places. The only thing connecting them is the conduit network." Gareth looked at the maps without touching them. "Something changed in the ritual six months ago. Something that altered the flow through the conduit lines. Changed how the load was carried or added a new draw on the network, something that reached all five stones at the same moment."

"Do you know what?"

"Not yet." He folded the paper with the note and placed it in his notebook. "I've been watching this pattern for two years. The pattern changes when the situation changes. This is a change. I'll keep watching."

Nibbles caught the *I'll keep watching* and knew it had been said before, to people who had wanted the pattern to hold for longer than it did. The rhythm resumed on his thigh. Tap. Pause. Tap. Nibbles got up and left Gareth to it.

Nibbles came back to the working room without quite having decided to. He had gotten as far as the building's entrance, watched a group of Ridgemarrow's remaining residents carrying furniture out of a house across the street, and then turned around.

Nori was at the table with Gareth. She had pulled a chair close to his and was leaning over the current boundary map, her paw hovering above the northernmost anchor site's marked radius. Gareth hadn't acknowledged her arrival, and she had not asked to be acknowledged. They held the same working space and the same problem.

"Your boundary ends at the crystallization front," Nori said. "The drainage runs northeast from that stone. The seeding gets carried ahead of the visible growth by the water table."

"Then where do you put the boundary?"

She moved her paw north of the marked radius and traced it with one claw, not pressing. "Here. Two hundred yards, minimum."

Gareth pulled a sheet from the stack at the table's edge, read a line, and set it down. He picked up his pen and made a correction to the map without resistance.

"The third marker on the second map is also off," he said. "Eastward."

"How far?"

"Fifty to a hundred yards. Same source. The two markers on either side give the radius. The third is out of line with them." He moved the pen to the second map and made the correction. "You'd have caught it if you'd been looking at the radii rather than the drainage lines."

"I was looking at the drainage lines."

"Yes. That's why we're both here."

Nori confirmed the correction, then looked back at the current boundary map. "The compass orientation on the third map is off by a few degrees as well."

"I noticed. It came from the Second District office. Their orientations run three to five degrees out. I've been correcting for it since year two."

"Does the Council know?"

"I sent it in twice. They asked for documents showing the error. I provided them. They asked for further documents from another source."

Nori looked up at Gareth. He continued making his correction.

"How long ago?" she asked.

"Four years."

She looked back at the map. "Further documents from another source."

"The same standard that took three months to accept the drainage finding," Gareth said. "It's the speed correct information moves."

Nibbles took his chair, away from the table, watching from that angle. They worked the way field partners worked after three years, useful disagreement, not consensus. Nori had field observation of water movement; Gareth had written-down surface measurements. Each could see the limits in the other's method. They exchanged corrections without apology and built on them without slowing down.

After a while, without anything passing between them, both of them moved to the same section of the current boundary map and worked on it side by side. Gareth updating the documented radius. Nori rechecking the drainage line she'd traced earlier.

Nori read a notation Gareth made, upside down from across the table. "That season's figure is off. Pull the spring numbers."

Gareth pulled the spring numbers. He looked at them. He crossed out the notation. They moved on.

At some point Gareth looked up and found Nibbles watching.

"She finds the third option," he said, in the tone he used for reporting measurements. "When two people are busy being right and not finding the answer, she looks for the third thing. We spent three months on opposite sides of the drainage question. I had the surface measurements written down. She had the field observation. The answer wasn't in either of them alone." He looked at his notes. "She looked at the spring water table numbers."

"You'd have found it," Nori said.

"Eventually."

"Probably not before we'd had the argument four more times."

"Definitely not before that." He looked at Nibbles. "The position that leads somewhere is more useful than the position that's right. She finds the one that leads somewhere. Three years means I show her my wrong answer faster, because the sooner she sees it the sooner we get to the right one."

"That's an extremely generous reading of how this works," Nori said.

"It's an accurate reading of how this works." He looked back down at his notes. "Which is what a compliment should be."

Nori stood and slung her crossbow across her back without looking at it. She looked at Nibbles. "The Bristlebaum argument is about to happen. You should probably be there."

Then she was through the door and down the hall.

Nibbles looked at Gareth. Gareth was already writing again, the pen moving down the margin, the rhythm on his thigh resuming in the deliberate tap-pause.

The argument was already running when Nibbles reached the briefing room. Bristlebaum stood at the near end of the table, Gareth's maps spread in front of him. Leonardo stood at the far end with his lance upright at his right side, his hand resting on the shaft just below the guard. He was in his formal-address register, the voice he used for parade grounds and briefings.

"Three drainage channels on the eastern approach," Leonardo said. "Stage 2 corruption active in each. Each crossing takes twenty to thirty minutes when the party moves correctly through it. Three consecutive crossings means an hour and a half of concentrated exposure before we've covered half the route." He had a hand-drawn sketch of the route beside Gareth's official maps, fork marks at the three channels, the northern path traced in clean lines. "The northern route avoids all three."

"At the cost of a day," Bristlebaum said.

"Yes. And I'm saying the eastern route may not save the full day the map suggests it saves." Leonardo's voice held level. "Stage 2 channel crossings at that intensity don't leave a party at full strength on the other side. They leave a party that has taken on significant void exposure and needs time to clear it. That recovery time belongs in the count alongside the transit time. Without it, the count is incomplete." He had a hand on the sketch, not pointing, just present. "I spent two years at a garrison inside a failing Wardstone zone. I watched groups use both routes. The groups that took the northern path arrived ready to work. The groups that used the eastern route needed a day's recovery before they were effective. In practice, the time difference was smaller than the map suggests."

"How many of those groups were running a schedule where the day wasn't available?"

A pause.

"I understand there's a timeline," Leonardo said. "What I'm asking is whether the recovery cost from three channel crossings is already in the count. If it's not—"

"It is," Bristlebaum said. "And the day that correction produces is still not available." He looked at the map. "The crossings cost what they cost," he said. "We build that into how we move through them. We absorb what remains in transit. We don't have the recovery day. We have the time between here and the Hollow, and we use it."

"With respect—"

"Sir Pondsworth." Quiet and final. "We take the eastern route. We move correctly. We reach the Hollow on schedule."

His claw moved to the eastern line on the map and traced it, the shorter path, three red marks at the drainage channels. Leonardo's hand-drawn sketch lay beside Gareth's annotated maps, the northern fork carefully drawn, where Leonardo had set it down twenty minutes ago.

Leonardo's hand lifted off the lance shaft and came to his side. His posture adjusted, a small military reset, holding the position rather than abandoning it. He reached for the hand-drawn sketch, folded it once with precision, and put it inside his breastplate.

"Understood," he said.

He picked up his lance, turned, and walked for the door. The lance's heel touched the floor twice as he went. The door came shut behind him.

Bristlebaum stood at the map. His claw traced the eastern line a second time, checking the count it rested on rather than reviewing the decision, the way a hand checks a knot before weight goes on it. The constraint still held. He turned and walked out through the building's side entrance without another word.

Nibbles stayed where he was. He had followed every word. The timeline Telia had given Bristlebaum this morning, the constraint that made the day unavailable, the route that arrived on schedule inside that constraint. He could see all of it. The decision was correct. Leonardo's case had been built on two years of watching groups cross those channels; Bristlebaum had answered with information Leonardo had not had when he built the case.

But the map had stayed under Bristlebaum's claw the entire time. Not when Leonardo named his two years at the garrison. Not when Leonardo tried to work inside the constraint. Not when the door shut.

He had weighed the route against the timeline and found the answer. The knight behind the route, what he knew, what it had cost him to learn it, had not been on the table.

They assembled in the street an hour before midday. Ridgemarrow had been a town of three hundred before the corruption began making itself felt in the water and the soil and in the slow numbers of households working through the cost of staying. A hundred of those three hundred had gone over the past year, some north, where family could take them in, some to the river towns, some simply gone, away from the flickering Wardstone on the hill. What remained had organized itself around the smaller number, but you could see where the missing third had been, the shuttered stalls in the market lane, the empty vendor slots, the houses whose windows stayed dark through the morning and into the afternoon.

In the windows that still had people in them, faces watched. No one came down. No one called anything out. They stood at their windows and watched the party gather in the street.

Telia stood at the street's edge with her staff in both hands and wrapped the cracked section with cord from her pack, tight, each loop placed deliberately beside the last.

Leonardo had a cloth from his saddle kit and was running it along the lance shaft in slow, even passes. When he tilted the lance to reach the lower section the plume flopped forward. He pushed it back with the heel of his hand without looking at it and kept polishing.

Dash had moved to the street's northern edge and was studying the road ahead the way he studied any road, exits, ground, what was on it. His ears were up. His whiskers worked without stopping. When he was satisfied, he moved back without comment.

Nibbles reached into his pocket and found the badge, warm. He held it a moment. He thought about the Wardstone on the hill at the northern edge of town, the veins cycling amber and violet and holding neither color even. He thought about the depression in the granite where Telia's paws had rested so many times the surface had worn to fit them. He put the badge back.

Acornimus confirmed the route from his journal, then closed it. Gareth folded the last map and tucked it away. Nori was already at the street's edge, facing north, and they moved.

The road north left Ridgemarrow through the gap in the low stone wall at the town's northern edge. Past it, the hedgerows ran overgrown on both sides of the track, uneven where they had not been tended for a season. The fields visible beyond them had gone the grey Nibbles had learned to read on sight, soil turned, the crops still standing but growing the wrong way.

He walked with his left side held stable, Whiskerbrand's weight across his right shoulder. The wound was tight, and no worse.

The party settled into its road order without discussion. Lark's shadow crossed the ground at intervals when the cloud cover thinned enough to cast one. Nori at the forward left, crossbow at her back. Gareth beside her with the maps folded and stowed. Leonardo in the rear position he'd been keeping since dawn.

Behind them, Ridgemarrow went out of sight in stages.

The mill roof went first around the first curve. The inn's weathervane (a rooster in iron, pointing roughly west) stayed visible above the hedgeline for longer, until the road curved again and the hedges ran higher and there was nothing behind them but overgrown green and grey sky.

Nibbles thought about the hoe on its hook. The corruption had not touched the hoe. It had taken the field around it, the water that fed the field, the soil that could grow anything, and the hoe was still on its hook, useless. That was what five inverted Wardstones did. They did not destroy things one by one. They took apart what you needed to use the things, and then the things were still there, and no one could use them.

The families who had left Ridgemarrow had not left because the corruption took their houses. The houses were still there. They had left because the houses were no longer in a place where life could be made.

Reaching Thornwall and stopping the ritual was the only thing big enough to give any of that back.

The town behind them (the watchers at the windows, the Wardstone still cycling on its hill, the stalls with their goods unminded) could not be held by anyone who stayed. Staying meant being there when it ended. Holding it meant getting to the seventh stone before Grimthorn finished what he had been working toward for thirty years.

Chapter Ten
The Mission Changes

THE BIRDSONG CHANGED TWO days north of Ridgemarrow. This wasn't the engineered silence of Wigglywood. Birds were still calling, still moving through the canopy, but perched too high. A thrush sat on a branch a thrush had no business using, ignoring the lower cover where it belonged. The midlevel had gone wrong, and the birds had given up on it. Bristlebaum marked it and kept moving.

The trail northeast ran through country that should have walked easier than the waterlogged farmland behind them, old forest floor, loam packed by centuries of root growth. The ground was solid. Something else about it wasn't. The familiar corruption signs (seeping purple, bark-growths, coordinated animal tracks) didn't account for whatever Telia had been catching since midmorning yesterday.

She walked near the center of the formation, paw trailing along exposed roots when the trail ran close to old growth. Not breaking stride. Not making a production of it. She was stopping more often this morning than yesterday. He waited.

Nibbles had settled into the march. His compound bite was healing cleanly (Bristlebaum checked it each morning without comment) and the boy walked now with the sword across his back the way he was beginning to walk with everything, alert without strain. Nori's work. She had him reading the terrain, not just the group. He still put the vest on backward half the time, but the sword was on straight.

Leonardo held the left flank. His left ankle had swollen after the river ford two days back and had not entirely forgiven the march since. His lance tapped the ground on his off-beat now, automatic, no longer something he was thinking about. He had adjusted his shield carry twice without prompting. Compensating cleanly. Lark was above. She had run two extra circuits that morning.

By the third afternoon, the trail crested a low ridge through birch and pale stone, and Bristlebaum stopped the column. The Hollow lay below them.

The valley had been left alone a long time. Soil and root and stone running at their own pace, the canopy closing where it wanted to close. Nothing wrong with it. Nothing dying. Just country no one had managed because nothing had asked to be managed.

The Ancient Willow stood at the valley's center. Hazel had never said how large it was. Bristlebaum had built an image from her letters over thirty years, a significant tree, old, the kind you could weave a detection net through if you had the patience. He had imagined a large tree. He had not imagined this. Everything else in the valley looked recent beside it.

He heard Telia's knees hit the ground before he turned to look. She had both paws pressed flat to an exposed root, a root as wide as Nibbles was tall, running along the ridgeline surface, bark worn smooth in oval patches, and the amber light had moved from her wrists outward, tracking through her fur to her fingertips.

He waited. The rest of the party settled behind him. Gareth unrolled a map without being asked. Nibbles kept his ears forward and had the sense not to speak. Lark banked above the valley's east end, ran her circuit, banked again, and ran a third.

The amber reached Telia's fingertips and held there. Two minutes. Three. She pulled her paws back.

"She's been running a net through the root system," Telia said. "The whole valley floor. Thirty years, maybe longer. The older contacts lie on top of the newer ones and I can't count them exactly. The Willow at the center is the hub, but the reach goes to both ridges." She caught her breath. "Anything that passes through this valley, anything that disturbs the soil, she would have felt it. The net was built to carry it back to her."

Bristlebaum looked at the worn patches on the bark. Not random. Two ovals at the width of a rabbit's paw span, in the same positions, worn smooth by years of the same contact returning to the same points. Thirty years of it, and he had not known.

"Still running?" he asked.

"Yes. The Willow is carrying it on its own momentum." Telia sat back. The amber faded. "She built it to run without her."

"The Caves."

Telia pointed northeast. "Below the valley floor, northeast end. The lines running from that location are older than anything Hazel built. The installation inside the Caves predates her whisper-net by generations. Someone built it for a different purpose." She looked at the valley a moment. "The crystals in the walls were placed deliberately. The pattern is complex. Whoever did it understood what they were doing."

"Good," he said.

Telia took it for dismissal and stood, brushing soil from her paws.

The courier had reached the column's tail while Telia was reading. Bristlebaum had tracked her along the eastern ridge approach for the last ten minutes, three days of hard travel behind her, the pace tightening now that she could see the column. Acornimus's cipher seal on the pouch at her hip.

He turned to meet her.

The courier was a young vole, trail-worn from three days of fast travel, the last of it spent finding the energy to stand still now that she had arrived. She presented the document pouch before Bristlebaum could speak, and he broke the seal.

The group had not dispersed. Nibbles with his ears angled forward. Nori three paces to the left, watching the document rather than his face. Gareth had closed his maps. Dash had turned from the eastern view. Acornimus had opened his journal. Telia had straightened from where she'd been resting, her paws still faintly amber.

He read the document. Hazel Willowbark. Taken three days ago. Two of the Herald's agents in their usual field pair, at the spring below the Ancient Willow, first light on equinox morning. Her cottage had been checked. She was not home. Her staff lay on the bank where it had fallen. Her morning bundle was still there. She had been taken to the Caves below the Hollow. A local informant had seen the entry. The informant was certain. Three days.

He turned to the second page. The informant's account. The cave mouth position. Sentry rotation, three at the entrance. He read it at the pace he read everything, line by line, evenly. Three days inside the Caves. He folded the document and put it away.

"The mission has changed," he said. "Sage Willowbark was taken from the Hollow three days ago. She is being held in the Whispering Caves below the valley."

He used the command voice, flat and level, nothing in it except what was necessary. Around him the group went very still.

Nibbles made a small sound. His paw had found Whiskerbrand's hilt.

"Taken," Nori said. How many, what force, what pairing, all of it folded into the one word.

"Two. Herald field pair. Matches what Gareth flagged from Ridgemarrow." He looked at the fox, who was already reaching for his maps. "At the spring. Equinox morning."

Gareth had the map open, already on the right spring.

"Why the Caves rather than transport north?" Nori asked.

"They wanted her contained locally. The Caves hold." He looked at the valley. "They use the walls. The crystals pull what a person carries (old regrets, old questions, the things she has not resolved) and put it in front of her. Over and over. It is a way of breaking someone."

Nibbles had not let go of the sword. "How long can she hold against it?"

"Hazel Willowbark has spent fifty years examining everything she has ever done," Bristlebaum said. "She will hold longer than most." Three days was still three days, and he let the rest stay where it was.

He had known about the spring. Hazel had mentioned it once, years ago. She went at dawn on solstice and equinox days because the ley lines ran most clearly then and the spring sat directly above a main conduit. Who else had known. Through which path the information had traveled. Those questions would keep until the operation closed.

"We move on the Hollow at first light tomorrow," he said. "The plan divides into a Caves operation and a perimeter hold. I want everyone fed and rested. We work the details tonight."

The courier was still standing there. "Sit," Bristlebaum said, not unkindly. "The third pack, near Nibbles. There's dried fruit."

She sat. Nibbles had already moved to retrieve the pack without being asked.

They gathered at the ridge's north end where the view of the Hollow gave them reference points. Gareth spread his map on a flat stone. Telia settled on the root she had been reading. Lark came down from her circuit and took a branch above the group. The valley lay below them in the fading light, the Ancient Willow enormous at its center, Hazel's net still running through every root in the floor.

The central question was obvious before anyone named it. Who goes into the Caves.

"I'll take the Caves operation," Bristlebaum said. "Nori, Acornimus, Dash, you hold the perimeter with Leonardo, Telia, and Nibbles. Gareth maps the ridge and keeps communication between both groups."

Leonardo was nodding slowly. Gareth was marking positions. Acornimus had his pen ready.

Nori said, "No." Quiet. Even. A statement.

"Walk me through it," Bristlebaum said.

Nori looked at him directly. "The Caves work on what hasn't been examined," she said. "That's what the reports say, and what Telia's read of the crystal installation confirms. They find the thing a person has been walking around and they put it in front of them. They don't stop." She kept her eyes on him. "You have examined nearly everything you've done and most things you haven't. There is one thing you haven't, and we both know what it is. I'm not going to say it. You don't need me to."

His quills had risen a fraction at the ridge of his shoulders before he caught the movement.

"The Caves will put you in that room within the first hour," Nori said. "And when they do, you will stop moving. Not permanently. But long enough."

Around him the group was very still. Nibbles had gone quiet the way he went quiet when something was costing someone and he didn't know where to put himself. Leonardo was looking at the valley. Gareth had set his pen down.

"Your alternative," Bristlebaum said.

"Acornimus, Dash, and myself go into the Caves. Acornimus has the network contact and the documentation skills. Dash has the instinct for closed places, the exits, the routes, the ways through that aren't marked on any plan. And I have what I have." What she had was six years of examined things.

"The Caves will find something in you as well," he said.

"Yes," she said.

"And you believe you can continue moving through it."

"I believe there is no one else for this task," she said. "If there were, I would send them." She had weighed it and arrived at the same answer more than once, and she was telling him so.

He was angry, at the correctness of what she had said, at the fact that the correctness did not make it easier to hear. He thought about Aldric at the summit, the sword warm in his paws for one moment, real and irreducible, and then the warmth leaving. He had concluded something from the leaving, and he had built on that conclusion for thirty years. The Ancient Willow was visible below, still carrying what Hazel had built. Nori was right, and the Caves would find that room and stop him in it.

"You have the assignment," he said.

The group did not scatter. Four weeks ago they would have been moving before Bristlebaum finished the sentence, people assembled by order and not yet by choice, each pulling to their own orbit. Tonight they stayed where they were. The decision needed a moment to settle, and they gave it the moment.

Dash had placed himself at the side of the main cluster from the moment Bristlebaum broke the courier's seal, angled to see all parties at once while appearing to watch the valley. He had been holding something since the document arrived. His lightning-bolt patch showed white through the mud at his chest, and when he stopped moving, it caught the light.

"Something I want to say," Dash said. "Whoever grabbed Hazel knew she'd be at the spring at equinox morning. Not that she lives in the Hollow. That she goes to the spring, on equinox, at first light. They were there at first light." He looked at Bristlebaum. "That's not something you learn from watching the valley for a week. That's a schedule."

Bristlebaum's quills rose before the implication had fully arrived. The lifting at the shoulder ridge happened ahead of any deliberate response. He felt it and left it. Nori had gone still. Gareth's pen was down.

"Source possibilities," Acornimus said, already writing. His pen moved in the small even letters he used for entries on the work. "Correspondence review covering anything confirming the equinox visit to any party outside the Hollow. Records held by parties with access to a mission schedule. Watching from a distance, though the root network would have caught a thirty-day prior approach before equinox." He wrote another line. "A field pair at this level does not improvise timing. The equinox hour is too specific for inference. The confirmation came before they left."

"Came before they left," Gareth said, not echoing but correcting what kind of knowing it was. Knowing on arrival was local; knowing before departure pointed back to origin.

Nibbles had gone very quiet. He was tracking the conversation without speaking, the way he tracked anything that moved faster than he could keep up with, when he still wanted the shape of it.

"The Guild routing system," Bristlebaum said.

"When I confirmed the mission, the Sage's contact passed through standard Guild channels. The equinox schedule went with it. That information moved through Ironhold before it reached any member of this group."

He knew whose archive held the routing records, the one who had spent thirty years keeping every mission that passed through Ironhold, every schedule, every contact confirmation, every agent's position, and who had done the work cleanly enough that the keeping looked like loyalty. He had one informant's account, one bent reading of it, and thirty years of a man doing his stated work. None of it was proof of the specific thing he was now holding next to the name. He kept the name to himself for now. He would write the inquiry tonight, phrased as a supply question about garrison movements northeast of the Hollow, and see what came back.

"Acornimus," he said. "Full entry. Source and timing."

"Done," Acornimus said. He was at the closing notation.

"Gareth. Field record."

"Already there."

Dash turned from the valley and shifted his angle. The lightning-bolt patch moved back into general shadow.

The courier was sitting at the third pack with dried fruit in one paw, eating at the careful pace of someone who had been moving for three days. She had heard things her clearance did not cover and had made the right decisions about her face.

Bristlebaum wrote the inquiry himself. Four lines in Guild cipher. Mission change confirmed, extraction required, request confirmation on all garrison units now posted northeast of the Hollow approach. Phrased as a supply question. No named subject. No stated urgency.

He folded it and pressed his ring to the wax.

"South to the Ridgemarrow relay," he told the courier. "Standard routing from there. Your task ends at the relay."

She took it, put it away, and started down the eastern ridge trail. Then they turned to the plan.

Gareth's map went back onto the flat stone at the ridge's north end. The late-afternoon light held long and level. The party gathered around the map without direction. Lark dropped from her circuit and took the branch above the map stone. Nibbles moved to the left of the map, the same position he had taken at Ridgemarrow when Nori was running an operation, taken now without being told.

"Two garrison units on the report," Bristlebaum said. He pointed to Gareth's marks. "One at the western approach to the Hollow, one rotating on the northern rim. Fixed-point deployment, Herald standard. The information is two days old. Exact positions may have shifted. The deployment pattern is what we've seen from the Herald every time."

"The northern rim unit covers the cave mouth," he said. "We cannot neutralize them and hold the western approach at the same time. We don't try. We fix the western unit at contact and use the rim rotation window for the Caves entry."

He looked at Telia.

She drew the descent route with her claw, northeast ridgeline, natural stair formation, descending to a shelf twenty paces above the cave entrance. "Stable enough. The shelf gives cover until you're twenty paces out. After that it's open ground to the mouth."

"Rim unit's rotation window," Nori said. "How long clear of the shelf?"

"Two and a half minutes," Telia said. "If the rotation interval is fixed. I read the paths in the root system. They have used that route the same way every time. The interval is fixed."

"We time it," Nori said.

"Caves team enters at the window," Bristlebaum confirmed. "Nori leads. Dash navigates the interior. Acornimus carries the communication kit and the writing kit. Forty-five minutes before I begin working from the assumption that the operation has changed."

"Three fixed sentries at the entrance," he said. "Separate deployment from the rim rotation, separate interval. They are present when the rim unit's rotation clears the shelf."

"Those are Dash," Nori said.

Dash was studying the map the way he studied any closed approach, reading what the drawn route did not show, the interior angles and the alternatives.

"Perimeter," Bristlebaum said. "Leonardo and I hold the western approach. We fix their unit there for the duration. Left and right of the approach. We don't engage unless they move toward the cave mouth."

Leonardo nodded, filing the assignment. "Left," he said.

"Nibbles and Gareth on the eastern ridge. Gareth keeps the maps current and relays between the perimeter units and the Caves team. Nibbles, you hold position between Gareth and the eastern descent."

Nibbles raised his paw. "Anything approaching the descent that isn't our team coming out—"

"Two short on the signal whistle," Bristlebaum said. "Gareth relays."

"Right," Nibbles said, and repeated it back in order.

"Telia, eastern anchor. You read the ground approach. Anything moving toward us through the root system before it breaks the surface, I want it with twenty seconds to spare."

"I'll have it," she said.

Lark adjusted her grip on the branch above.

Signal protocols. Three short for confirmed extraction, two for position change, one long for full abort. He went round the group for confirmation, and each gave it.

Acornimus wrote it for the record. Two garrison units confirmed; plan covers both.

"Eat," Bristlebaum said. "Sleep. First light, we move."

No fire. The Hollow's root network was still active and carrying, and what it carried, it carried back somewhere. Cold rations. They had done without fire in worse country.

The group found their positions without instruction, the way they had been finding them for three weeks. In the first week he had made two adjustments. Telia needed to be within sensing range of the eastern terrain, and Gareth needed to reach his maps in the dark without waking anyone. Both adjustments had been absorbed before he voiced them. By the second week he was no longer placing anyone.

Acornimus near his kit, back to stone. Dash along the ridgeline where the rock curved inward and gave him three angles of sight at once. Leonardo at the camp's north end where there was room to move without disturbing anyone. Nori at the perimeter's east edge. Her paw reached for the crossbow before she caught herself. The crossbow was going away in four hours. She had set it within reach for tonight.

Nibbles had the map stone. He had claimed it two weeks ago. Bristlebaum settled at the center.

"Nori," Acornimus said. His journal was open. The briefing was happening now rather than at morning. Morning would be equipment and movement.

Nori sat across from him. Dash moved from his ridgeline position to the edge of the group, close enough to hear everything but outside the circle itself.

"Six accounts in the Guild records," Nori said. "Thirty years, different agents, different assignments. The Caves generate voices. They sound like people the subject knows, someone trusted, someone feared, sometimes both in the same voice. The voice says the thing the subject most needs to hear, or most dreads." She kept her voice level. "Every subject who walked out says the same thing. They kept moving. They did not stop to answer what the voice said."

"Indistinguishable from the real person?" Acornimus asked.

"All four complete accounts say no. The voice knows the phrasing. The things only that person would say. It starts near something the subject has actually lived through, a conversation that happened or nearly happened. Then it moves." She paused. "It moves toward the thing the subject hasn't answered. By the time you notice the drift, you've stopped walking."

Acornimus wrote for a moment.

"What if the voice finds something true?" he asked. "Something the subject has worked through and knows was wrong, rather than unexamined."

"The accounts don't draw the line," Nori said. "The mechanism is the same either way. It uses whatever it finds to keep you stopped. The answer is the same. Keep moving."

She looked at Dash. "One of the four accounts says she spoke back to the voice. Several exchanges. Every answer she gave, the voice used to move closer. When she understood what she was doing, she stopped answering and moved. She was out before the voice stopped. It's using what you give it."

Dash had been watching her face through the briefing. "Has anyone been brought out from the inside?" he asked. "A second party going in after someone."

"The four complete accounts are all self-extractions," Nori said. "The subjects got themselves out, or went in voluntarily and came back. Nobody in the records was taken out by a second party."

Dash received this without changing his expression. "The Sage has had three days in there," he said.

"Yes."

"She knows what the voice does by now."

"She knows what it does," Nori said. "That doesn't make it easier. It means she has had three days of it."

Dash looked at the valley. "Move and don't answer it," he said. "I can do that."

"I know," Nori said.

Acornimus closed the journal with a quiet sound and placed the pen along the cover, aligned to the edge. "One more thing," he said. "The crystal installation. Telia confirmed it predates the Herald's occupation. If the Caves' working was not made for Grimthorn's purposes, there may be parts of it he cannot control or predict."

"Keep it," Nori said. "We are going in to bring Hazel out. The installation is a question for afterward."

Acornimus nodded and set it aside for later.

Across the camp, Gareth and Telia worked by the faintest amber Telia could hold, just enough to light the map between them and no further.

"Conduit below the eastern descent," Telia said. "Northeast bearing, thirty feet down. Pre-existing, same period as the crystals in the Caves, same working. Older than the Wardstone infrastructure."

Gareth marked it on his overlay layer, depth, bearing, period.

"What does it connect to?"

"I can't read it from the surface." She pressed her paw briefly to the ground. The amber traced through the contact and stopped. "The line goes northeast past the cave mouth, past what I can follow from here. Whatever's on the other end was built in the same period as the Caves themselves. Older than the Wardstone system."

Gareth wrote, *pre-existing conduit, installation-era, northeast bearing, connection point unknown.* He added a question mark and the note *recommend underground survey when operationally possible,* and put it with the file.

"You read something else," he said.

Telia looked at the ground between them. "The Willow is still carrying Hazel's net. The oval marks in the bark, where her paws have rested for thirty years, the most recent fresh contacts are three days old." She paused. "She hasn't touched it since she was taken."

"Thank you," Gareth said.

Telia closed the amber and lay down on the packed soil. Gareth put the file away.

At the camp's north end, Leonardo was working the lance through the slow practice form in the dark.

His armor was off, each piece set where he could find it without a lamp before first light. Without it he was thinner through the shoulders than he looked when geared. The marsh-damp had stained his fur dark across both shoulders. His bad ankle no longer interrupted the form; the compensation had gone automatic.

The lance moved through the positions at an unhurried tempo, practice for himself and not for anyone watching. In the dark his hands on the weapon were quiet and exact.

Nibbles was at the map stone with his belt knife and a whetstone. The rhythm was even and unhurried. Nori had shown him the angle on the second day of the march, the angle suited to the work the blade would do rather than the angle for sharpening alone. He had gotten it wrong twice before it started coming on its own.

Whiskerbrand rested against the stone beside him. The sword was warm the way banked coals were warm, steady, low, no edge to it. Its temperature had not changed since they reached the ridge. No void taint in the valley below.

He ran the whetstone along the blade one more time, set it down, and looked at the sword. Then he put the knife away and lay down, curling his tail around his leg before he closed his eyes.

Bristlebaum watched the whole of it. This was the work on the night before an operation, a circuit of the camp without leaving his place. Gareth asleep with the operational file under his paw. Telia slow in her breathing, her staff at her left side, the grey in her fur visible even in the dark. Acornimus lying still but not asleep, sorting what the evening had given him. Dash at the ridgeline, eyes open.

Nibbles was on his side at the map stone, tail curled, the belt knife sheathed and put away. Whiskerbrand rested against the stone beside him, the warmth unchanged.

Leonardo's slow form had stopped. He had set the lance carefully and lay down, the armor within reach, his bad ankle propped on his pack.

Nori was at the perimeter's east edge. Her crossbow was at her right side, close but not under her paw. She had set it where she wanted it for tonight.

He kept his anger where he had been keeping it, which was not the same as letting it go.

Lark dropped from her final circuit and settled in the birch directly above him. She tucked both wings close and arranged herself for the night.

Two extra passes after the briefing. He had counted them. She would be the first awake and the first in the air.

He lay on his back and looked up through the birch canopy. Above the ridgeline, just visible between branches, the uppermost canopy of the Ancient Willow rose above the surrounding trees, carrying what Hazel had built for thirty years.

He had known Hazel Willowbark for thirty years through letters. He knew the angle of her handwriting. He knew she wrote with more precision late at night than in the morning, and that she was careful with what she stated and more careful with what she implied.

She would hold in the Caves longer than most. The Caves found what had not yet been answered. With Hazel that left less to find than with most, but three days was three days, and first light was four hours away.

Chapter Eleven
Into the Caves

THE VALLEY MOUTH OPENED wide enough for six across. Nibbles watched Nori lead the descent into the Hollow. Acornimus followed her down the slope, journal tucked against his chest, his pressed vest still neat for the third day of the campaign. Dash came last. He paused at the lip of the slope, ears rotating once, and then the grade took all three and they dropped below the sight line.

Bristlebaum didn't watch them go. "Shoulder."

"I know," Nibbles said.

"Right flank."

He moved right without being asked twice. His left shoulder had been pulling since the valley crossing, still working on level ground, but overhead reach on that side was slower than it should be. Anyone watching him fight would see it. He went to the right anchor position. Telia settled at the far end of the line, her staff planted, paws already pressing toward the earth. The amber light moved faintly between her palms and into the soil.

Gareth took a position behind a low ridge of stone. Bristlebaum had placed him there, ten yards back from the line, out of the combat envelope where a pattern analyst belonged.

Leonardo stood at shield center. His lance was already leveled. The plume flopped. He shoved it back without looking. Lark was above, already banking east along the ridgeline.

Nibbles drew Whiskerbrand a half-inch and let it settle back. The blade was warm and steady, no blaze in it, just a low even hum that meant the air here was wrong somewhere he could not yet point to. He slid it back into the sheath.

"Hold until I call the contraction," he said.

"And if you can't call it?" Gareth asked. The tapping had already started on his thigh.

"Hold anyway," Nibbles said.

Seventy-three steps to the entrance. Dash counted them by habit. He counted anything he might have to walk back out of in a hurry.

The Caves opened at the base of the slope. Not a dramatic mouth, just a cut in the hillside, the stone worn smooth at the edges by decades of passage. The wear was too even for weather. Someone had walked through here often enough to leave a track in the rock.

Nori moved through the entrance first. Her crossbow was already off her back.

Dash went second. Acornimus brought up the rear, and Dash heard him pause just inside, a breath, then the scratch of a pen.

"You're drawing the entrance," Dash said.

"Recording it," Acornimus said.

Seventy-four.

The first passage ran level for thirty steps before curving left. The walls were carved stone, smooth on the outer face, rough where the tool had worked harder on the inner. Crystals were set into the ceiling at intervals, evenly spaced, placed with care. Whatever charge they had held was mostly spent now, the light at their centers gone grey.

Dash tracked the passage for exits and found two before the curve.

The whispers started at step thirty-eight.

The sounds were not words yet, just the hiss and murmur of voices too far off to resolve, arriving from every direction at once, the way sound moved through a large stone chamber. He tried to track the source by habit and couldn't find it. The stonework was moving it around.

Acornimus stopped. "The acoustic properties are deliberate," he said. He tilted his head. "Old work. The stone was shaped for it. Someone repurposed this place."

"Keep moving," Nori said.

Eighty-one. Eighty-two.

Nori was already walking again. Her paws were even on the crossbow.

Eighty-three.

The garrison came out of the tree line in a loose group, twenty maybe more, and Nibbles had several seconds to read them before they reached the forward markers. Purple eyes. The coordinated drift that field-animals didn't have, the kind that came of being moved by someone else's hand. Bark-growth thick on their shoulders and haunches, the secondary plating that built up from months inside an inverted Wardstone zone.

"Contact, left flank," Lark called from above. "Twenty-three. Moving to your markers."

Nibbles called the left side to close and took one step right to open his angle on the approach. His left shoulder pulled at the motion. He stopped the step at half-range and adjusted. The center was the priority; his left was secondary, and he had to choose.

"Gareth," he said.

"I see them," Gareth said.

He was behind the ridge, one paw on his map case, the tapping going fast on his thigh, somewhere working between the slow worry-rhythm and panic without being either. He was reading the approach angle, when the approach needed a body in front of it more than it needed reading.

Telia pressed both paws flat to the ground. The amber light rose through her palms and moved outward through the earth. Nibbles felt it underfoot, a slight tightening of the soil where it had been loose. The garrison hit the forward markers and the front group stopped. Redirected. The bark-plated animals began searching the line for the gap.

"Hold center," Nibbles said.

He stepped left, away from Gareth's position, to cover the angle Gareth wasn't watching. His shoulder pulled. He moved anyway.

Telia held. The light in her palms went from gold to yellow at the edges. The garrison hit the line three times in thirty seconds, and her breathing got harder with each press.

Bristlebaum drove the lead two back with his mace, three strikes, no wasted motion. Leonardo caught one on the circle with his lance. It went down.

"Nineteen left," Lark said. "Reading the formation. Coming back to your right."

Gareth's rhythm slowed. "They're testing for the thin point."

"Where," Nibbles said.

A pause. "Your right."

He was already stepping to cover it. The shoulder pulled hard at the extension, and the step landed under him anyway.

The garrison circled twice more and pressed once and found the line solid. On the third circuit they pulled back to the tree line and stopped. Not broken. Holding for whatever came next.

Telia lifted her paws from the ground. The amber light went out. She sat back on her heels a moment, her staff pressed into the earth at her side.

"How much did that cost?" Nibbles asked.

"Less than it will next time," she said.

They were sixty steps deeper when the first voice arrived.

The voice wasn't pitched at Dash. The Caves weren't interested in him yet. He heard it as a murmur pitched toward Acornimus, directed, quiet enough that Dash had to orient toward the squirrel rather than the stone to catch it properly. He watched Acornimus slow. One step. Two steps. Still moving, but no longer at the pace he had been moving at.

One hundred and two. One hundred and three.

"Acornimus," Nori said.

"A moment."

He had his journal out and the pen uncapped. He was not writing. His head was tilted the way it tilted when he was listening to something for the second time, comparing it against what he already knew rather than deciding whether to record it.

Dash caught fragments, not the words, just the rhythm of a formal voice, two sentences, the tone of a superior acknowledging good work. The stone was moving the sound around. It arrived from the left wall, the passage ahead, and faintly from underfoot, all at the same moment.

Acornimus wrote three quick words in the journal. He studied them. He crossed them out.

"It's wrong," he said.

"What is," Nori said.

"My supervisor uses 'noted' for acknowledgment and 'received' for information that has been recorded. This voice used 'received' for acknowledgment." His pen tapped once against the journal's cover. "That distinction is one my supervisor keeps precisely. The voice did not." He closed the journal. "Whatever this is, it isn't him. Moving."

"Can you keep going," Nori said.

"Moving," Acornimus said. He was already walking.

One hundred and ten. One hundred and eleven.

Nori set the pace again and Acornimus fell in behind her, journal tucked against his chest. He was still listening; Dash could see it in the forward set of his whiskers. But his paws stayed where they were. He was not reaching for the pen.

The voice came back at step one hundred and fourteen.

Different approach this time, from the right wall, the words pitched lower, slower, the kind of voice a person used when picking each word. The rhythm had changed. The same voice, adjusted.

Dash watched Acornimus slow again. Three steps. His paw moved toward his journal pocket and stopped. He looked at the right wall and then looked away from it.

One hundred and seventeen. One hundred and eighteen.

Acornimus did not reach for the journal. He kept moving, closed the gap to Nori, walked on with his whiskers forward and still.

Dash kept counting. He had been counting since he was sixteen, in new towns, on jobs he might need to walk back out of. The number kept him from running ahead of himself.

One hundred and nineteen.

Ahead of him, Acornimus closed the journal and opened it again. The voice was still speaking from somewhere in the stone. He left the page blank.

The garrison pulled back from the tree line and Nibbles had four seconds to wonder why before the second unit appeared from the eastern approach.

This one was different. The first garrison had moved in the loose drift of corrupted animals, testing the line for gaps. This unit came in formation, twelve soldiers in two ranks, moving in step, their armor intact. Deliberate where the bark-plated unit had been searching.

Nibbles was still counting the threat when Whiskerbrand changed.

The alert hum dropped into something lower, a vibration that moved through the leather of the grip and into the bones of his paw. He had felt it once before, on a mountain a long time ago.

"Contraction," he called. "Pull left, close the center."

The line began to move. Bristlebaum took the far right and drove inward. Gareth came off the ridge and stopped in the open field. The ridge had been his cover and there was no equivalent here. Nibbles pointed. Gareth moved to the new position, his map case still in hand.

Telia was already up. She'd lifted her paws from the earth when the second unit appeared. She'd seen them before Lark called them. She was standing, pressing her staff into the ground to hold herself upright, breathing harder than she had five minutes ago. She caught Nibbles looking.

"Still here," she said.

The twelve held their formation at fifty yards. Waiting.

At their center stood the void-knight.

Nibbles could not have said exactly what made it different from the corrupted soldiers around it. It was tall. It was patient in a way the rest of them were not. The corruption had been worked into the armor in deliberate lines, laid through the joints and the seams like inlay rather than spread across the surface. There was something at the eye-slit of the faceplate where the eyes should have been.

It looked across the formation.

It took in each of them in turn. Bristlebaum. Gareth. Telia. Nibbles. Brief looks. Counting, not threatening.

Then it looked at Leonardo and stayed.

"That one is fixed on Pondsworth," Lark called from above. "Not tracking the rest of the line."

"Leonardo," Nibbles said.

"I see it," Leonardo said. His voice was flat. He adjusted his lance grip. Adjusted it again. Then held. "This is not chance."

"The void-agent's report from Ridgemarrow," Nibbles said. "The Herald received it. This thing knows our composition. It knows your arm is hurt."

A pause. "Then it knows about your shoulder as well," Leonardo said.

Nibbles was already moving right. His left shoulder pulled hard at the first step. He gave it three steps and stopped at the range where the reach would still work, mostly, and where he'd have ground to fall back to if it didn't. He could cover the right side. Not at full strength, but he could cover it.

The void-knight crossed the fifty-yard mark.

It didn't rush. The twelve held the formation behind it, present and filling the count rather than pressing the line. If anyone broke to support Leonardo, the twelve had their opening. If everyone held, Leonardo had a problem that was only his.

There wasn't a third option.

"Hold the flanks," he said. "Do not break for Leonardo. If the formation opens for him, the twelve are inside it."

Bristlebaum's quills settled. Leonardo set his shield. Neither argued.

The void-knight kept walking, unhurried, toward Leonardo.

The blade's vibration changed again.

One hundred and fifty-two. One hundred and fifty-three.

The voices shifted at one hundred and fifty-eight.

The voices were no louder. What changed was the target. The register that had been directed at Acornimus turned toward Dash. He caught the shift in his ears the way he caught a lock clicking over the wrong way.

He kept walking. One hundred and fifty-nine.

The first voice was Sable's. The rhythm of it before the words arrived, the dry edge Sable put on everything that wasn't a joke but came out sounding like one. Two winters in the same hayloft. Before the lightning-bolt patch became a mark. Before strangers in new towns started recognizing him on the strength of it.

Three years.

One hundred and sixty-one. One hundred and sixty-two.

"Keep walking," Nori said from ahead.

He was walking. The feet were still going. The count was still in his head.

The second voice was Ferris's, and the Caves had moved closer with this one. The small exhale Ferris made before he laughed, when something genuinely caught him. Dash had been in enough small rooms with Ferris to know that breath.

One hundred and sixty-eight.

He let the voices arrive. He let them pass. He did not slow down. The Caves were looking for the thing he had not yet examined, and what they were finding in him was something he had already walked through. Three years was long enough to know where the loss lived. He had named it and set it down a long time back.

What he had not named yet was what came after the running, what it would look like to stop. He didn't have an answer for that one. The Caves seemed to know it.

But he was walking, and they could not find the answer if he wasn't standing still to give it to them.

One hundred and seventy-four. One hundred and seventy-five.

Acornimus was six steps ahead of him, his vest still pressed to military precision, his journal tucked against his chest. He was not reaching for the pen. He was walking the way Acornimus walked when he was refusing to write, paw deliberately turned away from the pocket, whiskers locked forward. It was a different shape of holding than Dash's, and harder to keep up.

He counted twelve more steps. The voices stopped.

The gap between them opened to six steps. Then seven. Then it held there. Nori had stopped. Not a slowing, not a hesitation. She was standing in the middle of the passage with her crossbow pointed at the ground, her paws correct on the grip, looking at the left wall. There was nothing on the left wall.

Dash stopped. He counted three more steps by habit (the count already moving before he'd made the decision) and then he was six steps back from her and the gap wasn't changing.

Acornimus had stopped ahead of them. He looked back at Nori, then at Dash, his paws still away from his pocket.

Dash went back. The whispers were still working around them in the stone. He'd been through his own version of it. Now the Caves had found Nori. He couldn't see what she was looking at; her eyes weren't tracking anything on the wall. Whatever they were showing her didn't live in the stone.

He stopped a step behind her. Her grip on the crossbow was correct. Six years of reflex holding the weapon steady while she stood still.

"Nori."

"Keep going," she said. Not an order. A request. She knew what was happening.

"I'm going to stand here."

"I'll catch up." Her voice was level the way it went level when she was working hard at level.

"I know you think that," Dash said.

She turned and looked at him. Her eyes focused on his face. "I'm fine."

"You stopped. You haven't stopped since Ironhold." He held her gaze. "I've been watching."

Something moved in her expression. She was deciding how to play it.

"The Caves found something," she said. "I'm handling it."

"You're standing still. In the Caves. That's not handling it."

"I don't need you to come back for me." Not sharp. Just flat.

"I know," Dash said. He didn't move. "But you need to be walking. The Caves will keep working on you as long as you're standing still. That's the mechanism. You've read the same word I have." He watched her. "Whatever it found in you, I'm not asking. I don't need to know. What I need is your paws moving."

The whispers worked around them in the stone. Patient. Coming from every direction the architecture could send them.

"It's an ordinary thing," Nori said.

"Most of them are," Dash said.

She let out a breath. She brought the crossbow back to working carry, re-settled the strap across her shoulder, and looked down the passage at Acornimus.

"Count if you want," she said. "I can hear you from here."

He counted one, out loud, and she started walking.

Two. Three.

He fell in behind her. Acornimus waited until they reached him and then turned and moved without comment. The whispers worked around them. Nori's pace was careful, each step placed. But her paws were moving. He started counting again.

The void-knight covered the fifty yards at a walk.

The twelve held their formation behind it, present and filling the count rather than pressing the contracted line. If anyone broke to support Leonardo, the twelve had an opening. If everyone held, Leonardo had a problem only slightly better than that. Nibbles had looked for a third option and not found one.

Leonardo was reading the approach, his lance adjusted to right-hand primary (the working arm) with the left taking the angle the damage permitted. He adjusted once and held. The void-knight came at his left side, the side it had already worked out was the weak one.

The first strike was a sweep at the lance, testing the grip. Leonardo held it (barely, the impact jolting up through his left arm hard enough that Nibbles saw the wince) and turned the sweep into a press, pushing the blade off-line. The void-knight stepped back and reset, the information filed.

The second strike came lower, at his legs. A horizontal sweep targeting his left leg at shin height, coming in flat and hard. Leonardo couldn't redirect the lance fast enough to cover it. His left arm was too slow.

The impact caught his left leg below the knee. The crack was clean and immediate. His leg buckled and he went to one knee, the lance swinging wide as his center of gravity dropped, and the follow-through swept the air above him, finding the space where an upright opponent should have been.

Leonardo was a full body-length lower than he should have been, on his knee, the lance already swinging back to center from the drop's momentum. His right arm brought it home.

The lance went in below the left pauldron, where the armor's movement required a gap at the shoulder joint, and drove through until it found resistance. The void-knight staggered back, the precision of its movement breaking for the first time in the exchange.

Nibbles held the formation.

Leonardo stayed on one knee. His left leg was wrong at the break. He kept the lance centered on the void-knight, tracking the pause as it weighed whether to come on again.

It came forward for one more exchange.

Straight approach this time, targeting the lance hand. Leonardo got the shaft up and caught the first strike. The second came from the opposite direction, the void-knight's off-hand sweeping across his hurt arm, a flat hard blow at the joint above the elbow that had already been bad. Something in there went further wrong.

The lance stayed in his hand.

The void-knight stepped back. It held for two seconds, its faceplate turned toward Leonardo, and then it turned and walked back toward the twelve.

The twelve folded around it and pulled north toward the tree line.

Leonardo stayed on one knee, lance planted, his left leg at the angle legs did not go at. He checked his grip. Right hand, fingers closed, shaft held. He looked at his left arm. The elbow joint had gone past hurt. He set the arm aside, the way you set aside a tool that has stopped working, and looked up at the sky.

"Clear," Lark called from above. "Full retreat. I'll track the void-knight west."

Hazel was in the deepest passage. She was sitting with her back against the stone, her paws in her lap, her ears held flat. Not distress. She had stopped registering anything else. The blood-bound scrolls were tucked against her side, bound in their cord. The cord was intact.

Her fur at the temples and around her ears had gone white. More than when they'd left her, more than the last time Acornimus had seen her. Three days of feeding earth-magic through the stone had cost her in fur and weight both. She was upright and breathing. Her paws, when Nori crouched beside her, were cold.

"I told you I was alive," Hazel said. Her voice had its precision still, only a little slower.

"You stopped answering after the second day," Nori said.

"I was busy."

Acornimus was already on his knees beside the scrolls, his pen moving in his journal as he wrote down their condition without touching them. "The outer cord shows no void-breach. The binding is intact."

"I held it," Hazel said. "That was the purpose of staying. The attuning signature will hold for another day, possibly two. We should not wait past that."

She paused. Nori was watching her.

"The Caves asked me questions," Hazel said. "I didn't answer them. The not-answering cost more than answering would have. I miscounted." The paws in her lap adjusted, a small precise movement. "I have been miscounting it that way for thirty years. Old habits."

Acornimus looked up from his journal, then went back to writing.

"Can you stand?" Nori asked.

"I would like to find out."

Nori put her arm around Hazel's shoulders and helped her up. The old rabbit was lighter than she had been, three days of giving had taken weight as well as color. She found her footing. She stood straight, smaller than she had been three days ago but still herself in the way she carried it.

She held on to Nori until her balance settled. Then she stepped away and tucked the blood-bound scrolls under her arm.

"Moving," she said.

Dash was already leading the way back toward the entrance.

The garrison held at the tree line for another twenty minutes after the void-knight withdrew.

Nibbles watched them from the perimeter and held the line. The twelve had folded back into the larger formation when the void-knight broke off, and they all stayed at the tree line in a loose grouping. They tested the line twice more, both probes weak, and the formation turned them back easily. Whatever hand had been moving them was no longer pushing.

Lark called circuit by circuit from above, holding east, holding north, no movement toward the valley.

Gareth was behind the ridge with his maps, the tapping rhythm on his thigh running slow and deliberate. Not the worry-rhythm. The reckoning one. The third unit had not been in his report, and he was working back through what else might be wrong because of it.

Telia sat at the base of a stone with her paws in the earth and her eyes open. The amber light was gone. Her fur looked greyer than it had this morning. She was breathing slow.

Leonardo had not moved from his knee. His lance was still planted.

The garrison drifted north, loose and aimless now that nothing was directing them. Then they were gone.

"Clear," Lark called. "Full retreat. The void-knight went west, not with the rest. I'll track it." She banked away.

Nibbles held the perimeter for another ten minutes. Then he called it down. He was at the Caves entrance when Dash came out.

The ferret emerged from the cut in the hillside at the same walking pace he'd gone in at. The mud on his lightning-bolt patch had dried and turned pale at the edges. Nori was with him, upright, the crossbow back in her grip.

She found a flat stone near the entrance and sat down against it. She placed the crossbow across her lap, both paws on the grip, the barrel pointing away from the group. Dash sat down beside her. Acornimus came out behind them with Hazel at his side.

Nibbles went to Leonardo first. The frog was still on one knee thirty yards out, lance planted in the earth, his left leg at the wrong angle. He had not moved since the void-knight pulled back.

"Don't try the leg yet," Nibbles said.

"I wasn't planning to," Leonardo said. The flatness in his voice was the flatness of someone managing pain and inventory at the same time. "The left leg is broken below the knee. The arm above the elbow has gone further wrong. I am still totalling it." He looked at the lance in his right hand. "The void-knight withdrew."

"Lark confirmed it."

"Then I held."

Nibbles got his shoulder under Leonardo's right arm (the working one) and helped him find a sitting position that didn't require the leg. The plume on his helmet flopped forward. He ignored it.

Gareth had come off the ridge and was standing at the perimeter's edge, map case open. The tapping rhythm on his thigh had gone quiet. He was looking at the map without really reading it. The third unit had not been in his report, and he was working out what that meant about him.

Telia sat with her staff across her knees and her paws flat in the soil. She was not channeling, only there. The grey at her temples had spread to her jaw. She was breathing slowly and not speaking.

Bristlebaum came off the perimeter at a walk. He went past Gareth, past Telia, past the entrance, and saw Nori sitting. His quills rose a fraction and settled, but not all the way. He looked at her for two seconds. She looked back and held his gaze.

He went past her toward Leonardo, his mace at his belt, his step measured. Nibbles watched him cross the distance. The quills were still up when he passed.

Chapter Twelve

The Tent

THE TENT HELD ALL of them, and Nibbles took the room in the way he'd learned to take rooms, the same way he checked for exits, automatic.

Hazel was against the far wall. She had settled there in the careful, small movements of someone still holding herself together by inches. Her pack was behind her. Her paws were folded in her lap. The fur around her muzzle had gone a shade greyer than it had been that morning, not enough that anyone would have caught it as it happened, but enough that you noticed when you looked back. She was smaller. Not in height but in fill, the way someone got when they had given out everything they had to give. Three days, and she had come out with the scrolls intact.

Nori sat beside her. The crossbow was still in her lap exactly as it had been when she walked in, stock near her wrist, one paw close. She was looking at nothing in particular.

From above, Nibbles heard the quiet sound of Lark settling on a roof beam, talons finding a grip and committing. From up there she had the whole tent in view.

The others filled in. Gareth to the corner with the most light, a map already spread across his knee. Telia with her back against the center support post, her cracked staff laid across her legs. Acornimus near the entrance, always with an exit at hand. Dash somewhere to Nibbles' right, his eyes tracking nothing in the visible room. Leonardo standing with his lance planted and his plume listing sideways. Bristlebaum at the tent's center, still in his equipment.

Nobody asked for food or a lamp.

Nibbles found a gap between Gareth's pack and the canvas and folded himself into it. The bite on his left shoulder ached, a low ache, present but bearable, the kind of pain that didn't get better with attention. He drew his knees up, put his back to the canvas, and felt Whiskerbrand settle across him in its sheath. The warmth was steady against his back.

He was carrying things he hadn't sorted yet. Acornimus's three words from the ridge (*the will behind the infection*) that had not fit anywhere since. Hazel's three days, and whatever it was she had kept the Caves from getting. The third unit Lark had called, the one Gareth had missed. The half-sentence Bristlebaum had cut off at the entrance to the Hollow about the seals. None of it resolved.

The argument from Ridgemarrow was in the tent. Nobody had named it. Leonardo wasn't looking at Bristlebaum, and Bristlebaum wasn't looking at Leonardo, and the two of them had decided, by not looking, that it could wait. Something heavier than that was in the room, and it was still coming.

Bristlebaum opened the count.

"The third unit." He didn't raise his voice. He didn't need to. "Three of our agents. Last confirmed position, the Whispering Hollow, two weeks before our arrival. They withdrew northwest. No signal given. No word filed. When we walked into the Hollow expecting clear ground, we had no warning of where they had gone because nobody in this camp was told they had moved."

He was looking at Acornimus. Acornimus had his journal on his knee. He had not opened it. His whiskers were level. His paw lay flat on the journal's cover.

"The unit's orders were issued through Main Hall," Acornimus said. "Their withdrawal went through the Quartermaster's office. The Quartermaster's records do not cross my desk. When an agent is reassigned through Main Hall, they leave my register. I have no way to track a withdrawal I have no record of receiving."

"I know where the orders began," Bristlebaum said.

"Then you understand the gap was already there," Acornimus said. "It sits between Main Hall and the field. It predates this mission."

"I understand where it sits." Bristlebaum's quills were at full extension. "That doesn't settle the matter. Ridgemarrow's void-agent reported our makeup north. The Hollow's third unit confirmed our destination. Grimthorn had our full situation before we arrived. The word that reached him passed through a gap in field intelligence. Your field intelligence."

"With respect," Acornimus said, formally, the way he always said it, "my work covers the agents I am told about. An agent reassigned out of my register is hidden from me from the moment the reassignment is filed. Naming this a failure of field intelligence would—"

"You've made that argument twice," Bristlebaum said.

Acornimus stopped. Bristlebaum was looking at him steadily. He had heard the argument, and he was telling Acornimus the argument was not the answer he wanted.

Nibbles watched Acornimus hold the journal closed. He could open it. The documentation was there. The case was clean. He'd already tried it twice.

Bristlebaum was angry at something he couldn't reach (the failure three levels above this tent) and he was turning it on someone who was within reach. He knew he was doing it. Nibbles could see that on his face.

Acornimus's paw shifted on the journal's cover, then settled again.

"I'll set down the chain of orders in the after-action," he said. "The records will show the gaps clearly."

Bristlebaum nodded once. The quills stayed up.

The tent went quiet. Nibbles looked at Acornimus (the journal closed on his knee, his face still) and saw the calculation finishing. Press the case and lose four days of working command. Or take the unjust line and put the truth in the after-action where it belonged. Acornimus had picked the second one before Bristlebaum had finished speaking, and the journal stayed closed.

The silence that followed had something waiting in it. Nibbles knew this was the wrong moment. He'd known it before at the Cheese Festival, watching a cart go over, the calculation finished before the choice had, his paws already moving. The cart was going over. He opened his mouth.

"The chain of orders," he said. "If the unit's withdrawal went through the Quartermaster's office, that's above what Acornimus is told. He can't read a record he never received. The gap is between Main Hall and the field. That's not in his work."

Bristlebaum looked at him. The tent was very still. Nibbles' whiskers had gone taut. His tail had wrapped once against his left leg without him deciding it should.

"I'm not saying the gap doesn't matter," he said, because the silence was getting worse, not better. "But if the order for the withdrawal went through Main Hall and never reached the field, that's a different failure than—"

"Tumblepatch," Bristlebaum said.

Nibbles stopped.

"I am aware," Bristlebaum said, "of where in the chain this failure began."

The pause after it was the kind of pause Bristlebaum used when he was telling someone the subject was closed.

He had been right, and the right answer had not landed any softer than a wrong one would have. The accounting had already been made; he had just interrupted it with the correct version, and the interruption had cost as much as the wrongness would have.

Across the tent, Acornimus had gone completely still. His paw was flat on the journal's cover. He had made his choice about absorbing this one and held to it. Now he was watching what happened to the person who hadn't. Nibbles had known it was the wrong moment and said it anyway.

A moment passed. Bristlebaum's quills came down half a notch. When he spoke his voice was controlled.

"Three weeks ago, you couldn't hold the blade through a half-guard pivot without Nori correcting your left footwork," he said. "You've come a long way in those three weeks. You've learned to compensate. You've learned to read situations and respond to them quickly." He paused. "But carrying information quickly and knowing when to use it are different skills. The second takes longer to develop. Two Guild trials were meant to give you that time. The sword didn't wait for you to be ready, and this situation hasn't either. That's not an accusation. But right now you are three weeks into a mission where the people around you have been working in the field for years. You spoke in their register before you'd earned it."

The tent went quiet.

Nibbles could follow every piece of it back to something real. The two trials. The blade choosing him before he was ready. The three weeks against everyone else's years. Bristlebaum had said most of it to him already, at Ironhold, when he'd laid out the probationary terms.

The sentence wasn't cruel. It wasn't even wrong. It just answered a different question than the one Nibbles had asked. *Is the chain of orders read right* was not *are you experienced enough to be speaking here*, and Bristlebaum had answered the second one as if it settled the first. Nibbles had watched him make the swap.

He didn't argue it. He had used his one go already. A second pass would be the third wrong move in the same direction tonight. He looked at Bristlebaum instead.

Bristlebaum had looked away before the last word finished, at the ground in front of him, at the space between where he stood and the side of the tent. Not at anything in particular.

His paw had moved to the head of the mace at his belt. Resting there, the way a hand goes to a familiar object after a sentence one cannot take back. The fingers were still and not gripping.

Nibbles watched him not take it back. Bristlebaum's weight resettled on both feet. The jaw pulled fractionally tighter. The eyes stayed on the middle distance. The control was real and the authority was real, and so was the rest of it, if you were watching.

The tent stayed quiet. Then Nori spoke from the far side. She had not moved. The crossbow was still in her lap. Her eyes stayed forward, on the space between the canvas walls, not on anyone in particular.

"Four days to the valley," she said. "Five, if the western approach is slower than Gareth's last guess."

Her voice came at the same level as everything else she said. The steadiness of it pulled the tent quiet.

"Whatever is wrong between people in this tent is going to stay wrong for however long we have left. I'm not asking anyone to resolve it." Her eyes moved briefly (past Nibbles, past Bristlebaum, past Leonardo) then forward again. "But it can't slow anyone's thinking when we reach the valley, and it can't land on anyone else."

The crossbow had not moved. Nibbles looked at it. Still in her lap, six years of reflex resting across her thighs. He didn't know what the Caves had shown her. Whatever it was, she was asking the rest of them to do what she was already doing.

Nobody contested her. Bristlebaum had not moved. His spectacles had slipped a fraction down his nose and he had not pushed them back. He was not looking at Nori. He was not looking at anyone.

Across the tent, Gareth had gone back to his map. Or had looked like he had. His eyes were on the parchment, but the tapping on his thigh had stopped. The tapping stopped when he had the answer.

He looked up. Not at the room. At Nibbles.

The eye contact was brief, direct, amber-eyed. He held the look for three seconds. Maybe four.

"Right again," Gareth said.

Two words. Flat, the same register he used to confirm a patrol count. He glanced back down and his paw moved to a route marker.

He had not been talking about Nori. Nibbles turned it over. *Right again.* Gareth was the one in this tent who counted things, patterns, mappings, the Wardstone inversion timeline before anyone else had it. If he said *again*, he had been counting more than one instance. The authorization chain was correct, and so was something else, and Gareth had been keeping track of how often being right and being heard came apart.

Nibbles didn't know what to do with any of it tonight. Gareth's paw moved along the route marking. The tapping stayed quiet.

The fire outside the tent cracked once. Wind shifted in the canvas. Somewhere at the camp's edge the guard rotation changed, two voices low, then quiet, then the new pair settling at their post. Inside the tent, no one moved for a long moment.

The bite on Nibbles' shoulder had gone steady again. Hazel had her eyes closed. Telia's paws were flat on the cracked staff and her breathing had slowed. Acornimus had not opened his journal. Dash's ears had eased a fraction off forward.

Bristlebaum's quills came down by a single notch. Not settled. Not full. The room felt the change without anyone marking it.

Hazel spoke into the quiet after Gareth's eyes went back to his map.

"There is something I've been keeping," she said, and the tent's attention moved to her without her asking for it.

Whiskerbrand went warm. It wasn't the alert hum. A different warmth, low and steady, coming through the leather of the sheath before he had taken in her first sentence. His paw had been resting near it, not gripping. He hadn't moved.

"When Grimthorn took me," Hazel said, "he wanted one thing. The sixth Wardstone's attuning signature, not the blood-bound scrolls. He couldn't use those without me, and taking them would have cost him more than leaving them. He wanted the signature."

"Each Wardstone has a resonance. A frequency in the earth, the way each stone sits in its conduit, the way it draws the anchor current toward itself. Every stone is its own. If you know a Wardstone's attuning signature, you can feel it through the ground from a distance. You can tell when the stone's resonance begins to change."

She looked at her folded paws. "When the inversion ritual reaches a certain point, the stone's resonance inverts with it. It stops drawing toward the anchor current and begins pushing against it. The change is readable, to someone who knows the signature."

Her ears stayed forward. "He wanted to confirm his own work without having to be present at the stone itself. If he had the sixth stone's signature, he could feel the inversion complete through any point of ground contact along the conduit line, from Thornwall, from the valley, from anywhere. That is what I kept from him for three days."

She paused.

"I am going to give it now," she said. "To Nibbles. Because the sword will be able to read it when the inversion begins."

Nibbles looked at her. "How does the sword—"

"Whiskerbrand was present at Shadowpeak," she said. "When Aldric drove the blade through Malachar at the summit, the sword's light channeled through all seven anchor points at once. The blade carries the resonance of that moment. It knows what the stones sound like when they are whole." Her paws shifted. "When the sixth stone's inversion begins, the blade will feel it because it knows the frequency it's changing from. It will know before you do. I am trusting that."

She reached up to the collar of her robe slowly, still holding herself together by inches, and drew out a small folded cloth. She unfolded it across her palm. There was nothing visible in it.

She turned her palm toward him and said a word.

He couldn't reproduce it afterward. He tried later and could not find the shape of it in his mouth. It was older than any tongue he had heard in traveling, older than the Wardstone conduits themselves, by the feel of it.

The blade vibrated.

This was deeper than the alert hum. He had felt this frequency twice before, once in the bedrock under Nettleflint's cellar when the purification light touched a conduit line, once in the tunnels below Ridgemarrow when the carved channels lit under Telia's paws. This was longer than either of those. Something being placed in him, not passing through. It moved up through the leather sheath into his spine, and it stayed there.

When it stopped, he could not have said how long it had been. The blade was still warm.

Hazel folded the cloth and set it on the ground beside her. She looked at it a moment.

"He did not get it," she said. "Three days, and he did not get it." She smoothed the cloth flat with two careful fingers. "I'm glad Brisk came."

Nobody spoke. Nibbles' paw was still at his side. He had not needed to grip the hilt.

Bristlebaum looked at Gareth. The look was the one he gave when he wanted the count, fast and complete.

Gareth set down the map. The tapping on his thigh had resumed during Hazel's explanation and stopped again when she finished.

"The third unit left the Hollow three weeks before we arrived," Gareth said. "That gap is between when Grimthorn received confirmation of our composition from Ridgemarrow and when he received confirmation of our destination from the Hollow. Two pieces of information, fully assembled. He had a complete picture before we reached the Caves." His paw moved to the map's route marking. "He has known for three weeks."

"The sixth stone," Bristlebaum said.

"He started the ritual sequence on the sixth stone before Ridgemarrow. We don't know the exact date, but the corruption pattern in the villages north of here suggests six to eight weeks at the least. The attuning signature will tell us when the inversion reaches its final stage." Gareth looked at the route. "Valley crossing is two days. Approach to Thornwall, one day. Approach terrain on the final day adds time." He paused. "Four days at the least to the ritual chamber."

Telia shifted against the center post. Her cracked staff was still across her legs, both paws resting on it. "If he finishes the sixth stone before we reach the chamber—"

"He moves to the seventh," Gareth said. "The sixth completing gives him the final momentum. The seventh Wardstone is the last anchor. That's the prison's keystone. If the seventh inverts, the prison fails." He looked at the route once more. "Our advantage is the attuning signature. We will know when the inversion enters its final stage."

"How long does the final stage take," Bristlebaum said. He looked at Hazel.

She had her eyes open. The same careful focus she'd held since she settled against the far wall.

"When the attuning signature begins to invert, the ritual is in its final stage," she said. "The stone will complete in twelve hours. Possibly sixteen, since the sixth stone has had more resistance than the others. Telia's work on the conduit kept it longer than the previous stones were kept before their inversions." She looked at Telia. "How much have you given it in the last month?"

"Enough," Telia said.

Hazel nodded. "Sixteen hours, then. On the outer edge, twenty. When the blade tells you the inversion has begun, you have twenty hours to reach the ritual chamber below Thornwall."

Bristlebaum's quills stayed at full extension. Nibbles watched him do the arithmetic. The quills had not settled; they were at the same extension they'd been at since before Nori spoke, full and held. Bristlebaum was setting the numbers against the map, against the four days of hard country, against the wounded people in this tent and what each of them could give and what each of them had already given.

Whatever he had built over thirty years was supposed to have caught this before it got here, and it hadn't. Now they were four days out, with twenty hours from the warning, and that was the operation.

Outside the tent, fire, wind against canvas, the sound of a guard rotation changing at the camp's edge. Inside, no one moved. Lark above on her beam, wings folded. Hazel with the folded cloth on the ground beside her. Nori with the crossbow in her lap, looking forward. Bristlebaum's quills stayed up, and the numbers stayed where Gareth had set them, four days to the chamber and twenty hours from the warning.

Chapter Thirteen

Before He Was the Herald

Bristlebaum had built the fire before anyone chose a place to sit, windward stone on the south side to block the draft off the ridge, wood stacked for a long burn rather than a hot one.

Nibbles sat cross-legged on his blanket and kept his paw from going to his side where the bite had healed most of the way closed. The marching had pulled at it through the afternoon.

The company settled in a wide, loose ring. Nori at the edge nearest the tree line, knees up, crossbow in her lap, her gaze still carrying the Caves. Gareth with his maps folded in his lap, one paw resting on the top. Acornimus's journal open, pen uncapped, but he wasn't writing. Dash against a root at the fire's edge, ears half-forward. Telia with the cracked staff across her knees, paws flat against the wood. Leonardo upright with his lance beside him, plume flopped. Lark somewhere in the branches above.

Bristlebaum sat on the far side of the fire. He had not looked at Nibbles since they sat down. They hadn't spoken since the night before, when the Guildmaster had said the wrong thing.

Hazel Willowbark settled her paws in her lap and looked at the ring of them.

"Before we cross the valley," she said, "you need to know who you are facing. Not the Herald. The creature who became the Herald. Those are different things, and walking into that chamber without understanding the difference is a mistake." She paused. "I'm going to start at the beginning. The beginning is a family."

She told it the way she wrote, in order, with the precision that made each part exact rather than rough.

"I was with him at Shadowpeak. I was the company's chronicler and healer. I stood in the same chamber with Vex Grimthorn and watched him be exactly what he was." Her ears were forward. "And I watched what happened after, what I could see myself, and what I have gathered since."

Vex Grimthorn. The Herald had a name now.

"Some of what I will tell you I witnessed. Some I had from his own letters during the campaign. The rest I assembled over thirty years, from those who went to Crumblewood after he had gone, from Guild researchers who reached the Bleakwood tower years later, from refugees who came through the Hollow with what they'd seen. Where I had to fill, I filled with the smallest assumption the evidence would carry." She looked at the fire. "This is the first time I have told it to people who need to act on it. So I will tell it accurately, with my sources where they matter, and with my own part included."

Nobody spoke. Gareth's paw stayed on his maps.

"Before I tell you what he became, you need to know what he was. When you face him below Thornwall, you will be facing a grief that has had thirty years to harden into purpose. If you go in thinking you are facing a monster, you will be wrong about what you're facing, and that wrongness will cost you." Her tone was even, the words placed with care. "He was a father. A warrior. A husband. He was called the Wolverine Wall because he held ground. Not because he was the strongest fighter, but because he would not yield when he was standing between danger and the creatures behind him."

She paused.

"He had a family. A wife. Three children. A farm in a valley called Crumblewood. An apple orchard. A practice yard where he taught his son the forms." The scrolls stayed closed in her lap. "I am going to name them. They deserve it, and you need their names to understand what comes next."

"Their names," she said, "are Rosemary, Bramble, Moss, and Clover."

"The eldest was called Bramble," Hazel said. "Twelve years old when Grimthorn left for Shadowpeak. Serious. He had watched his father carefully enough to understand that the forms he was being taught were not ceremony. The correct pivot step at the correct moment meant someone behind you lived."

She watched the fire. "Bramble had been working on his pivot step. He kept breaking it on the turn. The morning before Grimthorn's company assembled, Bramble was out early at the practice yard, just him, going through it over and over. He found the correction. He held the form, and a petal from one of the apple trees landed on his practice sword and stayed. It stayed because his arm was finally steady enough." Hazel's ears came forward slightly. "Grimthorn was watching from the doorway. He didn't say anything. He wrote to me about it later, on the march. He said he was afraid that if he spoke, the petal would move."

"The middle child was Moss," Hazel said. "Eight years old. Quiet. He saw patterns. He had a collection of stones, kept on his windowsill in a precise order he'd worked out himself at age six and had been refining and defending ever since. He could explain exactly why each stone sat where it did." She paused. "Anyone who moved them was corrected. He corrected his father once." Her voice didn't change. "Grimthorn thought he'd be a scholar."

Nibbles looked briefly at Gareth's maps, at the paw resting on the stack. He looked back at the fire.

"The youngest was Clover," Hazel said. "Five years old. Low through the center, built like her father in miniature. Fierce." Her paws shifted slightly in her lap. "The night before Grimthorn left, she made him make a pinky-promise that he'd be home for harvest. Apple cake, just the two of them. She told him *Papa always comes home.*"

"She had a yellow climbing rope," she said. "She used it to get into the apple trees. She wouldn't let anyone else use it. It was hers."

The fire cracked once, settling.

"And his wife was Rosemary," Hazel said. "I met her twice. She could feel a room shift before anyone in it had spoken. She always had a chipped teacup, one she'd used since before they were married. Grimthorn mentioned it in letters because she'd been offered new ones and refused every time." Hazel stopped. "That was her."

No one spoke. Acornimus had put his pen down without capping it.

"They were alive and they were specific," Hazel said. "I want that on record before the rest."

"While he was on campaign," Hazel said, "Malachar's corruption reached Crumblewood Valley."

She said it without softening. The facts were the account.

"The company that assembled at Thornwall Keep was led by a badger commander named Aldric Blackstone. He carried a sword called Whisker-brand. Cyan-blue fire, when it blazed. It transformed corruption's void energy. Aldric was the heart of that company. His voice didn't need to rise to hold a room. Short words. Warmth that came when it was needed." She paused. "Aldric saw in Grimthorn the center the company needed. He said so. Grimthorn carried it."

The warmth in Nibbles' sheath changed, a different note in the vibration, lower and slower. His paw was at the hilt without him deciding it.

"We defeated Malachar at Shadowpeak's summit," Hazel said. "We could not destroy him. Aldric drove Whiskerbrand through him and broke his form. What remained, the corruption he had become, the earth mages gathered. They carried it south, three weeks by road, to a chamber cut for the purpose beneath Thornwall Keep. They bound him there with seven weaves. We came to call that chamber the Crystal Sanctum. Each weave was anchored to a Wardstone placed at a point across the realm, where the ley lines ran strongest. The Wardstones held what the weaves bound. It held."

The blade's warmth deepened. Same warmth, sitting lower in his spine.

"In the final moment, as Whiskerbrand pierced him, Malachar's claws drove into Aldric's sword arm. The corruption spread visibly from the wound. His last act was to press Whiskerbrand into the paws of our company's hedgehog warrior." Hazel said it plainly. "He said *the heart is what wakes it. Not the sword. The heart.* And then he was gone. No body. Silver light in the chamber air, and then nothing."

Across the fire, Bristlebaum had not moved. His quills were fully extended and his whiskers did not twitch. His spectacles had slipped to the end of his nose. He was sitting through the part of the account where he had been someone called Brisk, who had received a sword from a dying badger's paws. He let Hazel tell it.

Nibbles looked at him once and then looked back at the fire.

"We celebrated," Hazel said. The word landed wrong. "The realm celebrated. Grimthorn had done what was asked of him. He had held the ground and the realm was safe. And while he was holding the ground, his family had died. Word reached him on the march."

She paused.

"He finished the campaign. At the first crossroads after Shadowpeak, when he turned north and walked away from the road home, our hedgehog warrior called after him. Once and then again. Over and over, until the last call was no longer a word, just his voice raw, aimed at a back that kept walking. Grimthorn kept walking."

Nobody said anything.

"And none of us followed," Hazel said. "We let him go."

"He went back to Crumblewood Valley," Hazel said. She paused. "The farmhouse had been preserved in void-stasis. Malachar's corruption had captured it at a specific moment and held it there. The breakfast table was still set for five. Five places, because Rosemary had set it the morning he left and then gone to wake the children. The food had turned to black stone. The room was unchanged, the same morning, kept."

"Clover's chair still held her impression from that morning," Hazel said. "She always curled her tail to the left. Small and deep in the cushion. Exactly as she'd left it." Her paws pressed together in her lap, then released. "He touched Rosemary's chipped teacup. It turned to ash in his paw. Immediately. He couldn't hold it."

Nibbles' tail had curled tight around his leg at some point in the last hour. He saw it and didn't move it.

"He was afraid," Hazel said plainly. "More afraid than he had ever been in his life. Not of dying. Of the room. Of a teacup that had outlasted a marriage and could not outlast his paw."

She stopped.

"He took what he could carry," she said. "The recipe box from beside the stove. Bramble's wooden badger from the children's room, and his practice sword from the yard. Moss's gray-blue river stone, the one he had given his father on the porch, the diagonal seam worn into its broad face. Clover's clay paw-print from the kitchen shelf. The ash where Rosemary's teacup had been, folded in cloth."

Hazel paused.

"And Clover's yellow climbing rope," she said. "He found it in her room. It was still bright. The fibres were still warm."

"Then he left Crumblewood Valley. Everything he didn't carry, he left behind."

"He went north to a tower in the Bleakwood," Hazel said. "A previous practitioner had attempted necromantic work there and failed. The failure was written down. Grimthorn found the texts, found where the previous work had broken down, and spent months understanding the failure before he built on it."

Dash's ears went flat against his head.

"His reasoning was this," Hazel said. Her voice had gone more precise, not softer. "His family had been taken while he fulfilled his obligation to the realm. He had given everything that was asked and the cost had been everyone he loved. He concluded this was wrong. He concluded a world where death could take them while he fought for others had a flaw at its center. And he intended to correct it."

She paused.

"His first successful animation was a dead sparrow," she said. "It sang backwards. It lasted less than an hour before it crumbled to ash. He found the error in the binding, where the vital current had failed to take hold. He wrote down the correction. He recorded what had worked and what had broken. He treated it as a technical problem."

She stopped again. The fire burned. "That was the part I wrote down three times," she said, "before I understood what I was writing. A scholar's notes read one way. A father's read differently. And those are not the same record."

"He built the full ritual from the tower texts," Hazel said. "Four anchor points at the cardinal positions. Rosemary's teacup at the north (rebuilt from ash, eleven months of work to put it back together). Bramble's practice sword at the east. Moss's seam-stone at the south. Clover's yellow rope at the west. At the center, Clover's drawing of the five of them holding paws, the last uncorrupted thing he had carried. The boundary line sealed in his own blood. He opened a connection to the Crystal Sanctum where Malachar was imprisoned."

The warmth in Nibbles' sheath pulled inward. It pressed down harder rather than cooling. The blade had recognized something.

"Malachar spoke through the connection," Hazel said. "He offered Grimthorn a world where families would never again be separated by death. In the four anchor flames, the shapes wore the right faces, Rosemary's protective stance, Bramble's squared shoulders, Moss's careful tilt, Clover's arms extended." Hazel's voice stayed exactly level. "Still reaching."

No one moved.

"He said yes," Hazel said.

"Clover's drawing crumbled to ash in the circle when he did."

The fire cracked once.

"What came out of that tower was no longer the Wolverine Wall," Hazel said. "He went to Thornwall Keep, where our company had first assembled thirty years before, killed the garrison, all of them, raised them as corrupted servants, and descended to the Crystal Sanctum to begin inverting the seven Wardstones. He has been doing that work ever since. He is very nearly finished."

The fire burned. The flames were low and clean, the embers built up at the base to a deep orange bed.

Hazel sat with her paws pressed together in her lap.

"I need to tell you my part of this," she said.

Nobody moved. The ring of them waited.

"When word came to the company on the march that his family had died, I watched him change," she said. "It wasn't the way grief usually changes a person. He didn't break open. He didn't weep. He closed. The grief went somewhere inside, the doors came down, and he finished the campaign. He ate, slept, kept his equipment in order. He fought better after the news than before, because there was nothing left in him to be afraid of losing." She paused. "I wrote that down. I was the company's chronicler. It was accurate."

Hazel was looking at her folded paws. Bristlebaum was looking at the fire.

"After Shadowpeak, after we came down from the summit, the company had six days of descent before we reached the crossroads. Grimthorn ate and slept and said almost nothing about his family or his grief or the direction either one was taking. I sat with him twice in those six days. I could see what was happening." She stopped. "I had spent enough time near him to know the difference between grief being carried and grief that had been given a direction. I knew which one I was looking at."

Her paws stayed folded. "I did nothing about it," she said. "I told myself I needed to be more certain before I spoke. I told myself he wasn't ready, and pressing too early would push him further. I told myself there would be more time, that reaching the crossroads would bring him back to people who knew him better than I did. Every one of those reasons was possible. I have had thirty years to examine which of them was the real one, and what I have found underneath all of them is this. I did not know what to say. I was afraid of saying the wrong thing. And I let those two fears tell me they were wisdom."

Nibbles watched her. He knew that pattern, good reasons stacking up until they passed for judgment.

She was quiet for a moment. The fire settled.

"I believed my own reasons," she said. Quietly, without heat. "The quill kept moving through all of it."

No one spoke, and the fire burned.

Then Leonardo asked his question. He had been still throughout the entire account. His armor hadn't shifted. The lance was on the ground beside him and his hands were folded in his lap.

"Was there something someone could have said?" he asked. "To him. In that camp after Shadowpeak."

Hazel looked at him. She took the question seriously.

"Yes," she said.

Leonardo's hands stayed folded.

"What would it have been?"

"I don't know the precise words," Hazel said. "Those would have come from whoever was saying them, from what they specifically knew of him. But the substance would have been this. *I see what's happening in you. I'm not going to look away from it. I'm not going to let you carry it alone into whatever comes next without standing here and trying.*"

Leonardo was quiet for a moment.

"The naming," he said.

Hazel's paws shifted.

"Yes," she said. "Not a solution. Not a way to bear it. Someone who looked directly at the wound and didn't step back from it."

"And you stepped back," he said.

"Yes," Hazel said. "I gave myself good reasons to. They were good reasons. They did not change what I did."

Leonardo took what he had just heard and set it somewhere in himself, the lance lying on the ground beside him, untouched. A long minute passed. Then he looked at the fire.

"Right," he said. Quietly. To himself, or to the fire, or to someone he had not been able to name back when it mattered. "Right."

The silence after Leonardo's voice went quiet lasted long enough for Nibbles to understand what his own question was. He had not planned to ask anything. He had been sitting with the account for the better part of two hours, carrying the images Hazel had put in him. The petal that stayed on Bramble's practice sword. The rope still bright in Clover's room. The sparrow singing backwards and treated as a technical problem.

A question had been building since Hazel said *he said yes*, and what it was had become clear in the space after Leonardo went quiet.

"Could someone have stopped it?" he asked. "The whole descent. Not the conversation in camp, but further along, or earlier, at some point when the direction was still open. Was there a moment where the right person in the right place could have changed the whole course of it?"

Hazel's ears came forward. She read him.

"You're asking two questions," she said.

Nibbles didn't argue with that.

"The answer to the first is no," Hazel said. "By the time he was in the Bleakwood tower, the descent had its own momentum. Before that, possibly. There were many points where things might have gone differently. But there is no single moment, no single right thing said by the right person, that would have guaranteed a different outcome. Grief doesn't work like that in a person who has decided to give it direction." She paused. "What might have changed things was a different gathering. Many small moments over many years. Many different choices by many different people. Not one intervention at one point."

"What's the second question?" he asked.

"You want to know if you can change anything," Hazel said. "Going into that chamber below Thornwall. Whether one creature with one sword can reach something in him that thirty years and everyone who loved him failed to reach."

Nibbles didn't agree or argue. He sat with the question being said out loud and found it was what he'd been carrying since she had named the family.

"I can't answer that," Hazel said. "I genuinely don't know it. What I can tell you is the thing I should have understood in that camp and didn't." She shifted slightly. "Grief goes somewhere. In every creature, always. It goes toward something or it goes into something, but it doesn't stay still. The question is whether there is anything around it (people, love for someone still living, responsibility, a reason to keep moving) that shapes where it ends up."

She looked at him steadily.

"You can't change where his grief went thirty years ago," she said. "But that is not the only grief in that chamber. His is one account. Yours is another. And some grief, met by something it didn't expect, can still change direction."

He thought about the valley and what was on the far side of it. Clover's drawing crumbling to ash in the ritual circle when the word *yes* was spoken.

Bristlebaum calling after Grimthorn at the crossroads, *not once. Over and over.*

He didn't know what was still possible for Grimthorn, but he thought something was. He couldn't prove it, and he wasn't going to know in advance, only when he was in that chamber, with the blade he'd been given, looking at whatever Grimthorn had become.

His paw was still on Whiskerbrand's hilt. The blade was warm and steady against his palm.

"Thank you," he said.

Hazel inclined her head.

The fire had gone deep orange by then. The outer logs were coals, and the last piece of wood Bristlebaum had placed was catching steadily, burning the way he had built it to burn. Nobody spoke for a time. Nibbles' tail was still curled around his leg. His paw was still on Whiskerbrand's hilt.

Nori sat at the fire's edge with her chin on her knees, watching the embers. Acornimus had his pen to the journal, moving it in small careful strokes while he watched the fire; he had stopped looking at the page somewhere in the family-naming. Telia's eyes were closed, her paws flat on the cracked staff, the purple lines threading her forearms gone darker in the firelight.

Across the fire, Bristlebaum had not moved for a long time. His spectacles had slipped to the end of his nose and he had not pushed them back. He had been the hedgehog in Hazel's account, the one who took the sword from a dying badger's paws, and he had sat through all of it.

Hazel's paws were folded in her lap. She was looking at the fire. The silence went on.

Then Bristlebaum's paw moved. He reached across (not far; they were sitting close on this side of the fire) and laid his paw over hers. He held it there a few heartbeats. Then both paws withdrew, and the fire burned.

Gareth had been waiting. He'd held the maps through the whole account, one paw resting on the folded stack. When the silence settled, he set the stack on the ground beside the fire.

He unfolded the first map and weighted the corners with four smooth stones from his pack. The map showed the seven anchor points, the conduit lines running between them, and the Crystal Sanctum at Thornwall where all seven converged. The notation in the margins was dense, weeks of work in a controlled hand, entries dated and layered.

He laid the second map over the first, offset slightly. Corruption spread, marked in charcoal, dated.

"The pattern makes sense now," he said, stating it rather than asking. "I've had five anchor points confirmed for three weeks. The sixth I confirmed at Ridgemarrow. The seventh is Thornwall. The anchor sits directly below the keep, in the Crystal Sanctum, where all seven conduit lines converge."

He tapped a notation at the edge, careful not to smear the ink.

"Each stone fully inverted increases the pressure on Malachar's prison," he said. "The prison wall doesn't fail at the last stone. It fails progressively, and the last stone completes the working. The sixth being held at partial inversion is the reason we're not already too late."

He pulled the charcoal from his vest pocket.

"He started the final ritual sequence on the sixth stone twelve days ago, near as I can tell. The coordination we saw in the valley, the way those animals moved, the directions they came from, isn't general corruption spreading outward. That's direction from a fully inverted stone, coordinating the others. He's no longer working on the sixth stone. He's working with what the five fully inverted stones can already do." He drew a line on the second map, direct, from their current position across the valley to Thornwall. "The window is not weeks."

He set the charcoal down.

"Days," he said. "Maybe less, depending on how long the partial hold at the sixth stone extends the timeline before it tips."

He looked up at the ring of them. His face had its working expression, careful and level.

No one asked him to repeat it. The maps were clear.

Nibbles' paw was still on Whiskerbrand's hilt. He thought about the valley and the western ridge, and about the figure that had been working below Thornwall all the time they had been walking north.

Gareth folded the maps carefully and returned them to his pack, the charcoal placed in the fold before closing it. He settled back, and the fire was still burning.

Chapter Fourteen

The Last Ordinary Time

THE ROAD NORTH RAN through open country, and the sky above it was just sky.

Nibbles had stopped noticing birdsong until it came back. A wren was carrying on from the bramble hedge along the eastern verge, a whole cascading run of notes, territorial and relentless. In the oak canopy above the slope, something large was moving, leaves shaking, a branch flexing, a twig cracking under real weight. He'd spent so long in country where those sounds were absent that quiet had become the thing he expected.

His left shoulder still pulled if he let the sword-strap sit wrong. He adjusted it with his right paw, not lifting his left arm above parallel. Six days of that habit now.

The column spread out on the open road the way it always did when there was nothing immediate to watch for. Hazel walked near the front with Bristlebaum, their pace matched. Telia's staff rang on the stone at a steady interval behind him. Nori was twenty paces ahead, scanning the high ground and the road's curve and the ridgeline to the east in slow rotation. Dash moved at the column's tail. Somewhere above, Lark's shadow crossed the road once, banking northeast, and was gone.

The smell was different today. No rot underneath. No iron sweetness below the surface. Just old leaf, dry stone, the road's dust warming in the morning sun.

He heard the stream before he reached it, fast and high, running over stone the way water did when it was just water. A low bridge crossed a cut bank, and he stopped at it and looked over the edge.

Clear to the bottom. The current ran over pale stone in a steady run.

He crouched and dipped his paw in anyway. The habit had settled in somewhere around Nettleflint's farm, when the stream at the field's edge had been slow and iridescent, the surface catching colors it shouldn't. He had checked every stream since, wrist-deep, paw flat, waiting.

Cold. Clean. Just water.

Whiskerbrand was quiet at his back. He stood, dried his paw on his vest, and caught up with the column.

Gareth crossed the bridge reading his notes and didn't look at the water. Dash came last, silent. The wren started up again from somewhere further along the hedge.

She dropped back from the column's head around midmorning and fell in beside him. Nibbles glanced over.

"Keep walking," Nori said.

He kept walking. She stayed at his left side for a time, watching him close enough that he was aware of her, and let the silence do its work. Her crossbow was across her back. Her eyes moved over the road ahead, the high ground, the eastern verge in slow rotation, steady and unhurried.

"Hold still," she said.

He stopped. She stepped to his left. His left shoulder moved before she'd done anything, a small rise, drawing back from her closeness, not quite a flinch but close. She reached out and tapped the outside of his left elbow once.

"That," she said. "You know you do it?"

"The shoulder —"

"I know about the shoulder." She raised her own right arm in a slow show, drawing it partway across her body in the guard position he'd been defaulting to. "You're protecting the bite. Anyone coming at you from that side reads you from ten paces out. They know exactly where to aim."

He looked at his arm. He'd thought of it as protection.

"So I stop guarding it?"

"Stop trying to protect it with your arm. Move so it doesn't need protecting." She stepped back and squared herself in the road. "Watch."

She took one step forward and pivoted on her left foot. The movement was small (hips and shoulders rotating on an axis, her whole frame coming around) and when it finished, her left shoulder was set back from the line of any strike coming from that side, not because her arm had moved but because her body's angle had changed.

"The threat has to change its line to reach you," she said. "Your arm was marking the target."

He tried it. The reflex fired first, shoulder tensed, arm started its rise. He caught himself mid-motion and the correction came out wrong, his weight ending up over his forward foot, the pivot late and uncentered.

She watched, saying nothing.

He tried again. This time he held the arm still by an act of will and the pivot dragged because he was fighting himself in two directions at once.

"Stop thinking about the arm," Nori said. "Think about the foot. Left foot comes back first. That happens before anything else moves."

He tried again. Left foot pulling back, then the rotation. His arm didn't need holding still because the hip turn had already committed it. His weight settled over his center. The shoulder had cleared the line.

She stepped in from his left at speed (not hard, but fast). His left foot pulled back on its own. The pivot happened. His shoulder was out of the line when she stopped.

"Again," she said.

He did it four more times. On the fourth she came in at a diagonal rather than straight from the side, and the footwork adjusted on its own.

"You'll still brace under pressure," she said, walking again. He fell in beside her. "When something comes in fast, the old reflex fires. What I'm giving you is a cleaner reflex, one that moves instead of braces. It works better than the guard once it's practiced enough."

"How many times is enough?"

"More than you'll do today." She looked north along the road. "Do it a hundred more times this afternoon. Don't count. Just do it."

She drifted back toward the column's head.

He walked and worked the pivot into his stride, left foot back, rotation, weight centered, the motion settling into him.

The camp that evening was quiet, tired and not afraid.

Nibbles ate and worked the pivot drill until the motion started to feel like his own, then sat near the fire. Telia had pressed her paws flat to the earth in the spot she chose every evening, eyes closed, her staff angled across her knees. Hazel was writing on a flat rock at the fire's edge, the quill moving in long careful strokes. Bristlebaum stood at the firelight's far edge with a map between his paws, studying something on it for the better part of twenty minutes. He didn't call anyone over. His quills were up.

Nori had finished eating and was sharpening one of her hand-axes in slow deliberate strokes, barely a sound to it, just the steady rhythm of metal on stone. Her crossbow was off her back and laid within reach. Sir

Leonardo worked through his lance forms on a flat section of ground, slow and deliberate, each one the same as the last. The plume flopped with each extended pivot. He pushed it back and continued. Dash wasn't in sight, which was usual.

Gareth sat cross-legged six feet from the fire with his notes spread in a semicircle around him. He'd been there since before supper. His paw tapped a rhythm on his thigh, faster than usual, uneven, the tempo he ran when he was working through something hard. It hadn't simplified yet.

On the other side of the fire, Acornimus sat with his journal open on his knee. His pen rested on the page. He was watching Gareth.

Gareth pulled two sections of notes together and laid them flat, then set a map on top and leaned forward to read all three at once. His paw went still on his thigh. He looked at the documents for a long moment, then reached past them, took a blank sheet, and wrote something short. He set the pen down and looked at what he'd written. Acornimus hadn't moved.

Gareth picked up his pen and returned to the notes. The tapping resumed, slower than before. Acornimus opened to a fresh page and began to write.

Nibbles stood and worked the pivot into a slow circuit of the fire's edge. Left foot, rotation, weight centered. He lost count somewhere in the middle and kept going.

They broke camp before first light and were on the road when the sun came up behind thin cloud.

The first hour looked the same as the previous day. Open fields, hedgerows, oak canopy on the higher slopes to the east. A pair of larger birds crossed the high ground to the west, riding the thermals in wide lazy banks. The morning felt like the morning before it, except the wrens were gone.

Nibbles caught the absence around the first mile. He'd been half-listening for the territorial run from the verge, and the silence had stretched long enough that he registered it. He scanned the hedge as he walked. No small brown movement. Nothing in the scrub. He walked on.

Around midmorning the road descended into a shallow cut and ran alongside a drainage ditch, the verge narrow on the right, the bank close. The water in the ditch was still from recent rain, sitting in the cut. He stopped.

The ditch ran downhill. The current should have been moving at a real pace on that slope. Instead it moved at the rate of flat ground. Slow. Wrong in a way he had a name for now, the same wrong he'd felt at Nettleflint's farm on the very first day out of Thimblewick.

He crouched and reached his paw toward the surface.

Whiskerbrand hummed once at his back. The alert hum, low and brief. He held his paw a finger's breadth above the water.

The hum faded. He stood.

Nori was beside him. He hadn't heard her come back along the road.

"Not yet," he said. "But the current is wrong."

She looked at the water. Then she looked north, toward where the road curved out of sight.

"We're getting closer," she said.

She walked back to the column's head. Nibbles followed. The ditch receded behind him. The birds that had been banking on the western thermals were gone when he looked up. He hadn't seen them leave.

She stepped off the road in the early afternoon, onto the verge beside a stretch of low ground where the field drainage had pooled in a shallow depression, and crouched. Nibbles stopped and looked at her.

"Come here," she said.

He stepped off the road. She was pressing her paws flat to the ground, through the thin root-mat to the packed earth beneath rather than to the grass. Her eyes were closed. He crouched beside her.

"Press flat," she said. "Both paws. Don't search. Hold and wait."

He pressed his paws flat. The soil was cool, the root-mat giving way to firmer ground an inch below. He held the way she'd said and waited.

After a moment, through the pads of his paws, something arrived, a warmth that wasn't quite heat, faint and even, the soil carrying what the sun had built up across the day. When he pressed and released, the ground returned to itself. Firm. Springy. The earth taking the contact and giving it back.

"That's healthy ground," Nori said. "The warmth comes toward you. The give returns when you let it."

He pressed and released again. It did.

"Now here."

She moved ten feet north along the verge, closer to where the road curved toward the valley, and crouched again. He followed and pressed his paws flat.

The ground was different. The texture was the same under his palms, the same packed feel. But the warmth was moving in the wrong direction, sliding away from the point of contact, neither cold nor dramatic. He pressed harder. The give didn't return. The earth held the impression of his paws and stayed pressed.

"The corruption hasn't broken the surface here yet," Nori said, still looking at the ground. "But the ground below is starting to change. The

Wardstone conduit lines run beneath us and the corruption follows the same channels. It draws the warmth down toward the source." She looked at the soil, not at him. "You're at the edge of the field around the valley. The earth has been changing here for at least a season."

"How do I read it when I don't have clean ground to compare?"

"You learn what the absence feels like. Once you've read soil that gives back, you'll know it when something isn't." She stood and brushed her paws on her thighs. "The canopy shows you where the corruption is right now. The soil shows you where it's been, and where it's moving."

She'd learned it from a groundhog she'd trained under, she said, the way she might have named who had tested a crossing. The groundhog was no longer alive. She moved past that and Nibbles didn't stop her.

"Where do I start?" he asked. "When I'm checking new ground."

"Low places. Anywhere water collects. The conduit lines run under the drainage channels, and the corruption finds the same paths water finds." She looked at him. "Press flat, hold, wait. Read which way the warmth moves. Read whether the give comes back. Do it every time you stop, making camp, checking a crossing, when something's wrong and you can't name it yet." She looked at the ground again. "The ground usually knows first."

He pressed flat one more time and held. The warmth was still sliding away, the give still not coming back. He could read it now. Nori was watching him.

"You'll teach it to someone else," she said.

He went through the faces of the group. Acornimus with his journal. Dash, who read ground better than he let on. Bristlebaum with thirty years of field knowledge worked so deep into him he wouldn't know how to break it down for a student. He tried to imagine standing where Nori was crouching, showing someone else how to press flat and wait. He set the question aside and walked back to the road.

The camp settled into the hollow between two low hills, the fire burning low because the wood was wet. Nibbles came back from the perimeter circuit (a wide walk looking for anything wrong in the tree line, the sky, the ground) and stopped at the edge of the firelight.

Gareth sat at the fire's edge with his notes in front of him, and the notes were stacked. He'd watched Gareth work every evening since Ironhold, long enough to know what the notes looked like in use, maps at the center, smaller sheets fanned out in reach, his paw moving between them as he pulled the work together. Tonight the papers were squared and aligned, sections ordered, the two maps folded and set on top. The stack looked ready to be handed over, not consulted.

Gareth wrote something on a fresh sheet, read it, added three lines below. He set the pen down and held the document for a moment before placing it on top of the stack. Across the fire, Acornimus sat with his journal open on his knee. He was watching Gareth.

Around the fire the others had settled. Telia pressed her paws to the earth in the spot she'd chosen, her staff across her knee. Hazel was writing in the last good light before the fire became the main source. Leonardo sat with his lance across his knees and ran his thumb along the shaft from grip to point and back again, slow and patient. Dash ate at the fire's edge, silent.

Acornimus closed his journal and stood. He crossed to Gareth's side of the fire and sat down close, the angle of his approach saying he had come for something specific.

Gareth lifted the stack and held it out. The full stack. Every section. The inversion timeline, the cross-references, the pattern Gareth had been closing in on for weeks.

Acornimus took it in both paws, balanced. He didn't open it immediately. He looked at Gareth.

"Field caution," Gareth said. "Call it that."

He opened the top sheet and read it with his whiskers forward and still, his working position, not the quick one he used for intelligence intake. He turned to the second sheet and slowed. The third he read more slowly still. He was reading the way he read things he intended to keep. He closed the stack.

He said something low to Gareth. Gareth reached across to the one remaining map and traced a line on it. Acornimus listened and asked a question. They went back and forth three or four times in the shorthand of two creatures who'd been working the same problem from different angles for a while now.

Acornimus opened his own journal and wrote something on the inside front cover. He closed it and laid it across the stack.

Gareth returned to his single remaining sheet of notes.

Nibbles watched them. He had a guess what the journal was for. The guess stayed with him.

They were an hour from camp, maybe less, walking the last stretch before the road began its descent toward the valley approach, when Nori dropped back and fell in beside him.

She'd been at the column's head for most of the afternoon, running the slow rotation between the tree line, the road's grade, and the eastern ridge. He'd watched her move forward and back three times in the last mile.

The road had narrowed here. The open-country track of the morning was behind them; this path had been worn into the hillside rather than built on it, the stones showing roots at the edges, the verge close on both sides. The country was quieter than the morning, and not the quiet of corrupted ground. The birds had stopped somewhere south of them.

Nori walked without speaking for a time.

"What do you go back to?" she asked.

He looked over. She was watching the road ahead, not him. He thought about the actual answer.

"My mother's garden," he said. "She keeps a kitchen plot, proper beds with labels for everything. She plants by moon phase and keeps a full record of what goes in on which day and what comes up after. She's been doing it long enough that she has a real case." He paused. "I've never learned which phase does what. The record's always available and she's happy to explain it to anyone who asks. The part I actually remember is the labels, small tiles pressed into the soil, different colors for each bed. She worked the system out over years and won't simplify it because the complexity is the point."

Nori was quiet.

"The apple tree," he said. "My father planted it the year before he died. The seedling was barely clearing the fence line when I left. I want to see how tall it is now."

He hadn't said that to anyone before. The words came out plain.

"And the fountain," he said. "In the square at Thimblewick. Someone used the wrong cleaning compound two summers ago and the water turned purple. The whole village voted on whether to pay to bleach it clean, and the vote came out eleven to seven in favor of keeping the color."

"Eleven to seven for purple," she said.

"Their reasoning was that the fountain had been there since the square was built and had been the same grey-beige for a hundred years, and something different might be worth having." He kept his eyes on the road. "The letter from my mother, the one that came before we left Ironhold, said someone had put fish in the fountain. The fish turned purple too. Which wasn't the plan."

"How are the fish doing?"

"There's a debate. My mother thinks they're an improvement. The baker thinks they're a bad sign. He'd been on the bleaching side from the start, and some people think this is affecting his view of the fish."

She laughed, real and brief, not for anyone else. It lasted a moment and then she was watching the road again, her face composed, eyes moving north.

"After the garden and the tree and the fish," she said. "What then?"

"Sleep in my own bed for about a week," he said. "And then probably go see what the Guildmaster has for me next. There'll always be something."

She didn't answer.

The road turned around a low rise. Past the turn, the ridgeline the valley sat behind was visible for the first time. Close and real now. The long shelf to the east. The lower saddle in the center where the road crested through. The air coming over it was colder than the air around them.

He waited. A few paces, then a few more. She walked beside him in silence.

The same question, turned around, would have been hers to answer. She didn't take it up, and he walked on without pressing it.

They reached camp forty minutes later, the column coming together as the road entered a hollow between two hills where the ground was flat enough to sleep on and the wind ran from the north.

Nibbles set his bedroll and ran the pivot drill at the fire's edge, left foot back, rotation, weight centered. He'd done it enough today that his body did it before his mind did. When it had settled he sat down.

The camp took its shape. Telia chose her spot and lowered herself to both knees and pressed her paws flat to the earth, her staff resting against her knee. Hazel was already writing, the quill moving in the long careful strokes she kept up regardless of light or fatigue. Leonardo worked his lance fittings with the methodical patience he'd kept since the ambush, the plume flopping at each angle change, each correction made and checked. Dash came in from the perimeter, ate in silence, and went back out.

Nibbles pressed his paw flat to the ground beside his bedroll. The warmth came toward his palm. The give came back when he lifted.

He pressed flat ten feet north and waited. The warmth still came. The give still returned. Good ground.

He held the comparison, this and what he'd felt at the drainage ditch that afternoon, the two different ways the earth came back. He could read it now. He did it once more with his eyes closed, the way Nori had shown him, press flat, hold, wait for the direction. Tomorrow, closer to the valley, the ground would tell him something different.

Bristlebaum stood at the far edge of the fire with the survey map, going over what he already knew for what tomorrow would ask of it.

Above the camp, Lark came over from east to west in a long pass and turned south without slowing. She didn't land.

He looked north. The ridgeline was close. The long shelf to the east. The lower saddle in the center. The black edge of it against a sky full of stars. The valley was on the other side of it. Tomorrow they'd reach the approach. He had the soil-reading, the footwork, Whiskerbrand at his back warm and steady. The sword had been quiet since the ditch this afternoon.

The fire burned to coals. One by one the others found their bedrolls. Hazel set her quill aside. Leonardo laid the lance down and was still.

Chapter Fifteen
The Valley

The thermal was gone.

Lark banked east and felt nothing, banked west and felt the same flat air. Every valley gave up heat. Warm ground, warm air moving upward, a column a crow could read as easily as a road. This valley's air moved sideways only, pushed by the wind off the northern ridge. Nothing rose from below.

She climbed on her own wings and gained altitude until the bowl spread open under her.

Purple haze lay over the valley floor, a tint in the air itself, sourceless, no smoke or fog behind it, thickening toward the center. Below the haze, every tree on the valley floor had leaned the same direction. She had caught it on her first pass and put it down to her angle of approach; on the second pass, coming in from the north, it was plain. Every trunk tilted toward the lake. Some gradually. Some at angles that should have toppled them seasons ago, the bark on the high side split from the tension, the bark on the low side smooth and pale, worn down by the slow continuous pull.

The lake sat at the lowest point. Its surface was black, light going into it and staying. It bubbled in long even pulses, slow and metronomic, the surface rising and breaking and rising. Something below was breathing. At the lake's center, a crystalline formation rose from the water, purple-grey, translucent, enormous, shaped like an arm from elbow to claw. Elbow-deep already. Whatever was below was pulling itself upward, slow and unhurried. She couldn't see the movement directly. There was only the difference between where the arm had been on her first pass and where it sat now.

The effigies lined the shoreline.

She came down lower on the third pass and read them. Deer mid-leap, forelegs extended toward ground that did not exist for them. Birds at the apex of a wingbeat, each primary feather at peak extension, the angle perfect for a stroke that would not finish. Rabbits in full sprint, haunches driving, ears flat, eyes wide.

They were still running.

She counted forty before the count stopped being useful.

She had flown over dying land before. Ridgemarrow's failing margins, the farms around Wigglywood in the early weeks. Dying land still moved. Animals fled. Corrupted things pushed at the perimeter.

This valley's floor held nothing. No animals, no corrupted things, no birds flushing from cover. The work here was done. It had been done long enough that the doing no longer showed on the surface.

She turned back toward the western ridge.

Her talons closed around the branch and the branch gave way, soft rot through to the core, powder where wood should have been. She dropped the last two feet to the rock and landed harder than intended, the impact jarring through both legs.

"Trees have quit too," she said. To no one in particular.

The party was on the outcrop below the ridgeline. Bristlebaum at the front with his quills at the partial elevation they'd held since the Caves. Nibbles at the ledge's edge with Whiskerbrand across his knees, the blade giving off its low steady warmth. Hazel against a boulder, ears forward and both paws on her knees, listening. Telia already down with a paw flat to the rock, eyes closed, reading through it. Acornimus had Gareth's notes spread open on his knees, a pen already moving in his other paw before he was fully seated. Dash had taken his position near the back of the outcrop, close to the fastest route down, paws at rest and tracking. Gareth stood slightly apart from the others, looking at the valley.

Nori was watching the valley-side treeline, not the party or the ledge but the treeline itself. The way she watched anything that might move. Automatically, for threats and exits.

The haze was visible from here, the lake a dark smear at the center. The effigies weren't readable at this distance. The shoreline looked like terrain, wrong and still.

Lark shook the wood-dust from her talons. The dead zone on the ridge had stretched further back than her last look had shown, another forty paces at least. The approach had narrowed.

"Gather in," she said. "I need to brief the route."

She had no map for the valley interior. The survey Gareth had been carrying showed the approach terrain and the ridgeline edges, nothing past that point. Whoever had done the original work hadn't gone in, or hadn't come back to write it down. She pointed at the terrain itself instead.

"Western ridge," she said. "Here's how it lies."

They had gathered in a close arc, near enough to hear without her raising her voice. Bristlebaum at the front. Nibbles beside him. Nori had moved up from the back and taken the arc's left edge, her crossbow slung at rest, her eyes moving in regular alternation between Lark and the valley-side treeline.

"The ridge runs along the valley's western edge." She showed the ridge-line's northeastern curve with her talon. "We stay on it until the creek crossing. The creek is about a third of the way through, there." The terrain depression on the northeast face was visible from where they stood. "The creek bed is wrong. I wouldn't drink from it. But it's fordable. The problem is the open ground on both banks, twenty paces of flat exposure each side before we get back to ridge cover."

"Approach angles?" Nori asked.

"From below, valley side. The ridge blocks approach from the west. The creek crossing is the exposure point." Lark looked at Nibbles. "Whisker-brand at point through the open section."

Nibbles nodded. He had stopped watching the valley.

"The other option is the basin." She showed the broad flat section of valley floor visible to the northeast. "Direct route. Faster by half a day. The corrupted animals in the basin have been moving in formation, co-ordinated paths, not scattered. The ridge limits how many angles they can approach from. The basin doesn't."

"Formation is consistent?" Gareth asked. He had his notes in his paws, holding them.

"The same since Ridgemarrow," Lark said. "Every contact has moved along pre-set paths. Basin terrain has more of those paths and no high ground to track them from."

Gareth looked at his notes. The small tapping rhythm started on his thigh (index finger, a count) and stopped.

"Two days on the ridge," Bristlebaum said.

"Two days," Lark said. "Night camp at the creek crossing if we make it by dark. The second day is shorter, mostly downslope once we're past the creek."

Telia had her staff in both paws and was looking at the valley floor rather than the party, her face level, the look she wore when she was still working something out.

Hazel's ears were fully forward. Acornimus's pen had started moving.

"Form up on the ridge," Bristlebaum said. "Two minutes."

They ran the codes before the descent.

Bristlebaum had brought the system in six days out of Ridgemarrow, on a quiet stretch of march when the formation had gotten loose. Four calls. Four responses. Simple enough to run in the dark, in noise, in the middle of something going wrong. Lark had watched the first drill from above, slow, uncertain on the phrasing, the timing uneven. By the fourth day of march it had tightened. By now it ran on its own.

"Scatter," Bristlebaum said.

"Ridge right." Three voices, nearly at once (Nibbles, Nori, Leonardo) and Telia a beat behind. Her paws had gone flat to the rock before the rest of her caught up to the direction. The earth-reading came in faster than her voice did. Bristlebaum had adjusted the formation to take account of it, Telia third from front, between Nibbles and Nori, where the brief delay cost least.

"Call," Bristlebaum said.

"Incoming, Lark, valley side." Nibbles. The full version. He'd used a shorter form in early drills; Bristlebaum had corrected him twice. On the third correction Nibbles had said "right, sorry, all of it," and had given the full response every time since.

"Anchor," Bristlebaum said.

Leonardo's hand went to his shield in a small settling motion. "Center locked." He'd developed a shorter command register for the codes, quieter than his parade-ground voice, deliberate and clear.

Dash had not spoken. He never did. His answer to every code was his position, taken first, before the calls were even finished. Lark had asked him once on a rest stop whether he knew the full responses or had simply assigned himself a role that didn't require them. He'd given her the look someone gives a question whose answer is already obvious. "I know them," he said.

"Again," Bristlebaum said. "Scatter."

The response came back faster. The beat between Telia's earth-read and her ridge-right movement had narrowed, narrower than yesterday without fully closing. Bristlebaum's quills made their small fractional adjustment downward.

"Move," he said.

She kept them in single file.

The ridge path was wide enough for two in the stable sections, and that width tempted pairs. Nibbles would drift toward Nori, Gareth would end up beside Acornimus working through notes on the move. Pairs spread the formation and complicated her sight lines from above. She had called them back to single file twice on the march out of Ridgemarrow before they'd stopped needing the correction.

Whiskerbrand was drawn at point. Bristlebaum's call, not Nibbles's, and Nibbles had taken it. He carried the blade across his body in the transit position, not raised, the sword resettling against his grip as the terrain changed beneath him. Each correction came in a half-beat ahead of his weight shift, the blade reading the ground before he did, and he moved with it.

She made a short double-bank over the column (the signal for the path narrowing) and watched the formation compress without having to fly down and say it directly.

The valley floor was visible in strips below the ridgeline, between the trees. The haze thickened from this angle, the purple deepening toward the basin. Every trunk on the slope had finished its lean, branches stripped on the high side where the growth cycle had broken. The valley floor below the tree line showed a regularity that natural terrain didn't produce, the same angular spacing between the crystal outcroppings, corridors running toward the lake at consistent intervals, arranged rather than grown.

She made a pass along the column's length. Leonardo was managing his limp on the steeper sections by shortening his stride, the lance angled to compensate. Nori moved without wasted motion, crossbow at her back, her eyes going to the valley floor on every other step. She was watching the floor.

Midway through the descent, Telia stopped. The earth-reading pause usually had her bowing forward, both paws to the ground, eyes closed. This was different. She had gone still while standing upright, the staff held but not pressed into the rock. Her paws were flat against the ridge stone, the amber at her palms thin. Not absent, but thin. The stone wasn't giving her enough to draw from. She held four breaths, lifted her paws, and walked on. She didn't look at Nori or speak.

Lark banked wider, gained altitude, read the ridge ahead. Clear for another half-mile before the steepening. She made a single-bank return (no correction needed) and continued her circuit.

She came in lower on the next pass.

The briefing had given the party the effigies in general terms. Shoreline, creatures, crystal formation. She needed the details now. How long the preservation had been in place, what the spread showed about when the valley's claim had completed.

Crystal corruption spread from source outward. The oldest effigies were always closest to the water, where the concentration had been highest first. She had learned the pattern watching Ridgemarrow's margins, where the link between effigy age and distance from the failing Wardstone was the same across every contact zone she had seen.

She came down to thirty feet and flew a slow arc along the shoreline.

The deer nearest the water had been standing for months. The first crystal capture had completed long enough ago that secondary formations had started, thin needles extending from the shoulder joint toward the jaw, a secondary plate beginning to form along the right flank. The corruption was layering onto what was already finished because it had used up the primary growth zone in this area. She had seen this stage once before, at a farm on Ridgemarrow's oldest affected edge. Secondary growth meant the primary capture was at the very least five months old. Probably six.

She moved northeast along the shoreline, watching the change.

The effigies furthest from the water showed none of that secondary formation. Clean crystal, clear, the preservation more recent, a month, maybe six weeks. The capture was still moving forward at the valley's margins, slowly. Most of what fed it was used up. It was working through what remained. The claim had completed at the center first and was still completing at the edges.

She pulled up, widened her circuit, gained altitude, and saw the party below.

They had reached the point on the descent where the full shoreline came into view at once. The formation had stopped. No code halt, no threat call. The column had just stopped moving.

Telia was standing with her staff in both paws, holding still. The earth-reading posture had her bowing forward, paws flat to the ground. She was upright instead, staff held vertical, looking at the shoreline. The grey in her fur caught the afternoon light from this angle. It had been moving on her for weeks; the last two days had moved it faster.

Lark had circled above the sixth Wardstone on Ridgemarrow's hill and watched Telia press her paws to it for hours at a stretch, feeding what she had into conduit channels that hadn't been properly tended in years. The stone flickered between amber and violet on its best days while Telia worked. Lark had seen the grey spread faster after the sessions that cost the most.

Telia had been holding a line. The valley below was what failure looked like. The line gone, the corruption past it, the deer and the birds and the rabbits caught running and held running.

Nori moved. Lark saw it from above. Nori came up beside Telia, said something, and put a paw on Telia's arm. Brief. Telia looked at the shoreline for another moment. Then she turned and started walking. She had spent three years shoring up the conduits between Ridgemarrow and here, and this was the first time she'd stood above the work that the shoring had been keeping back.

Lark banked wide and came back around.

The attack came from the valley floor, as she'd said it would.

She was three hundred feet up and climbing when she caught the first movement, corrupted animals coming out of the tree cover below, away from the ridgeline, moving along the wide corridors between the crystal outcroppings. Three distinct paths at consistent spacing. She had watched coordinated movement before (corrupted packs at Ridgemarrow's margins, the wolf-shapes that had taken to moving in rows) but this was more regular than those. Three columns. Equal intervals. Moving toward the ridge at the same pace.

She dropped altitude and made a hard bank over the formation.

"Valley floor. Three columns. Scattered approach, ridge base." She said it twice so the far end of the column had it.

The formation held the ridge.

Whiskerbrand's warmth went up. She couldn't feel it but she could see it in Nibbles. He'd planted his feet at the ridge edge and brought the blade across his body to a guard position, not raised, the sword pulling against his grip in small corrections. The hum she'd heard described was audible now, carried on the still valley air, a sustained note below speech.

Leonardo was at center. The shield was up and his lance was braced against the ridge stone. He'd found the low position that spread the weight properly on uneven ground rather than the parade-ground stance.

Telia had gone to her knees. Both paws flat to the stone, eyes closed, the amber at her palms thin and working. She was pressing harder into the stone to get what she could from it, her shoulders dropped from the effort. The ground-sense moved differently in this valley; she had said so at the briefing this morning, in plain terms. The stone gets confused here, it can't tell what's coming from which direction because it can't separate the corruption from the background. The thinning had gotten worse since the descent. She was giving it more to work with and getting less back.

The first column reached the ridge base.

They were mountain deer, or had been. The purple corruption had thickened through their coats to the point where the original coloring was visible only in patches at the face and along the belly. The coordination showed at the base of the ridge, the first column spread along the slope below the party's position without converging on a single target, two animals moving right and two moving left while three pushed up the center. Pressure spread across three points at once.

That was not pack behavior. Pack animals held to the line they'd learned. They did not reorganize around losses.

Nori's first bolt took the leftmost center animal in the chest. She was working the reload before it finished dropping, crossbow and hand-axes in alternation, shifting based on range. The animal that had been driving left stopped, pivoted, and moved back to center to close the gap its counterpart had left. The gap closed in four steps.

Gareth was on the high side of the ridge, above the formation's back rank, his notes wrapped inside his vest. He was not fighting. He was watching the columns. His right hand tapped his thigh in the rhythm Lark recognized from the marching camp, the beat he ran when he was matching things up, working a count against evidence, waiting for what he was missing.

The fight at the center was loud. Leonardo's shield took the weight of the first push, two animals together, the combined mass enough to drive his left foot back two inches in the loose stone. He held. Nibbles brought Whiskerbrand across in a purifying arc and the light blazed at contact, the corruption burning away from one animal's shoulder and flank in cyan-blue. The animal flinched back, the coordinated drive breaking for a single step, and Nori put a bolt through its neck on the break.

The right column reached the ridge.

Dash was there. He had been there before the animals arrived, which meant he'd read the approach vector from the first description. He worked economically in the tight space, two animals, one narrow gap in the rock formation to funnel them, his two daggers in alternation at the point where the gap forced them to single file. Clean, fast, unhurried.

The second push at the center came harder.

Nori took a blow across her left shoulder, a sweep she'd read late, the animal turning faster than her prediction. The impact spun her back half a step. She corrected and kept working. Lark, above, saw the half-step and the correction and Nori's next two shots going slightly wide on the lead. Not enough to stop her. But the shoulder was cost.

The attack broke the way coordinated attacks broke, all at once, on a signal that didn't come from anywhere Lark could see. The animals that were still moving pivoted and went back down the slope in the same paths they'd used to come up. Withdrawal across all three columns. The ones that were down or dead remained on the ridge.

Lark came down to confirmation altitude.

Nibbles was braced against a rock, Whiskerbrand still drawn, holding himself carefully. Nori rotated her left shoulder in a small deliberate circle, testing it, then picked up her crossbow.

Telia was still on her knees. She lifted her paws from the stone and pressed them flat against her thighs. The amber at her palms had gone out entirely. She sat for one breath. Then she got up.

They made camp in a cut in the ridge stone that broke the wind from the northeast, a natural recess, deep enough to hide the fire's light from below. Lark had flagged it on her afternoon circuits, contained, single approach, a clear sightline to the valley floor from the camp's rear. She had given up on good positions in corrupted land and settled for defensible ones.

The fire was small, contained to a ring of ridge stone that Telia had arranged without being asked. She arranged it, sat down at the fire's edge, and stayed there.

Hazel's ears were in the holding position, held neither forward nor back. She was watching Telia, not openly, her paws in her lap. She had picked a spot at the fire that put her nearest the warmth without showing she'd chosen it for that.

Nibbles was eating and watching the valley floor, his back to the rock wall and Whiskerbrand across his knees. He'd slept that way twice since Ridgemarrow and had worked out how to make it rest him. The sword was warm, low and steady, no blaze in it.

Dash had found his position against the far wall and had not moved from it. His gaze tracked the camp perimeter in slow regular intervals.

Gareth was writing. He had his maps and notes spread on the flat rock beside him, using the fire for light. The pen moved in the careful deliberate motion he used when he was setting something down for the record. His right hand had stopped its tapping rhythm about an hour before the camp was made; the count had finished. Whatever it had landed on, he had been carrying it since before they'd found the recess, and had kept it to himself.

He wrote for a long time. Added a line. Read it back. He set the pen down beside the page.

Acornimus had Gareth's prior notes and his own journal open, the pen moving in his neat sketching shorthand. He completed the record of what had already happened before committing the current day to anything permanent. He made one glance at Gareth's writing and returned to his own.

Leonardo was on the camp's outer edge, lance planted, visor up. He had taken the first watch on his own, the way he'd been taking positions since Ridgemarrow, quietly, before anyone could call it.

Bristlebaum was on the opposite side of the fire from Telia. His quills were still at partial elevation. He hadn't spoken a word since calling the halt.

The fire crackled. The valley below was dark. Nothing moved.

Gareth closed his notes. Opened them again. Closed them.

Lark had watched him run counts long enough to know when his certainty had landed but hadn't been spoken yet. Tonight was that. He had it. He was waiting for the second pass to come back with the same number before he committed to saying it aloud, the way he always waited, for two paths to land on the same answer. He would have that tomorrow.

Nori rotated her shoulder once in the firelight (the careful rotation, testing range) and let her arm settle at her side. Her crossbow stayed where it was. She had taken a blow that would have put most creatures on the ground, and now she was eating trail provisions at a fire in corrupted land with the economy she gave to everything.

Lark held altitude above the camp for a long moment, then banked north and began her circuit before settling for the night.

She told herself it was reconnaissance.

The night was cold, the ridge dark below her and the valley darker still. The thermal was absent; she had stopped expecting it on her third circuit of the day. She found her altitude on her own and held it.

The camp fire was the only light below. A small point in the recess, carefully contained.

She made the first circuit of the valley's western approach, the ground they would cover tomorrow, the creek crossing, the ridge's steeper descending section beyond it. She read what she could from the night, no movement on the valley floor near the ridge base, the corridors between the crystal formations still, the lake's surface pulsing in its slow steady rhythm. The crystal arm had moved again. She marked the change in angle.

She made the second circuit.

On the third she ran her sight lines over the territory they had not yet crossed, the middle and far sections of the ridge, the terrain that would matter on day two. She read what she could from altitude in the dark, which was less than in daylight, but she was a crow and her night-vision was good enough.

Nori's shoulder.

She had caught it at the moment of impact, the half-step back, the correction, the two shots that went slightly wide after. She had marked it as cost. The formation had been working. The operation was what mattered.

She came around on the fourth circuit.

The doctrine was what it was because the alternative was unworkable. A scout who formed attachments to her formation lost the distance that made the work useful. She had known this since before this company, had held to it across more operations than she had counted.

She gave herself another circuit.

The valley was the same. The corridors empty, the lake pulsing, the arm at its new angle. No threat to account for, nothing new to report. The camp was a cut of ridge stone with the fire still contained.

She had been adjusting her circuits around Nori's pace for the better part of a week. Not the formation's pace, but Nori's, because Nori's pace told her the most about the formation's condition. Nori was the marker.

She came around again.

She knew there was nothing left to confirm.

She banked west, picked up the wind off the northern ridge, and came around on a long descending arc toward camp.

She came back anyway.

Chapter Sixteen
The Second Wave

Nibbles had not slept well, and the valley had not pretended otherwise.

The last hour before dawn he lay on his bedroll trying to work out whether the ground was actually pressing upward against him or whether that was his body catching something it couldn't name. His whiskers had been moving all night, not the deliberate sweep Nori had taught him but the involuntary kind that happened when something kept arriving at the edge of what he could sense and never resolved into anything he could act on. By the time Bristlebaum said to rise, his face ached from it.

The air hadn't moved during the night. Two nights in the valley, and Nibbles had started to forget what moving air felt like.

Telia sat beside the cold fire pit with her paws pressed flat to the earth, eyes closed. She'd been doing that for nearly an hour before anyone else woke, listening in the way she listened when the ground needed talking to, neither sleeping nor praying. The amber light in her paws was thin this morning. Thinner than at the valley entrance. Thinner than yesterday.

Gareth was at his maps. He'd been there for most of the night; Nibbles had woken twice and found the fox crouched over parchment by the light of a candle stub, one claw tracing lines while his other paw tapped a slow rhythm against his thigh. Near dawn the rhythm had changed (the faster, deliberate one, the one that meant he'd arrived somewhere he didn't like) and Gareth had gone still a moment and then kept working.

Nori and Dash had their gear checked without speaking. Acornimus had his journal open and was writing before he'd eaten anything. Leonardo stood at the camp's eastern edge with his lance, watching the tree line. His limp was worse than yesterday. He kept his stance even on it. Hazel stood near the dying fire. She had not moved much. She would walk. She had been walking since the Caves. Lark was already gone, lifted before first light.

Bristlebaum handed Nibbles a piece of dried meat without comment. Nibbles ate it before Bristlebaum had to tell him to. The Guildmaster turned away without acknowledging it.

He shouldered Whiskerbrand. Steady warmth across his back, no alert hum yet, just present. The left shoulder pulled as it had since the bite. He fell into line.

The creek was thirty feet across, running low and brown, moving slower than water should. Even ten feet from the bank Nibbles could smell it, iron and something sweet underneath that sat wrong at the back of his throat. His whiskers swept toward the surface and pulled back. Corrupted water. The same family as the tar-black lake deeper in the valley, earlier in the spread, still water in structure, wrong in direction.

Telia went to the bank without being asked. She crouched at the water's edge, unlaced her boots, and pressed both paws flat against the mud and stone at the creek bed. Her eyes closed.

The amber light came up in her paws. Thinner than it had been at the valley entrance, more effortful than the steady gold from when she'd shored up the conduit below Ridgemarrow, a flame pulling against a headwind. She held it. The creek bed shifted. Stone moved against stone with a grinding Nibbles felt through his feet before he heard it, and sections of grey rock rose through the brown water in an uneven line, surfaces slick and tilted. The kind of bridge you took because the water was the alternative.

"Single file," Nori said. "Test each step before you commit."

They went across. Nibbles went second, behind Nori. The bridge shifted underfoot, resettling under each new load rather than failing, rock reading the weight. He kept his center low, paws spread, moving with the quick careful rhythm Nori had shown him, keep moving, let the forward motion carry the balance, don't stand still long enough for the stone to decide it was done. Nori was on the far bank before he reached the midpoint.

Dash came behind him without hesitation, light-footed across each shift. Then Leonardo, lance angled wide as a counterweight, his longer frame adjusting more than the others on the tilting surface. Hazel after him, deliberate and precise. Gareth. Acornimus, one paw on his journal by reflex. Bristlebaum last.

Telia came third from last. She had held at the bank while the others crossed, holding the bridge under the changing load.

Nibbles watched from the far side. Her left leg buckled. Whatever had been holding her up was gone. She caught herself on her staff, the wood flexing hard under the sudden load. Then her right leg went too.

Leonardo was two steps behind her. His hand shot out and caught her under the arm before she'd finished going down, immediate and ungraceful, no trained motion in it, and he held her upright and they covered the last ten feet to the bank together, his arm around her side. Neither of them spoke. He kept his arm where it was until she had her footing on solid ground. Then he took it back. He made nothing of it. Her eyes stayed on the ground ahead.

The bridge collapsed. The water took it quietly, each stone section settling back into the creek bed in sequence, the brown water closing over as the creek went back to thirty feet of wrong water. Stone on stone, then nothing.

Telia knelt at the far bank and pressed her paws to the earth. The amber light tried and didn't come. She held there a moment. Then she stood.

She laced her boots. She picked up her staff. She walked.

The eastern slope rose gradually from the creek bank, open ground scattered with corrupted scrub, the crystal formations smaller here than further into the valley, splinters pushing through grey-brown soil rather than the columns near the center. Two days inside the corruption and Nibbles had learned to read the stages, grey soil first, then the first crystal growths no bigger than a paw, then the second stage where bark-armored animals moved in coordinated circuits, then the fully claimed territory where nothing of what had been there before remained. The scrub on the slope leaned northeast, pulled the same direction as everything in the valley.

The ground read wrong underfoot. Soft wasn't the word. Corruption didn't make things soft, it redirected them. The soil had been told to care about something that wasn't soil. He'd been checking it since the creek bank. The ground had not had anything good to report since they entered.

His left shoulder was still pulling at every pivot. The void-touch had faded from the active burn of day one to a slower resistance, but it cost him a half-second at the start of any motion that crossed his body. He'd been compensating without thinking about it. On the bridge he'd used his right paw to test each step and his left to hold his sheath, which had meant his center of gravity was off for the whole crossing. Nori hadn't said anything. Either she hadn't seen it or she'd decided it wasn't the moment.

Gareth had his maps out before they were halfway up the slope. He walked and read at the same time, one claw tracing a notation while his other paw tapped a slow rhythm against his thigh. The working-through tempo. Nibbles had absorbed both rhythms over two days, the slow tap when the picture was still being built, and the faster, more deliberate one that meant the picture was finished and the news was bad. He'd heard the faster one near dawn.

"The attack at first light," Gareth said, without looking up from the parchment. "The interval between the western approach and the flanking units from the north. Twenty-eight seconds."

"Yesterday?" Nori asked.

"Forty-three. At the valley entrance, the day before, forty-one. Two days and the interval has tightened by thirteen seconds." His claw moved across the parchment. "That's not adaptation from yesterday's failed attacks."

His paw went flat on the map. "That's a ritual in active progress. When Grimthorn began the inversion ceremony for the sixth Wardstone, the stones he already controls started pulling harder on the corruption in sur-rounding territory. Everything being directed toward his will gets pulled more precisely. The animals here aren't learning. They're being directed with more force."

"How long," Bristlebaum said.

"Days." Gareth folded the main map. The faster rhythm returned against his thigh, steady. "If the rate of tightening holds, the sixth stone is days from full inversion. After that, everything in this region becomes what the valley's center already is."

The slope was a dozen yards from its crest. Nobody spoke for a moment.

"Then we move," Bristlebaum said.

"I have something else."

"Tell me while we move."

They moved. Gareth tucked the main map inside his vest and produced a second, smaller parchment, a column of entries, dates and unit designations, something he'd been compiling separately. His claw was at the top of it before the first map had fully disappeared. The slow working-through rhythm came back against his thigh.

Nibbles moved to his position in the forming line, watching. Gareth had named the main thing (the sixth Wardstone, the days) and was already inside something else. That second thing had been gathering in his paws since last night. Nibbles could see it in the way the fox's claw moved across the secondary parchment, unhurried, checking each entry twice before it moved to the next.

At the slope's crest, Lark dropped from the grey sky and landed on a dead branch forty yards ahead. She looked once at Bristlebaum, direct and hard, no settling in it, and lifted.

Bristlebaum said, "Formation."

The crest opened onto a long shelf of ground before the eastern tree line. Fifty yards across, the corrupted scrub thin and low here, fewer crystal formations, the ground more exposed. Past the tree line the corruption was deeper, bark-armored trunks visible even at distance, trunks leaning inward toward the valley's center.

Nori had the formation deployed before anyone had to ask. Her calls came low and certain. Dash to the right flank to cover the northern approach angle, Leonardo to the left where the tree line came in close, Nibbles at center-right with Bristlebaum, Gareth and Acornimus to center-left, Hazel and Telia behind the main line.

Nibbles moved to his position. His paw found Whiskerbrand's hilt through the sheath. Steady warmth, no hum yet, just present.

"Geometry's different from yesterday," Dash said from the right flank. He was crouched slightly, ears turned toward the eastern tree line, whiskers working. "Yesterday they came from three directions. These are coming from two."

"They're not trying to surround us," Nori said. She had the crossbow across her arm, bolt loaded, eyes on the northern tree line's edge. "Two parallel lines. They want to drive us toward the eastern edge."

"Or hold us on the shelf while something comes around behind," Dash said.

"We're not staying on the shelf."

Gareth was still working through the secondary parchment. He'd been talking as the formation deployed, not loudly, with the steady pace of someone following a chain of logic that kept giving way under his claw.

"—the unit's garrison assignment was Ridgemarrow, which puts them in the sixth Wardstone zone, which means any orders moving them out of that zone had to come through regional coordination, which means the authorization had to pass through Guild leadership at a level above field command, which means—"

"Gareth," Nori said, not loudly.

"—I'm almost there—"

The eastern tree line moved. The corrupted stillness they'd been watching gave way to actual motion, fast and coordinated, bark-armored shapes at the tree line's edge and more at the northern boundary, two parallel lines of approach, the interval between them tighter than anything they'd faced the day before. Twenty-eight seconds, the number Gareth had given them made real.

Nori said, "Here they come."

Gareth's claw was still on the parchment.

Whiskerbrand sharpened before Nibbles had finished catching the motion.

The warmth across his back went from steady to alert, vibration coming up through the sheath, urgency without direction, and his whiskers swept left before his eyes had turned, catching the air displacement from something large and fast, moving low through the gap between where he was standing and where Gareth was standing four feet to his left.

He'd drifted right during the deployment (the shoulder favoring the side that cost less) and Gareth had drifted forward from center-left while working through the parchment. The four feet between them was open.

He turned. His paw closed on the hilt.

His left shoulder caught at the pivot. The void-touch resistance cost him the rotation he needed. He drove through it, pulling the sword free, turning hard, but the shoulder had taken half a second he didn't have.

The animal that came through that half-second was a corrupted elk, bark-armored across the shoulders and neck, purple crystal fused into the ridge of its spine. It moved low and fast, angled under the height of any guard set for its natural profile, and Gareth heard it and turned.

The elk's shoulder caught him mid-turn. It hit him across the left side, ribs and arm together, and the force drove him sideways and down. He hit the ground on his left side. The secondary parchment went right. His pen went left. The sound the impact made was wrong.

The elk was still moving. Following through.

Nibbles drove himself between them. He drove Whiskerbrand into the gap where the bark ended at the elk's flank, under the armored shoulder. The blade caught and slid. The elk screamed in a sound with nothing elk in it and turned from Gareth toward the blade.

He gave it ground. Three steps back, resetting his center because the shoulder was pulling hard, and the elk pressed after him. He kept himself between it and where Gareth had fallen, led it along the gap, and when the elk lowered its head for a charge he dropped under the trajectory and came up on the left side with the sword at the unarmored neck.

The elk went down.

Two more from the northern approach (a corrupted boar and something smaller, faster) came in from his left. He moved to cover the gap before they could widen it. The shoulder was locked from the exertion now, not numb but fully present, costing him at every stroke that crossed his body. He paid it and kept moving.

The boar tested the gap twice, finding Nibbles there both times. On the third try Nori's bolt found its armored shoulder and the animal staggered. Nibbles stepped into the stagger and drove Whiskerbrand into the unarmored flank at the bolt's entry. The boar went sideways. He reset and held the gap.

Around him the second wave was fully arrived. Leonardo on the left flank, lance horizontal against a corrupted bear that was working the angles for the opening it needed, his limp worse than this morning but the lance steady and the ground-work sure. Dash at the right, a white blur finding gaps in armored shoulders. Bristlebaum's mace heavy and deliberate at center. Telia at the back, staff in paw, still standing.

"Left," Dash said.

Nibbles went left. A fast-moving shape came through the space he'd vacated and Bristlebaum's mace was already there, already completing its arc, and the impact dropped it.

The wave crested and broke. It broke hard, and it cost what it cost.

He sheathed Whiskerbrand. The alert in the blade settled back to warmth.

The fox was on his left side where he'd fallen, one paw still holding the secondary parchment, the other paw flat against the ground. His breathing was shallow and careful. Each breath deliberate, the left side of his chest held against motion, protecting the ribs. He was looking at Acornimus.

Acornimus moved without being directed. He was kneeling before Nibbles had finished turning away from the last animal, journal open in his right paw, left paw holding the cover back. The pen came out by touch (the pocket never changed, the pen never moved from it) and he held it over the open page. He looked at Gareth.

"The sixth Wardstone." Gareth's voice was level. "The rate of tightening confirms active inversion in progress. The timeline is days. Tell the Guildmaster."

"He heard you on the slope," Acornimus said.

"Then it's confirmed twice. Better." His eyes moved toward the secondary parchment. "Take that."

Acornimus picked it up and held it where Gareth could see it. Gareth looked at the entries without touching them, eyes moving across the page in the practiced way of someone going over work he'd already done.

"The third garrison unit," he said. He was reading from memory now; the parchment was confirmation, not source. "Assigned to Ridgemarrow. Sixth Wardstone zone. They weren't in position when the Herald's forces moved through the Whispering Hollow region. They'd been reassigned. Three weeks before the Hollow was taken."

Acornimus's pen touched the page.

"The reassignment came through Ironhold. Regional coordination. The order moved through channels above field command." He paused. One deliberate breath, the left side held still. "Somewhere inside the Guild. Or above it. Someone with reach across the institution. The unit was not supposed to be absent from that region during that window. Someone made sure it would be."

The pen moved in Acornimus's tight, precise hand. Each letter was set down carefully. He wrote the channel, the timeline, the conclusion. In the order it had been given. Nothing shortened. Gareth watched him write.

When the pen stopped, Gareth turned his head slightly toward the east. Past Acornimus and past the sky, toward the tree line, and past it, toward Thornwall somewhere in the haze. A small turning, nothing performed. He stayed looking that direction for a moment.

Then he said, "Good."

His breathing stayed careful after that, the left side held against motion, his right paw flat on the ground.

What Gareth had drawn sat in Nibbles' head with nowhere to put it. Someone inside the Guild, or somewhere above it in the Council's reach, had moved the third unit out of position three weeks before the Hollow was taken. Someone with that much authority, careful enough to leave no trail. He didn't know who.

Acornimus sat with his journal open on his knee. He read back through what he'd written, every word checked against what had been said. Then he read it through a second time.

He closed the journal. The clasp made a small sound. His paw rested on the cover.

Behind him the slope was quieter now. Bristlebaum's footsteps somewhere across the shelf. Nori at the tree line's edge. The second wave's noise gone. Somewhere above, Lark was on her circuit.

Then Acornimus opened the journal again. He found the last entry, the ink still drying on Gareth's name. He read it once more. At the line where the entry finished, he set the pen to the page below and wrote one sentence. He did not read it back.

He put the pen in its pocket and closed the journal.

The slope was clear. The last of the second wave was down, the ground strewn with corrupted dead. Dash was pulling his daggers free from the corrupted deer and checking each blade edge before he sheathed them. Leonardo stood at the western end of the shelf, weight on his lance, the limp worse than this morning. The arm that had caught Telia hung at his side, useable. Nori walked the tree line's edge in a tight perimeter, crossbow ready, making her passes visible to anything watching.

Telia sat in the dirt with her staff across her knees. The amber light was not coming, and she sat without trying to summon it. Her face was grey. She was breathing. Purple veined the inside of her forearms, faint but continuous, threading up from the wrists toward the elbows. Her eyes were on the tree line, not on her arms.

Nibbles stood in the middle of the shelf. He had walked three steps behind Gareth since the valley entrance, close enough to hear the slow tap of the fox's claw against his thigh when he was working something through. He had picked up the rhythm without meaning to.

The fox was on the ground twenty feet away. Acornimus was kneeling beside him, writing.

Three steps ahead of Nibbles on the line of march, there was nothing. His whiskers moved in the still air and found nothing there either. The trees on the eastern edge leaned northeast in the same coordinated pull, the same wrong direction they had been leaning all morning.

He went to where Gareth was.

Acornimus had stepped back three paces when Nibbles arrived. He stood with the journal in his paw, looking at the eastern tree line.

Nibbles sat down in the dirt beside Gareth. He hadn't planned to say anything. His body sat before the decision had been consciously made, and sitting turned out to be right. He set his paw on the ground beside Gareth's, not on top of it, just beside it.

Whiskerbrand was warm across his back. Just warmth, not the alert hum from before. The same warmth he'd felt on the worst night in the valley, on the watches where nothing moved, on the morning they'd crossed the tar-black lake's edge. The blade had been warm then too, and that had been the only thing offered, and it had been enough.

He had no words. He'd looked for them on the walk across the shelf and nothing came. No comfort, nothing adequate to Gareth being on the ground with his work finished. Whatever the right thing to say was, he wasn't carrying it. He sat. The sword was warm. Gareth was beside him.

Acornimus moved around them, giving them a perimeter. Nibbles heard his footsteps on the ground, the quiet sound of his pen moving, then footsteps again. He was writing it down, the site, the position, the aftermath. Nibbles was glad someone was doing it. His own body hadn't come here for that.

The secondary parchment was still in Gareth's right paw, the column of entries, unit designations and dates, the thing he had built through the night by candlelight. He'd had the full picture. He'd been mid-sentence when the elk found the gap.

The gap had been Nibbles' left shoulder. The void-touch resistance, the half-second it had cost him at the pivot. The shoulder was from the bite. The bite was from the valley. The valley had cost him a half-second, and the half-second had cost Gareth.

Gareth had worked it from animal attack data on a valley crossing with no access to anything except his maps and his paw tapping a rhythm on his thigh. He'd been right about the sixth Wardstone, and right about the institutional thread inside the Guild. Both, on a notebook page, while everyone else was watching the tree line.

He had told Nibbles once that the sword had chosen wrong if it needed someone without training. He hadn't said it unkindly. He'd said it the way he said all problems, as a thing to be worked. The question had followed Nibbles since, and was still following him now.

The sword's warmth did not shift. He stayed with the warmth and with the body beside him until he heard Bristlebaum crossing toward them.

He stood before the Guildmaster arrived.

"We need to move," Bristlebaum said.

"I know," Nibbles said.

Bristlebaum read what the body needed the way he read everything, quickly, without waste. The ground on the slope was uneven and the valley would not hold a burial. They needed a marker and they needed to move.

"We wrap him first," he said.

Nori had linen from the medical roll. She handed it to Nibbles without being asked. Nibbles took the secondary parchment from Gareth's right paw, carefully, with both paws, the way Gareth would have wanted it handled, and passed it to Acornimus, who tucked it inside his journal without opening it. Then Nibbles helped Nori with the wrapping. She guided the linen and he followed her lead, keeping it close but not tight, the same practical care she applied to wounds and crossbow strings. Neither of them spoke.

When they were done, the shape under the linen was still recognizably Gareth.

Dash and Leonardo carried him. Nibbles had turned toward Gareth to offer; Bristlebaum had looked at his left shoulder, and Dash had already moved to the other side. They went east together, toward where the tree line's edge thinned and the ground began to improve. Leonardo's limp was pronounced enough now that the lance was doing real work as a counterbalance, his arm adjusted the angle at each step, the same economy he'd been applying to every cost since the Hollow.

They found the place Telia had read before she'd stopped trying to read. At the tree line's eastern edge, past the last of the heavy crystal formations, was a patch of ground the corruption had thinned across. Not healthy ground, but ground that had held on.

Telia pressed both paws to it. The amber light came up thin and did not hold. She took her paws back and stood.

"This will hold," she said.

Leonardo set a stone from the tree line, flat and broad, at the head of the ground. He stood over it for a moment with his lance, upright. Then he stepped back.

Nibbles stood at the foot of the marker and looked at the stone and the ground it marked. Anything he could have said would have been inadequate. He stood there a moment longer and then he turned away.

Bristlebaum said, "We keep moving."

They moved. The eastern tree line opened onto the border country past the valley's deep corruption, terrain where the void's influence was thinner, the soil less fully claimed, the crystal formations small and scattered rather than column-dense. The trees did not lean here. The birds that had been silent in the valley's center had begun again, small and distant, at the edges of hearing.

They climbed the last rise to the eastern tree line's edge, and at the crest Thornwall was there.

Many miles out, the towers rose wrong against the sky, the wrong angles, the windows green-lit even in the afternoon, the iron-bound walls catching the light strangely. The land around the keep was barren, the soil pulled back from the stones. At this distance the scale wasn't fully readable. Up close it would be different.

Bristlebaum turned east and walked, and they followed.

Chapter Seventeen
The Night Before

NIBBLES HAD BEEN SITTING with his back to the camp fire looking at Thornwall Keep for most of an hour.

The towers were wrong against the sky. Two leaned inward at the tops, drawn toward something between them that couldn't be seen from outside. A third angled sharply east, leaning at a pitch no tower was meant to hold without falling. The windows along the upper story glowed green, cold and constant, lit before the sun went down and still lit now.

The land around the Keep was bare. Stripped rather than dead the way the valley had been dead, the soil pale and packed and giving nothing back to whatever tried to grow there.

The seventh Wardstone was below those towers. Seven conduit lines running through the ground beneath the Boroughs, all pointing to this convergence. The founding practitioners had built the Keep over the anchor point for their reasons. Grimthorn had chosen it for his. What he'd been doing with it in the thirty years since was why they were here.

The fire behind him was small. Light carried this close, and light drew attention. He could hear the others around it. A shift of weight. The small clink of someone setting a cup down. The steady draw of Nori sharpening a bolt-head. Lark was somewhere above.

Whiskerbrand sat warm against his back through the leather of the sheath.

He looked at them properly. He'd been avoiding the full count since they'd set camp.

His own left shoulder first. When he'd reached into his pack two hours ago, something had pulled under the blade, a sharp catch that hadn't been there before the valley. It was new. He'd know more about it by morning.

Leonardo was across the fire from him. The lance was wrong. Nibbles had watched him walk with it for six days and knew how he carried it (upright at the right shoulder, easy counterbalance) but tonight it was lower and braced differently, angled to take weight. The broken leg gave him a rhythm when he moved, step, plant the lance, step. The arm couldn't lift the lance properly; the lance was doing the work the arm couldn't. Nibbles had watched him lower himself to the fire using only the left arm and the lance together, breath held through the last part of the descent and released only when he was seated.

Telia's fur was mostly grey now. She'd been brown-grey when Nibbles met her in Ridgemarrow; almost none of the brown was left. The purple lines on her forearms were visible in the firelight when her sleeves fell back, two of them, threading up past the wrist toward the elbow. She'd been sitting in the same position for most of an hour, and Telia didn't usually sit still unless moving cost her too much.

The staff leaned against her at a careful angle. The crack running down its length hadn't grown. It would not take much more than it was already taking.

Nori sat without moving. Her shoulders were at the angle Nibbles had learned over two weeks. The managing angle. He didn't ask. She would have answered, and the answering would have cost her, and she needed what she had. Her crossbow was across her lap, where she'd had it since they'd set camp.

Willowbark sat at the edge of the fire's light, near Bristlebaum. She looked smaller than she had at the Hollow. Something in her had retreated and hadn't fully come back. Her ears were down but resting rather than distressed, and she was still attending to everything around her. Her eyes tracked each sound from the camp, sharp as they'd always been. The attending was costing her more than it used to.

Bristlebaum's quills were up. Partway and steady at that height, not the full extension of a fight. They had been at that level since the valley and had not come down. The spectacles sat straight on his face, which meant he'd put them on carefully and hadn't moved sharply enough since to dislodge them.

Dash was near Nori without quite being beside her. His ears were up and his whiskers were working through the dark. He'd been watching the perimeter since they'd set camp, the most useful thing he could do that wasn't Lark's job.

Acornimus had his journal closed in his lap, his paw resting on the cover. He hadn't opened it since sitting down.

The count was complete, and none of it was good.

Acornimus stood from his place by the fire. He tucked the journal under his arm, took three steps to where Bristlebaum was sitting, and said, "I need a word. Both of you." He glanced at Nibbles. "Somewhere quiet."

Nibbles got to his feet. His left shoulder caught when he pushed off the ground (the same sharp catch under the blade) and he moved through it.

They went to the edge of the camp light, far enough that the others wouldn't hear clearly, close enough to keep the fire in sight. Acornimus looked up at the dark above.

Lark dropped from somewhere overhead and landed on a dead branch at the edge of the light without sound. She tilted her head at a precise angle. "You could have asked."

"I am asking," Acornimus said. "Now."

He opened the journal and took a small travel lamp from his vest pocket. Guild issue, wick trimmed low. He held it over the page and waited until all three of them were attending.

"Gareth gave me his complete read of it before he died," Acornimus said. "I want to deliver it completely. Hold your questions until I'm finished."

No one spoke.

"The timeline." He looked at the page, then at Bristlebaum. "The corruption spread in the valley was consistent with the sixth Wardstone's inversion nearing completion. Not beginning. Gareth put the ritual sequence at roughly ten days running before we crossed. His conclusion was days remaining before the sixth stone reaches the same state as the other five. Not weeks."

"The Whispering Hollow." Acornimus turned the page. "Gareth confirmed the third garrison unit's presence in the Hollow before we arrived. The unit moved northwest roughly three weeks before we reached the Hollow. He obtained the coordination logs for that movement. The logs show the authorization, the date, and the scope of the reassignment. He had them in the field." He tapped the journal. "They're here."

The quills on Bristlebaum's back stayed where they had been since the valley.

"The movement was authorized," Acornimus said. "Authorized and signed, somewhere above field command, not unauthorized. The standing orders and the coordination logs match throughout. Gareth had the trail. He hadn't finished the cross-reference against the signature before—" He stopped. "The name behind the authorization isn't in the journal. The shape of it is."

Acornimus looked at the page. "Someone with reach inside the Guild," he said. "Or inside the Council. Someone with authority to move a garrison unit across Wardstone zones and the discretion to do it without leaving a question. Gareth had the channel. He didn't get to the name."

No one spoke. The travel lamp burned. Lark turned her head a quarter-turn and fixed one amber eye on the journal.

"The logs are in there," she said.

"Yes," Acornimus said.

She looked at Bristlebaum. Then she looked back at the dark above the camp.

Nibbles held the shape Acornimus had named and could not put it anywhere. Someone inside the institution. Someone with reach. He had no face for it. Looking at Bristlebaum, he could see that the Guildmaster did, more than one face, none of them spoken, none of them going to be spoken tonight.

Acornimus closed the journal. He set the lamp on the ground between them and sat back on his heels.

Nibbles looked at Bristlebaum. The Guildmaster sat very still, the spectacles still straight on his face.

Bristlebaum looked at the journal in Acornimus's lap, then past the fire, past the camp, at something that wasn't in the valley. His quills extended, every quill out and sharp and held there, all at once rather than in the quick spike of a fight.

No one spoke. Lark stayed on her branch. The travel lamp burned between them on the ground. From the camp came the sounds the camp made at night. Telia's low murmur when her legs needed adjusting. The shift of Nori's position. The lance settling against stone.

Nibbles held the shape in the coordination logs and could not resolve it. Someone inside the Guild. Someone above field command. That would have to wait.

Bristlebaum's eyes came back.

"The logs," he said. His command voice. The armor, intact. "Gareth confirmed them before he died."

"Yes," Acornimus said.

"Cross-referenced against the standing orders."

"Yes. Both sets matched throughout. The signature is in there. He did not get to the name." Acornimus paused. "He was thorough."

"He was always thorough," Bristlebaum said. He looked at the journal without reaching for it. "How many people know this."

"The four of us," Acornimus said. "As of tonight."

"It stays that way. Until we're through the Keep."

"Yes, Guildmaster."

Lark stayed on her branch, head tilted at a precise angle, watching Bristlebaum. She didn't ask another question. Neither did Acornimus.

Nibbles read what Bristlebaum was holding without needing to look at the quills. The journal sat on Acornimus's thigh, unreached for. The logs confirmed what Bristlebaum had already been carrying.

Bristlebaum looked at Nibbles. "Get some rest," he said, in the command voice.

His eyes had the same look Nibbles had seen once before, at the fire, when Willowbark had set her paw near Bristlebaum's and he had covered it briefly and pulled back.

"Guildmaster," Nibbles said.

Bristlebaum waited.

Whatever question had been forming in Nibbles' chest hadn't finished forming. He stood there, looked at the hedgehog, and said, "Nothing. I'll rest."

Bristlebaum nodded. He turned back toward the fire, the quills still out, every one of them.

Acornimus sat where they had left him at the edge of the camp light. The lamp was still lit. He listened to the camp settle back into what it was. Telia low and steady. The faint knock of the lance against stone. Nori not moving.

He uncapped the pen from his vest pocket and opened the journal.

The last entry was Gareth's. Two full pages and the top third of a third. Acornimus had written it as Gareth spoke, word for word. When Gareth stopped, Acornimus had read it back to him, and Gareth had said *that's right.* The account was accurate.

He read it once more from the beginning, slowly. He hadn't forgotten any of it, but he wanted his eye on it again before he did what he was about to do. He closed the journal.

Then he opened it again. He found the section on the coordination logs (the name, the signature, the authorization date) and below the final line of the entry he wrote one more line in his usual hand. Twelve words. He didn't pause before writing it, and he didn't read it back.

He underlined it, then closed the journal.

The lamp burned low. The Keep's green windows were visible at the camp's edge, cold and constant, unchanged since sunset.

He placed the journal inside his vest against his chest, where he kept it when sleeping somewhere uncertain, and left it there.

Nibbles walked back toward the fire and stopped before he reached his spot. Bristlebaum was standing a few paces short of the nearest bedroll, facing the camp but looking past it, eyes at the middle distance. He'd come back from the edge of the camp light and stopped here and stayed. One paw rested at the head of the mace at his belt, resting there rather than gripping, the way it had since Acornimus closed the journal.

"What do we do with it," Nibbles said. He'd meant to approach differently. The question arrived before the approach had finished.

Bristlebaum looked at him. "Nothing tonight."

Nibbles had expected that answer. He hadn't expected how much *tonight* was doing in the sentence.

"After the Keep," he said.

"After the Keep." Bristlebaum turned toward him fully. "The Council. The evidence complete, the logs, the standing orders, the prior documents bearing the same signature, all of it checked against each other before we say a word." He said the next sentence as something simply true. "Gareth had the full logs. He knew the documents well enough to trace the authorization all the way back and build the case from inside it. He's the one who should be presenting this." He paused. "He's not available to present it. That's one more reason it's not tonight."

Nibbles thought about Gareth in the field alone, finding the pattern in the corruption spread, building the timeline, working the coordination logs until the authorization was clear enough to follow to a name. Right about every piece of it, and not making it out of the valley. The case lived in Acornimus's journal now, underlined, waiting.

"You've been carrying the suspicion," Nibbles said. He wasn't certain enough about what he was naming to make it an accusation. But there was a difference between the held tension before Acornimus said the name and the held tension after it.

Bristlebaum looked at him for a moment. "Tonight is not the time."

"No," Nibbles said. "I know."

He stood there. The Keep's windows were steady in the dark. He thought about Gareth's voice giving way mid-sentence and what had been forming behind it. Someone inside the institution, with reach. No face for it yet, only the channel and the signature on a page Gareth hadn't finished reading.

"Get some rest," Bristlebaum said.

"Yes, Guildmaster," Nibbles said.

He walked back to his spot at the fire.

Later, when most of the camp had settled and the fire had burned to coals, Nori came and sat beside him.

She didn't speak first. She settled her crossbow across her knees, by habit, without looking, the way it had sat there for six years. The coals gave just enough light to see the Keep's green windows at the distance. Cold and constant, unchanged since sunset.

After a while, Nori asked, "What do you go back to?" The same question she'd asked before, in the same even voice.

"My mother's garden," Nibbles said. "There's an apple tree. Not a very good one. Most years it manages two apples, and they're small. My mother is very proud of it anyway." He could see the garden behind the house in Thimblewick, the apple tree at the far corner against the stone wall, the fountain at the center. "The fountain doesn't work very well anymore. It makes a sound like it can't quite decide whether to stop. I used to sit next to it when I was practicing the Guild forms. The sound helped me think."

He'd said all of this before. Not in those exact words, but close. The first time she'd asked, he'd said it without knowing what the saying would become. This time he knew. The apple tree was still the apple tree. The fountain still made the same sound. The place would be there.

Nori was listening. "The sound helps you think," she said.

"It's not the most heroic thing to miss," Nibbles said.

"It's real," Nori said. "That's what matters."

He looked at her. Her eyes were on the Keep. Her shoulders held the managing angle.

He thought about asking. She had asked him first, had been asking him since before the Hollow. He could turn the question around. She might answer, she might not. The Caves had found something in her. He'd been in those passages and he knew it. Whatever it was, it would cost her something to name, and she'd already spent enough getting back from the Caves on her own.

He didn't ask.

The coals shifted and sent a spray of sparks upward that died before they reached the height of any face. Somewhere above the camp, Lark was in the dark.

The garden came back to him. The fountain. The apple tree at the corner of the wall where the morning light came first.

Nori said, "You'll get back there." She said it the way she stated things she'd weighed and decided were true.

"I think so," Nibbles said.

She nodded. The small nod that registered something rather than answered it.

They sat there with the coals between them, and the apple tree where it had always been.

The fire had gone to coals.

Most of the camp was at rest. Leonardo lay with his lance beside him, parallel and within reach. Telia's breathing had the pattern of someone who could come back fast if needed. Willowbark was settled, ears down. Bristlebaum sat with his back against a rock, awake. Nori had returned to her spot, the crossbow still across her knees. Dash was at the perimeter.

The shape in the coordination logs sat in him without a place to go. The logs were in Acornimus's journal. The case would be built at a different time, with a Council to bring it to.

He thought of Hazel's voice at the Hollow fire. *I believed my own reasons.* Bristlebaum's paw covering hers briefly, and both of them pulling away.

Nori had asked the question again. He'd given the same answer. The garden. The fountain. The apple tree at the corner of the wall where the morning light came first.

Whiskerbrand was warm against his back. Just warm, the companion warmth he'd been carrying since the tent at the Cheese Festival.

He tilted his head back. The sky had gone fully dark and the stars were out in numbers, the way they came out when nothing was between you and the distance. He'd seen this sky before, from the roof of his mother's house in Thimblewick, late in summer when the weather went warm and clear at the same time and the fountain sound came from the garden below. He'd sat up there with the question of whether he'd fail the trial a third time turning over in his mind.

He was the same mouse he'd been on that roof. He'd failed a third time. Then the sword had woken. Then here he was at the edge of a valley looking at a keep that had been waiting for thirty years.

Thornwall Keep stood against the sky ahead of him. The wrong towers, the cold green windows. The seventh Wardstone underneath, and all seven conduit lines converging in the stone below.

Tomorrow they were going in there with what was left of this party to find whatever sat at the bottom of it and do what could be done.

Chapter Eighteen

The Ambush

THE PATH NARROWED BETWEEN two rises of broken rock before it reached the ridge, and Leonardo's eye went to the top of the right rise before his mind had finished deciding why. Twenty years of reading ground had its own way of pointing.

The party moved in a loose column. Lark was somewhere above the cloud ceiling, her circuit invisible from below. On the ground, Nibbles walked at the forward edge, the sword across his back dark in its sheath and still. Nori behind him and left, crossbow already unslung, her eyes moving between the rocks and the path ahead. Bristlebaum behind them both, the mace in his grip, quills not settled. Dash to the right, moving lean and close to the ground's irregularities, whiskers working, eyes flicking to each spot a body could be hidden before he'd finished his next step. Acornimus behind Dash with one paw free and one near the journal and both eyes on the ridge. Telia at the rear-right, the cracked staff finding each step carefully. Hazel beside her.

Leonardo held shield-center. His left arm ached. The Whispering Hollow engagement had cost him badly enough in the shoulder that the shield sat differently than it had for fifteen years, half an inch forward of where his training expected it, the forearm brace making up for what the joint no longer managed without effort. He had adjusted, and the adjustment was nearly invisible. Anyone who'd known him before the Hollow would still see it.

Forty yards to the ridge. The rock on either side too still. No birds, and not the silent-but-present absence of corrupted territory. The birds were elsewhere. He had learned the distinction in his second posting, when his sergeant had pointed at an empty rockface and said *hear that?* and he hadn't, and the sergeant had said, *That's the sound of trouble, boy. You'd better learn to listen for it.*

He looked at the right rise again. The high ground, the angle, the path channeled directly beneath it. It was where he would have set the ambush, if he'd been setting one.

"Close," he said.

The column tightened without discussion.

Lark's call came from above, two sharp notes, movement confirmed, and it arrived a half-beat before the first figure stepped out from between the boulders ahead.

Three of them came from between two boulders on the right rise, stepping into the path. Their armor was old and fouled with purple corruption along every seam. Their eyes burned the dim violet that everything the Herald had touched burned.

For a moment, as they cleared the boulders and straightened, Leonardo couldn't tell who they were. Corrupted figures moved wrong, the articulation off, the chest not lifting with breath.

Then the tallest one raised his head and looked directly at him.

Matthias.

Two years, three months, and sixteen days, and here he was.

He was barely more than a recruit when Misthaven happened, sixteen years old, already growing into his frame. The jaw. The slight crook at the bridge of the nose where a training blow had landed imperfectly in his second month with the unit. The brow that always furrowed when he was concentrating.

The violet burned behind the irises the way the corruption always burned. But the eyes were still his, the angle of the outer corners, the way the left tracked slightly faster than the right when he was paying attention to something.

The second figure was Thornberry. Shorter, broader, his stance already in his body, feet a little wide, weight balanced for a blow from either direction. He carried the same axe. The handle was worn smooth at the grip in the exact place his paw always found. Leonardo recognized it from thirty feet.

The third was Digby. Walking a little behind the other two, the way he always had. Digby watched before he committed, and that habit had saved Leonardo's arm twice at Misthaven.

All three advanced in step. Matthias had drilled coordinated advance until the footwork was reflexive, and the reflex was still in them.

The footfall was wrong. Left foot, a pause of half a heartbeat, then right foot. In a living soldier the weight shifted with momentum, one step flowing into the next. In these three the steps were separate, each motion finishing before the next began. The left arm completed its arc and stopped before the right arm started its own.

Matthias opened his mouth. The voice that came out was correct in pitch and cadence.

"Sir," Matthias said. "Sir, we need orders."

The voice he'd used a hundred times on the training field, the slight lift at the end that meant *waiting and ready.*

Two years, three months, and sixteen days since Misthaven. Leonardo was afraid. His arm had always moved to answer that voice, and it was moving now to answer it, in a way it should not have been.

The second construct, Thornberry, angled left without breaking the advance, the way Thornberry had always covered the weak side without being told. Digby came up the center behind Matthias.

Leonardo stood at the head of the column, his shield at half-extension, his arm still coming up. The gap to his right was widening.

"Shield line," Bristlebaum said, short and certain.

Leonardo was already trying.

Raise the shield.

His left arm had fifteen years of the same signal burned into it. Eyes find threat, arm comes up. The shield came up to intercept without thought. It came up slower than it should have. He felt the lag immediately, the way moving through cold water gives back a heartbeat less than you put in. The instruction reached the arm and the arm took longer with it than it had any right to.

"Pondsworth Credo," he started. "Dignity in the face of—"

Matthias covered the ground between them in two strides.

The stride was still wrong (set, step, set, step) but the pace was fine, the distance closed fast, and Leonardo's shield was still coming up and not yet where it needed to be when the construct's right arm swung.

The strike didn't reach Leonardo. Nibbles was two feet to his right, where he'd held since dawn, watching the ridge before any of them named it as wrong. The arm had slowed and the gap had opened, and the strike was aimed at the gap.

Leonardo pushed harder, trying to close the half-second between where the shield was and where it needed to be. The arm wouldn't give him the half-second.

Nibbles ducked, fast, practiced, already moving before the arc completed. The construct's blow caught his left shoulder, the bad one, and drove him left and hard into the rock face beside the path. He hit it, caught himself with one paw, and did not go down.

"Close left," Nori said.

Leonardo drove his shield forward into Matthias's follow-through and caught it. The impact traveled up through his compromised arm. The construct had its weight behind the blow and it hit hard, but Leonardo was braced and the iron rim turned the strike.

He pushed back. The construct stepped back (set, right foot retreating) and came forward again.

Thornberry was moving from the left, the footfall distinct, set, step, set, step. Behind Leonardo the sounds changed. Bristlebaum's mace ringing against Thornberry's axe, the impact flat and decisive; Dash's quick movement across loose stone; Nori's crossbow clicking.

He tried the credo again. Not for the others. For himself.

"Dignity in the face of doom. The lance is the line." His voice was reaching for the parade-ground voice and not finding it. "The line holds."

Matthias struck again, a short hooking blow aimed at the edge of the shield, trying to come around it. Leonardo tracked the angle and caught it. Barely. The iron rim took the impact. His hand went numb from the jarring up through the grip.

The eyes above the shield were still Matthias's. The trust in them was still right, the look they'd carried in fifty drills and two real engagements, the look that said *I know what we're doing and I'm ready.* Whatever direction Leonardo gave, Matthias had always been ready to follow. He was looking at Leonardo with that same look now.

Between Matthias and the next strike there was a half-second gap. Leonardo checked his position; he was three paces back from where he'd started. He had been retreating without meaning to. He planted his feet. His leg ached. He planted anyway.

Nibbles had recovered. The mouse was back up, the sword angled to catch rather than deliver, the bad shoulder staying low. He was holding a position that had been Leonardo's to hold.

Leonardo tried to step left to cover him and his leg reminded him it was wrong. The stride cost more than he expected. He planted the lance's butt against the rock for a half-second of stabilization and kept moving.

He tried the credo a third time. The lines came in his regular voice.

"Pondsworth Credo. Dignity in the face of doom. The lance is the line."

His arm was moving at two-thirds speed, and there was nothing he could do to make it move faster.

Nori put the first bolt into Thornberry's back left shoulder from eight feet.

It didn't stop the construct, but the drag of it pulled the next swing off-line. The arc came in four inches wider than it should have, and Bristlebaum shifted his weight in time to catch the blow with the mace rather than his arm.

Nori put the second bolt into the back of Thornberry's right knee, where the armor had a gap. The construct's right leg buckled on the next step, caught itself, and kept going, but the set-step rhythm broke. The next swing came wide.

Bristlebaum caught it anyway, quills fully out and steady. Nori was already reloading.

Dash appeared from behind the right boulder where he'd apparently been for the last minute, moving low and close to the rock face. He went for Digby. The third construct had been advancing steadily up the center toward Hazel.

He came in behind Digby's right and put both daggers into the back of the construct's right knee and right ankle at once.

Digby went down hard, both legs failed at once. The arms kept moving and the construct tried to push itself up, but neither arm could lift the body without the legs.

Dash stepped back, checked the construct, and moved to cover Hazel's left.

"Right side," Acornimus said. "Matthias is rotating."

The construct had fixed on Nibbles and was beginning a pivot that would take it off the direct line with Leonardo and put it on a diagonal toward the rear of the group. Leonardo stepped into the pivot's path.

His arm came up at two-thirds speed. The shield caught the construct's leading shoulder and turned the rotation forty-five degrees off its line. The impact traveled up through the compromised arm and his grip nearly failed. He locked the elbow against it.

The shield kept arriving late and going up again anyway. Each catch took the cost in the shoulder; the shoulder paid it and gave the arm back.

Nibbles covered his right. The bad shoulder was limiting the elevation of that arm, so the mouse was working low, the sword angled up from below, catching strikes before they fully extended. Each catch cost him too, but the catches were landing.

Nori put a third bolt into the back of Matthias's right elbow on the upswing. The arm short-armed the next strike, and the left hand arrived at Nibbles' guard instead of past it. Nibbles turned the blow, stepped inside, and brought the sword hilt up hard against the construct's chin.

Nibbles' left shoulder caught on the extension. He reset.

Telia was at the rear with her cracked staff between herself and Digby's prone form. The construct was pulling itself forward on its arms; the legs weren't working but the arms were strong enough to drag it if it found the right angle. She kept the staff between them, bringing the heel of it down on the reaching arm when it got close. The wood creaked under each impact but did not split.

Leonardo caught Matthias's next blow and felt the oak flex under it. The arm was past its immediate tolerance now, drawing on something that wasn't going to last much longer. He kept it up.

To his right, Nori's fourth bolt crossed the fifteen feet to Matthias's left knee. The construct's next step came half an inch short of where it needed to land. The advance stopped while the workings reset. Half an inch had bought them time, and Leonardo took it.

He had been at two-thirds speed for five minutes, and the arm was not correcting. He had been counting exchanges. The arm was not correcting. He accepted it the way he accepted any wound mid-engagement. See it, plan inside it, keep moving.

For two years, three months, and sixteen days, he had run the scenario. The garrison gave him plenty of quiet for it. He had played the moment out carefully, what he would do when the voices came back, how the credo would hold, what he'd learned at Misthaven that he hadn't understood while he was in it. He had been thorough about it. The credo was working at roughly the same rate as his arm.

Matthias was still looking at him.

He had thought, at various points in the garrison, that the hardest thing would be the surprise, seeing the faces without warning. There was no surprise. Somewhere below reasoning he had always known the Herald would use this, and the arm, on seeing the face, had slowed.

He caught the next strike.

Matthias, Thornberry, Digby. He had been carrying the three names forward from Misthaven, through the garrison, the corrupted valley, the Whispering Caves, the approach to Thornwall. They were standing in front of him now, the corruption burning in their eyes.

He thought about the unit name. Oakpaw. He'd given it to them, or they'd given it to themselves (the story had grown too many different shapes) after the crossing in the third month, where they'd held for six hours against twice their number until the relief column arrived. Most of them had been bleeding by the end, and the line had not given anywhere.

Matthias had taken a strike to the left arm in the third hour and kept fighting with the right, and Leonardo had not told him to fall back, because falling back would have widened the line past what the remaining unit could hold. He had made that call in the moment, and he had carried it forward without flinching since. Matthias had never asked him to account for it; neither had the others.

Afterward, Thornberry had appeared one morning with the shield covers laid out and the name painted on each of them in white, without asking permission or explaining what he'd done. Digby had looked at it and said *that's a tree, not an animal, and we're supposed to be a unit, not a tree* and Thornberry had said *trees don't run* and that had been the end of the discussion. The name had been on the shield cover Leonardo was still carrying when they went into Misthaven.

He caught the next strike.

He thought, *these three would not want to be here.* The thought was simple and clear, and he had been moving around it for five minutes without letting himself sit in it.

He looked at Matthias's face. Everything in it was Matthias except the footfall, set, step, set, step, each motion separate.

He could hear Nibbles to his right, the breath coming shorter, the footwork adjusting for the bad shoulder. Nori's crossbow, the reloads coming faster than she had reserves for. Telia's staff creaking at the rear.

The living were in the gap because his arm was at two-thirds. His arm was at two-thirds because the dead were looking at him.

The lance was in his right hand. It had been there the whole engagement, the butt against the ground, the shaft angled back. He closed his right hand around it properly, the grip he'd had ten thousand times, the weight and angle familiar as anything he owned.

He looked at Matthias. *Oakpaw held so the living could run,* he thought. *Not so the dead could walk.*

He raised the lance, and his arm raised it at full speed.

The construct's forelimb came in low and committed, the strike that had measured the range and decided. Matthias had thrown that strike before. Leonardo had watched him train it until the angle was automatic.

He brought the shield across. The arm gave him two-thirds speed.

The iron rim caught the strike, the oak took the impact, and everything behind it flexed, the straps, the forearm brace, the compromised shoulder. Leonardo locked the elbow and pushed back.

Matthias's forelimb came out of the follow-through and reset. Came in again, the same angle, more force behind it, because the construct had measured the resistance and adjusted.

Leonardo caught it.

The oak spoke on this one, a deeper sound than a crack, old dense wood giving up something it had been saving. The grip carried the warning to his hand before the sound reached his ear.

The third strike came while the shield was still moving across.

The impact drove through the brace and into the shoulder, and the shoulder, having no more to give, gave way. The arm continued in the direction it was already going. The shield didn't stop. The whole assembly (oak, leather, iron rim, brace, hand) swung in an arc, caught on the construct's follow-through, and came apart.

The sound was not the clean crack of reinforced oak breaking. It was the compound sound of everything attached to the wood letting go at once, straps cutting through leather, the brace tearing loose from the grip, the iron rim separating from the oak as the binding gave.

The pieces went across the path. Two sections of oak, the leather facing torn loose, the iron rim rolling and ringing against the stone before it stopped.

Leonardo's left arm swung free.

There was nothing to brace against. His forearm, which had been angled against the brace for the last fifteen years whenever he was in a formation, found air. The hand (which had been gripping the handle, which was also now separate and somewhere on the path) opened. He saw the blisters across his palm where the iron rim had broken the skin in the last exchange.

His knees found the ground. The braced weight in his legs released at the same moment the shield did, and the legs released with it. The ground came up against him, hard and cold.

He was on both knees with his left arm at his side and the lance still in his right hand.

He had carried the shield into every engagement since his second posting. He had carried it into Misthaven. He had carried it out of Misthaven, dented, the leather facing torn, the iron rim bent at the lower-left corner from a blow that had gotten under it during the third hour. He had had the rim repaired and the leather replaced, and he had not replaced the shield itself. He had carried it everywhere since.

He had thought he was carrying Misthaven, and the shield had been carrying it for him.

The construct was still advancing. Leonardo read it from the ground, Matthias's feet, the set-step-set, the right foot coming forward. The shield breaking had registered with no one but Leonardo. His right hand had the lance.

He shifted his weight and pushed to get upright. His left knee found the stone and pushed. His right leg took the load and reported, with no ambiguity, that it was no longer the leg it had been three minutes ago.

He had felt this before. The pain was there but not the main signal. The main signal was that the bone had moved somewhere it should not move and the ligaments around it were no longer doing the silent work they did when the joint was sound.

He was upright. The leg was holding, but the way a cracked hinge holds, working until weight tested it directly. He kept his weight off it.

Matthias was three feet away. Leonardo looked at the construct's center. The armor seams were all fouled with corruption. The chest did not move. The face was still Matthias's, the violet behind the eyes, the trust in them unchanged.

He planted the lance.

The angle his right leg was allowing was lower than standard, the butt against the stone, the shaft at sixty degrees from vertical instead of seventy-five. He took the angle the leg gave him.

He drove with his right arm.

The lance went in below the construct's sternum, at the seam between two plates. The resistance was something other than flesh, the resistance of the corruption itself, the held-together feel of something that wasn't held together by living tissue.

He kept driving.

His lower center had bought him the angle. The construct, set for an opponent standing square, had not accounted for the line coming from below. The forelimb came down and caught him on the left shoulder (the arm with nothing to brace) and the impact drove him down a few inches.

He drove the lance harder.

The corruption dispersed from the point of entry outward, the purple-black coming apart, the held-together feel going out of it. The articulation stopped before the construct fell. No dramatic collapse, only a stop, the limbs going slack, the forelimb lifting off Leonardo's shoulder.

Matthias fell forward.

Leonardo held the lance, took the weight of the fall, and kept himself on his feet through it. The right leg paid for it.

He pulled the lance free.

The second construct, Thornberry, had Nori's fourth bolt in the right knee and Bristlebaum between it and the rest of the formation, the mace working the construct's joints the way you worked an opponent who didn't feel the blow but still had to move after it. The bolt had degraded the knee. The mace had been working it down further. When the first construct fell, something passed out of the second one too. Leonardo couldn't have said how, only that the second construct's footfall changed and the set-step rhythm broke.

Bristlebaum hit the knee again. On the third impact, the leg buckled and didn't reset. The construct went down.

Digby had been on the ground since Dash's daggers, and the arms had been slowing for the last two minutes as Telia kept the cracked staff between herself and its reach. When the others fell, whatever ran the third went out with them, and the reaching stopped.

The path was quiet except for breathing.

Leonardo stood with the lance in his right hand. He put the lance's butt against the stone and adjusted his stance and found the point where the right leg could hold without the joint compressing in the direction it had started compressing.

He looked at Matthias. The face had gone. The corruption had taken the shape with it, the amber and violet both, the construct's coherence simply absent. What was on the path did not look like Matthias, which he was glad for.

"Anyone down," he said. It came out the way he wanted it to, taking inventory, not asking.

"Nibbles' shoulder," Nori said. "He's up."

"Staff is done," Telia said. The cracked staff was in two pieces. She held both pieces. "I'm up."

The others marked themselves in turn. All accounted for. Lark was still above.

He turned toward Thornwall.

Leonardo looked at the ridge.

The figure was there, and had been there for the duration. Standing at the crest between two outcroppings, the low morning light behind it, the outline massive and still. Leonardo's attention had been on the ground during the engagement, where it needed to be, and the figure had stood unbothered through every moment of it.

The Herald was a wolverine, massive, broad-shouldered, the frame built low and wide. He stood at the crest with no weapon drawn.

The purple-black ran through his fur all the way down, fully integrated. His armor had fused to him. The crystal growths at the shoulders and spine caught the morning light dull and dead.

His left hand was at his side, empty.

Leonardo had no way to read the face at this distance. He had only the stance and the stillness and the empty hand.

Lark's call came from above. One note, held, the call she used when she had something to say that wouldn't fit in flight, different from the two sharp notes she'd given before the constructs emerged. She landed on the rock face above them.

"He watched it," she said. "All of it. He was there when the arm slowed."

"What did he do when we drove the lance," Bristlebaum said.

Lark's head tilted. Her amber eyes fixed on the ridge.

"His face changed," she said. "Not much." She was working out how to name the right thing. "He looked at it the way someone looks at a choice they made a long time ago, when they see the choice going differently."

The figure on the ridge was still there, still unmoving.

"He didn't try to stop it," Nibbles said.

"No," Lark said. "He just watched."

Then the void-tear opened.

It came from behind the Herald, a line in the air, the edges pulling apart from a center point and widening. What showed inside was not dark. It was colorless in the way the corrupted valley had been soundless, something there holding the place that color was supposed to occupy.

The Herald stepped back into it. He did not hurry. His left hand was still at his side, still empty, when the tear closed behind him.

The ridge was bare rock again.

Lark spread her wings, caught the updraft, and went back up without being told. Her circuit of the ridgeline was visible for a moment before the cloud ceiling took her.

Leonardo looked at the empty rock. He was still holding his weight on the lance, the same way he had through the engagement.

He had expected something else, a speech, a second wave, some sign that the outcome had landed. None of it had come.

"He's been here before," Hazel said. Her voice was quiet and certain. She was looking at the ridge too. "On the other side of that choice."

Leonardo turned toward the Keep.

The gates were visible from the approach.

Thornwall Keep rose against the sky in the wrong way it had risen against it from a day's march out, towers at angles no tower should hold, the green glow in the windows the color of something that had been alive once and gone wrong. The iron-bound gates faced them across two hundred yards of barren ground, the soil cracked and pulled back, the air above the approach carrying the faint iron-and-rot Leonardo had learned to expect near any place the Herald had held for years.

He was walking. The right leg was bad and getting more vocal about it with each step, but it was moving.

The lance was making up for it. He had adjusted the angle, a walking angle rather than the fighting one, the butt-strike landing a foot further back from his natural stride. The rhythm was wrong, and he would have to learn the right one over the coming days.

"You'll want weight on the outer edge," Nori said. She was walking beside him, three feet to his left. She had been there since they moved off the ambush site. "Keeps the joint from loading on the compromised side."

He tried it. The leg complained at a different pitch.

"That's worse," he said.

"Give it ten steps," she said.

He gave it ten steps. The leg was still complaining at twelve, but at a slightly quieter pitch.

"Hm," he said.

She didn't comment. Nibbles came up on his right, the bad shoulder held close, the arm not swinging at its full arc. The sword sat differently in the sheath when the shoulder was compromised. Leonardo had seen this before in others, and didn't remark on it.

"Did you know he was watching?" Nibbles asked. He was asking about the ridge.

"I knew someone was on it," Leonardo said. "I didn't see him until after."

"Lark did," Nibbles said.

"Yes," Leonardo said. "That's what she's for."

"Pondsworth," Bristlebaum said. The hedgehog was behind him and to the left. He had not spoken since the ambush site.

"Sir," Leonardo said.

"You're limping."

"Yes, sir."

"You went through all that just to limp at the finish."

"The lance makes up the difference," Leonardo said. "I'm told."

The quills settled fractionally, which was the most they did anymore.

His boots found purchase on the cracked soil, and the lance found it after them. He moved through it.

The party moved without a formal formation, adapted rather than ragged, the shape of creatures who had been in each other's company long enough that the spacing was natural. Nori on his left, Nibbles on his right, the others in their places behind.

Lark called once from above, one note, the all-clear, her circuit completed.

Leonardo walked toward the gates.

Chapter Nineteen
The Guardians

The towers of Thornwall Keep were wrong against the sky in a way Nibbles' eyes had trouble holding. The stone wasn't crumbling (too precisely cut for that) but the towers angled at points where angles weren't meant to be, the lines departing from vertical in ways the builders couldn't have intended and the foundation shouldn't have permitted. Green light bled from windows that should have been dark. Wind moved along the battlements in a continuous low sound, like breath over a broken bottle.

His shoulder ached where the ambush had caught him. Flag-twelve, Bristlebaum had called it in the count they'd done while Leonardo's leg was being set, *carry it carefully, don't pretend.* Nibbles had been adjusting his grip since the valley, keeping Whiskerbrand's weight off the bruised joint, using the carry angle Nori had shown him on the second day of the march. She'd looked at how he was holding the sword and demonstrated with her own crossbow without saying a word. He still used the angle.

He'd been thinking about Gareth since they left the valley. The grief sat where he was keeping it, accurate, and bringing it up properly would mean stopping, and they couldn't stop. Alongside it sat Acornimus's voice the night after, naming someone inside the Guild, somewhere above field command, with the reach to move a garrison unit out of position and the discretion to do it clean. No name yet. Just the channel.

Whiskerbrand shifted. The alert hum came up through the hilt into his palm, the steady low cycle he'd learned to recognize. His whiskers went still, and his paw was on the hilt before he'd thought about reaching for it. He knew this hum. He'd felt it in the Underways below Nettleflint's cellar, when Telia had pressed her paws flat and the carved conduit lines had lit in the bedrock. The lines ran between the Wardstone anchors and the Crystal Sanctum, and all seven of them came together below the Keep.

He was walking faster than the grade required. He only caught it when Dash dropped half a step behind.

"Still alive back here," Dash said.

Nibbles shortened his stride. "Sorry."

Behind them, Leonardo's lance met stone in the rhythm that had changed since the ambush, making up for the broken leg rather than simply accompanying motion. Telia walked alongside him, her breath running slower than the climb accounted for. The soil around the Keep walls was bare, drawn back from the stone in a wide ring, the earth refusing to grow against the foundation. The cold coming off the battlements was wrong for the season.

Whiskerbrand kept humming.

They stopped at the gates.

The runes in the iron bars were moving deliberately, each line shifting in relation to the others, the pattern never settling. Nibbles looked long enough to confirm it and turned his eyes away.

"We knock?" he asked.

"The sword opens them," Bristlebaum said. His quills were at half-extension.

Nibbles stepped forward. He didn't draw Whiskerbrand. His paw had been on the hilt since the approach. The hum changed pitch as he got close to the gate, cleaner, rising from its sustained vibration into something closer to a single note.

The gates opened inward, without grinding or protest from the iron. They had only been waiting.

Nibbles stepped through. The floor inside held amber rune-channels, thin lines carved into the stone and filled with old light, running from some point deeper in the hall outward in all directions. The light was warm and faint, and it had been here a long time.

He looked at his shadow. The light came from below rather than overhead, and the shadow it cast ahead of him was wrong. His ears were right, his tail, the overall scale. But through the shoulders the shadow was broader than he was, heavier through the chest, longer in the arms. A creature significantly larger than a mouse who was small even by mouse standards. He had seen the silhouette before, in old illustrations. A badger's stance, low and wide. The shadow was not him, and the floor was showing him something else.

He stepped aside to let the others through. His shadow held the badger's shape while he waited.

The hall above was built for something grander than their party. Vaulted ceiling, arch following arch until they were lost in shadow at the far end. Old banners hung from iron chains, the fabric faded past recognition, pale suggestions of patterns that might have been campaign heraldry from companies who had once come this far. High near the ceiling, pale blue orbs drifted in slow arcs, edging closer and pulling back. They gave off little useful light, but they showed how big the hall was.

Bristlebaum came through. His quills shifted down by one fraction. Nori entered next, eyes moving to the exits and the upper gallery before they came to rest on anything closer. Acornimus had his journal in his paw, still closed, the journal waiting until he'd seen what he was going to see.

Telia crossed, her breath still running slow. Hazel came last. She walked steadily, but her ears were sitting low, neither forward nor attending. The Whispering Caves were still in her, and the ears showed it.

The gates closed behind them.

They walked deeper, and the floor woke.

Amber light rose under their feet, surfacing through the flagstones and taking shape as it rose. It was a tree. Roots ran from a center point deeper in the hall outward in all directions, each root branching and branching again until the pattern covered the full width of the floor. Branches rose into the carved columns lining the walls and climbed toward the vault above. The pattern lit in sequence, starting at the roots and rising through the trunk and out along the branches into the shadow overhead. It took perhaps thirty seconds. When it finished, the hall was warmer, the amber replacing the pale blue of the orbs with something more particular.

Nibbles looked at where the amber was brightest. The light wasn't even. Near the roots' convergence and along several branches midway through the hall, the amber was deeper and the stone beneath visibly smoother, worn, though not from foot traffic. The rune-channels in those sections had pressed their light through the same carved lines so many times that the stone had ground itself fractionally deeper, the way a wheel wears a groove in a road over years of carrying the same load.

"Telia," Acornimus said.

Telia had stopped walking. Her paws were flat on the floor, eyes closed. She opened her eyes.

"These aren't incidental," she said. "This is the convergence map. All seven Wardstone conduits running to this point. The Keep was built above the seventh anchor as part of the same system, not added afterward. By the same hands or the same tradition that built the Wardstones."

Bristlebaum's quills rose to full extension and came back down slowly.

"The seventh anchor's housing," Hazel said. She wasn't asking.

"Foundation stone and Keep are the same thing," Telia said. She pressed her palm flat to the floor. The amber under her paw brightened. "The corruption hasn't taken the structure because the stone knows what it is. It hasn't stopped being it."

Nibbles looked at the worn sections. The places where the amber ran deepest, where the same channels had lit ten thousand times. The Keep was still fighting, with the seventh Wardstone below it, and so was Grimthorn.

"The green in the columns," Nori said. She was looking at the carved stone where thin threads of a different light ran through the amber veins, threading along them without driving them out. The amber was still there, the green was still there, and neither had won.

"The Keep is fighting it," Telia said. "It hasn't lost yet."

Nibbles followed the amber deeper.

The mist came from between the columns. It moved with intent, not the drift of natural fog. Everything in this hall had been deliberate so far, and this was no different. It pooled at the column bases and rose into forms, soldiers, by the suggested armor, faces present if not detailed. Each one stood and looked at a specific person.

Nibbles found his. It was his size. He'd expected a figure that matched the hall's scale, since the hall was built for armies. The thing waiting a few paces ahead of him had instead been sized to him specifically, small, slight, no weapon in its paws. Its armor was clean, untouched by the green threading through the Keep's own stone.

He looked around. Bristlebaum's guardian was holding a mace. The proportions matched the one at Bristlebaum's belt exactly, same length, same iron-bound handle, same heft. The guardian held it forward in both paws, not as a threat but as a thing being returned to its owner. Bristlebaum stood looking at it, quills at full extension, and hadn't moved.

Leonardo's guardian was not a soldier. Three shapes stood at the edge of the mist near where the frog knight had stopped, unarmed and unarmored, their faces turned toward him. Leonardo had gone quiet. His lance had stopped its rhythm against the floor.

Nibbles watched Nori look at hers. Whatever she was meeting, she met it directly and didn't look away.

Acornimus's guardian held a journal, larger than his, spine cracked from heavy use, held open to a particular page. Acornimus had gone very still in the way he went still when the reading demanded everything.

Telia's guardian waited a few paces from her, head slightly inclined as if asking something.

Hazel's guardian took one step toward her, then stopped. Something passed across its face, recognition, then judgment. The guardian lowered its head briefly to her and stepped aside.

Hazel walked past it without slowing.

Dash had no guardian. Nibbles looked across the hall and found him at the far edge, no figure in front of him, no mist rising at the nearby column bases. The Keep had simply let him through, and he was already reading the walls, eyes tracing the joins between stone blocks, looking for the seams the architects had hidden.

Nibbles turned back to his own.

The amber rose from the floor around his feet, concentrated and local, rising from the rune-channels directly below him. He felt the warmth in his pads before he saw the light. Whiskerbrand's hum deepened, the way it did when the sword recognized where it was.

The mist soldier hadn't moved.

The amber climbed past his ankles. The floor was looking at him.

The first failure rose in the amber, and he knew it before the image finished forming. The cheese cart, rolling down the market square at the Cheese Festival, picking up speed where someone had thought the brake would hold. He'd run toward it without thinking. He'd tripped on his own feet, gone down, and watched from the cobblestones as the cart collected three decorative banners, a pyramid of sample wheels, and the Guild tent's left support pole before it stopped against the fountain base.

Bristlebaum had looked at him afterward with a face Nibbles had spent weeks turning over.

The amber held the image without verdict. *This happened. This is part of you.*

The second failure came alongside the first. The training yard, third morning. He'd put the vest on backward and worn it backward through the warm-up drills, through the first half of the first sword exercise, until Nori had said carefully that some vests were reversible but this one wasn't. He'd apologized and fixed it, and the heat had stayed in his ears for the rest of the morning. A small thing. But Nibbles kept a list of evidence that the sword had made a mistake in choosing him, and the backward vest was on it.

The amber held that too.

Then the third came. The cellar at Nettleflint's farm. The cold rising from the crack in the foundation stone, the blue-purple glow of corruption at the base of the wall. He'd gone down because he'd said he would and because the crack needed cleansing and because no one else was positioned to do it. But before his paw found the first step, his feet had moved toward the entrance, half a step, not exactly away, but not toward the stairs either. He'd caught them, turned them around, and gone down and done what needed doing.

But the feet had moved first.

The amber held all three failures in the same light, without distinction between them. The mist soldier was still.

His tail had curled tight against his leg.

He had been performing. Not just in this moment, but for months.

Performing at being the right choice. At being the creature the sword had meant to find. At being the version of himself who ran toward things instead of the version who ran toward things and tripped doing it. He had been building a self that was the correct answer to the question the sword had asked when it woke in his paws, making sure the running was what other people saw, keeping the falling somewhere private.

He pressed his paw flat to the floor beside him. The amber under his palm was warm and did not answer.

The cheese cart. The backward vest. The feet that had moved before he turned them back. Underneath those, also true. He was still in this hall. He had crossed the valley. He had got here. He had done all of that by running toward things, even when he fell, even when his feet moved the wrong direction first.

The amber held all of it as one creature.

Nibbles stopped performing.

The amber didn't ask what he was trying to be, only what he was, and it had already found that.

Nibbles looked up from the floor when his amber faded. His paw was still flat to the stone, the warmth still under it. He lifted it, found his feet, and looked for Nori.

She was eight or ten paces away, in the amber of the floor's center. The guardian before her was her height, her build, with the same practical set of the shoulders. The face wasn't hers and it wasn't quite a mirror. But the posture was a thing she recognized.

The guardian was asking by standing there. By not moving. By having arrived at a piece of ground Nori had been moving past for years.

Nori's crossbow was still on her back. Her paws were at her sides. She was watching the guardian with the attention she brought to exits and high ground, reading it before she answered. Then she stopped reading and went still.

She said something. He couldn't hear the words at this distance. Her voice was low and even.

The guardian didn't answer. Nori's head dropped. Whatever she'd been carrying alongside the crossbow and the axes (six years of being the one who didn't put it down) she was putting down now, because the guardian wasn't going to let her keep it past this hall.

Her eyes came back up. Something in her face had changed. He couldn't name what it was from across the hall, but he knew her face by now, and what had been in it since the Hollow if not before was no longer in it the same way.

She answered it. The guardian did not ask again.

Nibbles saw Dash before Nori turned around.

He was across the hall, almost to the far wall. He hadn't moved toward her during any of it. His paws were at his sides, daggers untouched. He was watching Nori with the steady attention he gave things he'd decided to stay with.

Nori turned. She saw him looking. She stayed where she was for one breath, then walked toward him.

Nibbles looked away.

The guardian held the mace in both paws, extended, the offer of something being returned. Bristlebaum stood two paces back. His quills were at full extension. They'd been at full extension since the guardian rose, which was the longest Nibbles had ever seen them stay that way. Usually they fell fractionally when Bristlebaum reassembled himself. They hadn't.

The mace was his, same length, same iron-bound head, same handle worn smooth from thirty years. Or it was the guardian's mace, made to look identical. Either way, the guardian was standing the way a soldier stands when he's been holding a post and the person it belongs to has arrived.

Nibbles watched Bristlebaum look at it. He'd seen Bristlebaum at the fire, the night Willowbark had told them the Grimthorn account. He'd heard *I gave up* spoken into the dark when Bristlebaum thought no one was listening. Whiskerbrand had been in the chest at the time, Bristlebaum had said. *Dead as stone in my grip.*

The guardian didn't speak. Bristlebaum's spectacles slipped. He didn't push them back up. His paw moved toward the mace and stopped before it reached.

Nibbles kept still.

Bristlebaum took the mace.

The guardian dissolved. The mist that had composed it came apart column by column and was gone. Bristlebaum was left holding two maces (his own and the guardian's) the second one losing its solidity as he held it, fading through his paw and out. He stood in the amber floor-light looking at his own paw afterward.

He looked up and found Nibbles watching. Nibbles didn't look away.

Bristlebaum's quills came down. Down but not flat, not the full flatness of a hedgehog whose news has resolved cleanly. He pushed his spectacles back into place, clipped his mace back to his belt, and turned toward the center of the hall.

Nibbles was still watching Bristlebaum when he saw Dash had moved.

He'd been tracking him in the background, the position count he'd been running since the ambush, the one Nori had taught him to keep going without losing the rest of his attention. Dash had been at the far wall. Now he was further along it, near a section where a carved column met a recessed arch Nibbles hadn't looked at directly since they entered.

Dash wasn't looking at the column. He was looking at the join between the arch and the wall behind it, paws tracing the edge of the stone without digging, just following the line the stonemason had cut.

His ears were up, his whiskers working. He found what he was looking for and went still over it, the way he'd gone still over the elbow-catch in the valley before the ambush. Then he looked down.

Below the arch, the floor stepped down into a passage. Narrower than the hall, the stone there darker and older, cut from below rather than set from above. The rune-channels in the hall didn't continue past the arch. The amber stopped at its edge. Nibbles couldn't see down the passage from this angle.

Dash looked over his shoulder, a quick sweep of the hall, taking in who was where. His gaze passed over Nibbles and moved on. He turned back to the passage, took one step into the shadow at the arch's edge to see the first section of the descent, and stopped there.

He didn't call out. He waited, giving the rest of the party time to finish.

The last guardians dissolved, and the hall changed around him.

The amber in the floor had been running at full waking since the tree pattern rose, all the rune channels lit, all the lines from root to branch burning amber. Now the brightness dropped, the channels keeping their light but pulling back from the trial-state to something steadier. The brighter patches at the worn sections were still brighter, the stone's record of past wakings still readable.

As the amber settled, the green became visible in its full proportion. It had been threading through the channels since they entered, following the same carved lines the amber followed (Nori had called it out earlier). The amber's trial-brightness had drowned most of it then. With the amber at its lower burn now, the green was plain to see.

It ran through nearly every channel. The amber still ran too, still held its light, still carried the Wardstone network's original purpose through the stone, but the green moved in the same channels, pressed against the amber along the carved lines, and neither was being driven out.

Nibbles walked to the center of the hall. He crouched and put his palm flat to the floor. The amber was warm. The green was something else, wrong in a direction without being cold, the way the corrupted valley's lake had been wrong in a direction. He could feel both through his pad, running in parallel, separated by the width of a carved channel.

He lifted his paw. Telia crouched beside him a moment later. She pressed both paws flat to the floor and closed her eyes.

"How long has it been like this?" he asked.

"Years," she said. She didn't open her eyes. "The green started when the Wardstones began failing. It followed the conduit lines in from the inverted anchors. The amber has held the channels because the seventh Wardstone is below us and the foundation is its housing. But the green keeps coming."

"What happens if the amber loses?"

"The conduit lines become the corruption's. The network that carries the prison's suppressive field out to the anchor sites becomes the network the corruption runs through instead." She lifted her paws. The amber under them didn't brighten; she had nothing left to give it. "The Keep has been holding the line, but it isn't winning."

He stood. Around him, the amber and green ran together through every line in the floor, the vast tree pattern of roots and branches, lit in two colors fighting over the same carved space. The columns showed it too, the green threading up through the amber toward the vault. High near the ceiling, the pale blue orbs drifted in their slow arcs.

Acornimus stood near the hall's center with his journal open and his pen moving. Hazel was attending to something Nibbles couldn't see, ears forward. Leonardo had found a column to set his lance against and was standing without it for the first time since the ambush, testing what the broken leg could hold. His face was even. After a moment he leaned back against the column, took the lance up again, and put it back to work.

Dash was still at the arch entrance, waiting.

The amber and the green were both still there, both still in the channels, neither retreating. The hall had burned clear amber for however many years it had been waking for those who came worthy, and now it ran two colors in the same lines.

Below the floor was the seventh Wardstone's anchor housing. Below that, the conduit lines converged into it. Below all of it, Grimthorn, and the Crystal Sanctum, and six Wardstones (five fully inverted, one half-repaired) and one more directly below his feet, which was the only reason the amber was still running at all.

He looked at the passage Dash had found. Then he looked back at the floor, at the channels running amber and green through the same stone, the Keep itself the ground they were contesting, and neither one had moved.

Chapter Twenty
The Laboratory

THE STAIRS WENT DOWN in a straight line, no curve, no landing, the stone cut by someone who had wanted to reach the bottom and not be delayed. Dash had found the entrance in the back wall of the great hall while the trial-light was still fading, and when Nibbles looked for him he was at the top of the stairs, waiting for the rest of them.

The smell arrived on the first step down. He smelled turned earth, the way a field smells when it's been opened in autumn, soil wet through to the dark layers underneath. Underneath that, iron gone sharp, the way long-uncleaned tools smell once the metal has started to take on what it cut.

Nibbles had smelled the second note before, at the crack in Nettleflint's cellar the night the corruption had pressed up through the stone. This was older, and denser.

Whiskerbrand shifted across his back, something sharpened, not the steady warmth it had held in the great hall, a hum that arrived at the base of his spine and held there. The sword was paying attention to the stairs, and so was Nibbles.

He followed Dash into the dark.

The walls were unfinished stone, working cut, deep grooves from the tools that had worked it, no smoothing for ceremony or appearance. The floor underfoot had been worn flat by decades of the same traffic moving the same direction. The ceiling was low; Nibbles' ears just cleared it. Above him he could hear the tap of Telia's staff on each step, the measured rhythm of someone rationing her effort.

The smell thickened as they went deeper. By the third landing, the earth-note had gone from turned to scorched. The iron-note was in every breath.

"The architecture stopped a few floors back," Dash said from ahead.

The walls weren't doing what walls were built to do anymore. They were bearing the keep's weight downward, and that was all.

The door was iron, not wood, and heavy enough that Dash had needed both paws on the latch. It opened with a sound like a blade coming out of a scabbard, slow, controlled.

Nibbles stepped through and looked up. Capsules ran from waist height to the vault along the far wall (glass, or thicker glass-like material) filled with a fluid that was amber near the top and grey-purple where it darkened toward the draw tube below. They were mounted in frames of black iron, eight columns across, and tubes ran from each capsule in descending lines, copper, oxidized green at the joints from long use. The tubes met at junction boxes bolted to the frames at intervals, and from there continued downward through holes cut in the stone floor. He couldn't see where the lines went below.

The room was wide. Wide enough for the full party to spread into, and they did. He heard them fan out behind him, heard the tap of Telia's staff on the stone, heard the scratch of Acornimus's pen-case coming open. The ceiling was high enough for Leonardo to stand straight with his lance vertical. It had been built to work in.

Three long workbenches ran the left wall, covered with instruments arranged with the order of regular use, vessels with residue dried in layers along the bottom, tools positioned and ready rather than cleaned and stored. Above the benches, shelves held smaller capsules and stacks of parchment weighted with stones. On the opposite wall, more frames, more capsules, more tubes descending.

At the center of the room, on a stand of black iron, sat a tablet the size of a large cutting board. Obsidian or something close to it. Covered on both visible faces with fine carved lines. Void-runes. Nibbles had seen those marks before, in the valley and in the caves. Here they weren't corruption's afterthought. They covered every flat surface in sight, the workbenches, the iron frames, the stone floor between the junction boxes.

His whiskers had gone still the moment he crossed the threshold. The cauterized-iron smell had a source in this room, and the source was every-thing in it.

Whiskerbrand's hum sharpened by half a step, but didn't push toward his paw.

He started with the tubes. Tubes went somewhere.

The copper had oxidized green along the joints, old work, but main-tained. He traced the nearest tube from its junction box down through the hole in the floor. The hole was sealed with a dark compound around the tube where it passed through the stone, sealed against leakage, which meant whatever the tubes carried was under pressure.

He looked at the nearest capsule. The fluid inside moved slowly, circu-lating in slow turns, drawn by something he couldn't see. Amber at the top, darkening to grey-purple at the bottom where the draw tube reached in. He had seen that color before. At Nettleflint's farm, in the crack below the cellar floor. In the stream water north of Thimblewick.

"Ley-fluid," Telia said from behind him. She wasn't close to the capsules yet, paws out slightly from her sides, not touching anything, just within range of what she could feel through the floor. "The world's own current, running through the stone. The Wardstone network was built to hold it in the right channels, moving the right direction. When a Wardstone inverts, the current it was anchoring doesn't stop. It backs up. And someone built a system to catch what backs up."

"And redirect it," Nibbles said.

"Down," she said.

He went back to the workbenches.

The instruments were arranged for measurement; he could read that from the way the parts were positioned, set and ready. The vessels held residue in layers, each layer a slightly different shade. The room had been built and used, repeatedly, for a long time.

He looked at the runes on the bench surface. He had assumed at first they were contamination marks, the same void-scarring he had seen on surfaces in the corrupted valley, random evidence of things that had been touched. But these weren't random. They ran from the bench's outer edge toward the center, inward, all in the same direction. The same kind of direction Telia had shown him in the conduit lines carved into the bedrock of the Underways. Something pulled from one place and sent to another.

He followed the rune-lines from the workbench to the nearest junction box to the tube and down to the hole in the floor.

The capsules collected ley-fluid from the inverted Wardstones. The tubes ran it down through the stone. The runes on every surface directed the flow toward one point.

Nibbles had spent the last month watching corruption spread across farms and water tables and dying fields. He had watched it move through the valley in the coordinated pattern Gareth had called *directed*. He had assumed it was the prison failing, seals degrading, old work wearing thin, the void seeping through gaps that were getting wider.

He had been looking at the exhaust and calling it a leak. The Boroughs hadn't been bleeding out. Someone had built the pipes.

Thirty years. A working system, full and maintained, running exactly the way it had been built to run. The corruption in Thimblewick's farmland, in Wigglywood, in the streams and cellar cracks and dying fields. It hadn't escaped from anything. It had been pumped there. Deliberate work, for thirty years.

He stood in the middle of the room.

Telia had already moved to the first capsule.

Acornimus had gone directly to the tablet. He had moved to the central stand before the room had been read, journal already in his paw, and by the time Nibbles finished tracing the first tube, Acornimus was bent over the tablet with his face close to the surface. The rest of them gave him room.

The tablet was covered edge to edge in handwriting, notation in a personal hand rather than rune-work, columns and rows of entries, each with a date-marker and a location code, marginal notes in smaller script pressing in from both sides. Acornimus was reading left to right across each line. His pen-case was open in his other paw but the pen was not yet drawn.

Nibbles found his eye returning to the tablet from across the room.

The handwriting at the top of the first face had faded to brown. The handwriting at the bottom of the second face was still dark, recent.

When Acornimus drew the pen, he didn't write. He held it. His paw made one small lateral motion, and the pen found a position above the tablet's surface and stopped there, not touching the runes.

Then he opened his journal. He turned to a particular page without searching. The journal's contents were as ordered as everything else he kept. He read an entry there, looked back at the tablet, and read the same entry again.

He went still. Not the stillness of attention. Something else.

He turned back three pages in the journal and read something else.

Nibbles returned to the tubes. He heard the pen move briefly, then the journal close. Then he heard it open again.

When he looked, Acornimus was standing at the tablet with the journal open in his paw and his pen suspended above a single page. He had stopped searching. He was looking at one entry on the tablet, his attention narrowed to it.

The pen moved once. A short lateral line.

Acornimus closed the journal and held it without moving for a moment. Then he opened it again, found the page, and wrote one line in the tight-spaced hand he used when he was being exact. He closed the journal and put it into the inner pocket of his vest.

He crossed to Bristlebaum. Nibbles didn't hear the full exchange; Acornimus kept it low, a private register. He heard one phrase clearly, a notation about an asset inside the coordination network at Ironhold. No name followed it.

Bristlebaum was quiet for several seconds. His quills had risen, not yet to full extension, the involuntary half-rise when something arrives before the body can decide not to react. They settled partway, the way they had been settling lately.

Acornimus moved to the workbench, pen still in his paw, whiskers forward and still.

Gareth had built his notation system from observation, months of tracking corruption across the Boroughs, working out a grid of markers that let him read inversion timelines from their effects alone. He had described the method to Nibbles once, the way someone described work they had developed alone because no one else had been working the same problem.

The tablet on the stand held a notation system that had been here for thirty years. Gareth hadn't been the only one who could see this way, and he hadn't known there was a map because the person who had built it was the man they had come here to stop.

Telia went to the capsules alone. She didn't ask for help or explain what she was going to do. She walked to the first frame on the left wall, set her staff against it, and put both paws flat against the junction box where the draw tube connected to the frame.

The amber light came slowly. It had been arriving this way all day, thinning rather than failing, what was left of the full channel she had been running in the Underways or the valley. She worked the first junction in silence, both paws pressed flat, the light running from her pads down through the seal points until the tube's flow quieted and the capsule above it stopped circulating.

She moved to the second.

Nibbles stayed where he was, the rune-pattern on the floor section still in front of him. But his attention kept moving back to Telia. She was working in a rhythm, paws on the junction, amber arrives, hold until the capsule quiets, move. She had measured what she had left and was spending it carefully.

By the fourth capsule, the amber was arriving thinner. The glow that had covered her pads at the first junction was thread-fine, just enough to reach the seal points.

She moved to the fifth.

Leonardo was standing to her right. He'd been positioned in the same general area since Telia reached the third capsule, lance planted, weight distributed between the good leg and the broken one. He hadn't moved any closer.

The sixth junction. The amber was hair-fine.

Telia was holding each junction longer now, taking the time the reduced light required to close the connection properly. The time it was taking went unremarked.

The grey in her fur had spread past her shoulders since the morning, down into the fur at her upper arms; the actual color of it, the brown-grey going white-grey.

She finished the seventh. Then the eighth.

Leonardo's position had shifted by half a step, an adjustment rather than a move toward her, the way a body adjusts when it has been tracking something and resolved on the best position to be ready.

The ninth capsule. The amber came as a single line.

Nibbles counted the frames. Three remaining in the second row. Fifteen capped, three circulating, the fluid in the sealed ones still. Telia had been at it less than ten minutes, and it had cost more than the walk down the stairs.

She pressed both paws to the tenth junction. The light arrived and stuttered. She held it. The stutter steadied into something cooler than amber but present, working through the junction in increments. The capsule above went still.

She moved to the eleventh.

Her right knee went as she reached it, a buckle, weight shifting wrong. She caught the frame with one paw and kept the other on the junction, and the light didn't break. She finished the seal. The capsule quieted. She straightened slowly.

Leonardo's arm was at her shoulder. His arm had simply been close enough to be there when the moment required it.

She didn't look at him. She moved to the twelfth.

At the twelfth junction, the amber had gone out of her pads entirely.

She pressed both paws flat. Her eyes closed. Her breathing was even, holding the one thing she still could.

Nibbles stopped pretending to look at the floor.

No one spoke. The room held the faint hum of the last circulating capsule and Telia's breathing.

The light didn't arrive.

She held the position. The stone against her paws, the junction box cold, the tube still running fluid through it the way it had been running for thirty years.

Then something arrived. Not the amber. Something thinner than thread, finding the seal points by some quieter route, working slowly through the junction until the last capsule was still.

When she let go, her legs gave at the same moment.

Leonardo had her.

He didn't make a sound. His arm had been close enough that catching her was a single motion, and she caught the wall with her other paw and stayed upright.

"I can still walk," she said. "Still fight." Her voice was steady.

He didn't answer. Neither did anyone else. The last capsule held its fluid; Telia leaned against the wall; Leonardo's arm stayed where it was.

The room had gone quiet after the last capsule stilled. The working sound that had been in the room since they entered was gone; Nibbles realized he hadn't registered it as a sound until it stopped.

He had moved to the center workbench while the room settled, standing at the edge without touching anything, looking. His mechanic's eye kept moving across the junction boxes, following the rune-lines from their outer edges toward the center, building the map of the system in his head the way he had always built maps of things he needed to understand. He was still at it when he saw Hazel.

She had been in the room since the descent but hadn't gone to the tablet or the capsule frames or the workbench. She had moved along the right wall, away from the apparatus, toward the far end of the room where the shelving had given up.

A rack had come down at some point, old enough that the iron brackets had rusted through before they failed, the parchment stored on it lying flattened and dried beneath the fallen wood. The collapse had pulled part of the wall frame with it, exposing a recess in the stone a handspan deeper than the surrounding surface. In the low light it read as nothing.

Hazel was crouched at the back of it. Her ears were fully forward. Her paws were held in front of her, not touching anything, the posture she took when she was reading a surface before deciding what to do with it. Nibbles had watched her use it at the Ancient Willow the morning Bristlebaum had first read her letter.

He didn't move toward her. He watched from across the room.

After a moment, she reached in with both paws together.

What she brought out was wrapped in black cloth. Small enough that her paws cupped it with room to spare, no larger than a river stone. The cloth was old, but in the particular way of something that hadn't been moved in a long time, the fold at the top had held its crease so long that the crease had set into the weave.

She stood slowly and held the bundle at a careful distance from herself.

Whiskerbrand gave one low pulse against his back, a lower, slower note than the alert hum it had been running since the laboratory threshold. Recognition rather than warning. He held the sheath still for a moment and let his paw drop.

Hazel moved to the edge of the center workbench and set the bundle on the clear section while she opened her satchel. She checked the inner compartment and moved a folded square of oilcloth to one side. Then she looked at the bundle for two full breaths before she picked it up and placed it inside.

She closed the clasp and adjusted the strap once.

She walked away from the wall without explaining it to anyone, ears still fully forward.

Telia had moved while Nibbles was watching Hazel.

She was near the center workbench now, a pace back from the surface, staff planted, paws free. She was reading the conduit lines through the stone below her feet without touching the bench's rune-work, and watching the bench itself the way she watched any surface she couldn't safely touch.

Nibbles was at the junction boxes along the bench. He had been working left to right along the row, an arm's length from the surface, reading each box by sight. The void-runes on the bench surface were directional, running toward the junctions from both sides. He had followed the logic far enough to understand the basic circuit, ley-fluid in from the capsules above, the rune-network directing the current through the junctions, the flow down through the floor-holes to the bedrock lines below.

The third junction box along held a pressure coupling, two main draw tubes meeting and becoming one. The fitting was larger than the others, the void-rune etching denser around it, pressed deeper into the iron.

His paw started moving before he'd thought about it. Eight years of mill work in Thimblewick. When you needed to read a pressure coupling, you put a paw at the fitting and a paw at the line below it and let the information arrive through the pads. His paw was doing what those eight years had taught it to do.

The coupling was four inches from his outstretched paw. Then three. Then two finger-widths from his pads.

Telia's paw caught his wrist.

"Don't," she said.

"Right." He held still. "I didn't think about the charge."

"The capsules are sealed. The current is still in the copper." She held his wrist. "When we stopped the flow, it backed up to the last points it could reach. Every coupling joint on this bench is sitting at pressure. The void-runes don't mark the joints; they feed them. The rune-work runs in a closed loop around each fitting and back to the surface."

He looked at the rune-pattern from a new angle. The lines ran inward (he had read that part correctly, toward the junctions) but they didn't stop there. They circled each coupling fitting and came back. He had traced the inward direction; he hadn't traced the return.

"Touch the fitting and the current completes through whatever is touching it," he said.

"Yes."

She released his wrist. He pulled his paw back to his side.

"How did you know I was reaching?"

"You did the same thing at the second box." Her eyes were on the bench. "You pulled back before contact. At the third, you didn't."

He looked at the second coupling along the row. Same position, same density of rune-work around it. He'd moved his paw away from it earlier without thinking about why. The warning had reached him in time for the second coupling. At the third, it hadn't.

He stepped back from the bench, kept his paws at his sides, and looked at the full row. Eight junction boxes, coupling joints at every third position, void-rune loops around every fitting.

"Thank you," he said.

"Don't reach for the fittings," she said. "That's the thanks."

He read the rest of the bench from where he stood.

Dash had read the apparatus while the others were still finding their positions in the room.

Nibbles had taken it in without thinking it through at the time, the ferret's amber eyes moving across the capsule frames, the floor-holes, the tubes, picking out the points where the whole thing would come apart fastest. By the time Telia had sealed the last junction, Dash already had his paws on the first coupling joint at the base of Column One.

He pulled it with a sharp twist at the lock-point. The tube came free with the sound of a joint giving up.

The fluid from the line hit the floor.

"Away from it," Telia said.

Everyone stepped back. The fluid spread across the stone (amber at the source, darkening fast as it spread) and at the edge of the nearest rune-line it stopped spreading randomly and began moving with direction, inward toward the junction boxes and the floor-holes. The channels carved into the stone took it and it followed them the way the system had always made it follow. It reached the nearest floor-hole and dropped through.

"The bedrock channels are still open," Telia said. "The current has somewhere to go. It will drain down."

Nibbles watched the fluid find the channels and follow them. The current hadn't stopped. The capsules were sealed and the draw lines severed, but the ley-current was still moving, finding the next available path.

"Break the apparatus above the floor," Telia said. "What's below is stone and it will hold."

Dash had already moved to Column Two.

He worked left to right along the first row without haste, coupling joint at the base of each frame, twist at the lock-point, tube separated, on to the next. The fluid from each column hit the floor, found the rune-channels, and drained. Eight on the first row. He moved to the second.

Nibbles worked the junction boxes on the workbench, the tube clamps holding each box to its mount, which were mechanical rather than charged, pins in slotted rails. He removed them left to right, lifted each freed box, and set it on the floor clear of the spreading fluid. When a box came free, the tubes it had been routing dropped and the remaining fluid in the upper sections followed gravity down, found the rune-channels, and drained through the holes below.

Nori worked the capsule mounts. Three strikes with the flat of her axe on each mounting bracket, placed deliberately. The brackets sheared. The capsules tilted and came down, and the glass (or whatever it was) shattered on the stone floor and the contents joined everything else moving along the rune-channels toward the floor-holes.

Acornimus stood at the far end of the workbench and wrote, slowly, taking the time to record each step accurately. He wrote down each column as it was dismantled, the direction of the fluid drainage, the position of the floor-holes, the behavior of the fluid in the rune-channels. He was standing exactly far enough from the spreading fluid to keep his shoes clear of it.

Leonardo was near the door they had come through. The broken leg kept him out of the dismantling work, but he wasn't standing idle; he faced the entrance, lance in hand, watching the stairs above. If something came through while the others worked, he would be between it and them.

The last coupling came free. Dash released it and stepped back. The fluid from the final tube section ran its channel and dropped through the floor.

The room went quiet, a different quiet than the one after the last capsule had been sealed. That had been a system paused. This was a system taken apart, frames bent and empty, glass on the floor, junction boxes set along the base of the wall, the bench stripped of everything that had been bolted to it.

Nibbles looked at what they had made of it. The capsule housings still stood (the iron frames weren't worth trying to move) but they were empty, stripped of their function. The workbench was bare. Only the obsidian tablet on its iron stand at the center of the room remained intact, the void-runes unchanged, the thirty years of notation in the margins untouched. Acornimus had the record in his pocket; the tablet itself could stay.

Telia pressed both paws flat to the bench surface and closed her eyes. She held the position. Her breathing was even.

"The ley-line is still running," she said. "The inverted Wardstones are still pushing the current through the bedrock channels and those channels still lead to the Sanctum below. What we've stopped is the routing, the part of the system that was taking what the inverted stones produced and sending it outward through the land." She opened her eyes. "The corruption in the Boroughs won't get worse from this room. The feeding is gone."

"But the stones are still inverted," Nibbles said.

"Five of them, fully. The sixth is partial. The seventh hasn't broken yet." She looked at the broken frames, the glass on the floor. "He can rebuild this. The bedrock channels are there and they won't stop being there. The rune-work on the surface can be re-etched. Given time and materials, the surface apparatus can be rebuilt above channels that never stopped working."

"He won't have the time," Bristlebaum said.

The mace was in his right paw.

Telia looked at him. "One level below," he said.

The stairs down to the Sanctum were not the same as the stairs to the laboratory. Those had been working stone, straight line, deep tool-cuts, no ceremony. These curved, following the bedrock beneath the Keep along the path of least resistance through stone older than the construction above. As they descended, the ceiling rose rather than pressed closer, and the walls spread by degrees. Less than a pace across the full descent, but the passage felt different, cut along what the stone allowed rather than against it.

He felt the Sanctum before he reached it. The sound came first, a vibration more than a sound, arriving in his chest, then in his ribs, then in the pads of his feet as they touched the stone. Low and constant, very old, without pain in it. It had been holding the same note for so long that the note had worn itself smooth. He felt it through three steps before his mind named it as sound.

Whiskerbrand went still, a stillness Nibbles hadn't felt from the blade before, neither the alert hum nor the low pulse near Hazel's bundle. It was the stillness of a sword at a threshold it had already crossed once, thirty years ago, in another bearer's paws. He felt that stillness through the sheath leather. He left his paw at his side and kept walking.

Behind him the party had gone quiet. They had stopped talking because there was nothing to say into the next step. Footfalls. The creak of Nori's crossbow strap. The soft clank of Leonardo's lance against the inner curve of the wall. Telia's staff at a slower cadence than the descent required, each step measured.

The amber light came up from below. Amber in contest, not clean. Pressing up through the dark of the stairwell from the level beneath, and the contest was visible in it, the same kind of amber Nibbles had seen in the corrupted valley at the failing Wardstone, except where that one had been losing by degrees, this one was holding. The Keep below them was still holding the line.

Bristlebaum moved to the front of the line. He had been walking in the middle of the party since the laboratory. He moved through them now without asking, and they stepped aside. His quills hadn't fully settled since the Hollow, but the mace was in his right paw and the paw was steady. He had finished deciding.

He went down into the amber light, and the others followed.

Chapter Twenty-One
The Crystal Sanctum

THE CRYSTAL SANCTUM ROSE three stories above the chamber floor. In each pillar, amber light pressed at the crystal's inner surface, and from inside the stone (in the places where the amber was thinnest) the darkness pushed the other way, slowly, without sign of slowing.

The pillars stood in concentric rings, each ring tighter toward the center, each pillar taller than two creatures end to end. The chamber hummed below hearing, felt in the chest more than caught by the ears. Bristlebaum knew the sound. Thirty years of Guild records had described it, scouts who'd reached the Keep's outer approaches, rangers who'd gotten close enough.

He had stood in this chamber once before, thirty years ago, after the battle at Shadowpeak's summit, when the prison had still been new and the amber in the pillars had filled them completely. He had not known then how much work the amber had ahead of it. The chamber was different now.

The mace was in his right paw. He adjusted his grip to the position he had carried since Shadowpeak, weighted toward the thumb, the groove in the leather worn smooth from years of the same adjustment. His quills were fully extended, and he made no effort to settle them.

He moved to the position between the main archway and the upper stair, checked the sight lines and the angles from the secondary passage at the eastern edge, and tested the floor under his boots. Solid.

The prison was not broken. It had been holding for thirty years.

He heard Nibbles's pads on the stairs a moment before the sound cut off, the light scrape of small pads on stone, then nothing as the descent carried him out of range.

Nori had been the last through the archway behind him, and she hadn't followed them down. She stood at the eastern edge of the pillar ring, her back to the stone, crossbow level at the secondary passage entrance, hand-axes at her belt. Her eyes moved between the three approach angles.

"You're sure," Bristlebaum said.

"Static defense at a chokepoint. That's what I do," she said.

He had asked anyway. It was the kind of question that mattered to ask out loud.

The others were below. He had tracked them by sound through the descent. Telia's cracked staff against stone, the heavier tread of Leonardo with the lance making up for the leg, Dash's near-silence which he had learned to register as its own signal over weeks of moving with him. Acornimus's pen had been scratching even as he walked. Hazel last in the line, moving with the economy of someone who had spent the last of what she had to spend. And ahead of all of them, Nibbles, with Whiskerbrand's light briefly visible at the archway's edge before the stairs cut it off. Then dark, then the Sanctum and the hum, and Nori at her position.

The main archway was forty feet from where she stood. Open stone between them, then the inner pillar ring, then the arch itself. Anything that pressed upward would come through the main arch first, and the secondary passage at the eastern edge was the second angle. Nori had placed herself to cover both.

Bristlebaum held the main arch. Nori covered the east.

Six constructs came through the main archway in a press.

The corruption had built them for mass and forward drive, broad forms, void-crystal layered through limbs and torso, moving the way something pushed from behind moves rather than something running toward a target. They came through the threshold without slowing.

Bristlebaum put the first one down before it had fully cleared the arch. The mace caught it across the chest and the form buckled left, void-crystal splintering at the point of impact, the whole construct folding and going dark. He was adjusting his angle for the second before the first had hit the ground.

Behind him and to his right, Nori's crossbow released. One of the constructs at the back of the press staggered and stopped.

The second came at him high. He dropped (hedgehog's center, low and stable) and drove the mace upward from below into its jaw. The impact ran through the grip into his paw and up to the elbow. The construct's head snapped back. He followed with a strike across its flank as it fell, and it dissolved.

Three remaining from the first six. Nori had crossed to his left without announcement, taking the eastern angle before two of the remaining three could split away from the press and use the open flank. Her hand-axe hit the nearest one in the shoulder joint where the void-crystal was thinnest, and the form sagged. Her second axe finished it.

That left two, and they came together.

He put himself at the stair archway. If either of them got past him, the party below lost its route back up. He took the first one's charge on his right shoulder (the impact drove him back two steps on the stone) but his extended quills caught in the construct's chest-crystal and the creature couldn't disengage cleanly. He turned hard left, and the construct's own momentum carried it into the pillar at his back. It shattered against the stone.

The last one pulled up short and watched him for a long second before it came in. He sidestepped the lunge and brought the mace across the back of its neck in a downward arc. It went dark before it hit the floor.

Six down in less than two minutes. Nori was at the eastern position, already reloading, paws moving through the crossbow sequence by feel.

"Probe," she said.

He had thought the same, the first wave had been measuring.

The second wave came before he had fully reset his footing, twelve through the archway, and the two outermost immediately curving toward Nori's flank. The wave that had watched the first six go down was adjusting.

He called to her (one sharp sound, a direction toward the gap) and she was already moving, pulling back from the eastern position to close the angle at the archway before the flanking pair could use the opening. He put his attention on the ten coming straight.

This wave was harder. The constructs pressed tight, using the bodies of the foremost to narrow his swing angles. The mace was built for reach and momentum; tight quarters reduced both. He shortened his grip and worked at the joins (the seams between the void-crystal layers) and the close-quarters work was slower and cost more per construct than the open-field strikes of the first wave.

His right shoulder caught a glancing blow from the third construct in line that deadened his rotation on that side. He shifted his lead to the left, put his left arm in front, used his right to drive the blows rather than direct them. The shoulder still worked, just slower than before.

At the archway, three came at once and he couldn't cover all three approach lines. The one on his far left slipped past his guard (the shoulder limit giving it the half-second it needed) and its claw caught across his upper arm, a burning line through the muscle. He turned into it instead of away from it, closing the angle, and the construct's second blow caught only his quills and lodged there. He used that grip, pulled the construct forward into his shoulder and drove it into the floor.

From the eastern position, Nori's crossbow, then her axe at a different angle.

In the grip of the mace, the Shadowpeak memory arrived. The summit chamber, thirty years ago. Aldric's light blazing at the center of the defense, then the light changing, then the sword passing to his paws, and the warmth already gone when he had closed his grip a moment later, the metal cooling against his palm before the chamber had finished settling. He had held the formation line on the summit, and held it after the warmth stopped.

The memory was there, and it didn't take over.

He drove the last three constructs down (the tail of the wave coming in without the same coordination as the bulk) and the second wave finished.

The cut on his arm burned. His right shoulder had less rotation in it than before. He looked across the chamber at Nori (still at the eastern position, reloading, no visible injury from this distance) and turned his eyes back to the archway.

They came again before the gap between waves had settled, eight through the main arch, four more immediately behind, and behind those a larger form that moved differently from the others. Denser. The corruption built thickly into it, layered rather than simply packed. He filed the larger form for later and started with the eight.

He was tired. His right arm had been working at reduced rotation since the shoulder bruise in the second wave. His left had been carrying more than it was built for, and each strike was costing him a little more than the last. The muscles holding his quills fully extended had been aching longer than that. He kept working; the position had no substitute.

Six of the eight were down when the grip went wrong.

He had aimed a downward strike at the seventh, a standard blow he'd thrown a hundred times in the past hour, and his right paw failed on the turn. The shoulder bruise had been reducing his rotation by degrees; on this strike, the rotation gave out entirely. The mace left his grip all at once.

The sound it made on the stone floor was a single flat note, specific rather than loud.

The seventh construct moved on the opening.

His left paw came up before he'd thought about it (the body acting first) and caught the construct's leading arm at the wrist. His claws found purchase in the void-crystal surface, enough to redirect the momentum sideways. He turned his shoulder into the construct's chest and drove it left, away from the stair arch. Without the mace there was no follow strike to make, so he slammed the construct into the pillar at his back, held it there with his left shoulder, and went to one knee.

His right paw closed around the mace handle on the floor.

He came up with both paws on the grip, weight forward.

He finished the seventh construct in two strikes and turned to the eighth before it had reached him. Two more strikes and the eighth went dark.

He had been off the mace perhaps five seconds. The construct that had moved on the opening was rising from where he had driven it into the pillar. He crossed to it and put it down, then stood in the Sanctum with both paws on the grip and his breathing hard, quills still fully extended.

The larger form waited at the archway threshold, watching. It was reading the cost of the dropped mace, the way the earlier waves had paused to watch.

Bristlebaum breathed. He checked his grip, right and left together, and found it solid.

He went to meet the larger form. It was built to absorb, the void-crystal laid in overlapping sheets rather than packed solid, each layer catching a blow and spreading it instead of taking it directly. His first two strikes confirmed it. The impacts sank in without the dissolution response he had been getting from the smaller constructs. He adjusted without stopping. Shorter strikes, aimed at the seams between the layers. His left arm drove the blows while the right directed the angle. Three strikes at the same seam before the crystal showed any response.

On the fourth strike, the seam cracked.

He pressed it, driving four more blows into the same point, each one reaching a fraction deeper. The fifth went all the way through.

The construct dissolved from the chest outward.

He straightened. Both arms ached from the shoulder down. His quills had been extended so long the muscles behind them were cramping. The cut on his upper arm had stopped burning and started pulling, drying out.

The archway was empty, and no sound rose from the descent.

The third wave came through the eastern passage.

He heard it half a second before the first construct appeared, the change in the Sanctum's sound, movement arriving from the wrong direction. Through the secondary passage at the eastern edge of the pillar ring, not the main archway. Tight formation, moving fast, the lead construct already through the passage mouth before Bristlebaum had taken six steps toward Nori.

He was too far. He moved anyway.

Nori had the crossbow level and released (the bolt took the lead construct before it cleared the entrance) and she was already stepping right as she released, using the eastern pillar as cover, the cover-and-strike rhythm she'd worked through dozens of these in the past two weeks. Two down in the first several seconds. The third she let come almost to striking range before her hand-axe hit the shoulder joint, and the form sagged and went still. Four remaining. He was fifteen feet away.

Her second axe took the fourth construct at the same joint. Three remaining. Ten feet.

The fifth construct through the passage had a face.

He was too far across the chamber to see it clearly. He saw Nori see it. Her left foot was mid-step, crossing toward the angle for the fifth, and the step didn't complete. Her weight stayed back on her right for a fraction of a second, a fraction her position couldn't afford.

The construct behind the fifth came through the gap.

It caught her across the ribs from the left side. She was already responding (her right arm bringing the axe up into the construct's line) but the blow landed before the axe did, and at an angle she hadn't braced against. The axe connected and the construct dissolved, but the ribs had already taken the hit.

He was still crossing the floor. He threw the mace (the wrong weapon for throwing, but it was what he had) and it hit the next construct in the column hard enough to knock it sideways and buy a second. He reached the eastern position, swept the last two constructs back with the recovered mace, drove both into the pillar ring, and turned.

Nori was on her feet. Her left arm pressed against her side, bracing the ribs from below. Her face had the flatness of six years of field work, but she was holding her torso carefully, keeping the ribs from expanding fully.

"Ribs," she said.

"How many."

"Two, maybe three." She breathed carefully. "Still working."

He had known she might hesitate. Grimthorn had used faces at the valley ambush too, with Leonardo's unit, the specific face aimed at the specific wound. Bristlebaum didn't ask whose face had been on the fifth construct.

He moved to her position.

He stood at Nori's position and checked the eastern entrance. No movement, no sound from inside the stone. He looked left to the main archway. Clear. He tracked the upper stair at his back; nothing had come from there through any of the three waves.

"Passage is clear," Nori said.

He kept his eyes on the main arch for three more breaths. The Sanctum's hum continued around them. The amber in the nearest pillar pressed at the crystal surface with the same patient rhythm it had held all night.

He looked at her. She was breathing carefully, each expansion measured. Her crossbow was still in her right paw, and she hadn't sat down.

"I have a field kit," he said.

"So do I," she said.

"I'll use mine."

She didn't argue. He had given her five directions since the great hall, and she had answered every one with a practical counter or a faster solution. This time she let him have it.

The ribs were worse than two or three. He moved close and opened the kit.

He crouched beside her and laid the kit open on the stone. The ribs needed a wrap, not stitches. He took the linen strips.

"Breathe in as far as you can manage," he said.

She breathed. He watched where the expansion stopped (the depth where the ribs pulled inward to protect themselves) and started the bandage two finger-widths below that point. He wound the first strip firm. Brace pressure, not compression. He pulled the second with both paws and checked the tension on each pass. The linen had to support without cutting into the breathing she still had.

Nori watched the eastern passage while he worked. He moved around her position, pausing when she shifted her weight to keep the sight line, working in the space she left. They had been doing this since the great hall.

He finished two strips, tucked the ends, and checked the tension with the flat of his paw. Even along the upper edge, a fraction less at the lower. Correct.

He wound the third, pulled it even, tucked it, and sat back on his heels. The Sanctum hummed.

"You tried to send Acornimus," she said.

He began putting the kit in order. Strips refolded, flask re-seated, needle and thread back in their wrapping.

"At the Hollow. When he was ready to go and you reviewed the reconnaissance a second time." She paused, careful with the ribs. "You sent me in instead because my field kit is better and I'm faster in close quarters and I can hold three angles at once. All of that is true."

He had one strip left to fold.

"The Caves find what you haven't examined," she said. "You'd read the construction. You knew what they would find in whoever went in." Another pause. "You tried to send someone else first."

He folded the strip and set it in the kit.

"I knew," he said.

He closed the kit's clasp. He had named her practical qualifications correctly to himself, in the quiet after he'd watched her go into the passage, and he had not named the other part. Not until now.

She had the approach angles in her sight lines. She had been covering his position since the great hall and she was still covering it.

"It's all right," she said.

His quills, fully extended since before the great hall, the muscles at their base aching, moved a fraction toward settling and stayed where they were.

He had let her go in carrying the full account without sharing it, because the practical reasons were true and because the rest was easier not to say. She had confirmed it and gone in and was telling him it was all right.

He accepted it.

He carried the field kit to the main arch, set it down where he could reach it, and resumed his position.

His paws closed on the mace. The haft was leather worn smooth, with the groove his thumb had worn over thirty years of the same hold. The Sanctum floor under his feet, the deep foundations beneath that, and the conduit lines running through the bedrock between every anchor site and the ritual chamber where the seven lines converged.

The warmth came up through the stone.

He had felt it exactly once before. The summit chamber above Shadowpeak, thirty years ago, Aldric pressing Whiskerbrand into his paws, the warmth already leaving before the grip had fully closed. The blade cooling to nothing as he held it. Thirty years since, the sword dormant in a chest in the corner of his office, cold whenever he touched it.

This was the same warmth. Arriving through the conduit lines from the ritual chamber below, from Nibbles's grip on the sword.

This wasn't the alert hum of void taint detected, and it wasn't the chest-deep drawing sensation Nibbles had described at full extension. The sword was engaged, working through whatever it was working through in the chamber below, and the warmth traveled upward through the stone the way the conduit lines carried the Wardstone network's suppressive field, following the channels already in the rock, arriving at whatever was in contact with the stone above.

He held still on the mace. The warmth stayed steady. Ten seconds, perhaps fifteen. Below him, Nibbles with Whiskerbrand at full extension, the others around him, Grimthorn and the ritual and whatever waited at the center of the chamber. Above, the amber pillars holding their level. Both ends of the Keep at once.

The sword knew he was here, and that was the closest he could get to it.

Thirty years with the blade dormant and cold. The months since this mission began, watching Nibbles hold Whiskerbrand and the sword answering. He had not thought the warmth would reach him here.

The warmth withdrew by degrees, the way heat fades in stone when the source moves away.

He stayed on the mace, watching the arch.

Nori was still watching the eastern passage, and the warmth was his to keep.

The waves did not come again.

He stood at the main archway through the silence that followed. His right shoulder would not turn as far as it used to and never would again. The cut on his arm had dried. His quills were still extended.

The amber in the pillars had changed since he came in. The darkness was still inside the stone, still pressing at the crystal, the prison straining as it had strained for thirty years. But the amber pressed back differently now, steadier, more even.

He could not hear the ritual chamber below. He could see the change in the pillars, and the pillars told him something had shifted down there.

Below were the others. Nibbles with Whiskerbrand forward. Telia at the conduit lines, whatever remained of her strength going into the stone. Leonardo without a shield, his lance adjusted for the broken leg. Hazel with the shard wrapped in cloth in her satchel. Acornimus and Dash on the angles. The party going in against what Grimthorn had spent thirty years building toward.

Bristlebaum had nothing to tell him what was happening down there. He had the pillars and the constructs that had stopped coming and, ten or fifteen seconds of it, the warmth that had reached him through the floor.

Nori was still at the eastern position, crossbow level, watching the passage. Her breathing was shallow.

Then she lowered the crossbow. "The Sanctum's quiet," she said. "The chamber isn't."

He had heard it the same way she had, the long silence above, the warmth still pulling through the stone from below. The fight down there was not finished.

"The stair," he said.

"I can take the stair."

He looked at her. The bandage was holding. Her face had the flatness of six years of field work. She had already made the call.

"Crossbow's better support down there than another body on the arch up here. You've got the arch."

He had the arch. He nodded once.

She went to the stair.

He swept the main arch, the upper stair, the eastern passage in turn. The level was holding, and below, the sword was still warm through the stone.

Chapter Twenty-Two
The Ritual Chamber

Grimthorn walked the groove.

Thirty years of the same circuit had worn the path into the mandala floor, a deep track through the inlaid stone. His pads found it without thought. Anchor point to anchor point, six steps to the sixth ring, three to the conduit marker, return. The pattern was in his body.

The sixth stone's inversion signal was close. He could feel it in the conduit lines beneath the floor, a vibration that had been building for three days and was reaching closer each hour to the resonance that would lock the inversion in place. He guessed one hour. He had been wrong about guesses before, so he kept working.

The crystal pillars in the outer ring did what they always did, amber light pressing against void-black in each column, neither side gaining, the structure holding what it had always held. The sound they made was constant, and he had stopped hearing it years ago.

A faint violet glow rested at the sixth ring's anchor point at the mandala's center, the inversion signal drawn up through the conduit lines and concentrated in the carved stone. Three days of uninterrupted work. The void-runes he had inscribed over thirty years of refinement had brightened as the signal built. He had gotten the pattern wrong twice in the first decade and corrected it, and the corrected version had been running for twenty years.

One more hour.

The party's approach was no mystery to him. Mouse with the divine blade. Otter who trained him. Rabbit with the shard. The hedgehog was holding something above. The rest would be here within minutes. The otter would be diminished from the Whispering Caves. It made no difference to the work. He needed his hour.

He was at the sixth ring's anchor point when the vibration reached him through the floor from above. Boots. Paws. A party moving with discipline rather than stealth. They were not hiding anymore.

His left paw hung at his side. He had carried four things in that paw once. He had not looked at it in a very long time.

He turned toward the stair.

The alert came through the hilt.

Whiskerbrand had been warm at Nibbles' back for the full descent. Three steps from the bottom of the stair, the warmth shifted, insistent now, a change that ran from the leather sheath through the strap across his back and into his spine before his eyes had adjusted to the chamber's light.

He stepped down from the last stair. His pads found the grooves first.

He crouched. His palm pressed flat to the stone, and the groove ran directly under it. Smooth. Deeper than he had expected, the edges worn round by repeated contact, not carved. He traced it with his paw. It was the kind of depth that took decades. He pressed harder and felt it through his pads.

He stood. The chamber was vast. The difference from the corrupted spaces he had walked through before was this. Nettleflint's cellar had been invaded, something growing in it that did not belong. This chamber had been worked. Daily, for thirty years. The crystal pillars in the outer ring threw amber light that pressed against void-black in each column, and the pressing was constant and worn, holding without advancing or retreating. The sound they made was a low sustained harmonic that had become part of the room.

"Seven rings," Hazel said, close to his shoulder, no louder than the space asked for. "One for each Wardstone. The outer ring anchors the seventh, the one that held. The center is where the conduit lines converge. He has walked this path until the stone remembers it."

Nibbles looked toward the center. The herald stood there, large the way a fortification was large, simply present rather than in motion. The corruption that patterned his fur was not the active spreading growth Nibbles had seen in the corrupted animals and the Corrupted Valley. It had settled into him. His armor had fused with his form at the shoulders and along the spine, crystal growths that no longer read as intrusions.

Grimthorn's eyes found Nibbles across the forty feet of mandala floor.

They were amber gone wrong, the gold of something old and preserved, still bright inside the preservation. He looked at Nibbles the way one looks at a problem already worked out.

Then he turned back to the sixth ring's anchor point and continued walking.

The ritual was still running.

Around Nibbles, the party had reached the bottom of the stair. Nori was the last down, slower than she had been before the Sanctum; she'd come down on the bandaged ribs, and the descent had cost her. She moved up to his right, crossbow level, eyes already reading exits. Acornimus had his journal out, pen moving. Telia pressed her paw flat to the floor at the base of the stair and closed her eyes, reading the conduit lines. Dash moved three steps to the left and stopped, whiskers forward. They had arrived in time.

Nibbles pulled Whiskerbrand from the sheath.

The blade came out warm, awake but not yet at full radiance. The amber light from the pillars moved across its surface, and the two lights stayed separate.

"He's not coming to us," Nori said, to his right. She had the crossbow level and her eyes had already worked the exits and the threats and what sat between them. "Everything he does in here is buying time for the ritual to finish. He doesn't need to beat us. He needs to hold us back long enough."

Grimthorn had turned from the sixth ring and taken up a position between the party and the anchor point. He was not advancing. His weight was on his back foot, his arms loose and low. He was set to hold ground until his ritual finished.

A fight against someone who wants to win was one thing. A fight against someone who only needed to keep them in place was another, and worse. They could not flank a position that adjusted instead of committing. Every move had to cover the ritual as much as the opponent, and every minute they spent on Grimthorn was a minute the inversion built.

"Spread to the outer ring," Nibbles said, already moving forward. "Don't give him ground toward the stair."

Acornimus went right, along the inner pillar ring, positioning between Hazel and the southern gap. Dash went left without instruction, to the outer wall, with a clear view across the chamber's full width. Telia went to the northeast corner, her paw never leaving the floor. Leonardo moved to the eastern gap between pillars, lance extended. Nori went to his left and low. He hadn't directed her. She'd seen the gap before he had.

Grimthorn watched them arrange themselves. He made no adjustment.

Nibbles walked toward him.

He was not fast and he was not large. He was a mouse with a divine blade, too many costs already in him, and very little margin for error, and the herald across the chamber had been practicing in this room for thirty years.

The first exchange was fast. Grimthorn moved to redirect rather than strike, one paw coming for Nibbles' sword arm at the angle that would push the blade wide and carry the momentum past him. Purification training had drilled Nibbles to extend and commit, and the last several months had drilled him to keep the two apart. He pulled the extension short. The redirect met empty air.

Grimthorn adjusted. The second attempt came lower, aimed at Nibbles' center, meant to drive him back toward the stair and free the ritual. Nibbles stepped sideways instead. His tail wrapped tight around his leg and he set his pads and held the ground.

"You know we're not leaving," Nibbles said.

Grimthorn's answer was the press forward, and the chamber filled with the sound of it.

The herald's attention moved to Hazel.

Nibbles saw it before Grimthorn moved, the amber eyes shifting from the sword in Nibbles' paw to the old rabbit three steps behind him. Hazel had the shard against her chest. Whatever could undo Grimthorn's work, the shard was the closest thing to it in the room.

He came fast for his size. Economical. He moved through Nibbles' guard, not around it. One paw deflected the blade left. The other came for the line to Hazel.

Nibbles stepped into it.

The blow caught him across the left shoulder (the old wound, not yet finished closing) and the pain went white and his left arm dropped for a beat before he got it back. He shoved into Grimthorn's chest with no technique, just mass, and it was enough to make the herald deal with him before going around.

Hazel stepped back. Acornimus was already there, leather journal gone into his vest, both paws free.

"Sage Willowbark holds the southern position," he said, whiskers forward. "She does not move from it."

Grimthorn looked at him a long moment. Then back at Nibbles. His weight stayed where it was.

From Nibbles' left, a crossbow bolt cracked into the stone at Grimthorn's feet, pushing his weight back toward the outer ring, away from Hazel. Nori was already reloading.

Grimthorn turned back to Nibbles and held his position.

At the chamber's western edge, Dash had stopped moving. He was at the outer pillar ring with his back to the wall, looking at something below eye level. Not at the fight. The base of the dark pillar.

Nibbles had watched Dash walk into three unfamiliar buildings and find the one thing inside the first ten minutes. He saw Dash's ears tilt forward and his weight shift onto his leading foot, and turned back to Grimthorn.

He pressed the herald back toward the sixth ring.

The void-knight came from the eastern gap between pillars.

It had been in the shadow there since the party entered. Leonardo had tracked it from his second step into the chamber. When it came, he was already turned toward it.

It moved for Hazel. The herald wanted her, and so did the rest of this chamber. The void-knight's motion was the wrong kind of coordinated (directed from somewhere outside itself) and it covered the distance between them faster than its size should have allowed.

Leonardo put himself between them.

He had no shield. Two years and three months had taught his body to expect less from his left side when a blow came from the right, and his body did the work on its own. The void-knight swung across his midsection. His left knee bent deeper than a sound leg should bend. His weight dropped into the bend. The swing passed over his helmet close enough to catch the plume.

The plume flopped sideways.

From the low position he drove the lance butt upward into the creature's right knee joint. The crack was loud in the chamber. The void-knight staggered left. Leonardo was already rising on his right leg, faster than the creature had braced for, and he laid the lance shaft across its neck and pressed to hold rather than to finish. A killing blow asked for commitment, and commitment meant losing this gap.

"Move," he said. His eyes stayed on the void-knight.

She had already moved. The void-knight recovered the way corrupted things did, and pressed forward, leaning its mass into him to drive him back toward the outer ring. Leonardo gave half a step, set his back foot on the seventh ring's groove, and stopped.

His left arm was shaking. The bad leg pushed too much of the work into his upper body, and the shaking would cost him before he wanted it to. But while he and the void-knight were locked in this gap, the void-knight was nowhere else.

Two years, three months, and sixteen days of standing in gaps like this one. Most of it alone in a deserted garrison, practicing the knight he had not yet had a chance to be. His hands had been rehearsing this for so long that they did not need him to think them through.

He pressed the lance forward. The void-knight pressed back.

The hollow-cost came faster than he expected.

Nibbles drove Whiskerbrand into the corrupted flank of a void-growth that had crept from the sixth ring's anchor point across three feet of stone toward the pillar where Hazel had retreated. The path had to be clear.

The blade hit the growth, the light came up hard and silver-white, and the hollow opened in his chest.

Four times before. Nettleflint's cellar, he had thought he was dying. The second time he knew what it was, and it dropped him to his knees anyway. The third time he had braced and walked through it. The fourth time he had moved through on momentum.

This time the hollow was deeper than the four put together.

All four were still in him, stacked, none of them paid down. He felt the hollow reach past them and keep reaching, past anything he could name, into ground he wasn't sure he still owned.

His vision greyed at the corners. His pads kept finding the stone.

The blade blazed. The corruption pulled away from the floor in threads that dissolved at the edge of the radiance, and the purification ran through the hilt and his paw and his arm and his chest, and the hollow deepened with it.

His vision narrowed further. The corners of the room went first, then the far edges, then the middle began to grey.

Grimthorn moved to cut him off, one paw extended to push him off-line so the void-growth could come back. Nibbles took the redirect on his left forearm, let himself stagger right, and turned the stagger into a step. His pads caught the worn groove in the mandala floor. The groove ran toward the sixth ring's anchor point.

He followed it.

His shoulder was screaming the old wound, white and clear. The hollow went deeper. Cold in his chest, then his arms, then his paws, moving toward his fingers on the hilt. He adjusted his grip. The hilt was warm. That was a thing to hold onto.

He pressed forward. The blade still blazed. The corruption pulled back from the light, and he stayed with the light the way he had been trained to stay with it, just moving, his pads on the stone and his grip on the hilt.

Grimthorn came for him again, lower this time, aimed at his legs. The herald had found that the longer Nibbles stayed inside the blazing, the more each step cost him. Nibbles felt the truth of it in his hip and his thighs.

He saw the attack through the grey.

His body responded before his mind caught up, a sidestep to the right, far enough but not fast. The strike caught his hip and numbed his left side from hip to knee. His pads stayed on the stone.

His vision was grey from corner to center now. The chamber had narrowed to a tunnel directly ahead. The grooves in the mandala floor. Grimthorn at the sixth ring. The sword's light, and where it touched corruption, the corruption fell back.

He kept walking.

He had failed the Guild trial twice. He had put his vest on backward the morning they left Thimblewick. He had tripped over his own sword sheath on the second day of the march and Nori had set him back on his feet without making a thing of it. He was also the creature that had run toward the cheese cart when everyone else had run the other way.

The vision narrowed further. He could still see Grimthorn, the path, the warmth in the hilt.

One pad in front of the other, the blade ahead of him, the light.

Dash was not watching the fight.

He had watched it long enough to read the pattern, the herald holding, the party pressing, the same exchange of advance and redirect since they entered. He had stopped finding anything new in it.

The dark pillar was a different matter.

Fourteen pillars at the outer ring. He had counted them coming in. Thirteen pulsed amber, irregular, working at something. The fourteenth, at the western edge, was dark, and had been dark since they entered.

He had noticed it the way he noticed a floorboard that didn't creak when every other one did. The why came after, once he had watched the fight long enough to know what he was looking for.

The loud exchanges at the chamber's center (Nibbles pressing toward the anchor point, Leonardo at the eastern gap, Acornimus covering Hazel at the south) left spaces between them that no one was watching. Dash crossed the chamber floor at a low diagonal and reached the dark pillar's base before the fight cycled again.

He crouched. The other pillars met the floor in sealed stone junctions, no gap. This one had a seam two fingers' breadth wide, running near-perfectly around the base, the cut too even for settling or damage. He pressed his paw into the seam and felt a mechanism under it, the kind that routed energy, not the kind that bore weight.

His ears went back against his skull. He had seen smaller versions of this in the Underways. The void energy flowing through the sixth ring's inversion ritual had to travel somewhere, and it traveled through the floor's conduit network from the anchor point outward, routed through pillar junctions toward the chambers below. The routing mechanism was here, in the base of this pillar. The pillar was dark because it was carrying the inversion signal, the whole of it, every conduit line in the chamber pulling through this one channel.

He held that knowledge a moment. Then he started looking for the weak place.

He reached for the thinner dagger at his belt (the prying blade) and worked the tip into the seam, angling it to feel where the mechanism took the most load. The metal resisted. He increased the angle. The resistance gave him a contour, and the contour gave him the break point.

A pulse came back through the blade. Cold and rhythmic. Thirty years of running without pause.

He braced his free paw flat against the pillar's base and drove the blade upward at the catch point.

The mechanism gave.

The sound was a single crack, sharp and immediate. He had the blade out and was moving before the echo finished. The dark pillar flared once, purple-black with the stored energy releasing through the break, and then went darker than before.

The chamber's harmonic shifted. The low sound the other pillars had been making deepened for one sustained moment (a resonance Dash felt through the floor in his paws) and then the amber light in the ring of pillars strengthened the way a fire strengthens when a blocked flue clears.

The sixth ring's groove stopped vibrating under his feet.

He was back at the southern edge of the chamber before anyone's eyes had moved.

"Done," he said.

The crack of the mechanism's break traveled through the chamber as sound, then through the floor as resonance.

The sixth ring's anchor point had been drawing void energy through the conduit lines and concentrating it in the carved inversion runes for three days. When the routing pillar broke, the energy had nowhere to flow. It pressed up against the broken channel, found no path forward, and reversed.

The mandala at the chamber's center flared purple-black. The inversion runes brightened, brightened further, and began to fragment from the outer ring inward in a fast cracking light. The amber harmonic the thirteen pillars had been holding surged, cracked, and turned wrong.

The shard in Hazel's paws split along its length.

The fracture ran base to apex, and the void energy the shard had carried (a decade of absorbed essence from corrupted zones across the Boroughs) released through the fracture into the air. A column of purple-black light rose three feet above her paws and spread at its crown. The cold that came with it was older than the hollow-cold of Whiskerbrand's purification. Deeper than that.

Hazel had not flinched. She was still holding the two halves, both paws open, cupped around the broken pieces, her ears flat against her skull and her eyes closed.

"Sage Willowbark—" Acornimus had come three steps forward from the southern gap before stopping himself.

"Hold your position," she said.

Her voice was steady. Her paws were shaking around the broken shard, not from effort yet but from what was pouring through the fracture and pressing against her palms.

She brought her paws together.

The void energy was pulling downward. Toward the mandala floor, the fractured inversion runes, the Wardstone conduit lines that had been routing the sixth stone's signal for three days. Those lines were still open at the anchor point. If the energy reached the network through the cracked runes, it would push outward through all of them, and the sixth stone's inversion would finish.

Hazel closed her paws around the shard's two halves.

The void energy was between her palms. She had nothing else to contain it with.

The light pulsed once, hard, and the cold went visible on her fur, faster than the creeping grey from days of carried cost, working from her paws inward by the second. The grey reached her wrists. Her forearms began to show it.

Her eyes stayed closed. "Telia," she said.

"Here." Telia was already beside her, flat to the floor, both paws pressed to the stone, reading the conduit lines beneath. Her cracked staff was down somewhere behind her, the grey through her own fur making plain how little she had left. "The seventh anchor is responding to the energy release. The conduit lines are running hot from the anchor base outward. If you can route it through the seventh conduit instead of the sixth, the anchor will take the load."

"How much can it hold?"

Telia's paws pressed harder to the floor. "More than the sixth has left. Less than what's in your paws."

Hazel opened her eyes. She looked at the column of light rising from her cupped paws, three feet of compressed void energy pressing against her palms. She turned her wrists, angling the energy's escape downward through the shard's fractured base toward the stone beneath her feet.

The nearest Wardstone conduit line was four inches below the floor.

She had no earth-magic and never had. Her work was chronicle and history, not the channeling earth-mages spent decades learning. What she had was thirty years of knowing the Wardstone network (every anchor point, every conduit junction, every load tolerance) because she had been present when it was built and had documented all of it. She knew where the seventh conduit ran and what it could hold.

She pressed the shard to the floor.

The void energy went through her on the way down.

Nibbles drew one sharp breath. The column of purple-black light reversed direction and drove down through Hazel's paws into the stone. The cords of her forearms went taut. The grey that had spread to her wrists over six days darkened and advanced past her elbows, toward her shoulders, the progression visible as it happened. Her ears stayed flat against her skull.

The seventh pillar blazed.

Amber light filled it from base to crown in a single surge, bright and sudden and total, brighter than any other light in the chamber. The seventh Wardstone conduit was taking what Hazel was routing through herself and into the floor, and the amber was the Wardstone answering it. The sound the seventh pillar made deepened, fuller now, no longer the exhausted holding Nibbles had stopped hearing since they entered.

The violet glow at the center of the sixth ring dimmed by half and held there. The inversion had stopped.

Hazel's paws shook against the floor.

The grey was at her shoulders, moving toward her throat. She was holding an opening through herself between the shard fragments and the conduit below the stone, and the opening was wider than she was. She kept her paws where they were.

The seventh pillar peaked. The amber threw shadows that did not match the torches at the stair, and then it held. The conduit was restored. The anchor was locked back into its work. The seventh stone's signal was running clear for the first time in thirty years.

The energy through Hazel's paws ran thin. Then it stopped.

She sat back from the floor. Her paws came away from the stone. The shard had crumbled further in the routing, a scatter of dark, dormant fragments across the carved stone where her palms had rested.

Her fur was white from paw to crown.

She looked at her paws. Then at Telia. "The seventh?"

Telia had both palms flat to the floor, eyes closed. "Whole. Full signal on the conduit. The sixth is half-restored. The interruption held at the halfway point. The inversion is stopped."

"Stable?"

"Long enough."

Hazel pressed her palms flat to her thighs and sat without moving. "That will have to do."

Grimthorn had not moved.

He stood at the sixth ring's anchor point and watched the seventh pillar reach its full amber blaze and the sixth ring's violet glow dim. The stillness in him was the kind a cord went into just before it pulled taut. Nibbles had learned that much across the fight.

He reached into the folds of his armor. The void-crystal was small, an inch across, irregular, with nothing on its dark surface for light to catch. He closed his right paw around it.

Nibbles still had Whiskerbrand in his paw. He could not feel his feet. He was standing because his legs had not given out yet, and he meant to keep standing until they did.

"Don't let him—" Nori said.

Grimthorn closed his paw on the crystal.

The transformation was total and immediate. The corruption integrated into his fur and armor flared outward, but it was nothing like the spreading growth Nibbles had seen in corrupted animals or the crystalline advance from Nettleflint's cellar. This drew energy inward, pulling through the soles of his feet and the mandala floor he had walked for thirty years, feeding from the conduit lines beneath. The crystal burned in his closed paw. The burning ran through his arm and into his chest. His amber-gold eyes went white.

Then dark, both lights gone for a suspended second, nothing in his face.

Then back to amber-gold, brighter than before. The age that had been working through him from previous void-crystal use spread visibly at his muzzle and the edges of his face. He had paid for what he was about to do.

Nibbles moved.

The hollow in his chest told him the sword had nothing left for full purification. He moved anyway. The herald was eight feet away, and the line to the stair ran between them.

He put his pads down on the seventh ring's groove and brought Whiskerbrand up.

The blade was warm. Warm and engaged, not blazing. The fifth use was spent and the hollow had run past where he had thought the bottom was. When Grimthorn's corrupted form came into the radiance, the blade's light pressed back. Not enough to stop him. Enough to make every step expensive.

Grimthorn came through it.

His right arm swept across in a redirect aimed at Nibbles' sword arm, and Nibbles took it on the forearm and went sideways. His knees hit the stone hard. His paws came down on the floor and the hilt was still in his right paw. He was on his knees between Grimthorn and the stair.

He brought the blade up. Grimthorn looked at him a long moment, at the mouse on his knees with the warm blade between them.

He raised his right paw, still closed around the crystal, and opened it.

The air in front of him opened with it.

The tear was vertical, three feet wide, rising toward the vault above. The inside was the absence of light in a particular direction, somewhere else laid over here. The sound it made was low and descending, the chamber's harmonics peeling away from the air around the tear and leaving silence behind.

Grimthorn stepped through.

As he turned toward the tear, Nibbles saw his left paw.

It hung at his side. The claws loose, the paw empty. Not braced for anything. In the moment before the tear closed, the seventh pillar's amber light fell across the herald's retreating form, and the empty paw was the clearest thing in it.

Nibbles noted it, and the meaning stayed past him.

The tear closed.

The chamber's harmonics returned. Nibbles was on his knees on the seventh ring's groove, the warm blade in his paw, the herald gone.

He got back to his feet.

His legs held.

The seventh pillar's amber light was steady and full, throwing clear shadows inward across the mandala's rings. The sixth ring's anchor point still held a trace of violet, the half-restored inversion signal sitting in stasis. The other five anchor rings were dark.

Five stones still inverted. Five regions still losing ground. But the seventh was whole, every Wardstone conduit line running to it live, the anchor locked, the signal clear. Grimthorn had walked this floor for thirty years to break what had been built here. It was still standing.

The sixth had stopped at the halfway point. Stopped, not recovered. The void energy that had been bleeding out into that anchor's surrounding country was no longer being fed.

Seventh whole. Sixth in stasis. Five inverted. A year, maybe two, before the prison started to give. Before this morning it had been weeks.

He put Whiskerbrand back in its sheath. The sword went in warm. Steady warmth, no draw on him. He had nothing left to give it.

He looked across the chamber. Leonardo was at the eastern gap, lance tip to the floor, the void-knight dark and still at his feet. Hazel was on the floor with Acornimus crouched beside her, one paw over both of hers. Telia was against the southern wall, knees drawn up, eyes closed, her cracked staff nowhere in sight. Dash was at the outer ring with his back to the dark pillar, watching the chamber.

Nori was at the western wall. He crossed the mandala floor toward her, his pads in one of the grooves.

She had found a space between two of the outer pillars, low to the floor. Her back was against the cold stone. The crossbow was in her lap, both paws resting on it, not raised. Her eyes were open.

He knelt beside her. The wound was in her right side, below the ribs. He had known since the descent that the bandage was bleeding through. The stair had finished it, twelve steps on an injury that should not have taken the stair. She had given no sign. She had kept the crossbow level and covered her angles and worked through to the end of it.

"How bad?" he asked.

"The stair," she said. "On the way down." Her voice was level. The same voice that had corrected his guard position on the second day of the march. "I managed. Didn't want to slow anyone down."

He sat down beside her. The stone was cold through his vest.

She had known before the descent. The chamber needed covering, she could cover it. That was the work. She had been right about all of it.

He reached out and took the paw not holding the crossbow. Her grip was still strong.

She looked at him the way she looked at exits.

"Bristlebaum's above," she said.

"Yes."

"He held the Sanctum?"

"He held it."

She made a small sound, and something in her face eased. Then she looked at the chamber, across the mandala floor, the pillar ring, the stair at the eastern wall.

"All right," she said. "Ask me what you want to ask."

"I don't have a question," he said.

"I know." She looked at him. "I do."

"Tell me again," Nori said. "What you go back to. You told me on the march. I want to hear it again."

He had told her in the third week, when the valley behind them still smelled of corruption and the road ahead was three hard days on an uneven track. She had asked why he hadn't turned back. Not unkindly. She had asked it the way she asked about exits, because she wanted accurate information. He had thought about it. Then he had told her.

His mother's garden at the edge of Thimblewick. The apple tree that dropped fruit on the roof in autumn, the sound of apples on thatch that had become the sound of autumn itself after enough years. The fountain in the village square, still tinted purple from the cleaning compound incident two years before the Cheese Festival, the one the village had voted to keep.

She had listened. She had said *that's a good enough reason.* Then she had kept walking, and at the next stream crossing she had corrected his footwork.

He had thought about it later.

"The garden," he said. "My mother's garden, at the edge of the village. The apple tree. In autumn it drops on the roof. The whole house sounds like autumn for a month." He kept his voice steady. "The fountain in the square is still purple. The whole village voted to keep it. Said the stain was Thimblewick's now and the bleaching fee was highway robbery besides."

Nori's paw tightened on his.

"That's a good enough reason," she said.

He held her paw. Her breathing slowed. Still careful, but settling. He watched the seventh pillar's amber light steady on the chamber floor.

"I told Bristlebaum you were the right choice," she said. "In Ironhold, after the first day. Before he'd decided."

He looked at her.

"Someone needed to say it plainly," she said. "He was going to bury it in a tier and call it unresolved. I told him the sword had chosen and the sword was right and if he needed two weeks to verify that, the two weeks were his to waste. He gave you two days."

"He gave me two days," Nibbles said.

"Still a bureaucrat." He felt it in her grip, the slight ease that meant she was almost smiling. "But the right call."

He had not known anyone had spoken for him in Ironhold. He was grateful and he was grieving at the same time, and the two were not separate things. He should have guessed it was her.

"You asked me about the garden," he said, "because you were checking."

"I was checking," she said. "Something worth going back to is something worth going forward for. That's what I needed to know. You passed. Mice who go back to purple fountains and apple trees don't abandon the work."

"I still put my vest on backward," he said.

"Twice this week," she said. "I counted."

He held her paw.

"You're going to be fine," she said.

He stayed quiet.

"Nibbles." She said it the way she said *hold your position*. "The work doesn't stop here. The five stones still out there don't stop because we had a hard day in a bad chamber. You know that."

"I know."

"The sword chose correctly. I knew it in the second week. I'm telling you now because you should carry it clearly from here, without the uncertainty." She paused. "You ran toward the cheese cart. Everything else followed from that. The sword knew what it was looking for and it found it and it was right. The doubt doesn't change that. Carry it with you if you have to, but carry it alongside the rest."

He could not tell her she was wrong.

He had been carrying the doubt since Thimblewick, in the pack with everything else, and that was likely how he was going to keep carrying it. But she had watched him do the work with it, and she was not telling him the doubt was wrong. She was telling him it was beside the point. The sword had already decided, and what remained was for him to catch up.

That was not the same as being told not to be afraid.

The seventh pillar's light held steady above them. Behind him, Leonardo set his lance tip to the floor. Acornimus's pen moved on parchment. Telia breathed against the southern wall.

Nori's paw was in his, and he did not let go.

Chapter Twenty-Three
The Aftermath

The Crystal Sanctum was quiet. It had not been quiet since they entered it.

The harmonic still lived in the pillars, low and cracked-open (thirty years of holding had left the structure that way and the fight had not improved it) but the active pressing and tearing was gone.

Bristlebaum stood at the nexus altar with his back to Nibbles, his thick paw passing slowly over each of the seven carved anchor points in the black stone. He was not pressing them. Reading them.

Nibbles waited near the wall. The first five anchor points were dark. From where he stood he could see the amber in the stone dead, replaced by the faint grey-violet of stones inverted and held inverted for years. Bristlebaum paused at each one. Two breaths, then on to the next. His quills were half-raised.

He stopped longest at the sixth. Amber ran along the lower half of its carved channel, present but neither bright nor certain. The upper half sat cold. Telia had pressed her paws to the conduit until her legs failed and the grey spread through her fur and the purple lines started up her forearms, and the half-restored stone was what that work had bought.

The seventh was different. The amber ran full, base to edge, bright enough to cast a faint shadow across Bristlebaum's outstretched paw. But the crystal pillar above it had fractured (hairline cracks running upward from the base) and the light pulsed unevenly, flaring and catching and flaring. The seventh stone was whole, and it was holding the prison by itself.

Bristlebaum stepped back from the altar and turned. "Five inverted." His Guildmaster voice, quieter than Nibbles had heard it. "The sixth, half restored. Telia's work held." He looked at the seventh's fractured pillar. "The seventh is intact. It will not hold indefinitely."

"How long?" Nibbles asked.

"A year," Bristlebaum said. "Perhaps two."

He looked at Nibbles directly, past the altar and the fractured column. He crossed the space between them and put his paw on Nibbles' shoulder, the grip deliberate.

"You bought time," Bristlebaum said. "That is what was done here. That is everything."

Nibbles' whiskers went still.

They found Hazel before they reached the laboratory door.

She had pulled herself to sitting on her own, back against a workbench in the outer passage, paws in her lap. The workbench held a row of Grimthorn's instruments, vials, measuring rods, a cracked-face compass. She had not touched them. She was awake when they came around the corner, her eyes tracking to them. The white fur across her face had gone grey at the temples before any of this. The grey reached past her brow now.

She looked at Bristlebaum. "The seventh weaving," she said. "Did it hold?"

"It held," he said.

She closed her eyes. When they opened, she turned toward the passage leading back to the Sanctum below. Her ears were fully down. "The sixth?"

Bristlebaum crouched to her level. "Half restored," he said. "Telia's work held."

Hazel took a moment. "Half," she said.

"Yes."

Her ears stayed down. Nibbles stood beside her and waited.

"I had hoped for more of it," she said.

Bristlebaum stood. "Can you stand?"

"Yes," she said.

It took longer than it should have. Nibbles kept his paw near her elbow without touching her. Her legs held once she had her feet under her. She straightened and looked through the open door at the laboratory.

Crystal capsules floor to ceiling, murky in the dim. The obsidian tablet on the central workbench with its two shades of ink. The smell of turned earth and cauterized iron.

"The scrolls," she said.

"I have them," Bristlebaum said.

She nodded once. "We should see to the others," she said, and walked toward the stairs.

Nibbles followed.

The outer wall faced east.

Nibbles thought Dash had chosen it. Dash had walked the base of the wall until the amber light from the seventh Wardstone's field reached the ground, and there he had stopped. The amber bled up through the foundations, faint and steady.

Nibbles dug on his knees with an iron bar taken from the laboratory. The wrong tool for the work, but his paws found a rhythm and the dirt gave way. The amber light lay across his paws when he reached the right angle. He kept his eyes on the work.

Dash had found a proper spade somewhere in the Keep's stores. He worked it steady and direct, each stroke even, his face toward the ground. The white lightning-bolt patch on his chest was smeared with earth. His whiskers worked the whole time.

Leonardo could not dig. His right arm was bound against his side, too recent from the chamber, and the broken leg made kneeling impossible. He had carried her from the Sanctum's threshold to this wall, her weight on his good arm, his lance scraping stone at every step to keep him upright. He had not stopped for the leg. He had brought her here and then planted his lance and stood.

Nobody asked him to do less.

Bristlebaum stood at the wall a few yards off, arms at his sides, quills half-raised. He had not come to dig. He watched the three of them work, and he stayed.

When the hole was right, Nibbles set the bar down in the dirt and got to his feet. His knees ached from the ground.

They placed her in the amber light.

Leonardo used his good arm and more of the bad arm than was careful. Dash was on the other side. Nibbles took the third position and kept the weight even.

She lay in the earth where the seventh Wardstone's field reached. The amber lay across the turned soil, the same steady pulse Nibbles had felt through his paws while digging.

He stood at the edge of the grave and looked at it. Dash stood at the foot of the grave and counted. Nibbles had seen him do it after every move, every camp, every time the group rearranged itself. The answer this time was one fewer.

They filled the grave. The amber light held through all of it.

Nibbles stood back and looked up at the wall of the Keep above them. The stone was cold and dark and the eastern sky beyond it was beginning to show the first faint lightening before dawn. His shoulder pulled at something when he lifted the bar to carry it back. He kept walking.

Bristlebaum was still at the wall, looking at the grave. His quills had not settled.

They walked back inside.

Acornimus had found a corner of the great hall where the pale blue orbs drifted close enough to read by.

He sat with his journal open across his knees and wrote. Nibbles came back from washing the earth from his paws in the passage basin, came through the hall entrance, and found him there. Vest still pressed. Pen moving. Pages turning.

Nibbles had not seen him write like this. The journal usually came out in short intervals, a name, a notation, a sketch. Tonight the pages kept turning. He had been writing since before the burial.

Nibbles sat against the opposite wall. He watched Acornimus write. The vest was still immaculate, the same as it had been when they stepped into Ironhold weeks ago.

After a while Acornimus stopped writing. He read the last page. Then he closed the journal.

He held it on his knees. Then he opened it again, turned to the last page, and his pen moved. One short line. He held the pen above the ink after.

He closed the journal and brought it to his chest.

Nibbles looked away.

Telia had not sat down.

The others had found places in the great hall. Hazel was near the door on a folded cloak. Leonardo had his back against one of the carved-tree columns, his lance across his knees. Dash was against the far wall with his eyes half-shut. Telia stood in the middle of the hall and looked at the floor.

She was grey. Grey through, not grey-streaked or grey at the temples, the brown remaining only at her muzzle and the edges of her paws. The colour had been changing since Ridgemarrow, and the Sanctum had brought it the rest of the way.

"Telia," Nibbles said.

She looked at him. Her sleeves were rolled up. The purple lines ran from her wrists to just below her elbows, the same corruption-threading he had seen in the valley's animals before the corruption fully took them. In her they were thin, faint as old ink, but they were there.

"I can still walk," she said, before he said anything else. "And fight if it's needed." She considered. "Less well on the fighting. The walking is still good."

The cracked staff was planted in the floor beside her. The preservation spell had been gone since before the valley, the crack running diagonal from grip to base. She was not leaning on the staff. It was standing where she had planted it.

She walked from the middle of the hall to the eastern wall and back. Steady. Even.

"Still," she said.

Nibbles looked at the purple lines on her forearms, and the grey, and the cracked staff, and the fact of her on her own feet.

Before the light failed, Bristlebaum walked out to the main gate and stood looking at the Keep from the outside.

Nibbles followed. The towers jutted at their wrong angles against the grey sky. The iron-bound gates stood open where the party had passed through, the runes in the iron still shifting in their slow patterns. The corruption in the stone would not leave because Grimthorn had. It had been here too long.

"We're not burning it," Bristlebaum said.

Nibbles looked at him. Bristlebaum was looking at the gates. His quills were lower than they had been all day. Not settled. Lower.

"It was built for something before Grimthorn took it," he said. "The stone reads the people who enter it. That is in the construction, not in the corruption." He paused. "There will come a time when someone needs a place built to ask the right questions. Whether they are ready. Whether they should be trusted with what they are carrying." His paw rested at his side. "We don't burn a proving ground."

He turned from the gate and walked back toward the entrance.

Nibbles followed.

The great hall was quiet by the second watch.

Hazel had gone still on her cloak. Leonardo was upright against his column, but the grip on his lance was too deliberate for sleep. Dash had gone still against the far wall, though his ears still moved in the dark. Telia was near the eastern door, finally seated, her cracked staff beside her.

Nibbles sat at the entrance passage with Whiskerbrand across his knees.

The blade was warm. The steady warmth it had been giving off since the Sanctum, no draw and no alert, just present. He kept both paws on the flat.

He was thinking about the five dark anchor points in the nexus altar. Five inverted. The sixth half-restored, the seventh holding everything alone and fracturing from the effort. A year, perhaps two, and the prison would fail, and everything they had spent to get here (the valley, the Caves, Gareth, Nori, Hazel on the laboratory floor, Telia's forearms) would have bought a year.

He was trying to decide if that was enough.

He heard Bristlebaum before he saw him, the heavy quiet tread of an older hedgehog who had learned a long time ago not to wake people on stone floors. Bristlebaum came through the inner passage and stopped when he saw Nibbles was awake.

"Thinking too loud again," Bristlebaum said.

"Sorry," Nibbles said.

"Don't apologize for thinking." Bristlebaum came and sat on the floor beside him, closer than a Guildmaster usually sat with a probationary recruit. His quills settled fractionally.

The pale blue orbs drifted near the ceiling.

"Did we win?" Nibbles asked. He had not planned to ask it.

Bristlebaum's answer waited while he looked at the dark amber runes in the floor, the great tree pattern carved into the stone with its roots and branches.

"Five Wardstones still inverted," he said. "The sixth half-restored, the seventh holding what it wasn't built to hold alone. Grimthorn alive and building toward whatever comes next." He paused. "And the seventh is whole. The sixth runs amber along half its length. Grimthorn does not have the prison." He was quiet a moment. His eyes moved from the runes to Nibbles' face. "That is because of what was done here."

Nibbles looked at the tree pattern in the floor. "The people who come after us," he said. "They'll have to finish it."

"Yes," Bristlebaum said. "They will."

"And we can't tell them where to start."

"They will find their own start," Bristlebaum said. "They will have a world to find it in. They will have time." He paused. "Do you understand what I mean by that?"

Nibbles looked at the runes. "Someone has to use the time," he said. "Or it doesn't mean anything."

"Yes. And that someone will exist because you were here. Because Telia was here, and Nori, and all of them." His paw rested on his knee. "The next people will not know your names, most likely. They will find the prison holding and they will not know who bought that. But the holding will have been bought. It will be real. Nothing that comes after can unmake it."

Nibbles' paws stayed on the warm flat of the blade.

Bristlebaum's paw came down on his shoulder, the same deliberate grip as in the Sanctum.

"You bought time," Bristlebaum said. "That is everything."

Nibbles' whiskers went still.

They left at first light.

Leonardo took the lead position at the base of the Keep's steps and set his lance against the ground at the new angle his leg required. Using it rather than carrying it, planting it ahead of him and walking up to it. He found the balance and moved, and the group fell in behind him.

The road north climbed for the first three hours. Nibbles felt the grade in his shoulder, the bandage pulling differently on a slope, the muscles either side of the wound making small adjustments that added up. He stopped tracking them after the first hour and let his body manage.

Hazel walked behind him. Deliberate as she had always been, each step placed with care, but slower between placements. The precision was intact. The pace was what she had left in the Sanctum.

Telia walked on his left. Grey through and through now, the brown only at her muzzle and the edges of her paws. When her wrists flexed on the cracked staff, the purple lines showed briefly past the cuff. She walked without stopping. She did not lean on the staff. The staff was planted beside her stride the way it had always been, cracked now.

Acornimus held his journal to his chest for most of the first day, pressed flat against his ribs with both paws on the cover. By the second morning it was back in his pack.

Dash walked at the rear, quiet. His ears moved more than the rest of him.

Lark came overhead every hour or so. She adjusted her arc, turned back north, and climbed again.

Three days. The grade eased. The barren cracked soil around the Keep gave way to scattered trees, then proper woodland, then the rolling country that meant they were almost home.

They came over the long ridge on the afternoon of the third day, and Nibbles stopped walking before his eyes had caught up with what his whiskers already had.

A mineral sharpness on the wind, old, familiar. His paw had already found Whiskerbrand's hilt by reflex.

This was not corruption. He knew corruption now, the iron-sweet edge of it, the way the blade would have warmed already against his palm.

He looked down. The village lay below them in the afternoon light. Chimneys against the pale sky. The mill wheel still turning at the far edge of town. The close-packed rooftops of the baker's and the chandler's and the wheelwright's and the rest. The Guild tent at the edge of the festival grounds, its patched tarpaulin and old-campaign banners.

And in the center of the market square, the fountain.

Still purple. The tint had not moved in two years of rain; the cleaning compound had gone deep into the stone. He could smell the mineral edge of the old dye from up on the ridge, faint on the afternoon wind. His whiskers had caught it before his eyes had.

He had grown up walking past that fountain. The color had stopped being remarkable after the first season. The village had voted to keep the stain rather than pay for the bleaching, and the joke about Thimblewick's stubbornness had been circulating since he was small.

He stood on the ridge and looked at it. The mistake sat in the center of the square. Every morning crossing to the baker's. Every evening coming back. Thimblewick's now, and they had kept it.

He stood on the ridge until the others caught up around him (Telia planting her cracked staff, Hazel at his shoulder, Leonardo straightening against his lance) and then he walked down.

Lark passed low over the rooftops and climbed back up without landing. Dash came down the last stretch beside him.

"Fountain's still purple," Dash said.

"Yes," Nibbles said.

Half the village had come out to the road.

Not the whole of it. The baker was at his ovens (which meant it was later in the afternoon than Nibbles had reckoned) and the mill was still turning, so someone had stayed back to mind it. But enough of them. A crowd stretching from the north road's edge in the fading light, people he had known his whole life, a few he could not place from this distance, all of them waiting and watching.

And at the front of it, his mother.

She found him before he found her.

He was still fifty yards out when he saw her posture change. The brace she had been holding in her shoulders went out of her. She did not run. She stood at the front of the crowd with her paws at her sides and her eyes on him and let him come to her.

The crowd opened to let the party through, voices rising in the low warm sound of a village reunion. Nibbles walked toward his mother.

She looked at him when he reached her, the full look, the one he had known since he was small. Her eyes moved over him the way they did when she was working through a list.

"There you are," she said.

He stopped in front of her. She reached up and took his face in both paws and looked at him the way she had after the mill wheel incident. He bore it.

"My brave, foolish, wonderful boy," she said.

She embraced him.

He had not thought about the ribs until her arms came around him. He had been managing the left side for three days, and it had not asked anything of him until now.

The cracked ribs from somewhere in the Sanctum screamed up his left side, bright and immediate.

He held his face still. He kept his arms around her and his breathing even. The familiar smell of her arrived in full, kitchen herbs, clean wool, the soap she had been using his whole life. His whiskers went still.

She held him a long time. Around them the crowd did the quiet work of reunion. Acornimus somewhere behind him, accepting something warm with formal thanks. Leonardo's voice rising too loud and then catching itself. Dash quiet, as Dash usually was.

His mother finally pulled back. Her paws stayed on his arms. She looked at him again, planning now.

"You need a meal," she said. "And a bath. Then you sleep for two days."

"In that order," he said.

"In that order."

She took his arm and walked him toward the village. He walked beside her with his breathing even and kept the ribs to himself.

The Guild tent had not changed.

Patched tarpaulin. Old-campaign banners. The quest board ten feet high in the dark, its enchanted driftwood frame catching faint sounds from the curling corners of old petitions. The chest in the far corner, dark with age, in its same place.

Empty now.

He had asked for first watch. Bristlebaum had looked at him a moment and then nodded, and the others had accepted the offer without comment. He sat at the tent entrance with his back against the frame and Whiskerbrand across his knees.

The blade was warm. The low steady warmth it had held since the Sanctum, no signal in it, no alert, just present. A fire banked for the night.

The village was quiet. The market square behind him held the fountain and the fountain held its purple. The night was the kind that came after.

He thought about the five dark stones in the nexus altar. Five inverted. The sixth running amber along half its length. The seventh whole and fracturing at its base, carrying what seven had been built to carry together. A year, perhaps two, and someone else would have to take up what they had started.

It would have been started, and nothing coming after could unmake that.

He had been sitting with the count since the Sanctum and he had not found a way to settle it, and he was not going to settle it tonight.

His whiskers were still.

Whiskerbrand rested warm across his knees. The sword had done its work, and so had he.

Somewhere east, past the ridge and three days of road, Thornwall Keep stood in the dark. Wrong-angled towers. Shifting runes in the iron. The amber tree in the floor of the great hall, waiting for whoever came after them.

The Keep stood dark against the eastern sky.

Chapter Twenty-Four
Home

THE QUEST BOARD WAS full again. Nibbles stood inside the tent entrance with Whiskerbrand across his back. The ribs were still tender when he moved wrong, and the shoulder where the purification cost had burned deepest was a tight knot of scar.

He counted seven new notices. A livestock concern from the eastern farms. A flooding report from a low district two valleys over. A request for escort on the coast road, merchants wanting someone to look imposing while they moved goods through a stretch of road that had grown inhospitable. None of it was corrupted valleys or inverted Wardstones.

The tent smelled the same. Leather polish, old sweat, and something in the far corner that had been edible at some point and was now its own concern. The enchanted driftwood frame had a few new burns where old notices had been pulled. New whispers in the wood. Smaller ones.

Two Guildmembers he did not know the names of were working at the dispatch table. One looked up when he came to the board, nodded, returned to the stack she had been sorting.

He moved to the board and read. The livestock concern was something killing fowl. The farmer had written "probably foxes" and crossed it out and left the line blank. The escort request was more specific. Three merchants, one cart, a road with three incidents in the past month. Standard Guild work, the kind that had been waiting on this board when he left for Ridgemarrow.

He reached up to take the escort notice down. His ribs pulled. His paw came back to his side.

One week home was not enough.

He checked the flooding notice. A low district, the record said. Water moving in ways the farmers had not seen before, which could mean the dam upstream, or a wet spring, or something else. He had spent enough time in the past weeks watching water do unfamiliar things to recognise dam trouble, and this was not that. Spring thaw. He moved the flooding notice to the advisory stack himself.

He turned to the left side of the board, the low corner where the half-burned scrap had been. It was gone. Someone had filed it, or pulled it, and he was not going to know which.

He turned back to the board and read the surveyor request from the south.

Outside, the festival grounds were quiet at this hour. Stalls not yet set up. The Thimblewick morning cool and grey. Birds called somewhere past the tent wall. His whiskers caught the smell of bread from the baker's across the square; she had her hours and she kept them.

He pulled the escort notice down carefully and carried it to the desk at the back of the tent.

Bristlebaum was already writing when Nibbles came through.

Not dictating. Writing himself, his paw moving slowly across the parchment in the careful script he used for official documents. Two sheets lay beside him, both with the Guild's standard commendation header at the top. The printed fields (name, rank, field service duration, citation date) had been filled in by a clerk. Bristlebaum was filling in the blank lines.

His quills sat at the middle register. Higher than the week before.

Nibbles set the escort notice on the far corner of the desk. One of Bristlebaum's ears tilted toward the sound.

"Flooding in the low district," Nibbles said. "Eastern farms want something about livestock. Escort request on the coast road."

"Coast road's already covered, routing notice, put it with the southern assignments," Bristlebaum said, still writing. "Flooding's in the advisory stack?"

"Already there."

"Good. Livestock concern, bring it in."

His pen kept moving. Nibbles moved the livestock notice to the incoming stack and stood watching Bristlebaum write.

The forms gave the Guild somewhere to put what had happened. Citation for outstanding field service. Commendation pending review. Standard procedure. Names went into the record, and after that there were procedures. Bristlebaum filled in a line, paused, read what he had written, continued.

"Will those go to the families?" Nibbles asked.

"Eventually." Bristlebaum's paw kept moving. "After review. There are families to locate. Records to cross-reference. The Guild has a process."

"How long?"

"Weeks. Possibly longer."

Nibbles watched him finish the citation for Nori Riverclaw. Six years of field service. Three prior citations. The form had a box for mission details, and Bristlebaum was filling it in himself.

"I'm going to write to their families," Nibbles said.

Bristlebaum's paw stopped. He set the pen down with care.

"It isn't required," he said.

"I know."

Bristlebaum looked at him, spectacles in place.

"Address records are in the east cabinet," he said. "Third shelf. Anything predating the current system will be in the supplemental ledger beside it."

He picked up the pen, and his quills did not settle.

The east cabinet was exactly where Bristlebaum had said. Nibbles spent a quarter of an hour with the third shelf and the supplemental ledger before he had what he needed. A family address for Gareth Redstone, with a next-of-kin notation in the Guild's standard format. One for Nori Riverclaw, updated two years prior.

He carried both records to the writing table at the back of the tent, found blank parchment in the second drawer, and sat down. Whiskerbrand he leaned against the table leg, within reach. He picked up the pen.

He started with Gareth. The first draft ran long. He wrote about the corrupted valley and the read Gareth had completed before anyone else understood the pattern. The way Gareth had reached for his notes when the situation was moving faster than notes could follow. The second assault. The ground, what had happened, who had been where. Gareth being right about everything, and what it had cost him. What Gareth had told him in the ritual chamber. He crossed out four sentences about grief and left one.

His whiskers had gone still by the time he read it back.

The letter was trying to explain. He could see it in every line. He had written it for strangers, putting the logic together as if the right arrangement of words would make Gareth's family understand. He tried again, shorter, cutting the valley and the maps and the weeks of travel, and read that back too. It was still trying to give the family an ordering of the events that would make the events make sense. The letter could not do that work, and the work was not what they needed.

He set both drafts aside. The final draft was half a page. Gareth's name at the top, then what had happened. Field analyst, assignment in the northern border country, identified the void corruption pattern before anyone understood what was being done to the Wardstone sites, right about all of it, died in the second assault protecting the party. One more line, the substance of what Gareth had said to him in the ritual chamber if not the exact words. That Nibbles being there had not been a mistake. He left the line as a statement.

He folded it and started Nori's.

The first draft for Nori went the way Gareth's first had, sentences reaching back toward the caves and the road and what she had taught him. He could feel it going wrong as he wrote and he wrote it anyway in case this one was different. It wasn't. He had written about what her teaching had done for him. It was true. It answered his grief, not hers.

He set it aside. The second draft said what had happened. Her name. Six years with the Guild. The best in the field at what she did. She had gone into the Whispering Caves knowing what it would cost her, because she was the right one to go. He was sorry for their loss.

He read it twice. What the letter meant was something her family would have to carry the way he was carrying it. He had spent one draft trying to do that work for them. He could not.

He folded both final drafts and went to find Bristlebaum.

The Guildmaster was still at the desk. He looked up when Nibbles came back, and Nibbles set both letters down in front of him.

"I don't know where they live," Nibbles said. "By feel, I mean. I found the addresses in the records. But you know the roads."

Bristlebaum looked at the letters a moment. He picked them up.

"I'll see they go out with the morning courier," he said.

Acornimus had requisitioned a room at the inn on the square instead of the Guildhouse cot his authorization tier covered. The inn had a table positioned beneath a window. The Guildhouse did not. On his first morning he had moved the table (door visible from the chair, window to his left, enough light to write without squinting) and he had not moved it since.

His vest was pressed. He had done it himself with a smooth stone, the way he had been doing it for most of the past several weeks. He had pressed it once this morning, looked at the result, and pressed it again. The creases sat the way they should.

The room had its own morning sounds. The inn's kitchen two floors below. The square filling with early customers. A cart somewhere behind the building. Seven days back from the field, and he could hear them as ordinary sounds again.

He sat at the table and opened the journal to the record he had written the night Gareth died. The page was toward the back of the current volume. He found the entry without looking for it, the coordination log thread, the garrison unit's reassignment, the exact words Gareth had used, the context, the date, the cadence of Gareth's voice as he had delivered the report. He had written it while the details were still precise.

He had closed the journal that night. Opened it before dawn the next morning and read it twice. Closed it. He had done that three mornings in sequence. This was the fourth.

The handwriting on the night-of entry was slightly different from his standard. Written at speed, by candlelight, with field ink nearly spent. The letters were correct. The angle was off by a few degrees. He had seen it on the second morning.

He read through the entry now. His whiskers were still throughout.

He picked up the pen. The addition was short. He wrote it at the bottom of the page, below everything else, leaving a clear gap between the existing record and the new notation. In his standard notation form. When he finished he read it over once, checking each word.

He set the pen down. The morning air was dry and the ink dried quickly. He watched it, read the line over once more, and closed the journal.

He buckled it into his satchel and went to the window. The square had filled while he was writing.

He put on his hat and went downstairs.

His mother's garden had a gate that stuck in damp weather and swung easy in dry. He lifted on the latch the way he always had, and it swung.

The apple tree was still there. His father had planted it the year before Nibbles was born, and it had grown tall, taller than the garden wall by three lengths now, branches spreading wide over the southern beds. The leaves were dark green in the afternoon, moving slightly in a wind too small to reach him at the gate. Fallen leaves from some earlier gust had drifted into the corner by the west wall. He would probably walk past them another ten times before he dealt with them.

The beds along the east wall held his mother's kitchen herbs, in tight rows, labeled with small flat stones carved in her slanting script. The gatepost had a crack in the stone at the base with a vine started in it, small when he had left, grown considerably since. His mother had been meaning to deal with it for two years. The vine had its own views on the matter.

He crossed the garden and sat on the bench beneath the tree. The wood was worn smooth in the two places where a person sat most often, the grain gone slick from years of the same weight.

The stone wall ran along the south edge, old fieldstone, laid before his grandmother's time, the mortar weathered and worn. The practice marks were at elbow height on his right. Long scratches in the mortar, repeated in the same spot, where a whittled stick had caught the same place over a season of the same incomplete form. He had stood here for three years when he was small. Seven, eight, nine. Working through forms he had copied from a drawing in a book, bracing his paw on the wall to find the balance the drawing showed. The marks had been there when he left for Ridgemarrow.

He drew Whiskerbrand and laid it across his knees.

The sword was warm. The steady warmth, no reach in it. He rested his paws on the flat. His whiskers had gone still somewhere between the gate and the bench.

His ribs pulled when he settled his back against the tree. He shifted and found the angle that did not wake them. The shoulder was the bigger problem, the tight knot of scar below the collarbone where the purification cost had burned deepest, sharp when he moved wrong. He found the position that asked nothing of it.

A bee moved through the herb beds along the east wall, working from stem to stem without hurry.

The sounds from the square came over the wall. Voices. A cart on the upper lane. The splash of the fountain. Someone calling a name toward the market end. None of it was about him. The village was running its own day.

He thought about Gareth. The ritual chamber. The second assault before it. Gareth carrying his notes right up to the moment the fight reached him, still reaching for them when it did.

A sparrow landed on the stone wall, looked at him without particular concern, and went.

He thought of Gareth's voice in the chamber, what he had said about why the sword had chosen what it chose. Gareth had been right about all of it.

He thought about Nori. She would have had something to say about the practice marks, something dry and accurate, the kind of observation she made before she decided whether the new information had changed anything. She would have read the angle of the scratches and said something he would think about for a day before he caught what it was also about. Six years in the Guild. The best in the field at what she did.

He looked up at the apple tree. The afternoon light had shifted through the branches. He had watched it shift like that from this bench when he was eight.

What she would actually have said stayed past him. She was gone, and he stayed where he was.

His tail had wrapped around his leg without his noticing.

The grief came up alongside the scar pulling, and the hollow-cost from the purifications still not entirely closed.

He looked at the practice marks in the stone wall. He had not cried yet, which surprised him sometimes and did not at others.

He shifted his grip on the sword. Whiskerbrand was warm across his knees.

Past the garden wall, the fountain in the square was still purple. The stain from the cleaning compound incident two years before the Cheese Festival; the village had voted to keep it rather than pay the bleaching fee. It had been purple when he left for Ridgemarrow, and it was purple now.

Epilogue

His whiskers caught morning before his eyes did. The garden lay still. Frost on the north side of the wall. Seedlings his mother had planted along the south-facing bed pushing up small and pale green.

The sword was across his back. The leather sheath had worn soft at the contact points over three months and he felt it the way he felt his own breathing. He lay on the garden bench where he had taken to sleeping when the nights were dry, the cold not quite gone from the stone but close. Birds in the eastern hedgerow. The drip from the rain-barrel spigot his mother kept meaning to fix.

He sat up. His left shoulder pulled at the angle it always did now, the scar from Thornwall, the one that would tighten in cold weather from here on. He adjusted the hilt position and the pull eased.

In the first week home, the sword had been active in ways that kept waking him. Warmth at odd hours. The alert hum at something in the soil that turned out to be the decay of a tree root. It had taken time for both of them to settle. He had learned the difference in the warmth (alert from present, working from at rest) and the sword had settled into the new pattern alongside him. By the second week it had stopped waking him, and it had not started again.

The sword was warm now, steady warmth, a fire banked for the day.

He was working at the base of the rose canes when she came out with two mugs. He smelled it before she reached him. Chamomile and honey, the thick amber kind from their own hive. She had made it this way when he was young and the thunder off the hills kept him awake. She would sit with him at the kitchen table until the storm moved east, not saying much, just there.

"You're up early," she said.

"Couldn't sleep past the birds."

She set one mug on the flat stone he used as a work rest and kept hers. He wrapped his paws around the warmth of it.

"You were dreaming," she said.

He nodded. "The old wielder. His memories come clearer than they used to. Pictures, not words. Like a teacher who only speaks in pictures. I had one like that. A hedgehog at the Guild when I was training, briefly. He'd show you the form and wait and never explain anything. Either you understood or you came back the next day and tried again."

"Were you any good at it?"

"At the time? No." He looked at the mug. "Getting better."

His mother was quiet. The chamomile had cooled enough to drink and he drank some.

"Are they difficult?" she asked. "The pictures?"

He thought about the one from this morning. A badger in firelight, a sword pressed from one pair of paws into another, silver light dispersing upward in the moment after. Plain, not dramatic. The face of the creature receiving the sword, knowing it already.

"They're getting easier to hold," he said.

She set down her mug and went back to the garden. She had a bed to weed on the west side. He finished his chamomile and went back to the rose canes.

Bristlebaum came through the garden gate mid-morning, mud still on his boots from the day before. The Guild tent was at the east edge of the village and the lane between there and the garden had not dried out. He walked the way he always walked. His quills had not gone fully flat since Thornwall.

"There's a report from the eastern reaches," Bristlebaum said. "A corruption pattern east of the Boroughs. Small. Moving north."

Nibbles set down the trowel. "How far east?"

"Two days past the Ridgemarrow fork." Bristlebaum's gaze moved across the seedlings along the south bed, then back to Nibbles. "The scout who brought it is thorough. The movement holds with early spread."

Early spread. Three months ago Nibbles had learned what early spread looked like. Wheat gone grey before ripening. The silence where birdsong should be. He knew what small became.

"When do we leave?" he asked.

Bristlebaum was still for a moment. The gate had swung half-closed behind him.

Behind Nibbles, his mother came out to collect the pruned canes he had bundled by the wall. He did not turn. She had known this was coming as long as he had.

"Five days," Bristlebaum said. "Equipment to collect. Word to send."

His mother set the bundle of canes by the wall. He heard the cord as she tied them. After Bristlebaum went through the gate, Nibbles picked up the trowel again. He turned the soil once more along the east edge of the bed and set it down properly.

She came and sat on the bench at the garden's far end. He had fixed that bench last autumn when one leg had gone soft with damp, spliced in new timber, sealed it with pine pitch. He went and sat with her.

The starling moved through the rose canes and out into the open garden. A cloud crossed the sun and the cold came back briefly and then the sun returned.

"I don't know what I'm doing," he said. "Most of the time."

"I know."

"That's not comforting."

"I didn't say it to comfort you." She looked at him. "When the world needed someone to say yes, you did. And then you came home. Both of those things."

"I'm proud of you," she said. "Because of you. Not the sword, not the mission."

She said it the way she said everything that mattered, plainly, looking at him. The first time he had failed the Guild trial she had sat with him at this same bench and told him he had been right to go and could go again, and that she believed he would get there. She had said that the same way. He had gone again, and he had gotten somewhere she had not imagined when she said it. Neither had he.

"I'll come home again," he said.

"I know you'll try." She looked at the south bed. The seedlings would need transplanting in two more weeks, once the last frost risk had passed.

She did not ask him to stay.

They came through the gate an hour before midday.

He heard Leonardo first, the uneven beat of the broken leg, the lance striking stone at the interval three months had settled into. Leonardo came through with his plume catching a gust and flopping sideways. He shoved it straight without breaking stride.

Bristlebaum's boots were still mudded from the morning.

Acornimus had his cravat knotted exactly as always, cream-coloured, precise, his journal in his breast pocket with the corner just visible. Somewhere in that journal was Gareth Redstone's last sentence, which Acornimus had recorded and was still working through. He had told Nibbles this once, at the end of a long evening at the Guild tent, the way a scholar mentions a problem he is interested in.

Dash appeared between two oak trees at the garden's edge. One moment the gap was empty. Then Dash was in it, paws loose at his sides, the lightning-bolt patch visible in the pale sun.

Telia came through the gate last of the main group, slower than at Thornwall, the grey settled further through her fur. Her staff, cracked at the base, was bound with new cord. Hazel walked at her shoulder, smaller than she had been, ears forward.

Lark landed on the garden wall without announcement, head tilted slightly east.

"Sir Tumblepatch," Leonardo said, and pressed his fist to his breastplate.

Nibbles had been receiving the title since Ironhold. He had learned to take it without flinching. Here in the garden, with the seedlings behind him and his mother on the bench and the smell of chamomile still on both of them, it landed somewhere different than it had anywhere else.

He looked at them. The lance leaning, the cravat precise, the lightning-bolt patch in the pale sun, the grey in Telia's fur, Hazel smaller and present, Lark tilted east.

He drew Whiskerbrand.

Not the way he had drawn it in the valley or below Thornwall, where the blade's alert had arrived ahead of his own thinking. This was a different kind of drawing. The morning was right for it. They were leaving in five days. The garden was the thing he was going back for.

He knelt at the center of the open bed, past the rose canes, in the turned earth where the seedlings were still small and the soil smelled of wet clay and something green just beginning. He pressed his paw flat to the ground. The top inch was cold from last night. Deeper, the earth was still holding yesterday's warmth.

The group had gone still around him. The lance, the wall, Bristlebaum's quiet. He was aware of them without looking. They had given him the ground without being asked.

He thought about Nori, who had taught him to read what the ground remembered of what had passed across it. He thought about Gareth, who had built the picture from evidence no one else knew to read, and who had given him the answer to the question he had carried since the Cheese Festival (*why me, why the sword, why someone without training*) by dying with it in his mouth. It was not the answer anyone had wanted. It was the clearest one anyone had given him.

He thought about the empty left paw resting at a wolverine's side in a chamber below Thornwall. The meaning was still past him.

He set Whiskerbrand's tip to the earth. The warmth came up through the grip before the light appeared.

The light found the roses first, then the low places, moving along the turned bed and through the roots of the seedlings and into the cold corners. No cost. No hollow pull from the chest. The warmth moved through the garden without hurry.

His mother watched from the bench.

When the light went, he lifted the blade. He waited for his shoulder to ease, and it did. He slid Whiskerbrand home in the sheath and stood.

"For luck," he said. "And so we remember what we're going back for."

He said it to the garden. He meant it for the people standing in it and for the ones who were not. For Nori, who had taught him to read the ground and the angle of a fight from the same instinct, and who had said *it's all right* at the end. For Gareth, who had been right all the way through, whose being right had not protected him, who had kept working anyway. For Aldric Blackstone, who had pressed a sword into someone else's paws thirty years ago in firelight and trusted the choice, and whose memories were arriving in pictures now, easier to hold each time.

They went through the gate. Leonardo led, walking at the front now. Acornimus beside him, journal in his pocket. Dash a few paces to the side where there was room to move. Telia and Hazel behind them. Bristlebaum at Nibbles' shoulder.

Lark lifted from the wall without announcement and caught the updraft east.

Nibbles followed them through the gate. The road curved away from the village, east through the morning mist.

His mother was at the garden's edge when he looked back, still working at the south bed where the seedlings needed the last of the dead matter cleared away. The mist was coming off the eastern field and the road was beginning to disappear into it. When the road curved, the garden went out of sight.

Afterword

A Note from the Author

Thank you for reading **The Shadow's Reach**. Every story finds its life not just in the writing, but in the readers who carry it forward—and you've given this one yours.

If Nibble's journey moved you, challenged you, or stayed with you long after the last page, I'd be deeply grateful if you'd take a few minutes to leave a review on Amazon and/or Goodreads. Even a sentence or two makes an enormous difference. Reviews help other readers discover the series, and for an indie author like me, that word-of-mouth is everything.

You can find all The Tumblepatch Chronicles Books on the Official Site – Scan to visit:

The Tumblepatch Chronicles still has a long road ahead, and knowing this world resonates with readers is what keeps me at the keyboard. Thank you for being part of it.

— Keith

9 798993 686707